## DESIRE'S DAWNING

"Oh!" Eden gasped as her patient suddenly grabbed her wrists and held them in his iron grip.

"What are you doing?" he said hoarsely.

"Lord Ramsay, I was merely bathing your face. You've been very ill." She expected to be released, but his grip tightened as his eyes narrowed.

"I don't *feel* ill." His voice grew huskier as he freed her wrists only to clasp her waist and draw her to the bunk. "But then perhaps I've died and gone to heaven."

"I assure you, sir, I am *not* an angel—and I shall be forced to prove it if you don't let me go immediately!"

But he pulled her head down and stopped her protest with his lips. Eden's heart quickened and her head spun as her resistance faded and the kiss gentled and deepened. When her glowing eyes opened, they could barely focus on his smoky blue gaze.

"You're no angel, wench," he whispered. "But I trust you know the way to paradise well enough. . . ."

# HIDDEN FIRES

## BETINA KRAHN

**ZEBRA BOOKS**
**KENSINGTON PUBLISHING CORP.**

ZEBRA BOOKS are published by

Kensington Publishing Corp.
850 Third Avenue
New York, NY 10022

Zebra and the Z logo Reg. U.S. Pat. & TM Off.

Third Printing: February, 1995

Printed in the United States of America

*for*
*Dorlinda Lee, H. Paul III, and Matthew David,*
*Paulo's and Sharon's children*

# Prologue

*Middle Scotland*
*Christmas Night, 1810*

The tallow candles guttered and the tankards were dry in the Great Hall of Skyelt. The yule log that had burned in the huge stone fireplace for most of the day and night was reduced to winks of glowing red that smoldered amid mounds of white ash. Shadows flickered lazily on the soaring gray stone walls, echoing the lethargy of the three kilt-clad figures sprawled in waning states of consciousness about the remains of their revelry on the great dining table.

"Bir-rth . . . that's what we're to be about, this s-season. Ye canna work the fields . . . canna hunt but starved rabbits . . . canna move yer flocks nor herds. Snow too deep to thatch a roof or even bury the daid. I say, the Good Laird did right well to be born o' a winter night. Time only fit for begettin' an' birthin'. What say ye, Terrance?" The burly Laird of Skyelt reached a meaty fist out to knock the boot of his steward from the table and bring the man's attention round.

"Uhhh?" Terrance started up, staring dully and blinking about him at the closing gloom.

"I said . . . a time for birthin'. It's all winter's good fer. What say ye?"

"Right, Laird Haskell, right as rain." Terrance gave the

expected response and both men turned restive looks upon the third member of the trio.

"Ye hear that, Ram, lad? Terrance agrees. 'Tis the season for birthin', lad. Or *begettin'*." Lord Haskell pushed himself straighter in his massive chair and slowly sat forward.

"Terrance always agrees. He's yer steward." Ramsay Paxton MacLean shook the fog from his faculties and prepared himself for what was bound to come. Why should he be spared just because it was Christmas?

"Aye, he's me steward . . . but a man o' sound judgment—a man wi' eight bairns! Eight! An' him likely not done yet." Haskell inched taller to meet his task full on and stroked his wiry, gray-flecked beard. Something kicked a spark into his piercing blue eyes. He raised his heavy pewter tankard, slammed it on the great planks of the table, and roared, *"Ale! more ale!"*

"Not me. I had enouf-f." Ram MacLean rose, steadying himself against the side of the table, smoothing his blouson sleeves and rumpled kilt with slightly exaggerated motions.

"Siddown, lad!" Haskell ordered, narrowing one eye to better glimpse his brawny, handsome son. "Ye've got naught better to do than listen to me. Siddown!"

"Old man—" Ram faced the laird, bracing himself on the tabletop with muscular fists that seemed only a younger version of those clenched on the table across from him.

"Sit . . . down!" Lord Haskell's chin jutted fiercely and Ram considered the older man for a long, rebellious moment before plopping down heavily in his chair and bracing himself anew.

A young and fresh-faced serving girl appeared, wiping the sleep from her eyes as she carried in a full pitcher of stout. She dipped wearily and set the vessel at the lord's hand, then reached for the empty one.

In an instant Laird Haskell's brawny arm clamped about the serving girl's rounded bottom and she was jerked full against him, in spite of her indignant protest. His other hand pulled down the top of her loosely tied blouse to reveal a firm, rose-tipped young breast.

"Here's a fine brae lass wi' a belly scarcely plumbed. Take 'er, lad—take 'er an' put me a bairn in her belly this verra night!"

"Damn you!" Ram thrust to his feet, his strong face raging red, his fist shaking furiously at his laird and father. "I'll not stand stud to yer kitchen wenches, ye lickerish old goat! Service 'er yerself—damn ye!"

The son's oath lay burning on the air for a long, bitter moment, then Haskell's face eased and a hoarse, ragged laugh issued forth.

"Might do jus' that," he leered. The young breast was conveniently at eye level, and he gave the taut, rosy nipple a playful tweak. The girl squealed in protest and he released her with a resounding thwack to her bottom. She pouted prettily as she gathered up her bodice and her empty pitcher and cast a speculative glance at the laird's handsome son before swaying out.

Ram narrowed his sky-blue eyes, knowing that the last lewd bit was for his benefit. His face reddened further and his generous lips curled in a sneer.

"I'd even take yer bastard, lad." Haskell grabbed the full pitcher and sloshed more ale into his tankard, gulping it noisily. "E'en a *female* bastard!"

Ram snorted his open disgust and it was Haskell's turn to stoke ire.

"Then marry, damn you! Marry an' make me a bairn for me knee!"

"You get a slew o' bairns from yer own loins every summer," Ram charged angrily. "Trounce *them* on yer bloody knee and leave me be."

"Aye, I've a slew o' bairns—but I've only one *son!* An'

9

I'll never have a *grandson* if it be left to you, boy!"

"Then so be it." Ram spoke with deadly determination as he leaned over the table and jerked the pitcher of ale up to pour his tankard full. He downed the brew with such vehemence that it overran the cup; dark streams dripped down the lean, hard planes of his cheeks and onto his dark vest, there to disappear.

"Take ye a wife, lad. Take her an' bed her an' make me a grandchild." The charge in Haskell's voice drained abruptly and the effects of the stout ale doused the spark that had animated his broad, graying face. He seemed older, more tired . . . more drunk.

"I'll marry when it suits me—if it ever suits me," Ram glowered, feeling the tide turning in his favor. His square chin jutted in a stubborn parody of the one across the table.

Haskell sat back in his great carved chair and looked at at his strong, capable son through eyes far too sober to suit the old laird. He stroked his beard and, as he often did, cast his thoughts into the past for comfort.

"I ken now where I went wrong, Terrance," Haskell spoke after a silence. Terrance gingerly turned his whole body in his chair to face his laird. He would scarce recall a word on the morrow, but he always managed to listen. "I shoulda married otherwise. Ach, I were a brash an' greedy young fool. Things woulda been different wi' a different wife. Shoulda married that young English lass . . . what were her name again?"

"Con-stance," Terrance supplied, feeling his mouth must surely be the only part of him yet capable of moving. None but a true MacLean could hold the monumental amounts of ale that his lairds did and still function . . . he was convinced it was a sign of their right to rule.

"Constance, aye, Constance. Beautiful, bonnie-haired Constance. Ne'er afore nor since have I met a female so created just for lovin'. An' just as enthusiastic as she were comely." Haskell's eyes drooped as he summoned some phantom image to his mind. "Breasts—smooth and cool like spring cream—makes me old mouth water just to remember. An' legs like a young colt—naemore than seventeen she were . . . an' o' good family. Ah, God, that lass could love me till I dropped . . . an' did, on several occasions."

"A fancy English whore," Ram pronounced pugnaciously.

"Nay." Haskell's eyes came crackling open, but quickly he retreated into his mellowing mood again. "She were a lass, a lady . . . my love th' summer I spent in London. I meant to go back to 'er after I settled my father's affairs here in Skyelt. But when I got back, she'd went off with some colonial an' her family weren't none too keen to tell me where."

"Then I were betrothed to yer ma, an' that were the end of it." Haskell sat forward and pointed at Ram. "Yer ma—she's to blame fer yer lack of interest in females. 'Twas her and 'er thin blue blood responsible fer yer lack o' juices. Why, by your age I had a string o' little bastards at me heels!"

"Like as not, she found your swinish ways so repulsive, she died to escape you!" Ram stood up, his features turning to stone as he trembled with scarcely contained rage. His blue eyes flashed silver and he stalked heavily from the hall.

Haskell let out a heavy sigh as he watched his son's manly stride and the rigid posture of his broad, muscular shoulders. He turned to his steward and propped his chin on his fist wearily.

"He be sharp as a razor." Haskell tapped his own temple. "Built like a fortress, hung like a bull—" He paused, shaking his head. "How can 'e be so lackin' in the finer points o' manhood? Is he . . ." Haskell swallowed

11

and lowered his voice as he leaned closer to the long-suffering Terrance. "Is 'e weak in th' wimple, ye think?"

"Nay." Terrance drew a huge breath and sighed. "He has a woman from time to time. I hear of it now and again. He's choosy, 'at's all. Ye push the lad hard by yer example, Laird Haskell." Sober, Terrance would never have dared such an observation. But strong spirits had a unique way of equalizing rank and he felt quite . . . equalized tonight.

" 'Tis so." Haskell nodded sagely.

A brief quiet settled over them and slowly a gleam appeared in old Haskell's drink-reddened eye.

"What I woulda give to see Constance have 'im a week or two. She'd a made a man outta 'im. Weren't a man around could keep his palms from itchin' when she walked by . . . not like my Edwina—were like hammerin' a board to bed that woman. Still," he became more reflective, "I suppose 'tweren't all her fault her ma raised 'er so deep in th' kirk. To go from lovin' the Lord to lovin' me—well, I s'pose it were a shock on 'er system."

Terrance's head dropped slightly before he caught it and jerked himself awake.

"I wonder where she be now, my Constance. She'd be some years older'n him . . ." His brow furrowed, then smoothed; then he tilted his head with interest.

*"Terrance!"* Haskell bellowed, pushing himself up from his great chair and snatching up his tankard for one last draught of ale. "Terrance . . . ye mon find her. Constance . . . ye mon find my Constance an' see what's become of her. A woman like that's got to be known somewheres. Send to London at first light, Terrance, an' find 'er, wherever she be!"

## Chapter One

*Dorset, England*
*May, 1811*

Eden Marlow emerged onto the massive circular steps of the old gray stone convent that now served as Mistress Dunleavy's exclusive School for Young Women and paused, breathing in the last traces of the morning's dewy breeze. The sun felt good on her cheeks and she smiled, gazing out over the lush, green Dorsetshire countryside that rolled like ocean waves around the old convent. The plowed fields and nodding orchards, the clear, wending streams banked with trees—they never seemed so lovely as when stirred to new life in the spring. It was a sight she would soon enjoy only in her memories.

Collecting herself, she rearranged her lacy cuffs and smoothed the fit of her golden velvet spencer over her bosom. Her thoughts were a tumult of memories and details of departure. But when her striking eyes fell on the masculine form approaching the bottom of the steps, these pressing concerns were abandoned.

Tall, clean-limbed, and graceful, James was the image of his father and thus a very grand sight on such a fine May morning. His caramel-colored frock coat was swept back into tails from waist to knee, his fashionable vest and breeches were of buff wool, and his throat was wrapped in an elegant blue silk cravat, tied in the obligatory Irish Tie. His every mannerism and every broadened Boston vowel shot the most intense longing through her: it was longing for her home across the Atlantic, longing for her family.

"There you are!" James Marlow's face lit with unabashed pleasure at the sight of his young sister on the steps above him. Her graceful, high-waisted dress with side-swept demicoat and a classic coif of extraordinary brown curls gave her a full, womanly appearance that took him aback for an instant. She had truly fulfilled the girlhood promise of loveliness her family had witnessed in her.

"Dede!" When he dashed up to meet her, he hugged her soundly, twirling her around with her toes barely touching the ground. He set her down and patted her cheek fondly, noting that she remained stiff — her eyes darted to two impeccably dressed young girls riding by, ogling the proceedings. And he felt her push away as his arms loosened about her.

But the sight of her glowing face soon supplanted his momentary uneasiness and he gave her yet another impetuous hug. Her skin blushed becomingly under his scrutiny and she lowered her long, sweeping lashes. He lifted her chin to bring her eyes up and marveled afresh at the fiery rings of molten copper at their centers and at the cooler, sweeter blue that rimmed their outer edges. Her eyes seemed to glow with the constant promise of the delight for which she was named. Never was there a young girl so fair, so sweet-tempered, so loving, James decided firmly.

"Let me go, James." Her lashes dipped again and her color heightened. "You can't just go about squeezing me! Whatever will people think?"

His laugh had a puzzled ring to it as he released all but her hand and led her down the broad steps to their

14

horses. He could have sworn she gasped when he put his hands to her waist to lift her onto her mount. He never thought to just give her a gentlemanly knee for climbing aboard.

"I could have used the mounting step in the stable yard," she observed quietly, accepting the reins from him as he held the stirrup for her slender foot. He paused and frowned teasingly up into her very polite face.

"Whatever happened to my little imp . . . the one who used to get walloped for trying to mount bareback?"

"James Marlow! I was never walloped in my life, and you know it." But her eyes warmed to sparkle with an old memory and he smiled, patting her hand before he went around to his horse.

"Besides," she lowered her voice to a loud whisper, "that imp was sent off to receive a lady's education." Then she intoned in her most cultured voice: "She's been . . . polished."

"Polished *off* is more like it," James muttered disagreeably, finally admitting to himself just what it was that had bothered him about his beautiful young sister since they'd been reunited two days ago. She'd been polished into a stiff, unrecognizable doll, the sort that decorated salons and parties admirably but was of little benefit otherwise.

His comment fell just short of her hearing, as he'd intended, but Eden read his sudden displeasure in his jerky mounting and in the nuance of tightness about his mouth as he spoke.

"Perhaps you'd best lead the way—you know the paths."

"Certainly." She looked down and adjusted her ladylike grip on the reins as she urged her horse into motion. James was her eldest brother, her favorite brother, her first love. She adored him and worshiped his manners, his wit and style, his zest for life. She had wanted to grow up

15

to be just like him . . . in those blissful days before she realized that a biological quirk of fate had ordained a very different life for her. And now something about her seemed either to disappoint or annoy him. She could feel it in the air.

There was a silence before she ventured a question.

"Do we still have Colleen . . . in the kitchen?"

" 'Aye, lassie, that we do.' " James imitated their family cook's Scottish burr and cocked a pleased grin at her. " 'Only now there be more o' her t'love than ever.' To smell her shortbread bakin' still makes my mouth water, and she still makes me wash my hands before she'll let me have any."

Eden gave out a sweet, musical laugh and her face softened with remembrance. "So many nights I lay there . . . alone in my bed . . . thinking about Colleen and wishing for a piece of her shortbread. . . ."

James shaded his eyes from the bright morning sun and searched her wan little smile. "Was it too lonely for you here?" He struggled to understand the changes in her.

"At first." She looked away, toward the approaching thicket of trees, trying to keep unseemly emotion from her voice. "But the other girls took me in rather quickly and after a while, this began to seem like home to me. The hardest parts were when I'd get letters and parcels from Mam-ma."

His heart jerked queerly at the elegant way she referred to their mother—*Mam-ma.*

"And that one Christmas when *Mam-ma* and *Pap-pa* came to England to see me . . . I thought I couldn't bear it when they left me here." Her lilting voice was smaller, flatter. "But I see now they were right to leave me here to continue my education. I was still untrained and had much to learn about being a lady."

"Sweet Jesus!" James snapped, furious at the ladylike restraint that overwhelmed her once-exuberant spirit.

"James!" Eden seemed genuinely alarmed. "You mustn't talk like that."

"Forgive my boorish ways, delicate lady." He put a sardonic hand on his dapper chest and bowed tauntingly, as far as his seat on the horse would allow. "I am only recently come from the crude and rustic colonies."

"It's not kind of you, James, to mock me." Eden felt her heart sinking slightly in her chest, corresponding to the rise of a lump in her throat. Moisture filled her lovely eyes to the rim and she set her jaw firmly against the untimely display of tears. "Ladies must never show their feelings in public," she could hear Dame Rosemary admonish. Indeed, the stern old mistress of deportment felt so strongly about it that when she died, her will and testament decreed, there was to be no weeping at her memorial services. And there was none.

Eden lifted her chin and screwed her courage up to improve her deportment.

"This path is where the older girls ride for pleasure," she said indicating the tree-lined path with a practiced, elegant sweep of her hand.

"Well, I'm shocked to hear that they allowed the word 'pleasure' to be bandied about so freely." James looked down his nose in a perfect parody of a dour schoolmaster. Then his handsome face broke into an enchantingly rakish grin that Eden couldn't resist.

"You're terrible!" Eden laughed, feeling the restraints within her snap. Suddenly she felt like little Eden Marlow again, galloping across the fields with her most beloved brother.

"You can't catch me!" She kicked her horse into a startled gallop down the broadening path, making for the rolling, open fields where rules and standards expanded to permit joy and pleasure.

They raced, one leading, the other trailing, then reversed positions so that the pursuer became the pursued.

Time was suspended, old enjoyments were revived and relived as the siblings rode and laughed and talked. James was vastly relieved to see Eden's strict training had done little to undermine her excellent seat on a mount, and Eden was equally relieved to feel James's regard for her warming again.

The breeze and the sun were magical, melting away clues as to time and place. Eden and James spent more than an hour in a spirited chase and shared remembrances, exchanging stories and family gossip.

Eden removed her scoop bonnet and tucked its long ribbons under her pommel. James watched the light shimmer on her lustrous brown curls. He cocked his head to one side; brown was too mundane a word for Eden's hair, he decided, letting his eyes flow over the gold and copper strands in her luminous locks. He admired the peach glow in her cheeks as she fanned herself with her hand and unbuttoned the top button of her spencer. Something in his chest swelled.

"Maybe we should stop in the shade." He pointed at the trees by the lazy stream that wandered through the little valley. "I wouldn't want to take a wilted young lady back to Mistress Dunleavy. Now there's a proper gorgon if ever I saw one."

"James, have you always been so irreverent? It's positively scandalous." She reined in under the trees beside his horse and waited for him to help her dismount.

"The Marlows do that as they age." He was quite serious as he tethered his horse and reached up to lift her down. "We pick up a certain saltiness as we barrel through life. Most of us do, anyway."

"You make us sound like sides of pork." She brushed the sides of her crumpled velvet as though brushing off his touch and caught his frown of displeasure as she turned toward the stream.

"Why do you do that?" he demanded. "Brush and

18

shush and stiffen? Are you suddenly scared of being touched?"

"Don't be absurd, James. I simply try to employ some bit of civilized restraint in my behavior and you worry that I'm frightened of being touched." And in a reckless rush she added, "I'm not a child to be patted and tussled about anymore. I expected that as a gentleman you'd recognize that."

"I *recognize* that I'm used to being treated with a bit more warmth and affection from you. What in heaven's name have they done to you here, Eden? I barely recognize you."

There it was, out in the open. Eden stared at James and a kaleidoscope of nameless feelings crowded into her heart, each clamoring for expression. The struggles she'd had overcoming her permissive upbringing and subverting her very nature to achieve that enviable status, refined womanhood! Sadness at leaving, remembrances of old home and new, and uncertainty for the future all crowded in on her at once. The din within her was unbearable, and she reverted to a response she hadn't made in these five long years with Mistress Dunleavy. She stuck out her tongue at him.

James blinked and straightened. She did it again, adding a nasty wrinkle to her pert and perfect nose.

"Eden!" He laughed shortly, but the change in her was too much of a shock to sustain humor.

She planted her hands on her waist and sent him a regal glare of challenge. Suddenly the only response he could muster was one from years long past. His eyes narrowed as the gauntlet was picked up and his shoulders jutted forward. His fingers came up to twitch ominously in a wriggly motion.

"The tickle bug is coming," he droned in a childish chant, "the tickle bug is coming . . . the tickle bug—"

"Oh *God,* James! *Not that!*" Eden squealed as she

recognized the purposeful glint in his eye and began to scramble away up the small incline. She snatched up her skirts and tried to run, but he caught her quite easily and applied his merciless, wriggling fingers to her ribs.

She wiggled and squirmed to escape him, but he held her with one strong arm as he tickled with the other. She was laughing so that it was hard to breathe.

"Please stop — James! Oh, please, stop! I can't stand it — " She set off on another round of laughter so pure, so releasing that it was almost painful. They thrashed and stumbled in that wild romp until Eden couldn't catch her breath at all. And with a newly acquired feminine instinct, she halted, surrendering to him utterly, but falsely.

Immediately the torturing fingers withdrew, James released her and staggered back a pace, drooping from exertion and weak with mirth. She attacked without drawing a breath, surprising him and knowing him down on his seat. She was on him in a flash, hiking up her elegant skirt and plopping down unceremoniously astride his belly.

Stunned, James watched her attack his immaculate cravat, pull it out, then apply her own vengeful version of his torture to his own ribs.

"Stop it, Eden! Good God — what are you doing, girl? *Oh — *" and he was off in peals of helpless laughter that weakened his defenses. He would have counterattacked, but her arms were stiff at her sides and there was nowhere else he could touch her within brotherly bounds. Her ripe young breasts strained her jacket and her shapely, silk-clad legs were bared to the knees. Suddenly he was acutely aware of her womanhood . . . and of how excruciatingly childish was their game.

Rearing ferociously, he dumped her to one side and grabbed her hands when she rolled back toward him in the lush new grass.

"I surrender!" he moaned, sitting up to catch her

crimson face and brilliant eyes in his sobering gaze. They sat looking at each other for a moment, each feeling the doors to childhood and their former relationship closing behind them.

"If you ever do that to me again . . ." Eden finally spoke in a husky rumble, "I'll . . . tell Mother." Inexplicably her eyes filled with tears and her chin trembled miserably.

James rose to his knees and snatched her in his arms, holding her tightly. His heart ground to a halt in his chest, willing relentless time to stop as well. He held her for a long moment, feeling her shoulders quaking.

"It won't ever be the same, James," she uttered against the satiny lapels of his coat.

"I know, Dede. I know."

High above them on the crest of the ridge, their reunion was watched carefully by a pair of piercing blue eyes that scowled darkly above a contemptuous sneer.

"The little whore — just like her mother." Ramsay MacLean spat his disgust and pointed to Eden, now enfolded in James's sheltering arms. "Merciful God! Look at her — rollin' and ruttin' about like a sow in a field. In broad daylight — as bold as sin itself. I can't stand to watch any more." He turned disgustedly and jerked his still rapt manservant by the arm, forcing him to quit the tawdry spectacle as well.

"Don' ye want to see what happens?" The stout, kilt-clad Scot gawked back over his shoulder as he was dragged along. He paused when they reached the horses and stared at his master's tightly reined wrath.

"I know what happens." Ramsay turned to him with that same dangerous glint in his eye. "I've known since I was a randy striplin'. An' I doubt those two could teach me *anythin'*. Women are a bother at best, Arlo, an' a boughten passage to hell's gate otherwise. And *that* one's a ticket first class."

He jerked the reins from their limb viciously and threw himself onto the back of his big horse. "Come, Arlo, we have work to do."

Arlo stood a minute, his broad mouth pursed as he glanced over his shoulder. He scowled; his young master had displayed a foul and dangerous mood since they left Skyelt a fortnight ago. And whenever the name Marlow was mentioned, his tall, well-favored laird went stiff with ire. They had thrashed about Dorsetshire, making inquiries about the Marlow lass. Even without seeing her up close, it was plain she was, as old Laird Haskell had insisted, "a fetchin' piece o' work." Today's little spectacle had enraged his usually fair and reasonable young master the way little could. Ramsay MacLean was a man whose loves and hates had been scored into him by the time he was breeched . . . and neither had changed a dot or tittle since. His disposition was always flawlessly controlled . . . until now. Arlo frowned, thinking that his laird's new ire had taken on a permanence since they'd learned last night in the local village that the Marlow lass was soon to leave England.

He shrugged his confusion, swung his stout, tartan-clad legs up onto his horse, and reined off to follow Laird Ramsay MacLean's broad, rigid back.


A week later, Eden stood on the forecastle of the good ship *Gideon's Lamp* and watched the bustle of last-minute loading underway. Her pulse jumped skittishly as she scanned the busy dock for sight of her brother. The droning din of movement and voices combined with the strong smells of waterfront salt and decay to threaten her stoutest resolve to be strong and true to her lady's training. She pulled a lacy bit of handkerchief from her

22

reticule and pressed its delicate fragrance against her nose, breathing deeply to calm her nerves.

James had deposited her on board without so much as an introduction to the captain and then hurried off to see to some nameless, but nonetheless "pressing," detail.

"Probably laying in a store of brandy for the voyage," she mused irritably. James, she had discovered in the last ten days, drank too much to suit her. Never mind that he remained the perfect gentleman when he drank—he still overindulged. And when she had delicately broached the subject, he had snapped at her nastily. Well, perhaps a discreet word to her father when they reached Boston. . . .

Again her thoughts flew back across the miles and years to her last remembrances of her home. It had been five long years since she'd seen it last, and she tried to prepare herself for the inevitable changes in it and in her family as well. It was painful to consider, but she made herself face it with true fortitude. And no matter how they received her, she must be gracious and set the example Mistress Dunleavy would expect. It shocked her that James could find the changes in her difficult to appreciate when her family had paid so handsomely to produce them in her. She sighed.

She could see clearly now that their family life had always been a bit unusual. They hugged incessantly and touched unseemly often. Eden was the most frequent recipient of such displays, the youngest of four and the only girl. It was the first of her "unsavory habits" to go when she arrived at school.

"Touching must be done only when strictly necessary—and then, purged of any carnal intent or connection," Dame Rosemary had declared. And Eden's raw enthusiasm for physical contact made her an early target and a prime challenge for Mistress Dunleavy's stern instruction. Whenever Eden argued that she always behaved so in her home in Boston, the elegant mistress remarked that such might pass without censure in the *colonies,* but that this was England, after all. Refinement was expected here.

Eden had overheard her parents' discussions of her need for proper lady's schooling. Her mother's term for her state was "wild as a hare," and her father asserted that at twelve years she was old enough to learn not to barge into her brothers' rooms while they dressing. So when Mistress Dunleavy spoke, it was with the added authority of parents determined enough about the disheveled state of her conduct to take the trouble to send her an ocean away in search of a remedy.

Reluctantly at first, she began to temper her outward displays and tame her instinctive physical nature. Gradually her scandals were limited to relating to the other girls the shocking sight of her parents embracing—kissing mouth on mouth and touching. In her most wicked moments, she related the details of her half-naked brothers' privies and toilet. The girls tittered and told tales and thereafter looked to Eden as the local authority on what happened between men and women. It was a role Eden relished until she began to garner inklings of just what those touchings and kisses and bare flesh probably led to. And as time went by, she rechanneled her youthful exuberance into zeal for proper conduct and eventually became one of Mistress Dunleavy's great successes.

Now she was going home, "a missionary of refinement," to use the old mistress's term. And just how formidable her task might prove had been revealed in James's odd and faintly resentful behavior.

A carriage rolled onto the dock and she squinted against the hazy brightness, tilting her head so that her stylish bonnet shaded her eyes better. Two familiar frocks descended; she hurried down the steps and across deck to the gangplank to greet her best friends from school, Laura Melton-Howard and Deborah Willingford. Her heart surged with joy at the sight of them.

They embraced and laughed and the girls admired her exquisite teal-blue velvet spencer and frilled bonnet. They had brought her a large tin of crusty sweets and a thoughtful bottle of fine sherry to ease the first days at sea. Laura glanced unabashedly about her and asked after James.

"He's gone off on some errand or other. He'll be returning soon, I think," Eden assured them, squeezing their hands tightly.

*"Look out!"* came a gruff shout from above them. They started, skittering to one side to admit a burly seaman struggling with one end of a huge sea chest. They stared as the other end was lowered onto the ship, supported by a stout pair of stockinged legs and stout, half-bare thighs. A wooly swirl of bold tartan was crushed between trunk and bearer, leaving a shocking expanse of male thigh passing by just at eye level.

"Oh—!" Laura jolted her face from the sight and all three girls flushed, rolling their eyes secretively and suppressing a giggle.

Eden's eyes alone flitted back for a second glimpse as the burly Scot bent over to set the cumbersome baggage on the dock. Horrified by her venal impulse, she jerked her gaze back and confronted another form, paused just above them on the loading deck.

It was another pair of male legs, a second fall of tartan that drew her eyes upward toward a black woolen coat and a carved marble countenance with eyes so blue they might have been snatches of the sky itself. Those bold blue eyes engaged hers brazenly and a smirk crept over the man's full, firm-set lips. Her reaction to the towering presence made the other women look up quickly to see what held her attention so. They flushed deeply when the tall figure strode lazily to the deck, their helpless eyes captive upon him. He turned to drop them a deep, courtly bow.

"Ladies." His badge-bearing tam was swept from his auburn hair and he paused, watching Eden's color heighten, scrutinizing the lovely evenness of her delicate features. He had never seen her so close and he found it mildly unsettling. He straightened and let the smirk on his lips show in her gaze as his eyes raked her pointedly. When she stiffened, he smiled; the little tart found the sight of a man's legs stimulating, did she? Perhaps his mission would not be so difficult after all.

Haughtiness made him move his broad shoulders about slowly and at his first step away, nervous whispers erupted from his feminine audience.

"Is *he* sailing with you?" Judith gasped. "Dear heaven above, Eden, the way he looked at you! So—so—"

"Primitive!" Laura supplied, gaining Judith's awed nod of agreement.

"The churl." Eden felt the heat of her flaming cheek through her glove. "You know what's said of the Scots. They're scarcely past barbarism. And he looks like a perfect example. Don't you dare look at him, Laura."

"It's not fair," Laura's eyes darted briefly in the Scot's direction, then were forced back by the pressure of Eden's hand on hers. "You're sailing with that incredibly handsome brother of yours—and now that strapping barbarian. Don't you think he's just terribly handsome, Eden?"

"Of course . . . but he *is* my brother, after all."

"Not James! The Scot." Judith tittered behind her hand, like a schoolgirl.

"I think both of you could use another year at Misstress Dunleavy's," Eden pronounced sternly, as if to make up for the wayward drift of her own interest.

"Oh, heaven forbid. Anything but another year there!" Laura wrinkled up her nose, then was instantly serious. "Please say we can come visit you. Are your other brothers half so handsome and manly as James?"

26

"Laura Melton-Howard, you're shameless!" Eden couldn't suppress a sisterly grin of pride. "Each is better looking than the last . . . and terribly dashing. And you're invited to Boston right now . . . both of you . . . whenever you can come."

"Good day, ladies," came James's familiar voice, setting two pulses aflutter and slowing the third to a steady rhythm of irritation.

They chatted politely until her friends had to leave, then James took her in hand to introduce her to Captain Henry Rogers and the other officers. As they stood together on the forecastle watching the last of the preparations for sailing, Eden was briefly overcome with a shiver of uncertainty. But James reached for her hand and smiled a fond reassurance. For all her ladylike veneer, the state of her emotions was still as readable to him as chalk upon a slate. Her mind was what genuinely puzzled him.

The heavy lines were cast off and the ship nudged out into the dark waters of Bristol Harbor. Eden swallowed hard and tried to fix her thoughts on the voyage . . . and the possibility that her friends might someday come to visit.

"Laura was most disappointed when she found you weren't here at first," she teased her brother as they made their way to the small cabins below. "I think you've captured her eye, James." Her primly coquettish teasing irritated him.

"Then it's just as well I was late." He reached the landing and turned to offer her a hand down. "You wouldn't want your dearest friend involved with a hedonistic cad like your brother. Imagine the scandal."

She jerked her hand back and straightened on the step above him. "Must you talk like that, James?"

"It's the pure, plain truth, Dede." He set his hands on his waist and rocked back on one leg to glower at her. "You'll learn it sooner or later, so be forewarned. I'm a

27

very *im*proper man sometimes, and if your affection for me hinges on mincing words and moderation, then I'll just have to forgo it. Because I'll not give up the raw and lusty pleasures of life to cosset your prim little sensibilities!"

"James!" Chagrin made her face crimson as her eyes widened, admitting a bright slash of red tartan at the edge of her vision. A throat cleared discreetly and Eden's face dropped in horror as she hurried down the last two steps to her brother's side.

"Your pardon," came a full-chested rumble as one of the Scots moved past them at the end of the passage to mount the stairs. Eden's eyes were lowered, but she could have sworn he'd paused as he passed beside her. She saw clearly the swing of his kilt, his strong calves beneath his knee-length woolen stockings, and his fine black shoes, with brass buckles that seemed to wink even in the dim passage. Instantly she knew which Scot it was and her recognition of such sundry parts of a total stranger appalled her. Surely a true lady would never remember such characteristics . . . she could only hope he hadn't heard much of James's heated reproach.

James showed her to her small, tidy cabin, pointing out the tallow lantern, the drawers beneath her narrow bunk, and a small metal brazier that could be used against the chill once they were at sea. He helped strap her cases at the end of her bunk and hung her oval mirror on the wall. After pointing out his cabin across the passage, he left her there to settle in.

When they went on deck again, the ship was well out into the channel, unfurling sail. There they met their fellow passengers; an older man from New York who professed to be a physician, and a graying Maryland planter on his way home from settling family business in Derbyshire. There were six passengers altogether, they learned. The other two were the Scots, who were nowhere to be seen while introductions were made. And so Eden had to wait until supper that night to learn the identity of the strapping, formidable man whose intensely personal stare had nearly taken her breath away.

"Ramsay Paxton MacLean, o' Skyelt, at the step of the highlands." The tall, auburn-haired Scot had to stoop whenever below decks and thus straightened only partway to take James's hand across the common supper table.

"James Marlow." Her brother's smile was formal and restrained. It made Eden smile adoringly at him when he turned to her. "And this is my sister, Eden."

"Your . . . sister," Ramsay MacLean responded with a chilled smile. "How convenient for you to be able to travel together."

The vibrating depth of his voice and the rolling burr of his speech blocked immediate recognition of just how odd was his comment. He reached for Eden's hand and as he held it a bit too tightly, she glanced into his striking blue eyes and felt some hidden barb in his remark.

"James came to England for me . . . to take me home, now that my schooling is finished." She bristled, tearing her eyes from his broad, black-clad shoulders.

Ram seemed to nod in understanding, but Eden felt his look was too knowing to be but simple agreement. The rangy, half-civilized Scot seemed to have taken an instant dislike to her. It rankled her fully and she sat straighter under those taunting eyes, refusing to look at him or allow his uncongenial attitude to bother her in any way.

"Are you traveling to Boston for business or for pleasure, Mr. MacLean?" James asked evenly, accepting the bottle of wine from white-haired Dr. Schoenwetter and pouring for Eden, then himself. Both Scots spoke at once.

"Business."

"Pleasure."

Ram looked at his stout companion, who reddened.

" 'Tis . . . a *family* matter, takes me so far from home."

"You have family in Boston, then?" James pursued a polite line of inquiry.

"No," and "Somethin' like that"; again they both answered at once. This time the tall, broad-shouldered young Scot scowled fiercely and Arlo looked away uncomfortably. Everyone looked at them expectantly, but Ram MacLean simply brushed their interest aside as Arlo accepted the wine bottle from James and poured for his master. The gesture confirmed the difference in their status; it was hinted at in the subtle differences in the quality and style of their clothing.

In the silence, Eden appraised both men surreptitiously. Ramsay MacLean wore a tartan kilt and a short, black woolen coat that fitted his muscular frame closely. Slung from shoulder to waist diagonally was a bright sash of the same tartan. It was caught and pinned at his waist, with a worked silver clan badge bearing a crest that was repeated in the silver buttons of his jacket.

The other Scot wore the same tartan and a similar jacket, coarser woven, without a sash. His buttons were of roughly polished horn.

"Have you ever been at sea before, Mr. MacLean?" the good doctor asked, pouring wine for Mr. Josephs, the planter, and himself.

"Nay, I've never been to sea," MacLean answered easily, sipping from his pewter cup.

Despite her irritation, Eden found herself staring at his throat as he swallowed. The play of tendons made her want to swallow, too, but strangely it robbed her of the power to do so.

"Concern myself wi' my lands and herds mostly," he continued matter-of-factly.

"Then you're likely in for a treat, sir," Dr. Schoenwetter pronounced, a mischievous glint in his eye. "Once you sprout sea legs, you'll find the spectacle of the ocean quite the most magnificent thing you've ever witnessed . . . with sunrises and sunsets rivaled nowhere on earth, sir."

"Except in Dede's eyes." James held up a finger of exception and his smooth face dimpled with irresistible humor. He drew the eyes of the table with his own gaze toward Eden's widened eyes and flushing face.

"James!" she protested, lowering her eyes quickly to deny them all confirmation of his roguish assertion. Why did he persist in calling attention to her by such unseemly observations? It was as though he enjoyed putting her on display—and seeing her disturbed.

" 'Tis true." James's laugh was utterly charming as he lifted her chin with one finger, deterred little by her refusal to unveil her eyes. "My Dede has eyes to shame the most glorious skies. And of late, I've even seen shooting stars and occasional lightning in their mysteries as well."

"James . . . please!" she whispered desperately, clenching her fists in her lap and wishing she could shrink and slither away through the cracks in the planking floor.

"Yes, well . . ." the gallant doctor came to her rescue, raising his cup, "let us drink a toast to fair eyes, fair skies, and an uneventful voyage."

"Here, here!" James's endorsement was heartfelt as every passenger and officer raised a cup and drank gustily. "And Mr. MacLean, should you need assistance finding those 'sea legs,' I've a keg of good brandy in my cabin that may help. I've found it speeds such an adjustment mightily."

Eden's face came up at last, her gaze filled instantly by Ramsay MacLean's piercing blue eyes. She looked away quickly and fresh color rushed into her face. At that first meeting on deck and now over supper, his looks were faintly taunting and undeniably disapproving. Never had anyone in her entire life taken so immediate a dislike to her.

No doubt it was that air of tightly reined resentment that made her want to look at him so. The need was becoming an itch that consumed her attention and demanded satisfaction. She tossed her lustrous curls and squared her shoulders, fastening her attentions on the great soup tureen being trundled to the table by the ship's cook.

The rest of the supper passed pleasantly enough. Dr. Schoenwetter engaged everyone in gentlemanly conversation, James controlled most of his outrageous impulses, and Mr. Josephs proved a banal and pleasant sort who agreed with everyone, even when they disagreed with him. Only the stiff-backed Scots were silent, though twice the servant had started to speak and was frowned into silence by his dour young master.

Eden found herself stiffening as the big Scot's eyes lingered on her whenever she spoke. Gradually she made it clear that her smiles, her melodious comments were for everyone at the common table *except* Mr. Ramsay Paxton MacLean. It was a small bit of ladylike revenge for his baffling attitude toward her.

Mr. Josephs was bragging about the size of his herds when MacLean's servant spoke up hastily.

"Me laird's flocks whiten the summer hills like snow!" His ruddy face glowed with the pride he was unable to suppress. "There be no finer sheep in all Scotland—"

"Arlo!" Ram MacLean stopped his garrulous companion with an expression that hardened his strongly chiseled features.

"Yea, laird?" Arlo sighed, tense with disappointment.

"You have duties . . . in the cabin." It was a command all the more potent for its supremely controlled tone.

"Yea, Laird Ram." The short, solid man rose abruptly and dropped a curt bow to the assembly, then left with greater than normal redness on his freckled countenance.

Eden suppressed a sympathetic shudder at her impres-

32

sion that Lord Ramsay MacLean never did or said anything that wasn't supremely controlled.

"Well, *my lord,*" James turned to the Scot with fresh interest, "where are your estates again?" Eden winced at the obvious change a peerage, even a Scottish peerage, produced in her brother. But she glanced at Mr. Josephs and at the doctor and realized that all about the table reassessments were being made of the brawny, taciturn Scot.

"Skyelt is at the step o' the highlands, not far from the Tay River." His firm mouth curled slightly as he noted the piqued interest in the faces now turned expectantly toward him; only Eden Marlow's eyes were averted. She was absorbed in running the tips of her tapered fingers around the rim of her scarcely touched wine cup. He watched her fingertips trace that circle over and over and felt as though someone was tracing the same lazy figures on the bare skin of his belly. He glowered and heaved a deep breath, jerking his attention back to what Mr. Josephs was saying.

". . . you see to your estates yourself?" Mr. Josephs sought to clarify their common impression that he was indeed a titled lord.

"My father is high laird, still." He sought Eden's gaze so determinedly that she could not escape looking at him for a brief moment. "Laird Haskell MacLean." His revelation was so pointed, it seemed he wielded it like a sword-thrust, meant for the very center of Eden. His muscular, sun-bronzed face was framed by a neat fall of unbound auburn hair that glowed with a violet cast in the lantern light. His pure blue eyes glinted knowingly above high, prominent cheekbones and a long, straight nose that gave his face a haughty cast.

The Scot's intensity rattled her so thoroughly that she jolted up from her chair and had to steady herself against the table. James rose to his feet beside her, scowling his

33

concern and confusion over her vague, lady-like dismay.

"Eden, what is it?"

"Nothing, James, truly. I'm . . . just in need of a breath of fresh air." She sent one fluttering hand up to the modestly tucked bosom of her stylish gown and smiled a feeble apology. The colonial gentlemen got to their feet quickly, but the Scot rose languidly, never taking his stormy eyes from the rounded feminine breast Eden's hand sought unconsciously to shield from him.

"I'll see you to your cabin, then." James pushed his chair back, but she stayed him with a hand upon his sleeve.

"No, I'll be fine, James. I'd best begin working on those 'sea limbs' good Dr. Schoenwetter spoke of." She smiled her leave of each gentleman, neglecting only Lord Ramsay MacLean as she went into the dim coolness outside. When the door thudded behind her, she leaned weakly against the paneled wall of the passage and drew a deep, shuddering breath.

"You're tired and unstrung a bit by all these changes—that's all," she muttered. A shiver ran through her shoulders, mocking her conclusion, and she stiffened irritably. "It has *nothing* to do with that churlish Scot!"

## Chapter Two

A tallow lantern provided a yellow light for Eden's simple toilette in her small cabin. She untied the stylish cording that bound her gown just beneath her rounded breasts and slid the bodice gently from her shoulders. Ignoring the chill, she held the teal velvet gown up to gaze on it before packing it away in her trunk. Her fingers traced the ecru lace on the scoop-necked bodice and drifted down the sinuous silk cording stitched like a twining vine amid the lace and tiny seed pearls. She couldn't remember ever owning a gown so grand, so womanly. And this was but one of several her family had ordered for her before they departed.

Sighing, she hurriedly donned a heavy woolen nightdress. Her heavy fall of hair was unpinned and dutifully brushed, her face scrubbed thoroughly and treated to a generous layer of rosewater cream. She shivered and climbed onto the high bunk, her feet dangling above the polished floor, and felt very girlish and uncertain.

She didn't want to think about it — going home. For the last six months it had been uppermost in her thoughts, this long-awaited reunion with her family. Her coming departure had focused every reading, every lesson, every quietly elegant meal into a critical opportunity for absorbing the last possible morsel of refinement and culture. She so wanted her family to be proud of her. She wanted them to see that she had indeed outgrown the wayward childishness that had seemed to disconcert them so.

And of course, there was the inconvenience of the voyage itself. She remembered very little of her voyage to England five years ago. She had imagined the first-rate accommodations James had mentioned would be bigger . . . certainly warmer. In her snug little bed at Mistress Dunleavy's, the journey had sounded so adventuresome, so romantic. It was turning out to be quite different . . . cold, cramped, and taxing of her charitable nature.

James, it seemed, found ocean travel so objectionable that he was prepared to endure it half-inebriated, and the other two respectable passengers dreaded it enough to hint at joining him. Well, it was no matter to her if they passed the time in each others' besotted company. She'd keep to her cabin and to more worthy pursuits . . . stitching, reading. . . . And she'd be relieved to escape the mystifying antagonism of that brawny, half-civilized Scot.

A strange, unsettled feeling crept into her stomach at the thought of those striking blue eyes turned upon her in intense and ungentlemanly scrutiny. He seemed to see little else when she was about, but his constant, simmering regard could hardly be called flattering. He obviously didn't like whatever his crude inspections revealed to him. She shivered suddenly. It was as if he tried to reach through her very clothing each time he looked upon her. A second shiver followed and her eyes widened in alarm. This was too akin to . . . excitement to suit her.

She drew a deep breath, trying unsuccessfully to tear her mind from the memory of his long, muscular legs and the smirk of his deplorably memorable lips. Why should she feel this compulsion to look at him . . . *stare* at him? It made her uneasy. Perhaps it was a tenacious remnant from her unbridled girlhood . . . resurrected by the old memories she and James had shared and by the prospect of going home at last.

If so, it was wise to recognize this potentially dangerous lapse in her sterling new character and deal with it sternly from the outset. Just having thought of it in such calm, rational terms was an immense comfort.

Scooting backward on the bunk, she drew her knees up under her chin and reached under the hem of her nightdress to loosen her garter. Deftly, she rolled the silken tube down her calf to her ankle and off.

An impulse seized her and she jerked up the nightdress to stare down her knees and over her shapely calves to her trim ankles and nicely arched feet. A swift pang of guilt pierced her at the brazen impulse and she tossed a guarded glance about the small, silent cabin. There was no tittering, girlish outrage, no stern, matronly reproof for such a bold exhibition.

Her chin jutted stubbornly, deepening its enchanting cleft, as she stared at her limbs, one swathed in finest silk and the other bare as it had been on her birthing day. She raised and flexed her bare foot, turning it from side to side, scrutinizing the shapely curve, the smooth, pale skin. It did not seem especially shameful or sensual just now.

Frowning in disgust at her unworthy thoughts, she dropped the silken rings in the top tray of her chest and snatched up the fresh sheets she had brought to spread over the raw, straw-filled ticking of her narrow bed.

She had nearly finished tucking her bed when the door of her cabin burst open. She was caught in the middle of the bunk on her hands and knees, her derrière facing the open door, clearly outlined by her nightdress. Aghast, she whirled in a brown cloud of hair, stretching her nightgown down over her bare feet. Her arms fluttered up to shield the high-buttoned neck of her demure garment.

"James!" Eden gasped, staring at her brother, now spreading across the gap from doorpost to door latch. His face was red and merry as he swayed between his supports, his gray eyes lidded and crinkled with guilt — or mischief.

"Dede, little love—" he muttered thickly.

"James, whatever are you doing? Are you drunk?"

"Nay, I'm but pleasantly . . . filled. I've come to t-tuck you in."

She slid from the bunk, hastily pushing the heavy nightdress back into place about her feet and ankles.

"It seems you're the one needs tucking, James. How could you?" Her tone of honest disappointment made him raise a handsome brow in rueful agreement.

"Dede, don't be c-cross with me." He wavered as the ship pitched slightly beneath them. "I *hate* sailing . . . but I couldn't allow anyone else to f-fetch you home, Mud-pie."

"James—" she took a step toward him but stopped to clasp and unclasp her hands anxiously. "You must put yourself to bed. It's really the best thing for you."

He swayed again with the ship's movement and the door flapped wildly as he strained to steady himself between it and the doorpost. She hurried to his side and slipped her arm about his waist awkwardly. Was it her imagination that the ship seemed to be rolling more underfoot?

"Let me help you to your cabin," she intoned primly. His lively gray eyes were dulled and bloodshot and she longed to give him a swift kick. Mistress Dunleavy's instruction on inebriated gentlemen was confined to how to camouflage them or escape them . . . nothing was mentioned about how to leverage one through two doors and onto his own bed before he was either unconscious or sick. And there would be the aftermath of his overindulgence to contend with the next morning as well. . . .

His fingers refused to leave the doorpost and she tightened her grip about his waist and peeled them off the wood one by one.

"Oh, hell, Dede—the f-first good hug I've had from you and I'm afraid to let go of the damned doorpost!"

"James, your language!" she muttered, loosening her hold on him as if he'd suddenly grown prickles.

"Oh yes . . . I f-fergot. Yer a lady now." He looked down into her eyes with an unfocused grin. "P-pardon my lan-guage, Mudpie. I s-said I was a hopeless d-degenerate. Do you s-still love me?"

"Lean on me, James, I'll . . . help you across." She was trying to be properly furious with him. But he had called her "Mudpie." She'd completely forgotten about ever being "Mudpie."

"Let go, James." She succeeded in prying his viselike grip open, dumping a good part of his weight on her shoulders.

"S-say you s-still love me, Dede. . . ."

"I still . . . love you, James."

Groaning and staggering beneath him, she managed to turn them both around and to edge out into the passageway. But they didn't get far.

The way was blocked by a huge, dark form set with eyes that burned like two points of blue light, trained intently on them.

"Might I be of assistance?" His deep voice was gentled by its rolling burr, but it carried an unmistakable taint of sarcasm.

Confusion rattled Eden as she felt the Scot's irksome stare roaming them freely.

"No." She tried to raise her chin to deflect his obvious amusement, but found it was impossible while bearing so much of her brother's weight about her neck.

"D-do me a turn, yer lord-ship." James managed with a lopsided grin. "O-open my door—"

"Gladly, sir." The Scot leaned one excessively broad shoulder against the wall beside James's door and flicked the latch up effortlessly. Then he pushed back the door with one muscular finger and crossed his arms over his chest to watch what would happen next. His eyes had never left Eden's comely form.

"Come, James," Eden snapped, anger and humiliation inflaming her cheeks. She pushed him through the doorway into the unlit cabin. She tottered with him toward the far wall and dumped him unceremoniously, then straightened with grim satisfaction. She paused and drew a deep breath, letting her eyes adjust in the gloom. One by one she gingerly lifted his stockinged legs onto the bunk. He rolled onto his side with a shudder and was still.

Light blossomed suddenly behind her and she wheeled, her heart sinking. The Scot had entered behind her and lighted the lantern. James's cabin was even smaller than hers—and it was nearly filled by Lord Ramsay MacLean's big, masculine frame. He hung the lantern from a peg overhead. His head and shoulders were bent forward to avoid the low ceiling and it seemed that he hovered over her like a predator ready to strike.

"E-excuse me, sir. I think he is best left. . . ." Her voice wavered in her ears and her cheeks were afire. Her heart pounded harder and she was agonizingly aware of her loosened hair and her bareness beneath the nightdress. Mortified, she fixed her lowered eyes on the door latch.

"Is 'e like this often?" came an unexpected query.

"No. . . ." Eden's eyes went to him up in spite of her and took in the expanse of his shoulders, the immaculate white shirt open at his throat. A small dark wisp peeked out just below the hollow at the base of his neck. . . . "That is, I think not." She jerked her head away so that her hair tossed about her shoulder, covering part of her breast. "He's usually . . . very gentlemanly."

"They always are . . . at first."

Eden frowned at his strange observation; then it struck her as a condemnation of James's higher nature. She pulled her shoulders back and recklessly looked straight at him, feeling the heat which emanated from his spread into her face. He was closer than she had realized.

"Sir, James is a gentleman of the first water. Perhaps he fares poorly at sea . . . but 'mal de ner' is a common enough affliction." Her eyes burned hotly in defense of both her brother and herself.

Ram MacLean stared down at her shamed, luminous face and felt an unaccustomed turmoil within him. Her eyes glowed strangely, with a molten gold center amid cooler rings of gray and blue—very like the setting sun on the heath. It hit him at once; they were indeed the sunsets this James Marlow had spoken of. Her hair waved and curled in a soft brown cascade over her shoulders and down toward her hips. He could smell its rose-like fragrance as he hovered above her and his fingers twitched with the urge to luxuriate in its softness.

"I think we'd best leave him to sleep now." She swallowed hard to free whatever had lodged in her throat. But Lord MacLean didn't move a muscle.

"You'd best loosen his clothing," he said without blinking, focused intently on the details of the startlingly beautiful young woman before him. In those brief seconds he mentally explored and claimed as his the soft oval of her delicate face, the creamy perfection of her skin, the ripe bow of her richly colored lips, the exquisite arch of her brows. Confusion threatened to boil up inside him again, but he forced it down savagely and his features hardened perceptibly.

"Loosen . . ." Eden stepped back, "his clothing?" His change from searching to sardonic jolted her and she flushed crimson, wondering how long she had been staring up at him. "I . . . think I can manage now, thank you."

41

Before she could move, his big form blocked her way to the bunk and with quick, skillful movements, he removed James's frock coat, unwrapped his blue silk cravat, unbuttoned his embroidered waistcoat, and removed his shoes. He hung the coat over the back of a chair and turned to Eden with an intriguing tilt to his firm, well-shaped mouth.

"I suggest, lady, that you learn quickly to nurse a sore and swollen head. I think you will often need such skills at his side."

"I have told you, sir, that this is not his usual custom." Her chin rose defensively and her lips tightened as ire surged through her afresh. "I am bound to thank you for your aid, but I will manage henceforth on my own."

He watched the flicker of pride in her eyes and noticed the unyielding squareness of her shoulders. She seemed younger, fresher than he had expected, and perhaps a bit more spirited.

"The man shows little sense, abandonin' you for drink's fickle pleasures. Were I your protector, Miss Marlow, I'd ne'er need assistance in *my* bed." The curl of his generous mouth counterfeited a smile. But his blue eyes sneered as they raked her, not bothering to conceal their interest in what lay beneath her nightdress.

"Then we may both be grateful that fate has spared us such a circumstance," she parried angrily. He stiffened and a line of displeasure developed at the corner of his mouth. "Good night, sir!"

He started for the door. She was close behind, reaching for the handle, when he turned to her. His hand reached for her hair and raised a lock of it to rub speculatively between his finger and thumb. The back of his knuckle brushed her cheekbone and she blushed furiously.

"Perhaps such a fate is neither so remote nor so disagreeable as it now seems, Miss Marlow." And with a brush of his bold, familiar gaze, he was gone.

Eden slammed the cabin door behind him pointedly. He had smirked, leered, and now taunted her openly! Her protector indeed!

As she glared resentfully at her brother's inert form and willed her heart to slow its breakneck pace, the second sense of his words came to mind. "Only *they* had "protectors." Fancy women, courtesans . . . the gall! He stood there in the presence of her brother, taunting her with the possibility of . . . bedding her. The foul-minded wretch!

She stopped suddenly, drawing herself up straight. Well, what more could be expected from a rude, coarse sheepherder . . . and a Scot at that. Let him ogle and smirk and make his crude comments . . . she'd not be baited into such a tawdry confrontation again. She'd see to it that James was at arm's reach whenever she left her cabin. Whatever James's flaws, he was fiercely loyal to her and would certainly protect her from such coarse attentions.

She turned, lurched across the tilting floor to pull a blanket up over James. Bracing against the bunk with her knee, she leaned over her blissfully unconscious brother and bestowed a dutiful kiss on his slackened cheek.

No one came to waken her; and in the dim, gray light of her chilly cabin, she nestled under her covers and slowly wakened to the rolling, lapping, and pattering sounds of water all about her. She had been dreaming of dancing, of moving in bold, graceful rhythms, gowned in splendid silk and basking in the admiration of countless eyes. She was floating and dipping and swirling, feeling warm waves of adoration breaking over her from all directions, buoying her up . . . up. . . .

*Thud!* She was suddenly jolted, dropped in her bed. She tried to sit up, but the cabin was rolling to one side, and it took both hands in a steadfast grip on the low sides of the bed to keep her from being tossed on the floor. It took a minute to make sense of this chaos: the ship bucked and wallowed in huge wave troughs now visible through the small window high above her bed. Rain and spray pounded against the side of the ship.

For a long, frightening moment, her heart stopped in her chest. They could founder in the storm and be lost at sea! They might even die! She swung her legs over the side of the bunk and struggled to rise.

"Eden Delight Marlow! Calm down and get a grip on yourself!"

Hand over hand, she dragged herself to the end of the bed and braced herself against the wall to reach into her trunk for some clothes. She wasn't going to drown without at least being properly dressed! Under her nightgown she couldn't tell . . . was her dress front to back?

"Damn it!" she groaned, then bit her lip. Her hands were shaking, but she managed to yank up the bodice of her dress and fasten some of the button loops at her back.

She fought her way to the door and clung to its handle and a nearby wall peg to gain her bearings. The passage was dark and ominously wet as she braced herself against the narrow walls and made her way along them. The common was empty, its lanterns swinging forlornly in the gloom above an overturned chair and a tin cup that rolled and clattered across the floor. Sinister black streaks of moisture seeped from the common-room windows and trickled across the polished floorboards.

"Ahoy, miss!" the voice booming just behind her booted her heart to a dead stop. She sagged against the door frame as she turned to face the first mate. "A ripe full snorter o' a gale out there." He was swathed in a heavy oilcloth that gushed water onto the floor of the passageway.

"The ship—" Eden gasped, clasping her hand to her

throat. "We're . . . not sinking?"

"Naw, miss. Th' worst is passing just now. Soon it'll be jus' these cursed swells and the miserable rains. We'll ride 'er out, miss. But there'll be no hot food for a while. Can't risk a fire in swells this size. Can ye see the other folk are told?"

Eden nodded, mute with relief, and started back toward James's cabin.

The smell of sickness assaulted her from the windowless gloom and she had to quell her stomach to enter the cabin and search for the lantern hanging above her. But what the light revealed was far from reassuring. James had evidently risen in the darkness, trying to make the door. The evidence of his struggle was on the floor . . . in three places. Eden averted her gaze and clamped her hand over her nose and mouth, forbidding her stomach to surge. She lifted her skirts and picked her way through the mess, having to steady herself precariously with each roll and yaw of the ship.

James lay with an arm flung over his pale, shadowed face. Beneath his rumpled clothes his lean, athletic form was limp.

"James," Eden drew a stifled breath, "are you all right?" She touched him and he groaned miserably, moving his arm to gaze blearily at her through reddened eyes.

"Dede . . . sorry . . . I'm sick. Everything . . . spinning and heaving and rolling—" His hand clamped over his mouth and his eyes went wide with panic. He sat up partway and pointed wildly about the cabin floor. In an instant Eden knew what he wanted and found the chamber pot at the bottom of his bed. Little remained in his stomach, and when he was finished, Eden helped him lie back down, managing a dose of sympathy for him.

"Dede—" he was hoarse and dry, "—get me a drink to settle my stomach, please." He lifted a shaky finger toward the empty corner. "From the keg."

"Really, James, what you need is rest, not liquor. I'll fetch some water for you—"

He grabbed her wrist.

"No Dede—it won't help. Brandy's what I need now—it's the only thing that will help—"

"It's the reason you're sick right now, James—that wretched drink."

"Oh, God, Dede, don't preach at me." He flopped backward. "Just get me a drink."

"No." She straightened, scowling. "I'll tend your illness, but I'll not contribute to your ruin."

"For God's sake—I'm seasick, not drunk—never mind!" He glared at her furiously and made to rise. "I'll get it myself!" His legs swung over the edge of the bunk and he grabbed his head as if it had tried to roll from his shoulders.

He buckled helplessly and she assisted him back onto the bunk without another word.

## Chapter Three

Eden made sure James was resting, then scoured the cabin floor before making her way down the heaving passage to Dr. Schoenwetter's door. She'd never have imagined that one night's drinking bout would put James down so low. But perhaps his manly vigor was deceptive; his drinking had probably weakened his constitution.

There was no response to her first knock on the physician's door. She braced herself in the sloshing wet passage and waited. She knocked again, her concern rising, then finally banged. The door opened a crack; she could see a single eye pressed to it.

"Doctor, I do hate to bother you—"

"You want the doctor." Mr. Josephs' voice was like gravel as he fled the opening.

Eden heard muttering, an uttered oath, and a groan. The doctor's gray face appeared. His white hair was disheveled, his eyes were red-rimmed and miserable.

"Yes, Miss Marlow?" he pressed a handkerchief to his lips as the ship underwent yet another pitching. Beads of sweat appeared on his august brow.

"I am sorry to disturb you, sir. But it's James, my brother. He's taken quite ill. I have no idea what to do for him. Can you come?"

"My regrets, Miss . . . I cannot. It's this wretched . . . sea—" He turned away abruptly and the door closed. The unmistakable sounds of sickness wafted through the door and Eden blanched. The doctor was ill, too! Just as she had raised her hand again, the door opened with a jerk and the white head leaned weakly against the door frame.

"Jus' . . . give 'em a tootful of watered brandy whenever he comes 'round," the physician gasped. "An' if your brother has some of that brandy to spare—it'd be . . ." he swallowed desperately, "a mercy to us as well." The door slammed and Eden was left in the dark hallway, stunned.

The doctor and Mr. Josephs were seasick . . . vilely so. Then James. . . . She felt criminally foolish as she made her way back down the passage toward her cabin. She emptied her water pitcher into the basin and set about filling it with brandy. She managed to get a fair cup of the stout liquor down his grateful throat. Then she bathed his hot face and hurried a pitcher of brandy to the ailing gentlemen.

She sat with James in the rolling cabin as long as she could, bathing his hot face, comforting his thrashings. It was a taxing duty, but keeping busy was better than sitting and listening to every shriek and shudder of the waterlogged timbers around her. First Mate Mallory was in the passage when she left James's cabin and she explained the passengers' plight. He scowled sympathetically and shrugged at her question, saying it was anybody's guess how long they'd have to endure the storm.

"An' them others, the Scots, are they struck, too? Ain't seen hide nor hair of 'em meself. Could ye be prevailed upon to check on 'em, miss? I got to get topside." He left her sputtering, trying to think of a good reason to avoid such duty. In the end, her better nature won out and she squared her shoulders, preparing for what she was sure would be a disagreeable task—confronting that sneering, conceited Scot.

When no answer came to her soft knock, she started to leave. But her sense of fairness made her turn back and apply her knuckles a bit harder. There was a scrape, a moan; the door creaked open.

The lord's man, Arlo, stood barefoot with a tartan blanket wrapped hastily about him. His rumpled shirt hung half off his shoulders. His eyes were dark-ringed and glazed with a now-familiar malady.

"Ah—miz! You be a merciful sight." His sturdy frame sagged markedly. "Me laird—he be a sick man. I tended 'im until I can—naemore—" This time he sagged to his knees, and Eden bolted forward to lend him an arm, helping him stumble toward the narrow bunk.

"You're sick as well? Both of you?" Eden glanced toward the other bunk, on which a large, very male form was sprawled. A strong glimpse of bare leg made her jerk her gaze back to the groaning Scot. They were *all* stricken . . . all except her!

Arlo clutched his belly and doubled up. Eden groped wildly about and grabbed up the chamber pot just in time. Arlo made use of it, then collapsed back on his bunk. Eden pulled the quilt up over his shaking shoulders.

"Help 'em, miz—" Arlo clutched her wrist frantically, his eyes wild with fear and sickness. "He be in a bad way—"

"I will," Eden agreed, pushing her new patient back down and covering him again. She fetched him some brandy and bathed his face with cool water. He lapsed into a restless sleep and Eden stared about the tiny cabin, noting with relief that the men had at least found their chamber pots. She turned to the other bunk and in the gray light of the small window she saw how the big Scot's frame hung over the end of the narrow bed. He was sprawled, barelegged almost to the hip and shirtless. His skin and hair were damp with fever and Eden tried not to look at him as she tugged the quilt from beneath his bulk and covered him quickly.

She wished she were uncivilized enough to let him stew in his own juices. But people of true breeding and real refinement went beyond their own baser instincts. Revenge was a petty motive when calamity was crashing all around. She sighed and lifted her chin. She'd been spared to minister mercy to these poor unfortunates, and she'd not be found lacking.

For the rest of the day she drew water from the rain barrel at the base of the hatch, bathed hot faces, and emptied the putrid chamber pots out the commons window. Managing to keep her own stomach calm, she mixed pitchers of diluted brandy and administered doses to all her patients.

Darkness seemed to tarry in grayness a long while before finally descending, and even then it brought her no relief. She was miserably tired, damp, cold, and aching. She finished one exhausting round of care and already they were in urgent need again. The smell of sickness and the cloying, pungent aroma of brandy clung to her clothes and filled her head.

Several times she rose in the night to pitiful moans or cries and finally left her meager lantern lighted. When the grayness filled her cabin again, she dragged herself from her bed to begin the monotony of nursing once more. The ship seemed no calmer than when she had gone to sleep. And when the mate checked on the doctor and Mr. Josephs that evening, he declared them to be in a dreadful way and Eden took them into her care.

James, Arlo, the doctor, and the planter proved docile enough patients. They accepted her cool touch stoically, mumbled gratitude, drank when spoken to, and quickly slept again. But the big Scot was another matter entirely. She never approached his sickbed without a quiver of fear.

A cold, wet cloth always shielded her fingers from the feel of his tight, sun-bronzed skin. When she wiped the damp wisps of hair from his face with the cloth, she jumped skittishly if a strand brushed her knuckle. Then she huffed with disgust and swallowed her nervousness, plying the cold cloth with firmer strokes. But more than once, her eyes followed her cloth over his temple, down his muscular cheek, around his square, stubbled jaw, and down the side of his muscular neck. The quilt sometimes slipped and the top of his broad shoulders gleamed in the pale light.

Once her fingers moved past the cloth over the hard ridge of his collarbone and touched with featherlight strokes the hard mound of muscle that rose tantalizingly toward a dark, forbidden peak concealed by the edge of the blanket. His skin was astonishingly smooth, hard in muscle and yet soft to the touch. As her fingertips circled gently, they encountered the fascinatingly crisp texture of the dark hair that trailed lazily from the base of his throat down his chest. Her downward gaze was stopped by the stark line of the quilt and Eden traced that edge speculatively. She was hypnotized.

Good Lord! She drew her hand back quickly and clasped it in her other one, shaking her head savagely and forcing her eyes away. Her breath was erratic, her pulse pounded in her temples, and her lips throbbed in the queerest way. She swallowed hard, aware of a frightening tightness in her throat.

Perhaps she was succumbing to the illness as well!

No, a sardonic voice rose inside her, the tossing waves outside were not the source of the strange prickling along the skin of her shoulders and the heavy rise and fall of her chest. It was him . . . and the intriguing helplessness of that powerful body. She'd never touched a man's body before . . . bare skin . . . nakedness. . . . Her teeth ground together when she realized that this arrogant Scot

51

could now claim such distinction in her life.

She pressed a cold hand to her flaming cheek and steadied herself against the end of the bed to pour a strong draught of the brandy for him. She stood a moment, wavering, but again her sense of duty overcame selfish considerations: she lifted his head and cradled it against one soft breast as she put the cup to his parched lips. The liquid dribbled from the corners of his mouth.

"Please," she groaned, feeling strangely queasy inside as she held his dark head against her intimately, "drink . . . swallow some . . . It'll help your poor stomach."

As if he understood her words, he managed a swallow or two and then several more. Relief and dismay mingled in her as she saw his dark lashes flutter open. The burden in her arms grew lighter briefly as his head turned toward her breast. She watched his glazed blue eyes with alarm, but quickly they shut and she dropped his head on the pillow as if she'd been bitten. Her breast was tingling strongly where he had pressed against it, especially at its rosy tip.

She slammed the tin cup down on the commode table in the corner, crossing her arms tightly over her bosom. "What's the matter with you, girl?" Mistress Dunleavy's voice had crept into her mind and she nodded obediently. "It's an act of mercy . . . a duty of pure humanity . . . nothing more."

All that day and the next, she went from bedside to bedside, snatching rest at odd hours when no one needed tending. James and Arlo seemed to be resting more comfortably, but the young lord remained hot and feverish. His head tossed and his lips sometimes worked soundlessly. He moved about restlessly and Eden worried that he'd roll from the bunk in his thrashings.

He sometimes rolled onto his side facing the wall, presenting her his broad back and moaning. She screwed up one side of her mouth, considering this warily. Then he cooled a cloth with more water and applied it to the right, smooth expanse of his back.

His movements uncovered his side and she glanced down to find his leg laid bare all the way to his hip. She gasped and grabbed the quilt to cover him, but not before the sight of his long, muscular leg was burned indelibly into her mind. Her heart began to pound queerly and she stood up, alarmed by the strange feelings he produced in her. Her stomach felt quivery and ached with a strange hollowness . . . and it was difficult for her to swallow. . . .

Eden Marlow did something she had never done in her life; she fled. In her cabin, she fell onto her bed, blaming her searing fatigue for her bizarre responses. She searched out the bottle of sherry that Laura and Deborah had given her, poured a ladylike portion, and downed it.

The warmth was marvelously comforting. But as she finished her third drink, her eyes filled with the image of broad shoulders and skin stretched tight over layers of muscle. Long, tapered legs appeared again in her mind and that worrisome tingling began again in her full young breasts, spreading alarmingly under her skin toward her other womanly places. She stared in horror at the bottle in her and, then dropped it down into her trunk as if it had burned her fingers.

The next morning the sea was like glass and the sun shone brilliantly. Eden awoke relieved and murmured a prayer of thanks. But James and the rest were frustratingly slow to mend, even on this calmest of seas. She asked the captain to be relieved of some of her burden and the cook was promptly assigned to see to the Scots. Her patients slept much, drank more, began to eat broth, then gruel, and then like petulant little boys, begged to be entertained by her melodious voice. They vied for her attention and pleaded their symptoms to keep her charming sympathies nearby. She had never imagined that grown men could act so childishly, her James included.

All seemed to be well on the mend until Arlo came staggering into James's cabin, where Eden sat reading to her brother from a book of apparently thirst-producing sonnets. The Scot's eyes were wide and his face was patchy with agitation.

"Ye got to come, miz—he be worse off by th' hour—"

"Who? Your master?" Eden's face flushed guiltily as she recalled how eagerly she had shed her disturbing duties with the big Scot.

"He be weak as a babe, Miss . . . takin' nary a bite an' ravin' an' feverish-like."

"But . . . I could do nothing the cook and Mr. Mallory haven't already done." She avoided James's heightened interest and hoped her reluctance would pass for modesty.

"Nay, miz—when ye tended 'im he were on the mend. Believe, it's a woman's healin' touch that's missin'." Arlo's ruddy, expectant face turned on James. "Some women has a way with horses an' creatures . . . a gentlin' and a healin' power. Belike yer sister 'as the gift." He nodded knowingly, compelling James's fascinated nod of agreement.

"Oh, by all means, Dede, you mustn't withhold your womanly gift from the man." James's mouth was twitching and Eden had to stifle the urge to slap him silly. How dare he taunt her with her own higher motives after she had tended him so devotedly!

"But James, I must see to you and the oth—"

"Don't let a worry mar your lovely brow, dear sister. You've done quite enough here for me . . . go and see to the young lord. I couldn't rest a wink knowing I had kept an angel of mercy from his side."

Eden's lovely eyes narrowed at him. So much for brotherly gratitude.

James waited until he heard them fade, then tossed his newfound sea legs over the side of his bunk and rose to

54

steal over to his brandy cask.

It was as Arlo had said and worse. Lord Ramsay MacLean was ashen as a death's-head, delirious with fever, and difficult to control in his ravings. The cook had, in the end, given up trying and Arlo was still too weakened to manage properly on his own.

Between the two of them, they wrestled him still on the bunk and managed to get some cool water into him. Eden spoke to him over and over, using his given name, *Ramsay*, at Arlo's suggestion. Slowly he seemed to fasten on her melodious, crooning tones and drifted deeper, into a more restful world. He was thinner; his heavy muscles were clearly outlined beneath once-taut skin, his eyes more deeply ringed. He looked as though he hadn't been bathed in days.

As soon as Arlo was tucked in, she climbed up on the end of the lord's bunk and opened the small window as wide as it would go. The cool air freshened the room markedly. And soon she was bathing that face she had sworn never to touch again.

She worked through the evening. When she left the room for even a few minutes, he became agitated again and in the end, she had to pass the night in a chair at his bedside. Responding to her ministrations, his fever subsided and by the following night he was sleeping deeply.

The doctor visited him on the second morning and prescribed the juice of oranges mixed with water as a tonic. But in his semiconscious state the Scot refused the mixture and faithful Arlo informed her that his laird had never fancied oranges. in sickness and in health, Lord Ramsay MacLean's will was unwavering, it seemed.

Undaunted, Eden fetched her tin of sweet biscuits and soaked them in the juice, feeding them to him with a spoon. As she held his head up and against her bosom, urging him to take the last of her sweet treats, she curled her nose irritably. Even desperately ill he was demanding, taking her very best as though it were his due.

She tried hard to recall his unpleasant, taunting tone or the first evening of the voyage, but for some reason it was difficult. As if to compensate for her uncharitable thoughts, she stroked his forehead gently and let her fingers trail through his damp, tangled hair. It was surprisingly soft, not at all like the crisp, wiry hair on his chest.

"Please . . . get well." She gave utterance to the strange longing growing inside her. It was just this uneasiness she had tried to forestall by avoiding him. She wanted him well, to rid herself of this dreadful duty, but then she would not be able to gaze secretly on his ruggedly handsome face . . . and the rest. Her unworthy thoughts shamed her and she drew back primly, clamping her arms about her waist. The man was a menace to her.

"He be restin' easy, miz," Arlo greeted her with a very relieved grin when she entered their cabin the next morning. She smiled and placed a cool hand upon the lord's hard cheek, feeling it somehow changed, firmer.

"His color is better, I think," was as noncommittal as she could be while her stomach was doing a slow turn. He did indeed look better. "I think I can leave him in your care now, Arlo MacCrenna," she said, turning toward the door, eager to escape. "I'll have Dr. Schoenwetter look in from time to time."

Arlo's eyes quickly narrowed as they rested on the bunk. Ramsay MacLean lifted his head and gave him a warning glare and a vigorous shake of the head. Then immediately the proud auburn head returned to the pillow in complete repose. Arlo blinked and jerked his attention back to the Marlow lass.

"Glory, miz. . . ." Arlo cast quickly about for an excuse. "He turned down before when ye left. If anythin' betakes me young laird—well, I'd as soon lay me down and cock up me own toes. Can ye not stay—"

The genuine grief in the man's broad face appealed to her much-burdened higher nature and she relented. Arlo left to go up on deck; she looked up at the small window longingly. She'd love a chance to stroll the placid deck, too. The sun was bright through the small window and she hitched up her skirts to climb up on the bunk and open it.

Beneath her, a pair of blue eyes widened to take in her curving form, her soft brown hair, the sweet swell of her full young breasts. The smooth, firm lips curved slightly, then quickly resumed a more passive expression.

Eden hopped down from the bunk and smoothed her skirts. She paused with clasped hands to study his face again. Those masterful cheekbones, that regally arched nose, that square jaw and stubborn chin . . . she had to tear her gaze away. As she returned to her stitching, she was unaware that the face she had just studied now studied her.

The delicate oval of her face was framed in rich brown hair. Wisps of the silken mane curled about her forehead and temples as if to caress her soft, perfect skin. Her creamy shoulders were half-hidden beneath her lace-edged chemise, but he followed their lines down over her maddeningly rounded breasts to her slender hands as they worked some strange magic with a length of scarlet thread. She seemed so girlish, so innocent, sitting there, waiting patiently for him to awaken.

He turned onto his side toward her, uncovering his long legs in the process. But when she looked up, her striking eyes wide with expectation, his face was quiet and she felt a wave of relief. A moment later, she scowled darkly and rose to cover him. In spite of her nobler impulses, she paused, staring at his strong legs. What was there about them that tightened her throat and made her heart thud faster in her chest? Again those sky-blue eyes widened and they crinkled knowingly.

She thought he groaned slightly in his sleep when she climbed onto the bunk to retrieve a bobbin she'd dropped when she opened the window. He rolled onto his back beneath her, brushing her legs, her stomach, and her breasts intimately. In her vulnerable posture, she had to fight to keep from being carried over with him. It was difficult composing herself afterward and she plopped angrily down into her chair, glaring at his sleeping form.

Since leaving England, she'd been assaulted by the most venal and unsavory thoughts and sensations. And most all of them had been connected to him. The seconds seemed to drag by until Arlo returned, when she could finally escape his overpowering presence.

"Laird Ram?" Arlo bent down near him as soon as Eden was gone. "Be you all right?"

Ram opened one eye stealthily and then the other when he was assured they were alone. "Yea, I'm mending fast, with such tender nursing. But I'm hungry as a bloody bear." His hand came up to rub his bristled chin and he frowned. "And I need a shave badly."

"Dam-me, ye had me half outta me mind w' worry. Why don't ye want the lass to know yer well. . . .?" But the answer came to him before the question was even out.

"I want her near me yet a while." Ram struggled up on one elbow, testing his weakened muscles. "I find her company quite . . . agreeable." A wry grin appeared as he recalled the pleasurable torture of having her nubile young body pressed against him. She'd never know how close she'd come to seeing much, much more of Ramsay MacLean.

"Then perhaps ye'll be wantin' a shave . . . and a bit o'bathin'—more'n she give ye."

"*She* bathed me?" Ram's eyes narrowed in speculation.

"Over an' over, when the fever was on ye. A true angel o' mercy, she was. She be as goodly hearted a lasts as ever—"

"I know exactly what she is, Arlo, and it's *not* an angel," Ram spoke curtly. "Get me a basin and my razor an' soap."

Eden resumed her vigil that afternoon, refreshed and fortified by a good meal, fresh air, and sunshine. The awful smells of sickness were finally fading from memory and with agreeable company the voyage was taking on a much more pleasant aspect. She stopped short at the sight of Ram's freshly shaven chin, throwing Arlo a questioning look.

"Me laird's a fastidious man." Arlo feigned responsibility for shaving his master and smiled his most guileless smile. "I'd not have 'im shamed by his appearance when he wakes, Miz."

"I see." Eden shook her head wonderingly at Arlo's complete devotion to his laird and took up her seat by the bunk. Her nimble fingers flew to her work and when she looked up moments later, she was once again alone in the cabin with Ramsay MacLean.

## Chapter Four

Ramsay MacLean's eyes opened stealthily and traced the top of her shoulders, flowing up the column of her neck, fastening on the perfect swirl of her shell-like ear. He felt a surge of heat through him as he lay there within arm's reach of her delectable softness. He hadn't expected to find her so attractive, so utterly appealing to his every sense. Her voice curled and floated and her fresh scent filled his head. Her womanly curves drew his eyes like a compass and his palms positively itched to touch her. He longed to test his idea of how warm and sweet her mouth would taste.

He frowned at his rambling thoughts, wondering if his recent sickness affected his logical capabilities. She was another man's mistress, and no matter how young and fresh she seemed, she still bought her keep on her back. And for her to respond to him as she obviously did, with her handsome young "protector" so close at hand, she must have the loyalties of an alley cat. Or perhaps she was one of those infamous creatures who was never satisfied, no matter how many men—

Eden turned suddenly in her chair and watched his sleeping face, feeling a chill run between her shoulder blades. Lord Ramsay's color seemed a bit ruddy and she put a cool palm against his cheek. It was a bit warmer than before, and she set her needlework aside to wet a cloth and bathe his face.

To ease the strain of bending, she settled her bottom on the very edge of the bunk as she stroked his face and proceeded down his throat to the edge of his shoulders. Her stomach was turning disconcerting somersaults as she leaned toward the end of the bunk to wet the cloth again. Her breast pressed gently against his shoulder and she swallowed hard to relieve that irksome lump in her throat. This was positively the last day she was going to—

*"Oh-h-!"* she squealed as he snatched her wrists and held them in his sturdy fingers. She tussled off the bunk and pulled away as far as his muscular hands would allow.

"What are you doing?" His voice seemed hoarse and his eyes had a dazed, defensive look.

"Lord Ramsay, I—" she strained in his grip, "I was merely bathing your face. You've been very ill and were put in my care by your man . . . Arlo." She expected to be released, but his grip tightened as his eyes narrowed suspiciously.

"I don't *feel* ill." His voice was husky as he released her wrist to clasp her waist and drag her against the bunk.

"I . . . I assure you, you are!" She planted her free hand on the hard warmth of his chest and pushed. "And this uncouth behavior is proof. Release me at once, sir!"

"Perhaps I've died and this is heaven." His blue eyes cleared remarkably fast as his arms flexed further and pulled her down across his now naked chest.

"I assure you sir, I am *not* an angel—and I shall be forced to prove it if you don't release me immediately!" She pushed against the treacherously warm flesh of his chest with the heels of her palms. But he held her securely, staring into her with a gaze that took her breath away.

"Then prove to me how just earthly a woman you are, wench."

Eden wrestled her arm up and bared her nails near his cheek in warning. Her eyes glowed with anger, snatching his concentration for an instant.

"Nay—there's a better way to prove it than that," he said, his crooked grin more like a smirk. Abruptly he released her other wrist and pulled her head down to his, capturing her lips.

Eden was too surprised to withdraw immediately. The contact was strange and confusing. . . .

"Sir—" she pushed up and as far away as she could against his forceful arms. He certainly didn't *seem* very sick just now. "You insult me and my good office—"

But he pulled her head back down and stopped her protest with his firm, well-formed lips, holding her head tightly as his mouth slanted and moved mesmerizingly beneath hers. This contact was too startling, too warm . . . and too wonderful—she could not let it end without trying to experience and understand it. Her resistance faded and his grasp on her head gentled as his kiss deepened.

His lips parted and Eden felt the moist tip of his tongue against her own lips, searching, exploring. Her lips were tingling, then everything began to swirl and darken. She was being lifted and spun about: her breath shortened. Kissing—this was being kissed . . . really kissed . . . by a man. . . .

This time it was Lord Ramsay who ended the splendid contact. When her glowing eyes opened, they could barely focus on his smoky blue gaze. His handsome face hardened into a humorless smile. In his eyes was a strange contempt for the savagely extinguished blaze of his own passions.

"You're no angel, wench. But I trust you know the way to paradise well enough." His deep utterance resonated through her, finally slapping her with the sense of his taunt.

The sun's savage heat leapt in her eyes and she poised a furious fist, then struck. And instantly his lordship was howling and grabbing for his nose. She backed toward the door, glaring.

"How dare you maul and insult me, you . . . you foul-minded . . . varlet!" Her breast was heaving and her heart pounded in her throat. "After the hours I spent tending you—"

He sat up, holding his nose and glaring at her angrily. She glowed like a brilliant flame and scorched just as surely. He still felt her warmth where her curves had pressed against him, even through the pain in his face.

"But surely your generosity had its compensations," he taunted with a harsh edge. Then he relaxed back on one elbow and propped up a leg, allowing the quilt to fall away unhindered. A muscular hand swept his bare frame from head to toe. "Or did you see nothing here to your liking?"

"I'd have done mankind a service to abandon you to the world beyond. But I doubt very much it would have been *heaven* you found." She jerked the door handle and ran out, banging the door savagely behind her.

Ram MacLean watched the portal for a long moment. In his mind he swept her stinging condemnation aside, but it was not so easy to rid himself of the lingering shock, the confusion in her fiery eyes. He glowered, rising to a sitting position and testing his nose with his fingers. She played the role well . . . the outraged lady of quality, the virtuous younger "sister." But he had seen her at play with her "brother" and had tasted her melting response on his own lips. She was a woman whose passions lay very near the surface. At the proper time, he could rouse them to further his ends.

He pushed his bare legs over the edge of the bunk and

stretched them stiffly. He vowed to take what he needed of her "sisterly" sport in days to come. But as the memory of her rounded breasts and soft lips returned to him, he sucked in his breath sharply. He was coming to truly want the wench; he had not bargained on that.


Eden bit her lip and leaned back against her cabin door, trying to calm her trembling shoulders and rubbery knees. Her fingers came up to trace her lip and she shuddered; she could feel her pulse throbbing in them.

Never in her life had anything like this happened to her. Hours upon hours of grueling, thankless vigil, only to be accused of doing it to take advantage of his manly magnificence! How dare that conceited bastard taunt and attack her after she had practically saved his worthless life!

She threw herself down in the chair. "The way to paradise:" she knew what he meant. He implied she was a woman of easy virtue, the type to roll up her skirts at a nobleman's nod, first in James's cabin and again in the very first moment of his waking. And he'd made it clear he'd be more than willing to oblige her presumed lusts.

Just wait until James—She stopped dead. James . . . would be compelled to avenge her honor. And whether onboard ship or after they docked, it could mean grievous injury to him. She thought of their collective illnesses and her heart sank. How likely would they be to believe an unwarranted attack on her person when the man had seemed near death just days before? She could scarcely believe it herself!

A sardonic voice rose to add another dismal stroke to the picture. Just how pure were own skirts, after all? Had she never wondered what it would be like to press her lips against the broad, generous ones she had so often attended? That kissing was a crazy upheaval of strange and wonderful sensations, mingled with a lingering fear. After all, it was her first kiss from a man on the mouth and—

She stopped dead: her first kiss. That brutal, arrogant, licentious Scot had stolen her first kiss. She wrung her slender hands together miserably as tears began to fall. She felt cheated and . . . soiled.

Some time later, James found her in her cabin, her eyes red-rimmed, her nose swollen. He pulled her to a seat on her bunk and took her hands in his.

"What's the matter?" He stroked her chin fondly. "You can tell me, Mudpie."

"It's nothing, James . . . just a silly, girlish. . . ." Her voice trailed off miserably and she refused to raise her face to him. "I'm just tired."

James watched her and his true gray eyes lit knowingly.

"I know this voyage has been sheer disaster, Dede. You've been a marvel, nursing us all back to health and vigor, with nary a complaint. Believe me, I'll do my very best to see the rest of the trip is better for you. I've even put in an order with the Almighty for good weather."

"James!" she admonished, her face quickly melting in the warmth of his mischeivous smile. "You're terrible."

"No I'm not." He grinned with relief to see her troubled face brightening. She was far too young to be so weary; it clutched at him. "I'm a little charming and a little decadent and quite adorable. Aren't I?" When she shook her head with fond disapproval, he jiggled her hands in his, "Aren't I?"

"Yes," she laughed softly, "you are." She squeezed his hand and felt him return the pressure reassuringly. "James, I can't wait to get home, to be off this ship. When we dock, I won't care if I never see another ship as long as I live."

"Here, here! You'd best get all the rest you can, Mudpie. Mother's got a schedule planned that would wear out a regiment of the king's finest. She plans to show you off to everybody."

"Tell me," Eden brightened, thinking of the beautif[u]
new gowns and dresses tucked away in her other trunk i[n]
the hold.

"Shall I start with the important things . . . potenti[al]
suitors?"

"Yes, do!" Her nose wrinkled impishly as some of th[e]
day's disturbing events fell away at last. The girlish glo[w]
returned to her face and James leaned down to brush on[e]
apple-blushed cheek with a brotherly kiss.

"Well, there's Farley Thorndyke . . . remember him?"
James stuck his front teeth out in a wickedly accura[te]
parody.

"Yes," she clapped her hands delightedly. "I *do* remem[-]
ber him."

"Well, he hasn't changed . . . only longer in the tooth[,]
if that's possible. He's been hanging about for the la[st]
year, pestering us about your arrival. He'll probably be a[t]
the dock to greet you. And Edward Brotherston . .[.]
remember him? The fat one with the runny nose?"

"Oooh, how could I forget?" she mimed, wiping he[r]
nose on her sleeve. He chuckled.

"Well, he's a big, strapping fellow now, quite elegant[,]
except he still. . . ." and James copied her motion.

"You make them sound a dreary lot, my husbandl[y]
prospects," Eden winced, dispirited.

"They all pale beside you, Dede," James smiled rue[-]
fully. "I'd marry you myself if I weren't your unworth[y]
brother and a hopeless degenerate. You're so beautifu[l]
and unselfish and . . . refined. You'll be the best thin[g]
old Beantown's seen in many a day."

"Flatterer," she charged, feeling her spirits lift as thei[r]
old banter returned.

"Cook's planning an extravagant one tonight, to cele[-]
brate everyone's survival. I hear even his lordship's finall[y]
come 'round."

"You heard?"

"Arlo, his man, brought us the news on deck. He's all for nominating you for sainthood straightaway. But the good doctor is of the opinion that you're already an angel—"

Eden drained of color and he frowned.

"Are you sure you're all right, Dede?"

"Fine, James," she straightened, back upon the wary edge of her nerves once more. "I'm perfectly fine."

Eden entered the common room the next night to a chorus of approval that brought a sparkle to her eyes and a blush to her cheeks. James made a show of escorting her to the table and she found herself seated opposite Lord Ramsay MacLean. The Scot was freshly shaven and wearing his best coat and a lace-ruffled shirt. He rose from his seat and reached gallantly for her hand.

"Your most humble servant, miss. I owe much to your kindness." His voice rolled in a cultured manner and with the others looking on, she could hardly deny him her hand. She extended it, then withdrew it primly when he'd done with his gentlemanly farce.

"Wi'out you, miz," Arlo supplied, taking his seat, "Laird Ram wouldn't be here. Lucky we had ye aboard, what wi' yer healin' touch."

Agreement was murmured all around and Eden found herself avoiding the taunt of Ramsay MacLean's serious gaze.

"Arlo thinks I have a gift with . . . beasts." She glanced pointedly at the young Scottish lord. "Perhaps he's right." A tight little smile crept over her face and she saw James's jaw go slack.

"Yer right as rain she does," Arlo supplied, happily ignorant of the nuances floating about him. "A touch an' a word and 'e was peaceful as a babe, me laird was."

"Remarkable," James said dryly, observing his sister' frosty air. "A touch and a word, you say. Dede, you neve cease to surprise me."

"Dede?" Ramsay MacLean's deep voice rumbled forth "I understood your christian name was Eden, Mis Marlow."

"Dede is my brother's pet name for me . . . from childhood," she managed politely, busying herself with her napkin to hide the color creeping into her face.

"A *pet* name. . . ." Lord Ramsay seemed to be rolling that around in his fertile mind.

"Actually it's derived from her middle name—"

"James—" she warned.

"Which is?" The lord cocked an interested brow.

"James—!"

"Delight." James's boyish charm fairly oozed as he smiled and patted her wrist as if it should pacify her "You see, my parents were so enraptured at having a gir child after three dreary, troublesome males, they named her for their primary emotion . . . delight. Either that, o they possessed the foresight of just how ravishing and perfect she would be in full womanhood and pronounced her a 'delight' to behold." He grinned at her teasingly and she feigned a lightness to counter her heartfelt disap proval.

"Indeed," Lord Ramsay gave her a rare, perfectly daz zling smile, "she is that . . . a delight for the senses."

Eden drew breath and sputtered, scarlet-faced. Bu James and his new playmate both found high humor in her irritation and there were chuckles aplenty around the table. There they sat, one speaking of her "delights" as i she were some prize breeding stock and the other as if she were a whore! It was in that moment that she first realized that all men were in league with one another— and loyal to their sex in spite of paltry things like blood ties and family honor.

By the time they quit the common room, Eden was speechless with pent-up fury. The big Scot had abandoned his gruffness, though still he spoke little. And whenever he did, the entire table stopped to listen to his deep, burred tones as though expecting a jewel of wisdom. His illness had made his intriguing face leaner, more dramatically chiseled, and he seemed to know it. Most distressing, she found her own traitorous gaze creeping back to him time and again and had to remain tightly on guard through the entire dinner. Once in her cabin, she sagged onto her bunk and vented her loathing in a string of adjectives that would have turned the rest of Mistress Dunleavy's hair white.

The next few days were no better. They breakfasted separately, Eden usually in her cabin, then ventured on deck to take the air. *He* was always there, his bloody kilt gaping in the wretched breeze . . . and him allowing it to do so. She tried to avoid him, speaking with the doctor, Mr. Josephs, or First Mate Mallory. But he managed to position himself nearby, or between her and the hatch, so that she had to pass near his bare, virile legs and witness the way the wind made his shirt caress those vulgarly broad shoulders. He watched her attempts to pointedly ignore him and they never failed to bring a knowing grin to his firm-set mouth.

Worse yet, James began to talk to the brawny Scot, seeking him out and conversing about a fascinating range of topics . . . things he never discussed with her. Their increasingly frequent laughter drew her eyes from wherever she was on deck and she straightened her posture and tried to seem absorbed in the details of Mr. Josephs' cows' hoof rot.

After nearly a week of her carefully maintained aloofness, the Scot finally planted himself by the hatch and managed to be the only one nearby as she made her way below deck. He extended his hand to assist her and Eden took pains to ignore it.

"You cannot avoid me forever, Eden." He seemed little perturbed as he ran his hand back through his burnished auburn hair. She glanced up from the top step of the hatch and took in his intense amusement full on. It was like stepping into a tub of deliciously hot water; chills rippled from her toes upward.

"Only for another week or so, sir. Then we'll be off this ship and need never trouble one another again." Her chin lifted, but it only brought her into fuller contact with those searching blue eyes.

"Perish the thought. You need not be so formal with me, Eden. My Christian name is Ramsay . . . or Ram, if you prefer."

"A *pet* name?" she smiled frostily, readying her thrust.

"You could say that." He bestowed a dazzling smile, but it didn't stop her.

"Given to you by your sheep, no doubt."

She was smiling wickedly when she reached her cabin. It was small retribution for his nasty, ungrateful attitude. She hugged her shoulders and set about straightening her trunk.

"What was that all about?" Her door swung open and James stepped inside, his face dusky with displeasure. He spread his lean legs and set his fists at his waist as if bracing himself for combat.

"What was what all about?" Eden stopped with a hand-painted talcum box in her hand.

"That business with Ramsay just now. What did you say to him?"

"Nothing, really. He asked me to address him by his Christian name and I declined." Eden felt a deep flush stealing into her cheeks.

"That's *all*? There had to be more than that. I saw his face—Eden, I won't have you being rude to my friends."

Her jaw dropped. "Your lordly 'friend' happens to be

70

no friend of mine, James. I find your Scot crude, boorish, and presumptuous. I will extend no more than the commonest of courtesies to him, title or no."

"By God . . . you're a bloody snob!" His arms rose and then flopped at his sides. "I knew you were too perfect to be true . . . you're a regular English-lady-snob. He's a Scot and therefore a barbarian, a lout . . . a bumpkin. That's it, isn't it?" But he gave her no chance to speak. "I never thought to hear my own sister spout such idiocy. Eden," he shook his finger at her righteously. "I'm gravely disappointed in you. . . ."

"Disappointed —" she sputtered, appalled at his conclusions. "See here, James, I don't have to answer to you for my likes and dislikes *or* for my manners. Nor do I have to swoon and titter and fawn over some uncouth nobleman just to enhance your status!" She was blazing, her eyes showering hot sparks.

"*My* status?"

"Don't suppose it's not obvious to everyone that you're cozying up to his title . . . his *supposed* title."

"Eden. . . ." James's face was florid with ire and he sputtered, "I . . . I would never have believed this if I hadn't heard it with my own two ears."

Eden's fists clenched at her sides and she was rigid with fury. How dare he accuse her of snobbery and an unladylike manner toward anyone! She drew breath for a hot retort, but it was another voice that filled the space between them.

"What's this? Trouble in paradise?" came the deep, rolling burr that always jangled Eden's taut nerves. During his outburst, James had barged in and left the door open. Now it was filled by Ramsay MacLean's annoyingly casual frame and and knowing blue eyes.

"Nothing, really," James jolted around fully and smoothed his vest, his face beet-red. "A brother-sister spat." He sent Eden a dark, forbidding scowl and she glared back at him icily.

"Now there's a shame. Nothing that can't be fixed, I hope." Ram's face broke into a charming grin that Eden could have sworn was aimed at her.

"I think I could use some fresh air." James glanced at her. "It's become quite stuffy in here." And he strode out, taking Ram with him.

On deck, Ram probed the reason for their "lover's" quarrel and was surprised to have James admit:

"You. She doesn't exactly approve of you, for some ungodly reason."

"That's strange," Ram mused with deceptive idleness, "I have only the warmest regard for her."

"She can be so sweet, sometimes . . . and so damned infuriating at others.

"That's a lass for you." Ram's mouth curled with lazy pleasure as he stretched his long legs out in front of the crate he was sitting on.

"Well, I'll be glad to be shed of her, come Boston. Let somebody else put up with her for a while," James huffed, drawing from Ram a startled look.

The sea was calm, the breeze balmy, and the passengers of *Gideon's Lamp* lounged about on deck after a cold supper. Lord Ramsay had gone below earlier and that accounted for Eden's pleasant, relaxed state. She sighed, gazing at the brilliant sunset, and joined James at the midship rail. Their quarrel had weighed heavily on her since yesterday afternoon.

"It won't be long now," she offered.

"No, it won't," he returned after a short silence. He glanced at her from the corner of his eye and stared back out at the gentle waves.

"James, please don't be angry with me," she blurted, biting her lip afterward. He drew a heavy breath and turned to her.

"I'm not angry with you, Dede. You can't help the way

72

you are, I know that."

"James, I am not a snob, contrary to what you may think. Not liking one of your friends shouldn't condemn me to live forever without your love and good graces. I didn't require you to adore my school friends . . . why must you let this one 'friend' come between us?"

"It's not just him, Dede . . . it's—" He stopped short. How could he tell her he found her extremes of refinement and elegance displeasing? She was a lady now, a true-bred, highly groomed lady, meant for the marriage trade. No doubt in a few short years she'd have set new standards for all of Boston society, standards he'd be obliged to break in order to live his own life. That was just the way she was, now, and it would be unfair of him to condemn her for it.

"It's all right, Dede. Let's forget it and enjoy what's left of our last voyage together." He took her hand between his and felt a catch in his throat as she turned her striking eyes to him; they were filled with liquid crystal that glowed golden in the evening light.

James opened her cabin door later and started inside with her.

"I'll light the lamp for you."

"That's all right, James," she turned quietly, eyes downcast in the gloom. "I can manage." She glanced up to his wan little smile.

"Good night, Dede." He kissed her upturned cheek and Eden was left feeling like the light had gone out of her life. She knew the truth of it now: James didn't like her anymore.

She fumbled for a splint and lit the lantern from one hanging in the passage. She felt hollow, utterly empty as she removed her knitted shawl and folded it with her customary precision. She turned to put it in her trunk and jolted back with a gasp.

Ramsay MacLean was sprawled in her chair in the

73

corner beside her trunk. He wore his kilt, shirt, and stockings, but his coat lay over the top of her trunk, beside him. He also wore a very pleased look as his eyes slid over her possessively.

"What are you doing here?" Eden stiffened, clutching her shawl to her chest as she crossed her arms over it. She was in no state to confront this man in her bedchamber.

"I came to talk with you."

"You can speak with me in the commons or on deck. Please be good enough to leave . . . immediately!" He showed no signs of moving and her heart began to pound harder in her chest.

"What I have to say is best spoken here." He crossed his arms over his chest as he surveyed her and one finger stroked his chin slowly. Eden felt as if it were stroking her. A sliver of excitement shot through her body and her eyes pulsed wider with alarm.

"I've not expressed my gratitude fully for your care of me. Arlo told me everythin'. . . ." He inched closer and Eden found herself shrinking backward.

"I'm not interested in your apologies, sir—"

"Ramsay," he interjected, leaning back slightly on one leg.

"—I'm interested only in your departure." She lifted her chin, suddenly finding it hard to swallow.

"You've done me a turn, Eden, and I've come to do you one. You see, I know you and James—or whatever his real name is—have argued of late—"

"Whatever his. . . ? Our arguments are absolutely none of your concern," she snapped, feeling her color rising. He was closing in on her, looming powerfully above her . . . and she smacked into the cabin wall.

"I've made you my concern, Eden Marlow." His hand came up to her cheek and he felt her skin respond to his fingertips as they explored the glowing curve of her cheek. "You're a very beautiful woman. . . ." A wry smile

74

tugged at the corner of his lips and he stepped closer, stopping her breadth in her throat. He watched the struggle of panic and excitement in her eyes and a hot shaft of desire shot upward through him. Another step and he was within a hair's breath of that maddeningly curved little body of hers.

"I like your James, but it's clear he's not man enough to handle a woman like you."·

A frown flitted over Eden's face as she tried feverishly to make sense of all this. James . . . what was he saying about James not being James?"

"Eden." Her name was like honey on his tongue. It was a summons to all those unknown realms where man and woman meet, and its impact was clear in the depthless centers of her unforgettable eyes. His big hands closed on her shoulders and he drew her close, lowering his head by degrees to her parted lips. That contact blotted everything else from her mind. She was drawn up to meet his kiss, wrapped in rugged arms that held her tight against that body she had come to know all too well.

The empty, aching chamber of her heart swung open to drink in the thrill of her womanly awakening. The void of girlhood lost was filled by startling new sensations that beckoned her toward womanhood's promise. Her arms circled his waist hesitantly, feeling him tighten against them. He was so hard, so powerful, so different from her. His lips were just like the rest of him, firm and smooth and unexpectedly gentle. They slanted intriguingly over hers, drawing her to fit her own against them in seductive patterns of exploration.

Her breasts tingled pleasurably where they pressed against his ribs. An intense itch inside her seemed to be relieved only where their bodies came together tightly.

"I know that James is plannin' to part company with you in Boston . . . leavin' you in other hands, as it were." Against her lips, his breath came harder. His hands slid up to toy with the back of her neck.

"James . . . what?" she managed to say while fighting the sensual storm that raged within.

"And as long as he seems bent on puttin' you in other hands, I think they might as well be mine." His hands began to roam her sides, searching through her clothes for her small waist, her ribs, her back.

"James . . . leaving me?" she breathed hotly, shaking her head desperately to clear her vision. Alarm finally penetrated those beguiling mists of pleasure. She couldn't understand what he was saying, but she managed to push back enough to look at him him. His eyes were lidded, almost black, frightening.

"It's a hazard of your trade." His lips bore a carnal fullness as they tilted in a sardonic grin. "Perhaps if you'd responded to him the way you have to me, your future would still be secure. A lady-love should always show a certain . . . *enthusiasm*."

"Lady . . . love?" she echoed, finally beginning to understand what she was hearing. Her *trade*. . . .

"It'll be easy enough, I think. James is a reasonable sort. I'll speak to him when we dock and see that your trunks are delivered to an inn near my host. You'll be made quite comfortable." He read the shock in her face, but knowing he possessed the ultimate persuasion, dismissed it. He pulled her against him easily, lowering his lips toward hers. How he had waited for this moment.

"You think I'm . . . we're. . . !" Eden exploded in his arms, shoving, wrestling with him—desperate to be free of his treacherous warm gasp.

"—*certainly* not brother and sister," Ram recovered just quickly enough to maintain his hold on her. "Tsk, tsk . . . you could have been a bit more inventive . . . say, husband and wife. Then you could have shared a cabin and you might have held his interest a bit longer. I won't make the same mistake with you, wench—"

"The same — ? Take your hands off me!" She grasped as he clamped her against his hard body, making her feel his overpowering strength and his aroused state. "James *is* my brother, you vile, degenerate wretch!" She shoved uselessly against the sturdy vise of his upper arms. "We didn't invent *anything!*"

"Of course he is, wench . . . an' I'm Good Saint Nicholas." Ram's features hardened against her fiery challenge. Silver sparks collected in his eyes and his breath came in hot bursts as they struggled.

"He's my brother, not my lover! *Let me go!*"

But he clamped her tight against him with her arms pinned safely at her sides. The silk net that had bound her heavenly cloud of hair had slipped and was slowly wriggling down that unwinding coil of silk. Her lips were the color of early apples and her eyes flashed with the summer lightning.

Her wriggling and twisting against him were excruciating and he sucked air in as white-hot desire exploded in him. Wanting her so and feeling her response to him, he hadn't expected her to take this change of patrons so hard. Uncertainty welled deep within him as those unheeded nuances of innocence now coalesced into doubt. Perhaps she wasn't so worldly, after all. . . .

"You're fond of James, but in time you'll come 'round to me. I've a pleasanter side —"

"In a pig's eye!" Her struggle were renewed and she tried to kick at him, finding she was held too tightly against him to muster force. "I'd sooner die than . . . serve your lusts."

"You think so, do you?" his eyes narrowed to a piercing gleam and his whole body began to ache for release. Perhaps she was the kind that required a strong hand to render her amorous. He'd heard of such women. . . .

"This is an old game, wench. You want a bit of persuadin'. . . ."

And before she knew what was happening, he had lifted her up and wrestled her over to her bunk. He pushed her down on it beneath him, crushing her into the thin mattress, covering her completely with his hard, unyielding body.

"Stop—!" She fought for breath and will under his massive power. "James will kill you for this!" She jerked her head to the side and gulped a breath to scream. But his lips covered hers again and again, robbing her of breath and forbidding her cry.

She stilled, drained of air and energy under his massive weight. And raw new sensations began to spread their loathsome tendrils through her, echoing her unanswered needs. He eased above her to allow her to breathe. But as her lips parted, he invaded them with the velvety tip of his tongue, tantalizing them until they twitched with response.

Ram's arms released her slowly. His hands came up to stroke her cheek, bringing her eyes open upon his dusky face. Beneath him, her insides were melting into a pool of fluid warmth. And as if his lips knew exactly what was happening to her, they began to move over her cheek and down her throat, in harmony with the strange rhythm undulating within her.

Her breath caught in her throat as his hand reached her tingling breast and began to caress its ripe fullness. Tongues of fire began to lick her belly from the inside, making her want to squirm away from—or toward—his manly hand. Ram's mouth lowered across her chest, leaving a trail of liquid fire along her skin. He tugged the bow of her chemise and gently nuzzled it aside, capturing her breast between his hand and the hot plane of his cheek. Soon her bodice was opened, too, freeing one pale, perfect globe to his eager mouth. He groaned and rained kisses over her taut, sensitive breast, then began to nibble the tantalizing bud gently at its tip.

Her name was ground from the very depths of his being, resonant and full of passion's sweetest demand. It called her to own her longing for him, to surrender to her passions and to him. She hadn't imagined that a man and a woman might do such things together—

"Tell me," he demanded huskily into her tingling ear and along her silken neck, "you'll come with me and be my mistress." His deep, intimate pleadings vibrated under her skin. "Let me have you now, Eden."

She had to conquer the pounding of her heart to hear him. Her sooty-lashed eyes drifted open to find him nuzzling the base of her throat and nibbling the skin of her shoulders. And his hand . . . his hand tantalized her naked breast. The sight of her own bare flesh jolted her as violently as the reality of his long, sun-bronzed fingers teasing her rosy nipple.

"Come . . . with you?" Eden was spiraling back to the present, careening wildly, dangerously from rapture's rare and unexplored peaks. "No . . . *no!* Get off me . . . leave me alone—"

He grabbed her panicky hands and forced them back on the bed next to her shoulders. His reactions were passion-dulled as he tried to stop her words. Her head strained away as her shoulders twisted and she began to thrash beneath him.

"Stop—you can't do this to me!"

"Wench—you want me as badly as I do you!" And to prove it his head dipped to her breast.

Intense shafts of shameful pleasure radiated through her and she shuddered to a halt beneath him. She was beyond the reach of those misty regions of pleasure that had once blocked her resistance to him. Now the same pleasurable brushes and kisses and tugs only filled her eyes and throat with salty shame.

"Stop . . . *please* . . . " she begged, squeezing her eyes shut against him and loathing both him and herself for

79

what was taking place inside her. "I'm not his mistress . . . I'm not anybody's whore. Please . . . don't . . . hurt me. . . ."

A frozen sob melted in her throat as she jerked her head away from his searching lips. Scalding tears slid down her cheeks toward refuge in her tousled hair. She went still beneath him, braced to bear his worst, and unable to contain the fear and tumult inside her.

Ram paused above her, his eyes black and hot with desire. A shudder ran through her breast, making her chin tremble as fresh tears slid from her eyes. His face stiffened as he touched the glassy ribbon of tears that trailed into her hair. He glared at the cool liquid on his fingertips and stifled what anger threatened to bloom within.

"Please," she felt his pause and, in desperation, cast away her last shred of pride. "Please . . . *don't make me*. . . ."

"Make you?" he echoed, feeling strange and thwarted. He touched her wet face again and lifted a tear to his lips, tasting it. In it was an icy blast that smacked him back to full reason. His muscular hands pinned her slender wrists to the bed and his heavy weight lay between the futile resistance of her thighs. Her hair was a tousled mass about her pale face and her modest gown was pulled down to expose one ripe young breast. His body was tensed and hard as it drove her down into the bed beneath him.

The realization of his position on her and of the force needed to maintain it shocked him. She was crying, almost sobbing. And he was poised to take her, regardless of her struggles. He rose fully onto his elbows and lifted more of his weight from her, scowling furiously when she drew a starved breath of relief. Her eyes fluttered open and their glazed, defenseless look was the final stroke. No tart was sly enough to mimic misery so well. . . .

"You really *don't* want it." It was half-question, half-conclusion, ground out of a growing fury.

Salty shame clogged her throat and she could only manage to shake her head, closing her eyes from his burning blue gaze. His face was granite-hard above her and she had read in his anger how little hope she had of escaping him.

He was suddenly in motion, flexing and rising above her, leaving the bunk. Eden's eyes flew open as cool air replaced his warm flesh against her. Disbelief paralyzed her for a moment, then she turned her head to look at him. He stood in the center of the cabin, stiff and braced, glaring at her as he smoothed his rumpled kilt.

"I'd rather have a willin' mistress." Something caught in his throat and he continued huskily, "My offer will stand, wench, while I am in Boston."

In the pause that followed, Eden sat up and curled her feet about her on the bunk. Every breath was a shuddering effort as she jerked her bodice up and wiped at her free-flowing tears with her palms. Her eyes were red and her cheeks stained with humiliation. A cloud of sable hair clung protectively about her shoulders.

Ramsay MacLean watched her in the yellow lantern light and his churning stomach warred with his desire. She seemed so innocent, sitting there crying. And yet only minutes before, she had returned his kisses, pressed herself against him as only a woman in need would have done. One feel of her in his arms and he'd lost his grip on himself.

That was the worst; raw appetite had taken him to the brink of oblivion. He'd never come close to forcing a woman before now—he'd never needed to. Such a thing was beneath even Haskell, the randy old goat. It was she . . . it was Eden Marlow who'd done this to him. She'd disrupted his future, his senses, and now his self-possession as well. And he was bound irrevocably to her.

81

"Damn!" he swore aloud, reaching for his coat and running his fingers through his hair. He tried to glower at her without really looking at her. But he saw her luminous, crystalline eyes, still moist, and the jerking of her shoulders as she trembled.

"When you change your mind, you know the way to my cabin." He savagely jerked open the door and was gone.

## Chapter Five

The polished black coach drew up to the dock not long after *Gideon's Lamp* nudged the stone wharf and settled into a secure berth. Adam Marlow , fashionable in frock coat, descended the steps and then lent assistance to his wife, Constance. Behind them, two gentlemen rode up to the coach and dismounted, tethering their horses. They joined Adam and Constance, quickly, brushing their brown riding coats and adjusting their fawn-colored vests and blue cravats. Under their mother's appraising eye, they dusted their tall boots with their gloves and stood a bit straighter.

"No, dear," Adam restrained his wife by the arm when she started for the gangway that was being lowered into place. He turned to his middle son, the taller. "Ethan, you go . . . let them know we're here." And as Ethan grinned and jolted into motion, Adam lowered his head near Constance's ear. "Wouldn't want to appear too eager."

"I *am* too eager," Constance muttered, sighing. "I've never been good at stifling my impulses."

"I know," Adam's grin was meant only for Constance and she lowered her lashes briefly to acknowledge it.

"I haven't seen my daughter in three years. I think I'm entitled to be a little swept away."

"A little," he agreed indulgently, squeezing her delicately gloved hand. Constance realized his hand was trembling in hers and shot him a teasing glance. He smiled ruefully and smoothed his other hand down his vest front.

Together they watched the top of the gangway anxiously for sight of Eden and James. Adam's arm slipped about his wife's waist and he pulled her to his side. Her hand flitted up over her elegant coiffure and came to flutter above the bows of the spencer she wore over her polished print gown. She sighed raggedly and felt Adam's arm tightened her about again.

A moment later Ethan came striding down the gangway, his face red with excitement, his eyes twinkling. "They're coming!" he called to the little party on the dock.

"What does she look like?" Constance left Adam's support to meet her son halfway. She grasped his sleeve and looked anxiously into his square, pleasant face.

"She's beautiful—all grown up and quite the lady!" he beamed, looking over his shoulder at the empty gangway.

James appeared at the top of the ramp and waved, looking behind him, then frowning after a moment. He turned to them and let his arms rise and fall at his sides in exasperation. He took two steps down the gangway then stopped and retraced them.

A confused minute passed in silence and Adam and Chase, the youngest son, hurried to where Constance and Ethan waited. All eyes were riveted on the spectacle of their eldest son and brother's irritation. He finally turned to them and called out, "Her bonnet. She's forgot her damned bonnet!"

He disappeared but in short order reappeared with Eden in tow; she was still making final adjustments to the canted bow of her velvet scoop bonnet.

She paused, stunned by the sight of her beloved family's faces, and she flushed with excitement . . . and all manner of wonderful and confusing feelings. For a moment she couldn't move.

James took charge and ushered her down the incline and into their waiting arms. Instantly, she was engulfed by hugs and kisses, and passed from embrace to embrace and back again: she was bobbing in a sea of affection. She smiled demurely under the crushing hugs of her brothers and father and in her mother's possessive grasp. She managed to blush appropriately and return compliment for teasing compliment. But their raw enthusiasm for her was overwhelming: she wasn't used to this touching, this bold display of feeling — it was like being plunged into a cold river — it took her breath away.

At last Constance called a halt and drew Eden before her, absorbing every detail of her delicate features and elegant clothes. She touched her daughter's cheek with tender restraint.

"*Look* at you! You're so beautiful, Eden! And I'm so proud to have you home. You don't know how we've longed for you. And you're so grown up, such . . . a l-lady. . . ." Constance's eyes were wet suddenly, and she stammered to a halt, searching her reticule, then dabbing at her tears with her handkerchief.

Eden felt a great lump in her throat and clamped a tight hand on her wavering emotions. She squeezed her mother's hand and looked at her brothers longingly.

"It's so good to be home, *Mam-ma,*" she managed with subdued joy, reaching a hand to her father and squeezing his tightly. "This is all a bit . . . overwhelming. Ethan, Chase — they're so handsome. And Father, you've grown so distinguished — "

"Gray, Eden — I've grown gray in your absence," Adam corrected good-naturedly.

"And *Mam-ma* . . . you're *still* the most beautiful woman in Boston." Eden tried to put the pride that

85

swelled in her heart into her eyes. Her mother had not a streak of gray in her luxurious brown hair and her skin was dewy and smooth.

"Oh, Eden!" Her mother hugged her again with great exuberance. Caught off guard, Eden remained somewhat stiff in her arms and Constance released her with a fleeting glance at Adam. "Come, dear," she put her arm about Eden's small waist to turn her toward the coach, "we'll leave the men to fuss with the baggage. I can't wait for you to see the house and your room—I've redone it with Chinese printed paper and—"

But as they turned, a pair of tartan kilts appeared between the little group and the coach. Eden stiffened noticeably.

"Ramsay, my friend, this is the rest of our family . . ." James was grinning broadly, oblivious to Eden's sudden chill. "My father, Adam Marlow; my mother, Constance; my brothers Ethan and Chase . . . and this is Lord Ramsay MacLean, a fellow passenger—and fellow sufferer during our voyage."

Ram MacLean smiled engagingly as he took Adam's hand, then Constance's. "My pleasure to meet you at last, Mr. Marlow, madam. I've heard much about you." His smile swept the family group with deceptive lightness. "You have an uncommonly fine-lookin' family, madam." His accent seemed almost a purr as he spoke to Constance, whose face was paling even as her daughter's was reddening. Ramsay MacLean's dress and handsome features were jarring long-buried memories. "And as generous an' noble of spirit as they are pleasin' to the eye," Ram went on. "I owe yer daughter more than I can say."

"Uh-hum—" James cleared his throat hastily, seeing his mother's distress and thinking that Ramsay might have put it more gracefully. "We had terrible storms at sea and I'm afraid Dede here was stuck with abominably good health while the lot of us were sick. Ramsay was stricken

86

worst and Dede pulled him through like a regular angel of mercy."

"How perfectly horrible for you, Eden, dear." Constance managed to peel her eyes from Ram's shockingly familiar countenance to glance at Eden's crimson face and lowered eyes. "But how fortunate you were spared and able to assist . . . his lordship."

"Wasn't it?" Eden approximated a smile, then met Ram's taunting gaze with a spark of retribution. "I was glad to be able to help *my dear brother* . . . and the others." Ram's genial expression hardened visibly.

"Yes, well," Adam took up the unsettling exchange just as it threatened to unravel, "your lordship must call upon us for supper some evening."

"That would be *delightful*," Ram nodded regally and all pretense of pleasantness left Eden's face. "James knows where I'll be stayin'. Good day, sirs, madam . . . Eden." He turned and strode down the dock with Arlo at his side.

"I hope it wasn't too taxing for you, Eden." White-faced, Constance ushered her daughter to the coach once more, managing to steal a glance at the Scot's retreating back. The familiar twitch to his kilt and the conquering stride of those long, muscular legs roused in her a genuine anxiety. Lord Ramsay *MacLean* . . . even the name and rank were the same. The strained exchange between the regrettably familiar young lord and her own lovely daughter briefly made her weak in the knees. A twinge of uneasiness swept through her as she watched Eden's stiff posture and controlled air. It had been many years, she tried to tell herself. But perhaps she was wrong. . . .

From a distance Ram watched the coach lurch into motion and disappear around a corner. His face and thoughts were both dark with ire . . . mostly for his own pigheaded behavior. Earlier, watching from the ship's railing, he had been stunned by the reunion he witnessed. Constance Marlow was an older version of his own tempting quarry—there was no mistaking her as Eden's mother. And the others—they, too, shared a strong resemblance to Eden. Only James had escaped this assessment; he alone favored his father. They truly were brother and sister . . . Eden and James Marlow!

Chagrin and disgust warred with an annoying sense of relief inside him. She wasn't James's mistress . . . why should that please him so? He'd made a damnable fool of himself, assuming *like mother, like daughter,* assuming Eden had to be raising her skirts for somebody. Still, her behavior—he'd had provocation for his conclusions. And she had responded to him readily enough . . . despite that last evening's disaster.

Damn! Now he had his work cut out for him. Like as not, the only way to get a child from her was to marry her. And from her reaction today, it was going to take a small miracle to make her agree to that.


"Well, James, you've been with her for several weeks. What do you think?" Late that night, Adam Marlow watched his eldest son slide into the high-backed leather chair in his dim, oak-paneled study. He settled back in his great tapestried wing chair and sent a sidelong glance at Constance, who had paused in the midst of pouring three very stout brandies.

James sighed and ran a hand over his eyes, collecting his thoughts and deciding on the truth. He smiled briefly as he accepted a heavy crystal goblet from his mother, sniffing it appreciatively.

He sipped the potent amber liquid and raw pleasure shone in his features. "She's lovely and gracious, the epitome of elegance and refinement," and here the approval suddenly evaporated, "and she's a prig, a snob . . . nauseatingly proper."

"Oh!" Constance's exotic blue eyes flew wide open and she drank the full balance of her potent drink in one draught.

"Yes, well. . . ." Adam murmured, copying her mode of drinking. Then he rolled his empty goblet between his hands, seemingly at a loss for words.

"Not that she isn't a perfectly wonderful and splendid person." James sat forward and sipped determinedly until his glass was dry. He took a deep breath and rested his elbows on his knees. "She's incredibly well bred, often downright witty, and noble as hell. She went without sleep for days while nursing us all back to health. You can't help admiring that." He handed his glass back to Constance, who rose and refilled all three glasses, with a liberal hand.

"She's eighteen, I know," he continued miserably, "but I can't be around her for very long without feeling as if I'm being chaperoned. I feel I'm being given marks on deportment . . . and hygiene."

"Yes, well. . . ." Adam slouched a bit in his chair and glanced warily at Constance. "All evening I had the feeling I should be holding my stomach in."

"Adam!" Constance admonished him.

"It's the truth, Mother . . . *Mam-ma,*" James mimicked Eden's high-toned pronounciation. "She's got a good heart, but she's been polished till she's cold. She doesn't like being touched . . . well, not much, anyhow. Just dry little pecks on the cheek and stiff little squeezes. And she's very choosy about who she considers 'proper' folk to know."

"She does seem a bit stiff and uncomfortable when I hug her," Adam mused. "But a snob? Our Mudpie a lady-snob?" He dispatched his second glass just as he had the first.

"Honest, I swear it. Took an *instant* dislike to my friend Ramsay—on account of his being a 'crude, uncouth Scot.' Those were her very words."

"Well, there are many reasons a young woman might object to a man," Constance put in, feeling slightly ill at her own conclusion. There was only one reason a woman might object to a MacLean. She finished her glass with an unladylike gulp. "That doesn't prove she's a snob."

"Why else, then?" James scooted forward in his chair and finished his glass before handing it back to his mother. "Look, Ramsay is one of the brightest, most congenial fellows I ever met. Tall, well-favored . . . of nobility, and a gentleman's gentleman. What else could it be but snobbery?"

Constance poured another round in uneasy silence, carrying the decanter back with her and setting it by her feet on the rug. What else, indeed? Adam had never actually seen her old lover, Haskell MacLean, though he certainly knew the name—*and* the reputation. So he wouldn't understand . . . Good Lord! She was letting her imagination run amok. The man might prove a distant nephew . . . or one of any number of far relations!

"She seemed a bit distant—strained—on the dock this afternoon." Constance clamped a stern hand on her motherly fears and observed, swirling her drink and watching it. "Are you quite sure she wasn't ill during the voyage?"

"Come to think on it," James finally sat back and scratched his beard-shadowed chin, "she complained of her head the last three days or so and stayed in her cabin most of the time. Wouldn't let the physician near, so I just figured it was a feminine complaint . . . nothing to really worry about."

Constance leveled an impaling look at her eldest son while Adam Marlow sent him a now-you've-done-it wince of sympathy.

"James Atherton Marlow, sometimes you're an insensitive lout. No wonder no decent woman will wed you. Feminine complaint, indeed!" With no small sense of guilt, Constance rose valiantly to her daughter's defense. "She's been through a harrowing experience . . . and she's undoubtedly exhausted. And with the strain of coming home—it's natural that she's keyed up and feeling out of sorts. Mark my word, some rest and a little time to adjust—and she'll be back to her vibrant old self in no time."

Late in the next afternoon Eden stood at the door of her bed chamber, one hand on the latch, the other clasped against her cheek in indecision. She started back yet again and was stopped by the graying upstairs maid who stepped in her path.

"Honest, Miss Eden, I'll manage," Charity assured her, looking at the half-empty trunks, strewn dresses and linen, and piles of other feminine paraphernalia that had inundated Eden's room. The place looked worse than a dressmaker's workroom.

"Well—be sure the heavy velvets and any dresses with quilt bodices are wrapped in paper before they're put in the wardrobe."

"Yes, Miss Eden, I know all about 'em," Charity smiled tightly, containing her slow-stoked indignation.

Eden read her thinning patience and sighed, clasping her hands together to keep them from interfering again. "I'm sorry, Charity. I'm used to doing everything myself. I suppose it will take me a while to leave my schoolgirl ways behind, now that I'm home." She looked so wistful that Charity came to put an ample arm about her shoulders and give her a fleeting hug.

"Ye'll get the hang of it again, quick enough. Just

remember, if ye think it ought to be done, there's someone to do it. An' if you think it ought to be left alone there's someone to do that, too."

Eden laughed and gave Charity's hand a squeeze. "That should be easy enough." She left then, feeling another small hurdle behind her. There were so many things to get used to again . . . servants . . . brothers . . . parents.

She wandered through the second floor, peering into room after room of the stately brick home. She compared it all with the long-cherished images that had comforted her so far away, noting each new coverlet or vase or painting. From the upstairs parlor, she looked out over the gardens below and saw her mother cutting flowers for the evening's table. It was so placid and genteel a sight that she melted onto the windowseat and leaned her head against the windowpane. Her home: how dearly she had remembered it. It still seemed grand, even through the discerning eyes of an adult. Perhaps someday her own home would prove just as heartwarming. . . .

She stopped, watching her mother enter the house, her wicker basket laden with bright blossoms. This had been her home . . . and was her home now. But for how long? How long would it be before a marriage bargain would be struck and she'd be shuttled off again, this time for good? Tears pooled in her eyes and to quell the trembling of her chin, she raised it determinedly and made herself think of Mistress Dunleavy, and of duty. She'd not allow sentiment to erode her finer sense of place and purpose. She'd take her place by her husband when she found one, and that was that. Until then, she could enjoy her home and repay her parents' faith in her by displaying and sharing some of the refinement the colonies needed so urgently.

Sniffing and dabbing at her eyes with a lacy handkerchief, she straightened her back and rose with an extra effort at grace. Perhaps she could begin by helping *Mam-*

*ma* with her flowers.

Constance, still carrying her basket, crossed the entry hall and went toward her husband's study. Eden saw her from the top of the staircase, but had been raised to understand that calling out over such a long distance was gauche, and so she simply made note of where her mother was bound. Her leisurely descent gave her a chance to study the subtle changes in the entry hall: she noted with pleasure the charming use of Federal blues, the new Belgian rug, the marble-topped table. She paused a moment, smiling bountifully and feeling a long-needed peace settling over her.

Rounding the corner of the hall near her father's secluded study she heard his raised voice through the half-open door.

"Constance!"

But it did not sound angry . . . more surprised, or pleased. Eden smiled, thinking what a fine and striking pair her parents made: her tall, distinguished father beside her petite, enchanting mother. And they always got on so well—

"Constance, really . . . what if someone should come—" Adam's voice was unmistakable, bringing Eden to a dead stop.

"No one's going to come, Adam," Constance assured him breathily. Her giggle sounded positively naughty. "The boys are out pillaging the local economy—or the local young women. Eden's setting her things aright or resting . . . and the servants know better than to disturb you in your inner sanctum."

"Really, Constance—I have a whole raft of figure that need attending," Adam's voice was growing husky. "Ohhh. . . ."

"I have a figure that needs attending, too, Adam." There was an electric silence before her velvety voice issued forth again. "Here. You won't see anything this absorbing on parchment."

"God, Constance, what are you. . . . Oh—oh, you insatiable minx! I'll probably be penniless by supper. . . ." His voice became hoarse and barely audible, "and I won't give a damn."

Constance's laugh was husky and triumphant. In the long pause that followed, there was an unmistakable rustle of silk and the scrape of a chair. Eden stood, paralyzed, unable to swallow the tightness in her throat. Breaths and small groans of pleasure washed over her and her eyes burned dryly. Murmurs and whispers followed and there was movement.

"All right, I'll close the dratted door," Constance laughed huskily.

Eden jolted to the side just in time to avoid being seen, but not in time to avoid seeing her mother, skirts awry and bodice loosened, sway into view. She paused a moment and Eden almost gasped at her earthy, seductive air.

The door closed with a thud; Eden's heart pounded wildly. Those were her parents, her precious mother, her dignified father! She bolted and ran straight through the morning room for the gardens.

In the farthest corner of the winding, tree-lined garden, she collapsed on a stone bench and clasped her forehead with one hand and her heaving chest with the other.

A flood of memories came rushing over her. How many times had she stumbled on similar scenes in her childhood—her mother ensconced in her father's lap, her hair or buttons loosened and her body molding to his as they kissed. She had liked watching them, giggling until they acknowledged her presence and gave chase or swept her up to cuddle between them. Then she'd had no idea their behavior was a prelude to other, more carnal pursuits.

But now . . . now she knew exactly what they had been doing. And from the frequency of such remembrances, her parents must have engaged often in such . . . escapades. And they were obviously still at it! It made her face sting with shame. How could her own parents behave in such a lewd and vulgar manner?

Her father's voice sounded again in her head, "Constance!" It was filled with surprise and delight.

Delight. *Delight!* She shuddered physically as the awful possibility washed over her. The inquiries and sly looks whenever her middle name was mentioned . . . it was *this* delight she was undoubtedly named for! And if there was anything in a name—as her family so often proclaimed there was—likely she was tainted with some unholy licentious streak as well. "Blood will tell," she'd heard it said over and over.

Another awful wave of recognition buffeted her. It was true! Blood did tell. And there was clear evidence already that she was indeed her mother's daughter. Her strange feelings on board ship when that crude, rutting Scot looked at her . . . the way she felt when he kissed her and touched her . . . and the shameless, humiliating way she participated in those degrading encounters! She'd abandoned all reason, all decorum, at the first hint of pleasure in his arms. No doubt he sensed it, the weakness, the venal streak in her, the way an animal senses its prey. Perhaps that was why he thought James must be her lover, not her brother.

Vulnerable to temptation, to the pleasures of the flesh . . . it seemed an unbearable burden the cruel fates had cast upon her. No doubt if she were tainted, then her brothers must be doubly cursed . . . men's passions always surpassed those of women. James's testy remarks about his degenerate state and his love of drink were all she needed to confirm it.

Her family was at the mercy of its own unspeakable carnality: it rang like a challenge through her. A spur of determination made her shoulders rise and her chin set solidly. It was her family, after all. She had to *do* something . . . she couldn't just sit by and watch them dwindle into the profligate jaws of oblivion.

It was a fortnight later that Constance entered her husband's study one evening and paused just inside the doorway to survey a family gathering—save one member of the household. Her three sons and her husband were draped over chairs as if they had been poured there and hardened. They lolled, thick-lidded and miserable, each sighing or nodding weakly to acknowledge her presence, none with enough energy to rise. She bit the inner corner of her lip knowingly and forged her way through the jumble of her tall sons' legs, forcing them to withdraw to let her pass. Never had she seen them sunk so low.

"Colleen's quit," James informed her morosely.

"Threatened to," Adam corrected, looking like the distinction gave him little comfort.

"When?" Constance deposited her bonnet on the table and started to pour herself a tall brandy. The decanter was stone dry and she glared at her profligate sons. "I was only gone an hour, to see Mrs. Perkins—"

"She came storming in not ten minutes after you left, raving that someone had marked her sherry bottles with wax," Adam lifted his head from his palm long enough to explain. "Says she won't work where she's not trusted."

"That's absurd. Everyone *knows* she guzzles the cooking sherry. Why would we mark her bottles?"

"She had the proof in her hand, Mother," Ethan grumbled.

"It's *her* again," Chase charged glumly.

"Who else?" James chimed in. "Eden's on a one-woman crusade to reform us all."

"Lord help us," Ethan proclaimed, "she's got Brigit walkin' around with a bloody book on her head, sayin' 'Miss Eden scolds me if I don't.' My bed's not been made n a week and a half."

"She just needs something to occupy her." Constance defended Eden with less conviction than previously. Brigit could walk under a book for the rest of her life, for all Constance cared, but losing a splendid cook like Colleen was an entirely different matter.

"*And —*" Adam straightened in his chair and raised an indignant finger as he took the offensive, "she informed me sweetly that in England, gentlemen retire to a 'less public arena' to foul the air with their cigars."

Constance chewed her lip to stifle her amusement at the sight of Adam's wounded dignity. "Really, dear, she only needs —"

"A good strapping!" Ethan volunteered sourly. "Ever since she learned what the Rotterdam Club is, she's made it her vocation to drop comments around me and quote sages and proverbs about the horrors of gambling."

"And if Chase here is kept away from Madame Rochelle's another week by her cleverly timed evening entertainments, he may take to assaulting women in the streets," James offered, receiving a sharp *thwack* from Chase across the shoulder.

Constance glared at Chase, then at James. "Madame Rochelle's?" She tensed visibly and clasped her hands tightly before her. "Your sister is trying, however, awkwardly, to help. And from the sound of things," she glared at Chase's sprawled, masculine frame, "we could do with a bit of it."

"What we could do with," Chase's tone was surly, "is something to get her out of our hair."

"Your sister needs —"

"A man," James declared hotly. "She needs a man to work some of that godawful starch out of her."

"Here, here!" Ethan cried.

"She needs — a husband," Constance corrected. Then she thought of irate Colleen and added, "and I'm working

97

on that. Her 'come-out' is Saturday, and till then, you'll—
we'll all just have to bear it. After that, she'll have plenty
of invitations and callers to keep her busy."

James sighed, thinking of Eden's sweetly prim manner,
and gave the project little hope. "Let's pray she can find a
suitor to suit her."

## Chapter Six

"Have you met Mr. and Mrs. Vervoort, Eden dear?" Constance drew her from one scarcely begun conversation into yet another introduction. "You know . . . Hildy Vervoort's aunt and uncle . . . from New York. And of course, this is Anders Vervoort, their son."

Eden smiled up into a fleshy male face and extended her hand, wincing as it was crushed in the young man's soft, sweaty one. It was the thousandth time that evening though it was scarcely ten o'clock. Eden was sure everyone present had at least one eligible son or brother in tow . . . and every one of them had feet like lead and a grip like ironmonger.

Every eye in the grand parlor was fastened on her as she chatted and laughed demurely with both new and renewed acquaintances. Her beauty and grace were remarkable enough, but her wit and refined charm were positively mesmerizing. All about the room, mothers were squinting to recall the name of that marvelous English school that would shortly see an influx of gawky adolescent Bostonians. Quickly it was buzzed about that this Marlow girl was truly the find of the season . . . she would not last long in the marriage market. And the mothers all sighed gratefully behind their fans, relieved it would take only one man to end her tantalizing eligibility.

Boston's wealthiest families were represented in Adam Marlow's gracious house that night. The men looked splendid in fawn-colored breeches, frock coats with swooping tails and high collars, colorful cravats, and showy embroidered vests. Marriageable girls wore thin-strapped French chemises beneath their daringly cut, high-waisted gowns of moire satin, flowered brocade, flowing damascene, or embroidered summer voile. With coifs inspired by the classical Greeks, and fans of exotic silk and ivory, they bared and displayed their attractions as completely and appealingly as nature and the dress-maker's art would allow. The older ladies, with fortunes already set and standards to uphold, sedately revealed less of themselves, and allowed their love of bold color, lacy starched ruffs, and jewels to tout their taste and status. They came to feast and play, to make a new family alliance or further an illicit dalliance.

Amidst this sea of intrigue and finery, Eden floated like a pristine jewel in a gown of embroidered fawn silk, trimmed with seed pearls and rimmed at bodice and sleeve with sweetly feminine tambour-work frills. A small cameo on a silk ribbon graced her throat and her thick brown hair shone gloriously in a cascade of curls that trailed down her back.

Chase suddenly appeared at her elbow and whisked her off for a promised dance.

"Thank you!" she breathed, smiling politely and taking her place beside him for the stately gavotte.

"Selfish of me, really," Chase winked a rakish hazel eye at her and grinned. "I couldn't stand the thought of that ham-fisted freight-hauler as my brother-in-law."

"You were in no danger," Eden laughed with a twinkle. "There are far more appealing fish in this sea." Her gaze swept the room and caught on two knots of fashionable young men. Sure of their interest, she lowered her eyes inconspicuously and flushed with pleasure.

"And just which of these fish have you set your hook for?" Chase teased, watching the veritable tide of interest his young sister generated in Boston's blooded eligibles. A surge of protectiveness surprised him as he noted the gleam of appraisal in his spirited friends' eyes.

"All of them," she laughed, gazing at her handsome youngest brother. "But it is difficult, you know, having to settle for second best."

"Second best?" Chase frowned.

"The very best are all my brothers." She gazed fondly up into his angular features and feared that she spoke the truth. Despite their flawed morals, a man would have to go a long way to compare favorably with her virile, intelligent, and charming siblings.

"Indeed?" Chase seemed genuinely surprised by her approval. He watched her as she twirled and dipped gracefully beside him. She was positively enchanting, and really very sweet, he decided, to be so concerned for her wayward brothers. Yes, she really was quite special, their little Eden.

"Where is James? I haven't seen much of him about. I hope he's not emptying the punch bowl."

Chase laughed roundly, drawing her surprise. "No . . . he's drawn duty as official greeter for this evening. And I believe he's regrettably sober."

"Oh," Eden reddened becomingly, then recovered. "Well, I'm counting on a dance with him to help mend fences between us. Lately I can't seem to say or do anything to suit him."

Chase swallowed hard and recalled guiltily how he had avoided her himself of late. And as if to make up for it, he put forth his broadest smile and most skillful leg.

Eden relaxed in Chase's charming company, enjoying both the dance and the flattery of the growing interest in her. Her eyes lingered discreetly on several young men of impeccable dress and suitably gentle manner. Then, as the dance ended, her eyes lit briefly on the back of a man engaged in earnest conversation with Ethan. The man was even taller than her tall middle brother, and his shoulders were broader. His long limbs were clean and straight beneath fashionable tight velvet breeches and silk hose. His frock coat was of the latest continental cut and his wrists, when he gestured, were circled with rows of starched linen frills.

Eden turned several times to gather additional details and the peach-like flush of her cheeks betrayed an unmistakable interest. Chase heartened and watched her eyes for clues as to who had captured them so completely. He was going to lend that fortunate young man all the covert aid he could muster.

Then their dance was over and Chase had to relinquish her to Farley Thorndyke for a promised country dance, noting with pleasure that her eyes betrayed the object of her fascination: the tall, muscular man Ethan was leading toward a group of ladies for introductions.

Before he could follow, James entered and Chase collared his thirsty brother to inquire about the newcomer.

"Over there, with Ethan," he jerked his head surreptitiously in that direction. "Who is that bloke? I can't remember ever seeing him around here. Yet he's something familiar. . . ."

"Oh," James grinned delightedly, "that's Lord Ram MacLean, my nobleman friend from the voyage. I wasn't sure he'd come—"

"The Scotsman?" Chase's eye widened, "the one Dede tended on his deathbed?"

"The same."

"Where's his bloody tartan? I didn't recognize him in civilized clothes."

"I took him to old Bendleton, my tailor," James brushed his own immaculate lapel and beamed. "I told him he couldn't just go about half-naked in that scrap of plaid. Had to have some proper clothes. Then—" he leaned closer and lowered his voice conspiratorially, "I took him to Madame Rochelle's."

Chase brightened at the mention of Boston's most noteworthy house of pleasure, only to have his enthusiasm doused at James's conclusion.

". . . but he wasn't much interested in that particular sport. Strange," his gaze raked the Scot speculatively, "he's carryin' enough to keep the Madam's whole damn house happy—but he's not much inclined toward the pleasures of the flesh. Sports a mean hand at cards and the bones, though—"

"Excellent," Chase's grin reappeared and his eyes widened with mischief. "Then neither he nor our little sister are particularly afflicted with rampaging passions. They're well matched . . . they'll be perfect for each other." He reeled off toward Ram.

"Whoa—" James grabbed his sleeve and pulled him back. "Dede hates him. She thinks he's a bloody barbarian."

Chase sighed and faced his older brother squarely. "Drink is your vice; women is mine. Look at him," he nodded at Ram's tall, purely elegant and manly frame. "Do you honestly think *any* woman could really *hate* him? You spend too much time at the Madam's . . . you've been away from innocents too long. A woman's never more susceptible than when she's at war with a man."

James stared at Ram's beguiling smile and recalled Eden's furtive looks and puzzling aggitation whenever the Scot had appeared on deck. And she had nursed him in his hour of need. . . . Was it just possible that he might prove the answer to their prayers?

Across the room, Eden turned and dipped around rich but scrawny Farley Thorndyke, her eyes scanning the crowd for a glimpse of the tall, courtly fellow who had set Ethan to laughing minutes earlier. Something about him had positively conquered her eyes, inciting her curiosity unbearably. His broad shoulders, regal posture, and exquisite clothing . . . even without seeing his face, she knew he would be handsome . . . he must be. Something in her vibrated with excitement and she aimed a generous smile around her while she concentrated on finding that interesting form again.

Mercifully, the music stopped and she plied her silk and ivory fan briskly while Farley escorted her from the dance floor. She was greeted and hailed and welcomed home several times as they progressed toward the dining room. Impatience spread a becoming color under her liberally exposed skin and she fidgeted to be away from her well-wishers.

There he was, chatting amicably with Chase, near the buffet. Again his shoulder was to her. Brightening, she excused herself from Farley's bemused escort and nudged her way toward them. She reminded herself of her best lady's manners—to indicate only mild interest, even though her hands were dampening her gloves and her heart was thumping energetically in her chest. Show only mild, flirtatious interest until—

"There you are!" James caught her elbow. His face was beaming merrily at her. "You promised me a dance, Dede, and I'm here to collect."

Eden managed a wan smile and out of habit, sniffed inconspicuously. Strangely, she could detect no telltale whiff of liquor, and she nodded, puzzled at his cheery mood in the grip of sobriety.

"You're in fine spirits tonight," she observed as they wound through the crowd toward the grand parlor again.

"Indeed, excellent spirits. It's the company I keep that

pleases me so," James positively twinkled, seeing her furtive glance over her shoulder in the unmistakable direction of her youngest brother and his lordship. Perhaps Chase was right.

They were taking their place in the dance when Eden looked up to see Chase bearing down on them, the stranger in tow. An overpowering urge to stare made her flush with consternation and fix her eyes on the floor. A pair of long, muscular legs moved into sight and she had to raise her gaze quickly . . . up a snug pair of cunningly cut velvet breeches, over a shot-silk brocade vest, to a stunning royal-blue cravat and a square masterpiece of a face. Her heart stopped as she was instantly absorbed into the pools of sky blue she had seen over and over in her hot, disturbing dreams.

"Y—your lordship," she stammered. "I—whatever are *you* doing here?" Her face burned with chagrin and she snapped her fan open nervously, trying to hide her violent blushing.

"I invited him, Dede," James beamed. "Splendid of him to come to celebrate your—"

"James," Chase broke in, "Mother's in a regular stew and sent me for you. Something about the wine—"

"Ah, the wine." He raised a mischievous finger. "Now here's where my long experience with liquids becomes valuable! Do me a turn, Ramsay, old man." He plopped Eden's hand in Ram's. "Spin her once around the floor for me. I shall return shortly." After a brotherly tweak to Eden's pert nose, he moved off with Chase in his wake.

"Nothing would please me more." Ram wasted no time in pulling her hand through his arm and leading to the center of the floor. He looked down at her blushed cheeks and her wide, blue-rimmed eyes and felt a pleasurable ache flood through him. Her scent wafted up to him, lightening his head. He had forgotten—or had wanted to forget—just how lovely, how desirable she truly was.

"I . . ." she glanced about her trying to avoid looking directly up into his face, "hardly recognized you, your lordship." Her pulse was frantic as she scanned the nearby guests, trying to find an avenue of escape.

"Ramsay," he corrected, staring down at her.

"Lord . . . Ramsay," she repeated helplessly. It was a potent experience, calling him by name; her heart nearly jumped out of her chest. "Your dress . . . you look so . . . different. I wouldn't have taken you for the same man." She finally surrendered to the unbearable urge to look at his strong, perfectly molded face. Her knees weakened and she could barely swallow. Close on the heels of these disturbing sensations came a wave of irritation. James! He'd left her in this barbarian's clutches—

"You like my clothes, then?" He arched a brow in question as he extended his arms a bit to invite a closer inspection.

"They're . . . you're . . ." she averted her gaze pointedly, "just so different."

"If, as it's said, clothes make th' man, then I am different."

Eden's eyes grew stormy as she tried to decipher the levels of meaning in *that* pronouncement. He had the most annoying way of saying things that had multiple interpretations.

"Any difference could be an improvement," she observed tartly, lifting her chin and preparing for the ire she expected her remark to produce. But instead, a slow, fascinated smile spread over his full lips and his eyes reflected the dancing light from the great chandelier overhead.

"You are an enchanting woman, Eden. It is easy to forget the edge of your tongue when I gaze on you." His grin barely covered the intensity she felt in his gaze as it swept her exposed shoulders and lingered on the sweetly rounded tops of her breasts.

"Then I shall be pleased to remind you."

She was jostled slightly by another couple. The dancing had begun and there she stood gaping at him in the middle of the floor. Whatever would these people think of her untoward behavior?

Quickly, they caught up with the steps and took their place in line. Unfortunately, it was the stately gavotte again and she spent far too much time in his very warm hands to suit her. He danced with surprising grace, considering his height and muscular frame. He seemed the elegant, titled gentleman in every annoying aspect. And he smiled a secretive little smile at every turn.

She couldn't help looking at him. He was too . . . handsome, too interesting. Every other man in the room paled to insignificance beside his fascinating frame . . . drat and blast him!

"Your visit to Boston, has it gone well?" Eden finally broke the silence, trying to seem only politely interested in his reply.

"No."

She glanced irritably at him, catching the square cast of his jaw and the play of crimson highlights in his soft hair as he turned. It made her fingers tingle with memory.

"Where . . . are you staying?" she tried again, wondering if it were worth the effort.

"With friends."

"And who are these friends? Might we know them?"

"No."

"Be mysterious, then," she snapped, flinching as his muscular hand returned to her waist, "I was only trying to be polite."

"I know what you're tryin' to do." He leaned a fraction closer and grinned. "And it's not workin', is it?"

"Work—" she went rigid and glared openly at him. He knew! Somehow he knew that her politeness, her strained attempts at ladylike behavior, hid the raw, shameful excitement that he produced in her. "I don't know what you refer to, sir," her head tossed and she fixed a smile on her face as he turned her toward the others again.

"Ah, but you do, Eden." His voice lowered as she came nearer with a step. "I can feel your pulse racin' and see the color floodin' into yer skin. You don' hate me half as much as you'd like to."

Color exploded in Eden's face and she strained to pull away from his relentless hands. She would have left him standing, but for a sudden glimpse of her mother and the infamous gossip, Mrs. Perkins, looking on. And a taunting deep rumble from Ram's throat further tempered her outward display. She couldn't run from him, shrink from him, and still live with herself. But to stay was positively dangerous. He knew about her terrible weakness and every comment, every movement he made was calculated to prey mercilessly upon it.

"Honesty," his voice washed over her, "is a virtue without gender or class. I'd prefer an honest tart to a deceitful lady."

"Then go and find one!" she growled, pulling her hands from his. The music stopped just as she turned away and she was trapped in the crush of dispersing couples. A strong hand gripped her elbow from behind and pulled her back a step to set her on a freer course. She ground her teeth and tried covertly to wrest her arm free as they left the dance floor.

"There you are!" James approached, beaming jovially. "Sorry I was called away. It's all straight now. I hope Dede's giving you a taste of our hospitality."

"She is indeed," Ram stopped beside her, taking her slender hand and forcibly threading it through the crook of his arm, holding it there. "I'm glad of a chance to prove we Scots are not th' barbarians we're made out. But I think she needs a bit of convincin', yet. Another dance—"

"I simply couldn't," Eden flicked a searing look at Ram and raised her dangling fan, plying it with savage intensity. "I'm positively parched and I couldn't possibly dance another step in this heat." A noticeable tug on Ram's arm drew James's searching eye and she ceased trying to retrieve her hand.

Her face was flushed a becoming, deep peach and the damp tendrils of hair at her temples attracted Ram's gaze. His blue eyes slid downward over her like a blatant caress. The glistening of her moist skin betrayed the delectable warmth of her ripely curved form. Suddenly every nerve in his big body sprang to life, trained on the sensual promise of the woman beside him.

"Then a bit of refreshment and a breath o' fresh air in the garden is what you need," Ram declared, starting for the punch table.

"I could use a dram myself," James offered, beaming. "Why don't you take Dede outside and I'll get the punch and join you."

"No, really—" and "Excellent!" Eden and Ram spoke at once. Ram turned sharply toward the door, cutting off Eden's path and forcing her to turn and accompany him. She sputtered, appalled by his brute tactics, and finally managed to dig her heels into the rug just before the open garden doors.

"Take your hands off me, *your lordship!*" she spat with all the force she could muster while trying to maintain an even expression for the score of guests that watched them intently. From the corner of her eye she saw Millie Perkins staring at them and began to shrivel inside at the damaging gossip that was even now being generated. This big, lecherous boor was intent on ruining her!

"I'm not your *lord*ship, Eden. I'm a *laird*. A *lord* prances and flounces, 'as soft hands and pretends to be richer than 'e is. A *laird* looks 'is people in th' eye and calls every one of 'em by name. A *laird* works his lands an' flocks as well as his people and makes them proud to wear his plaid. A *laird's* hands are never soft." He held up one big, ruggedly tapered hand for her inspection. The skin of his big palm was pale and toughened. Eden stared in helpless fascination as he flexed his muscular hand before her eyes, then lowered it to brush the side of her cheek. A spark of raw excitement leapt from his hand into her skin and she jerked back, glaring at him as if he'd bitten her.

"Lord . . . laird, whatever you call yourself—you're the same *loathsome* churl." She pulled at her hand again and found it still firmly entrapped over his perfectly elegant sleeve. And now she could feel the relentless strength and sinewy hardness of his arm beneath it.

Ram stared into her through the dazzling molten copper rings of her eyes. Involuntarily, his breath quickened and his palms began to itch. His generous lips tilted up on one side in rueful acknowledgment of this all-too-familiar rush of feeling that threatened his self-possession. But to Eden it was a knowing smirk that goaded her to remember that he had treated her like a common trull and assaulted her.

"I said before, you may call me Ramsay. Or Ram, if you prefer." His voice had dropped to a husky purr that caressed her ears and made them burn for more.

"I don't want to call you anything! Least of all what your bloody sheep do!" She jolted back toward the parlor, but he held her securely. She changed directions and strained toward the cool sanity of the darkened gardens. To her surprise, his hands then released her and she suddenly found herself at the edge of the brick terrace overlooking the gardens. A soft scrape on the brick behind her sent her down the broad, curved steps nearby, into the heavy sweetness of the night garden.

In the semidark, purple wisteria hung in fertile abandon over the trellis arches that spanned the paths. Lavender was brushed by her hem as she passed and showered sweetness over lupines and straw like bachelor's buttons. The perfume of roses drew her forward and seemed to promise shelter amidst their forbidding thorns. The night buzzed with the muffled merriment of the party inside and with sensual expectation, spurring her pulse faster with each stealthy turn of the garden path. Chosing the least-used path, she made for the farthest corner, the place where she had often sought refuge as a child. The path narrowed, with branches that had overgrown their bounds clutching at her gown.

She stopped at the very farthest corner of the walled gardens. All was quiet, and her shoulders rounded with relief. She sank onto a heavy stone bench and pressed her hands over her eyes, trying desperately to collect herself.

"Eden—" the deep voice seemed to rumble from inside her own head, but she braced and turned. He was standing there, hands on hips, rocking back on one shamefully well-tapered leg. He anticipated her next movement. In an instant his powerful legs were braced against her knees, trapping them against the bench and preventing her from rising.

"Let me up!" she demanded. Her stomach was doing strange little flips that were followed by unnerving quivers through her loins.

"Or perhaps I should come down an' join you. I've a thing or two to say to you."

"Nothing you could say would interest me in the least, sir." She leaned back to avoid him and had to brace herself on her arms to keep from tumbling over backward.

"Now, have you no fairness in your heart, Eden, lass? Not even enough charity to forebear an apology?" His tone teetered between sincerity and sarcasm so effectively that even he was not entirely sure how it was meant. And she was braced distractingly, half-reclining, beneath him. Her soft, satin dress molded tightly over her full breasts, her small waist, and her rounded hips. Her shoulders gleamed in the moonlight and her eyes flashed seductively. . . . His manly cunning collected like a wad in his throat and he swallowed it.

"Apology?" her voice was strangely husky in her own ears. "For taunting and harrassing me? For misusing my charity and Christian duty toward you? For mistaking me for a cheap trollop and nearly . . . taking me against my will?" A recount of his wrongs bolstered her flagging spirit and made her sit up straighter on the bench. But it brought her closer to his potent maleness as well.

"I . . . never mistook you for *cheap,* lass."

It took a moment for the resulting spurt of ire to set her blood ablaze. Both fists came up and she half-pushed, half-pounded against his thighs. He jolted his pelvis back with a protective reflex and she managed to gain her feet before he could grab her.

"Let me *go,* you scurrilous lout!" She pushed and squirmed, nearly succeeding in wrestling free of his determined hands, but he relinquished one hold only to find a more secure one. And relentlessly she was drawn against him. "You hurt me and I swear . . . I'll see you rot unburied after hanging!"

*"Eden!"* he thundered with such ferocity that it rattled some of the fight out of her. Then he grabbed her mutinous chin in one hand and stilled it, forcing her to look at him. "It's not *hurtin'* I want to be about with you, lass! I'm no beast! I want to talk wi' you."

"To . . . to talk with me?" It seemed incredible as she said it. "I don't believe you . . . why should I?" She tensed afresh in his grasp and against her better judgment, allowed her gaze to be drawn into his. The warm lights in his true blue eyes melted another layer of her resistance. She was already at his mercy if he really meant

112

her harm. *Harm?* a voice inside her sneered. She was behaving like a ninny. Hurt her, indeed. She was a grown woman, after all, and reposing in her own gardens. Would he dare assault her here, under her family's very noses?

"Then let me go." She gambled on her insight and nearly collapsed with relief when he released her altogether. He turned a bit to one side, straightening his vest and smoothing his velvet sleeves, and Eden sank onto the bench to relieve her wobbly knees. She felt unexplainably giddy.

A moment later, he eased his tall frame down on the bench beside her, careful to avoid all contact with her. A muscle jumped in the side of his jaw. A deep, slow breathing belied the riot that was occurring in his loins. Moisture beaded on his forehead and he quietly tensed his hands and lips to still their cravings.

"My conduct toward you has not been without fault," his low tones invaded Eden's skin and drew her eyes to his strong, angular profile. "But a man seldom sees all beauty and temptation arrayed in one woman's flesh before him. And you are that, Eden . . . beauty in th' flesh . . . and temptin'. I never seen eyes to rival the sun on the heath before now, nor smelled hair like a field of blossomin' heather. Your skin is like sweet cream over summer peaches and yer soft —." He stopped abruptly, swallowing with difficulty and sneaking a glance at her from the corner of his lowered eye. This was far more difficult that he had expected. The more he spoke of his passion for her, the more keenly he felt it!

"Do ye see what I'm sayin'?" he put his elbows on his knees and clasped his hands together rigidly in front of him.

"I . . . I don't know." She swallowed hard, watching his hands turning white with the effort needed to control them and wondering whether it signified anything that she'd gone from *wench* to *lass*.

"I'm sayin' I cannot help my manly feelin's for you, lass. An' I must tell you how I feel about you, make you understand. You're a woman fashioned to please a man's eye . . . an' to turn his thoughts toward . . . other heavens." He turned to her slowly; her eyes were wide and wondering in the pale moonlight. He straightened and took her reluctant hand between his, noting its coldness, its trembling.

A thrill of excitement fluttered down her spine and tingled her fingertips. He was speaking to her as no man ever had . . . as a lover, baring his soul's passion to her. Astonishment banished every response from her tongue. This of all things she had not expected from him. He implored her to understand the unstoppable tide of his manly needs. . . .

"I pluck a ripe cherry from a tree an' it tastes of your lips. I swim in the river an' the swirl of water against me feels like your cool skin." His hand traced the upturned curve of her cheek, feeling it warm under his touch. Raw desire hit him with gale force, making tatters of his resolve. He opened his mouth to continue his well-rehearsed wooing, but instead revealed his truest longing. "Let me taste, Eden. . . ."

His eyes probed hers as his head lowered. Then that soft, splendid contact obliterated all else for her. His firm lips moved gently over hers, drawing forth that secret need she had never felt except in his arms. She gripped the hard edge of the bench with her free hand, trying in vain to keep the world from spinning crazily around her. She must have swayed, for his arms came out to steady her, then enfold her.

The divine pressure of his lips increased, demanding, coaxing a response that she could not withhold. Lips parting, yielding their inner softness, she responded in the most basic and utterly feminine way. Her hands found his

114

lapels, then his vest, tracing the exotic twining of its embroidery over his chest and slowly down his stomach and around his ribs. Tendrils of excitement traced similar patterns on the underside of her passion-blushed skin. The warmth of his body flowed into her arms and body, melting her last resistance. An ache rose from her loins and spread in all directions through her. It was that peculiar ache that was assuaged only by the touch of his body against hers and she sought relief in the only way she could.

Ram felt her ripening breasts pressing harder against his ribs as she moved closer and knew the moment he had been waiting for was near. She wanted him, he felt it in every screaming muscle, every straining sinew of his body. And he wanted her, ached with madness to possess that soft, silken flesh he had once explored and had craved ever after. It was a need he had grown to dread and even now he clung desperately to the threads of his unraveling control. He wanted to plunge into the sweet depths of her fragrant mouth, lose himself in the tempting valleys of her lush body. . . . But he needed to decide it now, here, before he lost control completely over his traitoious desires. . . .

"Eden," he murmured hoarsely against her lips, "let me love you. . . ." The unveiled turmoil of his soul found resonance in the empty chamber of her heart. He meant to say more, but the soft eagerness of her mouth beneath his hammered a final stroke on the iron bonds of his passions. His heart pounded with fierce demand and he clasped her to him hungrily, feeling her molding seductively against him.

Time and place were banished, leaving reason no footing, and it retreated abruptly. Eden felt herself being lifted soaring into his arms, engulfed in his warmth, his tenderness with her. Her arms caressed his broad shoulders, then threaded about his neck as he carried her. He

115

held her against him easily as his lips showered adoration over her temple, her cheek, the arch of her throat. Shivers of delight trembled through her as she felt herself being lowered and glimpsed his handsome face, his entrancing blue eyes above her. The last of her maidenly fears fled; she abandoned propriety and exiled reason. For this moment, he was her universe, and she was his completely, yielding and entrusting all her womanly treasures to him.

There were earthy smells, damp soil and greenery, lush and soft beneath and around her. It was ground ivy; she managed that one impression before he filled her eyes, her arms, her mind once more. And again she rose on pleasure's breathtaking spiral.

Ram stretched out beside her in the secluded bower, trapping her skirts beneath his long legs and covering her creamy breasts with his chest. His hand traced her throat, her breasts; and his lips followed, nibbling, caressing. Her breath caught in Eden's throat as she drank in these startling new sensations hungrily. When his hand moved, she moved with it, arching against him to renew his touch, responding with desire that had fermented and grown potent in her dormant flesh.

Her eager fingers flew over his soft hair, his square jaw, the fascinating muscularity of his neck. They pushed down his immaculate blue Irish tie to explore those hidden reaches of his throat that so often claimed her eyes on board ship. She wanted to touch him, explore him, revel in his virile pleasures even as he taught her the joys of new sensation, new sensuality.

Ram's hand trembled with eager heat as it slid down the elegant satin drape of her skirt and raised the hem, slipping beneath it. His breath was ragged as he touched the bare silk of her stocking, the lacy ring of her garter, and the satiny skin of her thigh. His hand rose on her; she was silky smooth, as he somehow knew she would be. She was firm, enticingly rounded, yielding. She was pli-

116

ant, fitting herself against him, beneath him, around him.

Eden felt his weight shifting onto her, parting her legs with its compelling intimacy. Every touch, every movement of his body on hers answered an aching need within her. She quivered in his arms, gasping with virgin delight at the shockingly pleasurably feel of his mouth at her breasts. Instinctively she met the rhythm of his hard, bulging breeches against her, shivering with anticipation of that unknown ecstasy that lay just beyond, in the next turn of pleasure's spiral.

Then he moved away for a moment and returned to meet her soft, moist flesh with his bare, hardened shaft. The feel of him pressing intimately against her was intoxicating and she wriggled upward to meet his delicious force. He parted her throbbing flesh slowly and when he encountered that virgin barrier some unmolten part of his mind took control, gentling his forward motion to let her absorb him slowly. The stinging, the sharp discomfort of being opened, molded to his potent manhood, washed over her in shuddering, intense waves that were transmuted into gentler fullness by the tenderness of his hands and lips. Further and further, he penetrated her virgin reaches, moving with breathtaking restraint against her straining, untried flesh.

Eden felt him begin to move within her and was drowning in conflicting sensations. A hot, burning fullness invaded her loins with every thrust and a steamy, bone-melting pleasure radiated through her as he withdrew partway to thrust again. Each shocking, sublime sensation was a passage to a paradise her body had craved but her maidenly intelligence hadn't dreamed existed. Marlow blood roared triumphant in her head. Filling her arms, her body, her heart was the one Destiny had fashioned just for her.

"Dede?" It came so soft, so distant, that it was easy to ignore at first. "Dede? Ramsay, old man . . . where are you?"

Ram fought through the clouds of reverie that suffused his senses to reclaim a foothold in reality. That voice called not to pleasure, but to warning. Alarm surfaced into his awareness and he tried to cover Eden further with his burning body. He had to blot out that awareness, to keep that voice from penetrating their paradise.

But Eden had heard; now she groped through pleasure's bright mists toward a more solid realm. Her arms, her heart were full; she still wanted nothing but the tantalizing pinnacle of the tightening spiral she'd ridden.

"Dede—" It came closer, and like a garish flash of light, shot through her passion-sated senses. Instantly Ram's weight above her became heavier, harder. His lips became more demanding and his hands gripped her more possessively. He drove her deeper beneath him into their bed of ivy, bringing his lips beside her ear. She could scarcely make out what he said through the pounding of her blood in her head.

"Shhh. Quiet and he'll ne'er know we're here."

"Shhh. . . ." It hissed in her ears with the taint of betrayal . . . of sin.

# Chapter Seven

Shock numbed Eden's responses for what seemed an eternity. One by one the details of her state righted themselves in her mind. It was dark . . . the darkest corner of the gardens . . . in the ivy . . . on her back . . . her legs spread beneath the arrogant and carnal Ramsay MacLean! Her body ached and throbbed where it was being invaded in a lustful, unthinkable way! She was . . . they were . . . *joined*.

She moaned, sending her hands in panicky flight down her raised and rumpled gown. They touched her naked hip and the side of Ram's pelvis as it pressed hard against her, verifying her worst fears. Those shameful, hot sensations . . . that was him . . . forcing himself inside . . . hurting her! Her panicky eyes flew open to meet Ram's shadowed features.

"Eden." He stroked wisps of hair back from her burning face as he tried to discern her state. "He's gone, darlin'." His head lowered to claim her lips again, pulling back quickly when she jerked her face away in horror. "Eden . . . don' worry, lass, no one will disturb us—"

*"Get off me!"* Eden shrieked in a raging whisper. She groaned, pushing violently against his huge chest. Her nails came up, bared, but he grabbed her wrists before

she could strike and pinned them back beside her head

"Eden, it changes nothin'—" But he knew as he said that he was wrong. Everything was changed, and anger blew through the burning middle of him—anger at his own stupidity.

"Dearest God," she moaned, thrashing to end that unspeakable contact with his body. "Let me up—*please* let me go!"

"Eden, love." He tried to control her wriggling and resistance enough to claim her lips and recover that lost moment of yielding. But the more he tried, the more she struggled.

"You're hurting me!" she pleaded, then commanded "Let me up or I'll scream bloody murder—I swear to God Almighty I will!"

Frustration boiled up in Ram's stomach and he released his punishing grip on her wrists, rising and covering himself. His hands shook violently as he raked them back through his hair and ruthlessly quelled his body's screaming protest. Lord—what had he done?

Eden pushed up, shrinking from his hot, powerful form as she scrambled to shove her debutante satin down over the burning flesh of her exposed legs. He reached for her and she dodged his hands unsuccessfully.

"No! You can't . . . not again . . . don't make me," she ordered and pleaded, scarcely understanding that he was dragging her from their secluded bower onto the brick path again.

"I didn't have to *make you,* wench." His voice was rough with frustrated passion. His coarse defense savaged her tattered pride. He was unforgivably right—

"I despise you . . . you and your disgusting rut!" She was on her feet in the moonlight, tussling against Ram's determined hands even as horror bloomed in her heart "Look what you've done to me!" she wailed, ceasing attempts to right her crumpled and contrary bodice to

120

shove against him. The sight of her exposed breasts poured white-hot shame through her veins. He'd taken her virtue and—merciful lord—she hadn't even put up a struggle! "You crude, degenerate *rogue!*"

"*Rogue,* am I?" his eyes flashed with new flame. "No more than you're a *lady,* wench. It appears to me, we're matched an' paired." His hands tightened on her shoulders and he pressed her against him, forcing her to feel his body's unvented heat. But his face was like cold granite in the moonlight. "You're not badly damaged— nor could anyone know how I've *misused* you. I'll marry you, then, an' set an end to both our misery."

For an instant, as Eden's eyes flew wide open and her jaw dropped, Ram wondered if his taunt might actually bear fruit. But he was not deluded for long.

*"Marry? You?"* She shoved and pounded furiously against his chest and won surprised release. She lurched backward, her eyes blazing coppery fire as she searched for the vilest fate her sanitary mind could summon. "I'd sooner die . . . of the bloody flux!"

She jolted around his startled form and ran down the twisting path, her heart beating in her throat at the thought that he might pursue her. Only on the steps of the terrace did she recover enough to think rationally. Her trembling hands flew over her rumpled gown and rose to her mussed hair. Abetted by the shadows, she slipped unnoticed from the terrace and entered the house by a servants' entrance, bound for her room.

Ram MacLean, heir of Skyelt, drew a deep, furious breath and finally let out his bottled frustration with a rare and virulent oath. He threw himself down on the stone bench and grasped its raw edges savagely.

"Damn and be damned!" he swore again, then continued to rant to himself. "What a jackass you are, MacLean! No better'n that disgustin' old reprobate who sired you." His face hardened and his eyes became like cold sapphires at the thought of his father; he had to shake the ire from his tight shoulders.

He'd planned it all so carefully. The invitation, the clothes, the dancing, the earnest speech of apology . . . all were calculated to flatter a woman's vanity. And at the proper time, he was to go down on his knee and ask her to marry him . . . and relieve his manly pain. Then he had given in to that momentary weakness for a taste of her womanly flesh—and it was all for naught.

"Damn!" he raged, grinding one impotent fist in the other and feeling the rebellion of his thwarted loins. God knew he'd tried. But there were some things no mortal man should be expected to resist . . . and Eden Marlow, warmed and willing, was one of them. His whole flesh was screeching disappointment.

He'd never felt anything akin to this before. Was this the driving lust that afflicted old Haskell and made him want to bed every skirt that flicked by him? And if it were—did it mean *like father, like son?* Was he doomed to truckle after the tawdry and transient pleasures of the flesh until his own men laughed at him behind his back, too?

He snorted furiously and pushed up, smoothing his coat sleeves and resettling his vest at his waist. He inspected his costly raiment and began furiously brushing leaves from his knees and elbows. No woman should have that much power. A double jackass he was, for letting her wreck his control a second time. Once bitten, twice shy. But twice bitten—then what?

Eden did not reach her room before being intercepted by two ladies in the hallway. She raised her chin and smiled politely, cringing inside as she felt the rasp of their close scrutiny. She was sure the ignominy of her ruin must be fairly painted upon her. A second wave of ladies entering the hall sent her scurrying up the servants' stairs toward her room.

Charity appeared in the hallway and caught a glimpse of Eden's pale face and devastated eyes. "What is it, missy? Ye look pale as death an' ashes." She came to take Eden's icy hands and the warm concern of her touch wilted Eden's stiff control. The servant's eyes flew over Eden's mussed hair and took in the new crinkles in the satin she had pressed herself just hours ago. She put a protective arm about Eden's slender waist, leading her young mistress off.

In the thick silence, Eden fought back her tears and concentrated on making herself presentable again. She relinquished her dress to Charity for pressing and washed hastily. The maidenly joy with which she had started this evening's festivities was in tatters. Her heart felt like a stone in her chest. What was to have been the glorious beginning of her new life in Boston was now destroyed by the callous lusts of that despicable Scot. Lord—how was she to get through the rest of this evening?

Eden slipped through the upper hall, pulling at the tambour-work frills that rimmed her deep neckline and hearing Mistress Dunleavy's drone on a lady's decorum, a lady's duty. She had betrayed both . . . and she must now pretend to embody their epitome. She took a breath and swallowed her rebellion. Pale as ashes, gray as death . . . she remembered and pinched some color into her cheeks. Her face felt stiff and numb.

At the bottom of the graceful staircase, Chase intercepted her, surveying her cool rigidity with puzzlement.

"We've been scouring the house for you, Eden."

"I was freshening up," she managed politely; her expression looked strangely like a grimace to her perceptive brother.

"Mother is asking for you . . . has a passel of folk for you to meet." He held out his arm and Eden accepted it gratefully. Her desperate inner state was confirmed by her frantic grip on his arm. "And I've been beleaguered by my friends for an introduction to Boston's fairest flower." His full smile warmed her a bit and her resulting sigh shuddered demurely.

He straightened and patted her hand. The protectiveness he had experienced before now flooded back with a vengeance. What in the devil was the matter with his little sister on this night of all nights?

James joined them as they searched for Constance. He read in Chase's serious look and Eden's blanched countenance that all was not well.

"There you are." He exuded a determined humor. "I looked for you and Ramsay out on the terrace but couldn't find a trace. Where did you disappear so thoroughly?"

A tide of humiliating color washed under Eden's liberally exposed skin and her dark lashes lowered to veil the turmoil in her eyes.

"I . . . we parted on . . . less than amicable terms." Her voice wavered and she had to temper her ire to manage facing him. There was an accusing mist in her eyes when she raised them to James's sobering face. "If you have no brotherly care for me, James, then at least refrain from tossing me into that degenerate's clutches."

The shamed hurt in her luminous eyes cut James to the core. She released Chase's arm and brushed past them both, but not before Chase filched a tuft of green from the deep gathers at the seam of her puffed sleeve.

Chase held aloft a tiny ivy leaf and both he and James stared at it as if expecting an oracle.

"Damn!" James swore, glaring at his younger brother. "What woman could hate *him,* you said. Damn you for a man who knows women!"

"Well, he's *your* bloody friend." Chase lowered his voice to avoid the inquisitive eyes that turned on them.

They turned as one man and followed in Eden's troubled wake.

She took refuge by her mother in a circle of Boston's grand doyens, listening to the names they dropped and trying hard to maintain a illusion of pleasure. The group flowed about the room and wherever she appeared, there was a flurry of young men's attention. She found herself the object of earnest offers for dances.

"You flatter me no small amount, sirs . . . I'm overwhelmed." She managed a dazzling smile at each suitor, but inside she was cringing. "But I am too fatigued to move . . . perhaps later." Neither Chase's rakish entreaty nor James's subdued request could dislodge her from that august coven. But her brothers stayed in attendance, exchanging inquisitive looks with Constance.

Shortly they were engulfed by a second wave of handsome, elegant males. And this time several of the older women were flattered into taking a turn on the floor. In the flurry of pairing and departing, Eden was distracted and failed to see Ram's approach until he was within arm's reach. To their credit, James and Chase stepped forward, thwarting his intention of addressing Eden again.

"Ramsay, old man!" James was the picture of hale fellow, well met. "Where did you get to? None of your monkish habits tonight, my friend. I have a lady or two who'd give their toes for a turn about the floor with you—"

"No, thank you, James." Ram looked past James's shoulder to Eden's drained face. "I'll have only the best. I've come to beg another dance with yer sister." He had to have her alone with him for a few minutes . . . he had to talk with her. Now that his body was cooled and his reason had returned, he realized their unfortunate tryst in the garden only made the necessity of marrying her even more urgent. He had no taste for bearing a woman's ruin

125

upon his head . . . not even when she so clearly asked for it.

Blood flooded Eden's vacant skin and her chin tilted up with unmistakable defiance. The contemptuous look she leveled at him was so passionately loathing that her brothers and mother stared at her. They'd never imagined their incessantly proper and annoyingly polished little Eden capable of such depth of feeling.

"No thank you, *sir!*" her melodious voice was half a growl. "I'd rather d—"

"Dance with her brother!" Chase broke in, "We were just about to—." Taking her firmly by the elbow, he steered her from their midst and toward the dance floor in the grand parlor. She managed one last withering glare at Ram's red-granite face before swaying off.

"I. . . ." Constance stopped at the sight of Ram's well-controlled ire and forced a correct but bloodless smile. Anxiety flooded through her. "I am promised to none, sir. And my feet itch for a dance."

Ram nodded with all grace and extended his arm to Constance, bearing her to the parlor. It was a lively dance, with no occasion for talk. Whenever Eden twirled by in the next group of dancers, Ram stiffened and his look became steadily more dour. He executed each step with courtly precision, but he looked like a man being led to the rope.

When it was over, Constance implored him to accompany her to the dining room for a drink. She had to know the reason for Eden's passionate dislike of this handsome and stunningly virile MacLean.

"I understand from my son that you're a laird," she decided to brave the topic and the tension that made him seem so formidable. "Where is your home, Laird Ramsay, and who are your people? I've had some acquaintance with Scottish families."

"My father," Ram handed her a cup of wine punch and

-126-

leveled his response at her as if it were a musket, "is Haskell MacLean of Skyelt. My home is on the step of the highlands, near the Tay River."

The crystal cup slipped in Constance's fingers, spilling a trickle of red liquid down her richly embroidered gown. She fumbled and swiped at it uselessly, swirling about nervously to find a place to set the cup. When she turned back, Ram was staring down at her with those relentless blue eyes that seemed to penetrate her social self, discovering all her secrets, all her past.

"H-Haskell MacLean?" she queried with a sickly smile, finally admitting the reason for her concern over her daughter. "I knew a Haskell MacLean once . . . long, long before I was married."

"The very same." Ram's taunting scrutiny informed her that he knew a great deal about her former association with the Laird of Skyelt.

"Well . . . how interesting. Imagine you . . . Haskell's son." Her fan flicked open and she wielded it expertly to veil her discomfort. What was she to do now?

"Then imagine that I might 'ave been your son as well," Ram's deep voice vibrated quietly through her as he leaned back on a leg that grew understandably familiar.

Constance stared at his handsome face and supremely well-knit frame, at the flinty resolve visible in every aspect of his countenance. He was wrong, she realized; he could never have been *her* son. He was a man honed to hardness against something stern and unyielding. And for the first time in years, she wondered what had become of Haskell MacLean. Resistance straightened her spine.

"So, you know about your father and me," she smiled, taking a deep breath and meeting his implied threat full on. "And just what do you intend to do with this *knowledge* of yours?"

Ram appraised the satiny strength of the woman before him and allowed his eyes the freedom of her still-attractive form. His recent experience with her daughter had tutored him sternly in the strength of fleshly desire. Only weeks before, he had sneered and judged this Constance Marlow a high-flown whore . . . and assumed her daughter was cut of the same cloth. That he had been so wrong about the daughter gave him pause to wonder at this gracious and unflinching woman before him. She was none of that trollop he had come to despise for her effect on his own life. Perhaps it was his recent struggle with fervent passions and yearnings that made him willing to consider his father's youthful folly in a less condemning light.

"Nothing, madam . . . I shall do nothing with it," his burr rolled as he nodded to her.

A softer cast crept over her face as she searched him in the silence, reading his stubborn honesty in the square set of his jaw.

"You are a gentleman, then, sir," Constance nodded in return, acknowledging his silence. She was surprised when one of his brows lifted, transforming his sober face into a rakish mask.

"Not entirely, madam." His generous mouth curled with disguised self-deprecation. "No more than my old father was."

"That would make you an interesting man indeed, Laird Ramsay." Constance's relieved laugh had Eden's low, musical quality and Ram's chest felt suddenly crowded. "I must tell you: my husband knows my past well . . . it has been no hindrance to a long and fruitful marriage."

"Then you are both most fortunate, Mrs. Marlow. Would that old Haskell had been so blessed." He bowed with a gallantry that stunned Constance and then turned upon his heel, and strode for the front door.

Twice after Ram's abrupt departure, Constance tried to closet Eden and discover what had set her against the young MacLean with such virulence. But both times, Eden found an excuse to avoid her, throwing herself into the escalating merriment with abandon. So Constance watched as Boston danced her daughter's feet off and she formed her own conclusions.

The heavy dampness of the predawn hour muffled the sound of footsteps on the rough cobblestones of the alley behind Marlow House. Here and there the unwieldy wooden ladder dragged and scraped the ground and a harsh glare at Arlo MacCrenna brought it quickly under control once more. After what seemed a torturously long time, in and out of alleyways and up and down hills, Ram MacLean paused and raised a silent hand to stop his companion. In the gloom, a thick weed patch hid most of a brick garden wall. He proceeded more slowly, beckoning Arlo after him until he came upon a narrow break in the overgrowth.

"Here it is."

"Are ye sure this is what ye have to do, Laird Ram?" Arlo grabbed the sleeve of Ram's fitted black shortcoat and held him from entering. Even in the darkness, it was easy to read the frown that creased Arlo's broad face. Only a stubborn Scot like Arlo would dare risk a stubborn Scottish Laird's ire at so critical a time.

"I'm *sure*. Now bring the ladder an' come on."

"She be a good lass . . . couldn't ye just talk wi' her?" Arlo didn't budge.

*"No!"* Ram thundered raggedly. He raked a hand back through his hair and ground his teeth. "The wench'll not set eyes on me again. This is the only way . . . I have to make her marry me. Now come on!"

He whirled and pushed angrily through the bushes that overhung and narrowed the path. And it was a moment before he reappeared with a furious gleam in his eye to

hold back the greenery and make room for Arlo and th
ladder.

The rusty hinges of the garden gate screeched hid
eously. Ram glimpsed Arlo's no-more-than-you-deserve
look and waved him angrily toward the central garde:
path. They slipped around the edge of the terrace, keep
ing to the keep shadows at the side of the huge house

Arlo grasped Ram's sleeve and pointed soundlessly to :
set of windows nearly three floors above them. Ram
squinted and frowned as he studied the height. He *hate*
this. It was low and conniving . . . even if it *was* neces
sary. He was infuriated that his inheritance was hopelessl;
tied to a woman's skirts . . . especially that he had t(
crawl under them to get it. And he was further humiliate(
by his unprecedented lapses of control where Eder
Marlow's delectable self was concerned.

"You're sure that's her window," Ram leaned close a
Arlo positioned the ladder in the shrubbery.

"Dead sure," Arlo whispered, testing the bottom rung

"How do ye know th' old woman wasn't just talkins
out her ear?" Ram fidgeted, watching Arlo reposition th(
ladder.

"Old Colleen's been cook 'ere for nigh on to eternity
And she give me the truth all right," Arlo whispered
disgustedly; his voice lowered. "By the time we wus
through, she'da give me her virtue."

Ram glared down at his manservant and Arlo stuck out
his jaw. "I didn't want it." He added under his breath, "I
ain't a MacLean, thank the Good Laird."

Ram paused on the bottom rung and scowled at him,
knowing his mumbling must have been some further bit
of vexation over Ram's course of action. He jerked up
the next step and turned to whisper, "Remember,
tomorrow—"

"Call with a carriage for ye!" Arlo waved him on sourly
and muttered, ". . . if there be anything left alive to

collect."

Ram climbed the ladder and was quickly onto a parament over the little-used side door. From there he edged sideways and up onto the ledge of the window, clinging to a wooden trellis. It was a long minute until he found suitable hand and footholds in the brick to allow him to swing over on the trellis to Eden's window. He teetered for a heartbeat on the windowsill and then secured his position by grabbing the wooden sash. He swallowed hard as he looked below to where Arlo had been only a moment earlier. The servant and the ladder were both gone. He drew a determined breath and set about exploring the window sash with his hands.

He sat gingerly on the windowsill and threaded himself through the opening a bit at a time. Finding himself behind a heavy brocade drape, he felt his way to the edge and finally stood in Eden's darkened room.

His eyes adjusted slowly, and the darkness soon revealed the outline of her big poster bed; he was drawn there on silent feet. Twice he closed his eyes, forcing them to admit more light each time they reopened. His heart thudded impatiently in his chest and his jaw clenched as he recognized the faint mingling of lavender and roses that now meant Eden Marlow to him. He tensed, his senses coming alive in the improving light.

It was indeed her, curled under a light coverlet, her hair spread over the pillows to relieve the summer heat. He edged closer until his thighs brushed the side of the bed. His hands on his waist, he leaned back on one leg, his jaws clenched tight. She wore a thin summer nightdress that bared most of her chest and all of her arms. Even in the dimness, he could see the smooth elegance of her skin and delicate features. He stared at her with narrow eyes and began to remove his coat.

Methodically the buttons gave under his strong fingers, and with each unbuttoning a knot of tension drew tighter inside him. He folded the coat carefully, laying it neatly on the bench at the foot of the bed. His soft linen shirt followed, then his sturdy woolen hose. He stood bare-chested in his burnt-red tartan, listening to Eden's slow untroubled breathing. He scowled, deciding that his kilt must go, too, for it to be truly convincing. Leather buckles gave and he paused, stark naked, the sturdy woolen in his hand. He laid it on the floor beside the bed to have it close at hand later on. And he reached for the coverlet.

The soft sheets were pleasantly cool against his bare skin and he inched further into the bed, never taking his eyes from Eden. She conveniently slept on one side of her big bed and he lowered himself onto the other, tucking his muscular arms back under his head and exhaling quietly.

He went over it in his mind, forcing himself to review his purpose as a charm against the allure of the soft skin and days he'd conconcted and had to discard half a dozen schemes. How was he supposed to marry her if she wouldn't see him or even accept a note from him? It was her own doing, now . . . forcing him to such a desperate measure.

The die was cast. He was in her bed, naked as on birthing day, and they'd be found that way, together, when the house awoke. She had a penchant for sleeping to a ladylike hour and so the maid woke her well after sunrise. The maid would run for the master, screaming bloody hell, and *she* would likely exercise her lungs a bit as well. Everyone would jump to the proper conclusion. *She*'d be pitching furious, Mama and Papa would be appalled, James would threaten to bash him—or call him out, which, of course, he would refuse to honor. The other sons, Ethan and Chase, might have to be dealt with, but neither was his match for strength . . . too much the city gentlemen, those two. The house would be in turmoil for half the day, then one of these bright folk would see the obvious solution to this horrrendous disgrace and mention the word "marriage."

*Marriage.* He stiffened, feeling a shiver to down his muscular body. He'd marry Eden Marlow and bed her and he'd have his child . . . and Skyelt. He'd take her back to Scotland, give her a pension or something, and be done with this whole damnable business. It soured in his mind as he thought about it in such cut-and-dried terms. What had started out as a simple exercise in carnal blackmail had gotten deucedly complicated. She was supposed to be a whore; she wasn't. She was supposed to be easy to persuade, with money or with charm; she was and she wasn't. She wasn't supposed to get under his skin; but damn it, she had. And the only way to get her out was to have her and be done with it once and for all! Then he could get back to his land, his books, his farming . . . and perhaps someday to Parliament. But this was no time to think about all that.

He turned his head and looked at her briefly. Maybe this was the perfect time to think about Parliament and his future . . . or anything that might help him ignore the sleepy innocence of the enchanting face on the pillow beside him. He turned from her then, forcing his thoughts as far away from Boston as he could . . . Bombay: saffron and strange cows that roamed streets and houses freely; Cairo: the making of papyrus into paper; Ceylon: the way they dried tea for shipping. He went through his repertoire of metaphysical poets, the wording of the Magna Carta, and four Latin declensions before resorting to sonnets. Why did sonnet writers all feel compelled to burden the already overexcitable world with their delirious notions of connubial rapture? Back to that again . . .

He huffed quietly and turned his head a bit further from her, but it did little good. He knew she was still there, with her cool, bare skin and dark hair spread about

133

her like a sea wave. It was an excruciatingly long hour before gray light would begin to seep around the heavy window drapes and fill the room.

Eden's breathing changed and she turned in her sleep, resettling comfortably against Ram's bare side. He groaned silently and released the breath he'd been holding. What would he do if she sensed the change in her bed and woke early? Likely she'd scream, he reasoned, and the end result would prove the same: it would change nothing. She'd have to marry him, one way or another, and sooner or later she'd bear him a child . . . as planned. Damn Haskell for the base old lecher he was! He couldn't stand to see his blood bottled up by decent morals, even in his son.

Eden moved again, bringing her buttocks full against his hip, her legs stretched along his warm length. The breath died in Ram's throat and he waited for her to move. But she relaxed and gave no indication of moving further.

This was what he hated most, he decided, the way she weakened his self-possession. She appealed to something primal in him that sprang to a life of its own, impervious to his moral training and even the stern exercise of his hitherto invincible will.

His body tightened, muscle and tendon and nerve. The softness of her thinly clad bottom against him was torture refined. He peeled himself away from her, biting his lip as he felt the edge of the bed at his shoulder. He glared at her blissful form and jammed his tensed arms back under his head. Fastening his eyes on the wooden braces of the canopy above them, he tried again to turn his mind to worthier pursuits.

Eden turned again, drawing much of the coverlet with her. He put out a stern hand to snatch some of it back, but remembered and grimaced, gentling his grip. His hand returned for a second hold and brushed her thin lawn nightgown, feeling the warm, smooth flesh of her side beneath it.

He froze. His knuckles touched the dip of her small waist. It was soft, tapered, utterly and beguilingly feminine.

His hand turned over, hovering on her side and finally touching her. A bolt of fire shot through his chest, sending his heart racing and his blood pounding in his head. Every sense, every facet of concentration was trained on that enthralling curve. And with a true explorer's instinct, his hand began to move.

The side of her hip was a lush rounded curve, and below came the taper of her silken thighs. Memory dried his mouth as he recalled the way those thighs had looked just two days ago in the garden: firm and exotically tapered above her dainty garter. He reversed direction and slid his hand gingerly up her side to the edge of her full breasts. His fingertips dipped forward to brush the rose-tipped peaks that strained her twisted nightdress. The light fabric proved no hindrance to appreciation of the shape and erotic texture of her tightening nipple.

He held his breath as she roused and turned over once more, landing this time on her back, her nightdress twisted hopelessly about her. Fearing she was wakening, he watched, tensed and aching, as she settled back into rest. He propped his head on his arm and studied her in the gathering light.

She was too lovely for his or any man's good. Her lips were arched like Cupid's bow, her slender nose had an impudent little roundness at the tip that kept her from seeming unearthly perfect. Her hair—he lifted a lock of its tousled mass and rubbed it against his cheek—was like heaven's softest cloud.

*Eden.* They had named her well. She was a garden of delights, of pleasures to be claimed and savored. . . .

* * *

Deep in her dreams, Eden had found herself in the midst of her family's garden, seated on a white linen cloth beneath a great elm. Nearby were bowers of fragrant phlox, colorful nasturtiums, and elegant lilies. Beside her was a willow hamper that made sense as she felt pangs of hunger come and go: this was a picnic, she realized with the convenient logic of dreams . . . how lovely.

The sky above was dappled with clouds that provided some protection from the warm sun; the breeze was gentle and dry. It was a perfect setting, one of her favorite places in the world. Heedless of the threat of dreaded freckles or sun-reddened skin, she sank back onto her elbows and closed her eyes, drinking in the warmth on her face. But a hungry, insistent ache in the middle of her made her reach for the lid of the hamper, pulling it closer and peering in.

Instantly she was paralyzed. Staring back at her from the bottom of the bare hamper was a fat black snake with glowing golden eyes. And as she sat staring in fascinated horror, its glossy coils began to unwind.

Fear made her heart pump frantically. She tried to move, to scream, but couldn't budge a muscle. Panic welled in her chest, beating against her nerves and crowding her lungs to make breathing impossible. For long and agonizing moments, she watched the languid movements of the snake's iridescent body, now growing closer and closer to her.

It was near her hand on the basket rim, its devil-red tongue gleefully anticipating some unspeakable horror. It seemed to smile, its eyes dancing with infernal lights that called to Eden, belying the hideous shape that cloaked them.

Gasping, she summoned the strength to jerk her hand from the basket. But she was unbearably slow, despite her wild inner state. Terror swelled in her throat as she watched the heavy coils drop over the side of the basket onto the cloth and begin to undulate toward her. She tried to scream but it came closer to her feet, rippling, slithering . . . closer. . . .

Brawny hands appeared, pouncing on the loathsome thing as it made to wrap itself about her ankle. The movement slashed through the bonds of her fear to free her and she scrambled away. In a the blink of an eye, the snake was gone, flung far away. And those hands that had saved her now comforted and caressed her. Then arms, a chest, a body enfolded her protectively and gratitude flowed through her quaking body, making her wilt with relief against her muscular palladin.

She raised her face to find Ram MacLean's blue eyes, auburn hair, and strong features above her. Strangely, she was not surprised. His eyes were filled with tenderness and a tide of pleasure swirled about her. Sighing deeply, she touched the hard plane of his cheek and watched his face turn to nuzzle her hand. She lifted her face and his lips covered hers with honest desire. This feeling was achingly familiar. How often it had tormented her dreams with its sweetness, its shocking delight. And always it was Ram that held her, rousing her wild and primitive responses.

Eden's arms slipped about him, reveling in the massive feel of his muscular body under her slender fingers. The warmth of his body flooded through her thin clothing as they kissed. There were no clues to time and place; there were just the two of them caught in passion's protective mists. His lips nibbled hers eagerly, then meandered over her face and throat and downward to her breasts.

Her light muslin gown was swept aside and he showered intense devotion on those twin peaks whose crests she yearned for him to conquer. They quivered under his nibbling and nuzzling, and liquid fire spread into her loins. His hands traced her contours and caressed every inch of her delectable frame.

Eden ached for the feel of him covering her and, as if in response to her unspoken desire, he began to slide gently over her. His hard weight drove her beneath him, making her want him to assuage that strangely familiar hunger mounting in her loins. She craved greater closeness with his beautiful, fascinating maleness and fitted herself fuller, tighter against him as he slipped between her yielding knees. If only she could take that hard, potent essence of him inside her again, hold him there. . . .

"Charity!" James hailed the aging maid in the upstairs hall. "Is that Miss Eden's?" He nodded at the cloth-draped silver tray in the woman's hands.

"That it is, sir. I was just bringing it up."

"Well, I'll take it in to her." He relieved her of the burden and shushed her protests. "I must have a word with her and this is as good a time as any. She's been off her feed and furious with me since the night of the party—"

"Very good, sir." Charity bobbed, smiling at James's rueful expression. "Best to 'not let the sun go down upon thy wrath.' " She straightened and brushed her apron with tidy hands. "I've plenty to do downstairs." Her heels clacked on the hard wooden floor and James stretched his neck above his impeccable royal blue cravat and squared his shoulders, striding for Eden's door.

James was dimly aware that a door opened nearby and that it was Ethan who stepped into the hall just as he reached for the door handle. A muffled sound seeped through the paneled door as he balanced the tray on his knees to turn the handle. He was concentrating on equilibrium and on what he would say to try to mend fences with his little sister.

*"Dede!"* he called cheerily, absorbed in the bobbling vessels beneath the cloth, "get decent! You and I have a few things to disc—"

He stopped dead at the sight that greeted him. Muffled sounds came from the entwined figures in the midst of Dede's canopied bed. Wide-eyed, James jolted forward, then jerked to an absurd halt, feeling his eyes bulging from his head. It was a man, naked, flesh on naked flesh, on—Dede!

The tray slipped from James's hands, crashing on the floor, splashing hot cocoa and scattering fragments of bone china in every direction. The crash brought the man's passion-bloated face up in dull, angry surprise. His grip on Eden slackened and her head tossed to one side long enough for her to draw air and moan, "No!" In the twinkling of an eye, James took it in. Ramsay . . . his friend . . . his sister . . . betrayal!

*"Damn you!"* He jolted forward just as Ram rolled from Eden and off the far side of the bed. Even in the dim light, the result of his enflamed passions were all too visible. *"Damn* you for a mangy whoremonger . . . raping my own sister! I swear, I'll kill you for this!"

James launched himself around the bed at Ram just as Ram pulled the top buckle of his kilt tight. The move came as no surprise, but Ram made no move to avoid it, meeting James head on. They grappled to a standstill, both slackening and then intensifying afresh as Eden's wail rose.

She rolled onto her side, hiding her horror-struck face beneath her maidenly curtain of hair. She shook violently as shivering moans gave way to anguished sobs. Her body screamed with shame. Tears now burned her face where his raspy cheek had nuzzled it just moments before. Her heart was shrinking, dying inside her with the humiliation of what had befallen her. Her virtue was gone . . . stolen! And now she was found with him . . . ruined!

Her misery insulated her from the struggle at the foot of her bed. She did not hear Ethan and then Chase storm into her room and rush to James's aid. The sickening dull thuds of bone on flesh, the scraping of boots, the grunts and moans — all fell short of her hearing. The sounds of Ram being wrestled from the room were lost in the noise of calamity within her.

Then she was being covered, lifted, embraced. Warm feminine hands stroked her hair, cradled her face. Soft, motherly tones comforted her through her grief. Her mother, she managed to realize — it was her mother who held her. And somehow the consolation of her mother's tender presence worsened the pain she felt inside. *Ruined* . . . it beat a refrain in her brain. . . . Ruined . . . *ruined*.

Her mother and Charity helped her from the bed and half-carried her into the master suite, tucking her into bed. Constance charged Charity with absolute secrecy and sent her for the physician and then for Adam, who had left for his offices only a short while before. Their muffled tones and the air of hushed tension were like hot coals on Eden's burning head.

Constance gave her a strong sleeping draught and sat with her a long time, stroking her hair and murmuring reassurances. Eden slowly surrendered to the swirling darkness of rest. Mercifully she was sleeping when old Dr. Reynard arrived and examined her, confirming the change in her womanly state. And mercifully she slept through the rest of the day.

# Chapter Eight

It was mid-morning the next day when Ram MacLean, tied and trussed like a bird to be roasted, was shoved through the door of Adam Marlow's study. He stumbled but righted himself, wincing as he straightened to his full, towering height. Ethan Marlow pushed him further into the hushed room and closed the door behind them. Ram stopped after two steps and spread his muscular legs in a stubborn gesture of resolve. His shoulders squared and beneath the ropes that bound him, the power of his bare chest and upper arms was undeniable. He meant to show that he was still a force to be reckoned with, but the effect was fatally undercut by his bruised and battered face and by another merciless prod at his ribs from a equally mauled Ethan.

Ram's silent snarl was one of sheer bravado as he moved toward Adam Marlow's desk, feeling the other Marlow sons falling into place behind him. He stopped a pace away from Adam's desk and from the side heard Constance Marlow's indrawn gasp.

"Good God!" Adam growled, glaring at his sons, "what did you do to him?"

"Less than he deserved, the filthy raping *bastard!*" James hissed.

141

"'Twas not rape—" Ram declared yet again, bracing for another blow.

"You slimy—" James lunged at him, only to be caught and restrained by Chase.

"Enough!" Adam rose, shaking with anger. "Leave, if you cannot control yourself, James." He turned to Ram with eyes hot enough to cauterize. "He looks like a bloody piece of meat already."

"Sit down," Constance addressed Ram, shuddering slightly and averting her eyes. "All of you, sit down."

Ram edged to the chair placed before the desk and eased down into it, grimacing, then sat again, rigid with self-possession. He glanced at Constance white face and wondered fleetingly just how bad he really looked. A cursory inspection with his stiff, aching fingers had told him his nose was probably broken and one eye was swollen shut. His lips felt mashed and still bled when he touched their bruised corners. His face throbbed and ached, but it was his bruised and perhaps cracked ribs that pained him most. Fortunately he had lost no teeth in the mad fracas that followed his removal from Eden's room.

They had dragged him to the stable and had come at him, pounding and kicking. He'd defended himself admirably, seeking to inflict no permanent damage, yet hold them at bay. After all, he'd expected some outrage, some brotherly fury. But he hadn't expected raw bloodlust from this city-bred lot. They'd fought like devils and finally abandoned all pretense of couth to come at him all at once. In short, he found himself on his back and on the receiving, rather than the dealing end. And when he woke some hours later, he lay on the dark stable floor in a spatter of mingled blood, bound hand and foot. There was hardly an inch of him that didn't howl with pain.

He glanced about at his punishers. They had cut lips, black and swollen eyes, bruises aplenty. At least he had given an honorable account of himself; and so a grim satisfaction settled over him.

Adam had thudded stiffly into his tall chair and now studied the battered visage before him with undiluted approval: the man had gotten what he deserved. His usually genial voice was cold and hard.

"You say there was no force in my daughter's bed. How could there have been anything else?"

"Did she say she was forced?" Ram only now wondered what had happened to Eden since that regrettably timed intrusion on his bedding of her. He'd had no luxury to think about her since. No doubt she was suitably outraged.

Adam glanced at Constance in the charged silence and Constance lowered her eyes and her voice. "She's said nothing," she whispered.

"James witnessed it with his own eyes," Adam declared, his fatherly anger on a perilously short tether. "You call my son a liar and insult my family's honor yet again?"

"I don' dispute what he saw, sir." Ram glared back, his jaw set as determinedly as his injuries would allow. He seemed to grow before their eyes as he straightened, clenching his big fists. He risked all on this next, reckless gambit. "But it is well known a lass's first time is not the easiest. And Eden is not the first to express . . . regret."

"You dare say she *welcomed* you to her bed? The gall—the nerve—" Adam sputtered, jarred by Ram's bluntness.

"I say we're lovers, the same as any unmarried man," he stared at Constance meaningfully, "and his lass."

"Liar!" James stalked angrily toward Ram and Chase bounded up to grab him by the shirt sleeves and strain to hold him. "Dede doesn't have the juice to be anybody's lover—"

"That's the God's truth," Ethan muttered, feeling ashamed of himself seconds later when they turned to

143

stare at him. "She's . . . a fine lady," he tried to redeem himself, "who would never stoop to such."

"Believe me," Ram asserted, astonished at their denial of Eden's obvious sensuality, " . . . she stooped."

"Damn you!" James drew back a fist.

*"Enough!"*

Every muscle in the room froze. Constance stood beside the desk, pale and trembling. Between tending Eden and preventing bloody mayhem in her household, she was near the limit of her endurance.

"There's been enough brutality," she snapped. Why was she saddled with a whole family of men who lived at the edge of their cursed male reflexes? All they could think of at a time like this was bashing and thrashing!

"What's done is done. There's Eden to consider . . . or had you failed to think how the gruesome murder of a Scottish lord and the hanging of her brothers might affect her? Good Lord . . . don't you think she's been through enough?"

A stunned silence prevailed. In spite of her strained attempts at calmness, motherly tears welled in Constance's eyes and clogged her throat as she buried her face in her hands. She'd watched Eden's agony of shame these last hours and the image of that sweet, devastated face had burned into her heart.

"My little Eden . . . sweet, loving little Dede . . . what's to become of her?" She sagged against the edge of the desk, her shoulders slumped. Instantly Adam was on his feet, gathering her into his arms, pulling her to his broad chest protectively. His face was grave as he tried to control his own spiraling emotions.

Ethan's eyes were fixed on his boots and James turned away to slouch back into his chair. Chase despondently scuffled over to the window and leaned heavily against it as though the fight had just drained out of him. Ram stared at them one by one, his eyes burning strangely as they returned to Constance's quiet sobs and Adam's husbandly tenderness.

This wasn't supposed to happen. They were supposed to rant savagely and demand he do the right thing by the girl, not stand there clinging to one another as if all the spirit had been crushed from them . . . it made him feel like the biggest wretch in the world, like the base and loathsome lecher he was. It was all going wrong! He'd never have the wench . . . .

"I'll marry her." His deep voice came thick and choked. For a long moment there was silence. Ram began to wonder if he'd actually said it or only thought it. He said it again: "I'll marry her."

Adam's piercing gaze fixed him on its point as Constance lifted her tear-streaked face to Ram. James was on his feet again, jamming his lacerated fists into his pockets and staring at Ram incredulously. Ethan and Chase turned as one man to verify what they'd heard.

"Don't be absurd." Chase finally expressed their common disbelief. "She despises you . . . and with every good reason, since you betrayed our friendship, forcing yourself on her like a damned animal!"

"She was never forced . . . ever!" Ram defended himself, feeling this defense leave a foul taste in his mouth. Good God! Here he was parading and defending his revolting lusts — worse than old Haskell!

"I'll not deny we were lovers. But many a lass has been tried before being led to altar," he stared at Constance pointedly, "and none the worse for it. An' you'd not think of callin' the girl a whore nor her man a criminal."

Constance turned toward him, brushing away the last vestiges of tears, stung by his unmistakable reference to her own past. How dare this audacious buck toss her past up to her in the midst of such hurt! But the sting was immensely productive. She was suddenly remembering: Laird Ramsay MacLean had all the raw, sensual magnetism of a younger Haskell MacLean . . . and unfortunately, about as much finesse. Eden's strange vehemence toward this virile Scot began to make perfect sense. It was just possible . . . .

"It takes more than climbing into a girl's bed to make a man her lover . . . as I well know." A much clearer pair of eyes narrowed in covert appraisal of the strapping young nobleman who had somehow managed to bed her prudish daughter.

"My sons will take you to your lodgings," Adam interjected abruptly, feeling his grip on the situation slipping; it all seemed such a hopeless muddle. "Count yourself fortunate and quit Boston on the first available packet." He turned to Chase. "Untie him."

"Just like that?" Ram scowled, pushing to his feet as Chase began to work loose the strong knots. "You're letting me go? But . . . what about Eden?" Ram's mind was whirring. "I said I'd marry her," he proclaimed, rubbing his rope-chafed wrists, scowling until the blood in his face began to pound anew.

"We'll see to our daughter," Adam scoffed indignantly. "We'd not sentence her to a life of abuse at your hands just because of your sin against her!"

"Abuse?" Ram jerked his arm from Chase's insistent grasp and leaned across the desk on his cut and swollen knuckles. "You don't understand . . . I *want* to marry Eden."

The strange tenor of his voice roused Constance's feminine instincts to fever pitch. There was more here than met the eye, she was sure of it. The rich velvety blue of her gaze bored into Ram, sorting and examining the possibilities with the exceptional clarity of a mother's sight.

"Marry and make a life with a girl you've insulted and degraded before her family's very eyes?" Constance questioned, seeming to dismiss his assertions. "She'd never

146

agree to marry you . . . especially after this humiliation."

Ram's stomach lurched. He'd never considered that she could be given a choice in the matter. What kind of family was this, anyway?

"She'll like the life of a spinster less, I trow," he charged. "Of a certainty she cannot be mated to any other. With me she'll have an honorable name, a home, and . . . comforts."

"That sounds a cold transaction." Constance'a gaze raked him, finding there a spark of desperation that intrigued her and made her believe he really wanted Eden in the way Haskell had once wanted her. "And what makes you think she must end her days a spinster? God willing, she'll find a true mate and put both you and this sordid episode behind her."

"Constance—" Adam stared down at his wife, baffled by her cool pronouncement.

"And when she marries, she'll not be dragged to the altar just to salve a careless nobleman's conscience or an outraged society. She's my daughter and I'll not let that happen to her anymore that I'd have accepted it myself, years ago."

"Constance, really—" Adam scowled, unable to hide his surprise.

"You can't do this!" The swelling and bruises of Ram's battered face hid its furious reddening. "I'm her true mate—she must marry me!" He finally blurted out, feeling his stomach do a slow grind at the thought of anyone else beholding Eden Marlow's silky hair spread over her pillows, or feeling her lush young curves . . . . Furiously he dragged a hand back through his hair and braced his knuckles on his hips determinedly. His only chance now was to make them think him besotted of their daughter . . . and robbed of judgment by his passion for her.

"I want Eden." The Good Lord knew *that* was the unvarnished truth! "I want to marry her and make a

147

home with her . . ." Questionable ground, there. He'd never really thought much past bedding her when he was around her. And when he wasn't around her he tried very hard not to think of her at all. "And despite what humiliation may lead her to deny, she wants me as well." That truth had undoubtedly expired, but how would they know?

Unwittingly, he lent credence to his cause by the tortured tension of his big muscular frame. He was the very picture of a man beset by a woman.

"The state of Eden's feelings has yet to be determined." Constance pushed away from Adam's slack arms and faced Ram squarely. She raised her chin in regal challenge. "And just *why* should we give our only and most precious daughter to *you?*"

"Because," Ram thundered, "I . . . I *love* her!"

His declaration reverberated about the room, settling on each set of ears differently. Adam stared at him with astonishment; James's jaw set with disbelief; Ethan scratched his head, bemused; and Chase's mouth began to twitch with a hint of a grin. Constance relaxed visibly, her expression softening.

"That puts a whole new complexion on things," she demurred. She clasped her hands patiently as she flicked a sidelong glance at Adam's open consternation. "Of course, Eden's feelings in the matter will have to be verified."

"Well . . . of course." Ram's chin jutted determinedly, but he could barely hear what was said for the pounding of his heart. What had he said? Something in his chest began to shrink. What an unregenerate cad he was . . . the lie rolled so easily from his tongue! And what an unbelievably stupid bastard he was. It would serve him right when Eden denounced him and his *love* and he had to forfeit Skyelt altogether.

"We shall speak with her this afternoon." Constance

148

reached for Adam's hands and nestled once again at his side. She smiled with new confidence into her husband's blank face before turning to Ram again. "If it is as you say, then this may all be resolved very quickly. Expect word at your lodgings tonight, sir. Good day."

Ram's big arms slid to his sides and his impossibly square shoulders rounded slightly. It was no good protesting further. His cause was lost, irretrievably lost. He nodded as nobly as his injuries would allow and grimly backed two steps before wheeling and striding painfully for the door.

"Just what in bloody hell was that all about?" Adam swiped a hand over his crinkled forehead as soon as the study had cleared. He glared in confusion at his wife's enigmatic smile. "All that about finding Eden a true soul mate . . . not caring what society says—"

"*We* didn't care," Constance showed not a drop of contrition, "and we've been quite happy. It was an effective bargaining point, I thought."

"Bargaining . . .? God, Constance, what are you up to? You don't honestly swallow this business of them being lovers!" He watched as she cocked a brow knowingly. "Well, excuse me, but Eden is just not capable. Can you imagine it? 'Take me, Ramsay, darling-- but be sure to say *please* and *thank you'*."

"She is *our* daughter, after all," Constance countered. "She must have *some* blood in her veins. And he positively enrages her for some unexplainable reasons. It's the closest I've seen to real passion in her since she arrived."

"Maybe she just despises him, pure and simple."

"Nothing's ever pure and simple about a woman's passion, Adam. I would have thought you'd have learned that by now." A mischievous dimple appeared in Constance's cheek and Adam harrumphed irritably, plopping

149

down into his big leather chair.

"Even if she agreed to a match, which she won't, what kind of marriage would they have? Whatever happened upstairs, I say she won't let him ever touch her again . . ever."

"Oh, he'll touch her. And I doubt she'll resist for long." Constance swayed over to the arm of his chair and pulled his arm about her waist, holding it there as she gazed down into his melting determination. "He's Haskell Mac-Lean's son."

"*Haskell . . . MacLean's . . . son?*" Adam blanched with shock.

"The very same."

"Then the man's a randy menace to all womanhood! And we're throwing our sheltered and . . . genteel little Eden into his slavering jaws!"

"Really, Adam." Constance's mouth pursed in mock annoyance. "Last week she was stuffy, prudish, and insufferable. Find a man in her bed and she's suddenly sheltered, maidenly, and too delicate for such carnal shenanigans. Will you make up your mind?"

He opened his mouth to protest, but it worked soundlessly and then closed. Perturbation furrowed his brow.

"He seems honorable . . . in all other respects. He'll be quite presentable, healed and cleaned up a bit, and he's got a title—albeit a Scottish one. I believe he really wants Eden. And if, as I suspect, he's roused a scandalous bit of pleasure in her, then who better to mate her with? If anyone can teach her to enjoy the marriage bed, Haskell MacLean's son can."

Adam frowned thoughtfully and tried to imagine Eden's reaction to such a proposal. And only one scene came to mind.

"She'll never agree to it, Constance. She'll declare him a pillaging villain and vow never to marry, ever." He sighed, staring into the gloomy future. "And I'll have a martyr to chastity under my roof for the rest of my days."

"You have an astonishing lack of faith in your own daughter, Adam Marlow. I know she's seemed cool and formal and obsessed with propriety since she's come home. But somewhere inside her is that little brown-haired moppet who used to hide under James's bed to catch a glimpse of him shaving shirtless." Constance's lips turned up fondly at the corners as she recalled it. "All it takes is the right man to wrench it out of her. And I think perhaps Ramsay MacLean has the right tool for the job."

"Constance!" Adam looked at her unbelievingly. But the absolute assurance on her face made the corner of his mouth purse in consideration of her motherly scheming. His brows raised in one last question before surrendering.

She smiled beatifically and patted him.

"Just leave it to me, dear."


"We were greatly shocked, Eden. This gentleman had never even asked permission to call on you . . . and to find him in your bed . . . . Well, it really was *most* distressing."

Eden raised her crimson face to object, but met her mother's probing eye and quickly lowered in it deeper humiliation. She had trouble breathing and squeezed her bloodless hands together harder in her lap as her heart shrank further inside her. It had come at last, the time for facing the awful consequences of that horrible night.

She squirmed on the parlor window seat and wished she could just slink back to her room and quietly die. But after the living nightmare of the past two days, it would almost be a relief to have it out and in the open. The sheer weight of everyone's kindness bore heavier and heavier on her heart. Thankfully, it was her mother who had sent for her. At least she'd be spared her father's open wrath and her brother's indignation.

"How perfectly horrid of you to keep your courtship such a secret from us all," Constance sniffed for effect, scrutinizing every nuance of her daughter's posture. "Of course, once we psoke with his lordship . . . and he declared how very much in love with you he is . . . some of the sting is gone now."

"Courtship? Love?" Eden's face came up to stay this time, draining some of its furious color. They somehow believed she had welcomed him to her bed? She shook her head numbly. "He declared—"

"Perhaps it's understandable," Constance swept her reaction aside with a purposeful hand. "Such a strong love can cloud a man's judgment, men being what they are. But I might have expected more from you." She had glanced at Eden and looked away, satisfied that her parental disapproval was working its intended charm on Eden's pride and sense of duty.

And worked it had. Eden shriveled inside at the realization that not only was she disgraced, but her family was again adrift, just when they needed her strength and her good example most! She bowed her head and her shoulders sagged miserably.

Constance felt completely torn as she watched and she wanted nothing more than to take her daughter into her arms and comfort her again. But she recognized the danger present in her surge of sentiment: if she failed to take advantage of Eden's shame and persuade her take vows with Lord Ramsay, what would her future be? A shamed and bitter spinsterhood that disavowed all pleasure to atone for her one sin? Not her daughter, Constance vowed with a silent oath. Eden would have a marriage, a true marriage, if she had to be hoodwinked into it!

In the brief silence, Eden sorted the incredible facts of her ruin yet again. The viper had tempted and ravished her in the garden, then slithered his way into her window,

152

into her bed—and very nearly into her body again! The humiliation and hurt were overwhelming; but they turned to rage when she realized Ram's conniving treachery. And the depth of his degradation was only now clear—in order to escape the consequences, he claimed he did it for love! How dare that surly bastard try to put a noble face on his lust!

"I have to say, when he *begged* for your hand, your father and I were every bit as surprised as we were relieved." Constance feared giving Eden too much time to think.

"Relieved?" Eden gasped, feeling her stomach tense. But the word *"begged"* exploded in her mind. Lord Ramsay had *begged* for her hand? Declared his love for her to her family and actually begged for her hand in marriage? She struggled to grasp that tumbling revelation in her mind. This was a shocking new wrinkle. His words in the garden came storming back over her . . . he'd spoken of his "manly feelin's" for her . . .. Had he honestly ben trying to tell her that he . . .?

"Yes!" Constance straightened and primly fluffed the lace at her wrists, "relieved and fortunate. Not every gentleman of his station would feel compelled to right . . . such an indiscretion. It's not difficult to see how his manly qualities impressed you . . . for he is courtly, handsome, honorable. And having just come from Mistress Dunleavy's, you would naturally be drawn to a man with such a strong sense of duty. She paused and rearranged herself on the window seat beside Eden, clasping her knees with her hands, her mouth pursed with a judicious amount of resignation.

"I am disappointed . . . *very* disappointed that you did not confide in me from the outset, Eden. It would have saved us all much heartache . . . not to mention the humiliation of . . . you being found together . . . clandestinely." Her emphasis on that last word sent a sliver of pain into Eden's chest.

There was no use denying it, she had allowed her lustful imaginings to beguile her into responding to his . . . assault. Every time they met, he set hands to her and her stubborn, sensual nature always responded quite wantonly. What else could he think but that she secretly wanted him? He had sneaked into her room but not without some assurance that he would be welcomed by her willing flesh. Was it possible for a man to love a woman and yet force himself on her lustfully at their every meeting? The questions all swirled hopelessly in her head.

"Our only course is clear, Eden." Constance straightened, her voice huskier than usual. "The vows cannot be read before two weeks, to allow for the banns. Special dispensation there would cause comment, and Lord knows there will be plenty enough of that as is."

"Vows?" Eden lifted her luminous, coppery eyes to her mother's softening gaze. "Marry him? How could I even face him—" Her voice cracked and tears rolled slowly down her burning cheeks. "Oh, Mama—" She buried her face in trembling hands and Constance felt as if she'd been impaled.

"Dear, sweet, Eden!" She impulsively gathered her daughter into her arms and rocked her, shushing her softly and trying to staunch the tears in her own eyes. Little sobs shook Eden's shoulders. Constance's chin quivered above Eden's head and she brushed Eden's silky curls with her cheek, feeling a wave of painful remembrance sweeping over her. She'd held her sweet little daughter just so on that day they'd sent her off to school over five years ago. It had nearly broken her heart then and was doubly painful now, for when Eden left her house this time, it would be forever.

"Dede," Constance reassured her, "it'll be all right."

"Mama, what kind of marriage would it be?" Eden

154

shuddered, trying to draw a breath. "How could he forget . . . how could I forget that our marriage was forced by disgrace, not allowed by love?"

Constance's heart was wringing inside her.

"But he does love you, Mudpie." She stroked Eden's soft cascade of hair and prayed she was right. Please, God, let him be an honorable man who spoke the truth when he spoke of loving Eden.

"But how could he love a woman who . . . was disgraced in the eyes of her own fam—" The little sobs were renewed and Constance closed her eyes, trying to think of Eden's good and to swallow her misgivings. Her heart was near to breaking—she had to do something!

"Dede," she lifted Eden away from her and clasped her trembling chin to make Eden meet her eyes. "You mustn't think that way. A man doesn't feel the way a woman does about these things, believe me. Men . . . take a certain pride in their . . . manly persuasions. What does it matter to him how he gained a sweet, beautiful wife to grace his life? And Dede, you will most certainly grace his life; there's no mistaking that."

"But Mama, I've been . . . ruined."

Constance groaned inwardly, knowing now she'd done her job too well.

"Eden, listen to me: you've not been ruined . . . you're still the same gentle, refined young lady you were before this happened." She reached for Eden's hands and squeezed them. "You can still make a good and loving marriage with Lord Ramsay. There's absolutely no reason—"

"But I'm . . . not pure anymore," Eden's face lowered under the disgrace.

"Eden—" Constance groaned openly with frustration. She rose and paced, measuring her words through tightened lips. "Then I see I must tell you my secret, though it may well cost me your respect, perhaps even . . . your

155

love. If it will settle your mind and ease your troubled heart, it will be worth it to me." She turned and stood before Eden, clasping her hands tightly and bracing herself.

"I . . . was not a virgin at my vows, either."

Eden's jaw dropped as she lifted her head to verify what she'd heard. Her eyes were wide with shock.

*"Not,"* she swallowed hard, *"a virgin?"*

"No."

"You mean you and Father . . ."

"Yes." Constance killed the fleeting urge to reveal even more when she saw how deeply her news had affected Eden. She could see the wheels spinning in Eden's mind and knew she risked much with her daughter by this confession. But a desperate situation called for desperate measures . . . like the truth.

"I allowed him . . . before our vows. And we have enjoyed a good and faithful marriage all these years since. God help me, I still do not regret it." Heaven knew that was the truth at its barest! She lifted her chin, feeling a startling pang of new conscience for the licentious behavior of her youth. She couldn't escape the growing feeling that her sensual past with Haskell MacLean played some role in all this. And once expressed in her mind, the guilty tendrils of that thought were soon entrenched.

"You . . . and Papa." Eden turned it over in her mind and it seemed a strange but real comfort to her that her parents had been lovers before their vows. They did indeed have a loving marriage, a harmonious household, a respected life. Only one cloud remained on her horizon: despite what he'd proclaimed before her family, she and Lord Ramsay were not true lovers, sweet and longing and wistful. And that secret, shameful knowledge weakened her voice as she spoke.

"Then it shall be as you say, Mam-ma," she reverted to her elegant, flattened tone. "If I must marry, then I'll try hard to be a good and proper wife. Let me know . . . when I must make ready."

Constance watched her sweet young daughter glide slowly toward the door and wished she could crawl under the nearest rug.

## Chapter Nine

Two weeks and two days later, Eden descended the grand staircase of Marlow House for the last time as an unmarried woman. She felt like a wooden puppet moving inside her elegant ensemble of beautiful yellow and ivory shot-silk brocade and matching veiled bonnet. She checked the wrist buttons of her kid gloves for the tenth time and clamped her fingers tightly about her nosegay of pink and yellow summer roses. Every impression, every sensation was magnified and meaningful; the carpet was exceptionally soft beneath her slippers, the crystal chandelier sparkled with more brilliance, the blues and crimsons of the furnishings in the hall vibrated richly. She paused at the top of the stairs and looked around her with wondering eyes, hoping to capture it in her heart.

Constance paused behind her and squeezed her fan mercilessly. She could almost feel the thudding of Eden's heart, the dryness of her eyes, the coldness of her hands. And she felt a ruthless stab of pain at recalling how very different her own hurried and eager vows had been. She'd been laughing, sighing into Adam's handsome face, melting at his warm, loving touch. She'd never wanted anything more than she wanted to be married and joined to Adam Marlow . . . no matter what her parents or hypo-

158

critical London society said. And her lovely daughter, her sweet little Dede, would have none of that joy on her wedding day.

"Eden—" Constance moved up beside her, frowning uncertainly.

"I know, Mama, it's time. I'm . . . ready." Eden lifted her chin bravely and Constance felt her insides quiver. Then Eden turned back to put a hand on her mother's arm and give it a brief, reassuring squeeze before moving down the steps to take Adam's arm. Constance recovered just enough to glide down the steps and enter the parlor ahead of them, starting the music with a nod to the violinist.

Eden managed a quavery little smile at her serious father and nervously fluffed the lace frills that rimmed the low bodice of her empire gown. She absently recalled her dismay at the last fitting in England: she had thought the gown cut scandalously low. Now it seemed particularly fitting as her wedding gown . . . low and scandalous.

The music wafted toward them and Adam patted her hand on his arm and drew her along toward her fate. They paused in the graceful arch of the wide doorway and Eden's knees almost buckled when she saw Ram MacLean standing with old Reverend Gilworthy before the cold fireplace. He wore his fitted black coat with the tartan sash and silver badge and his bold, burnt-red tartan kilt. Her eyes widened as they flew over his hard, manly form and came to rest inescapably on his strong, fascinating legs. She swallowed with difficulty and tore her eyes away, fastening them on her roses. But a guilty stain washed her pale cheeks and transformed her into a true blushing bride.

Adam retired to Constance's side and she clung tightly to his hands, her eyes already filled before the first words were spoken. Eden looked so terribly young, so vulnerable, so . . . *small* beside that hulking, self-possessed Scot. Constance sought her sons' faces and read identical thoughts in them.

Feeling Ram's gaze on her, Eden raised her face, first to the good Reverend, then to the man who was to become her husband and master. She might have withstood the assault of his arrogance, his smug possessiveness, even his cold appraisal; but nothing could have prepared her for the sensual revolt of her own body in his male presence.

He was so near, she could feel his breath on her upturned face, could see the newly faded scar at the corner of his generous lips, could smell soap and warm wool and even a trace of the brandy he'd shared with Arlo just before arriving to claim her. The scenet was draining every bit of resistance from her, and she ached with that pleasurable hollowness that afflicted her only in his arms. Her skin came alive under his azure gaze, tingling all the way to the tips of her sweetly exposed breasts. Her breath came harder and it was impossible to swallow, but she managed to moisten her lips.

The burnished glow of his thick hair, the strength of his neck, the width of his shoulders . . . his beauty engulfed her, sending her thoughts spiraling. A chill fluttered up her spine, followed by a frightening surge of heat in her most womanly places. He was so handsome, so compelling, so proudly, even arrogantly, male. Then it struck her . . . it was this very desire . . . this *sin* of wanting . . . that had brought her to such dire straits in the first place.

She made herself nod dutifully at the Reverend and helplessly returned her eyes to Ram, wondering how he could want her for his wife and hoping against her better judgment that he did, for both their sakes. Shamed color stole into her cheeks again as she watched his big hands with their callused palms share their warmth with hers.

160

Ram traced the demure oval of her face with aching eyes, his gaze catching on her lustrous curls and then descending to caress the creamy fullness of her bosom. The hard lines of his face softened under the warmth of her eyes and a smile pulled at the corner of his lips. Never, not in all his life, had he seen a woman more beautiful, more appealing to his every sense. She was like a fever in his blood. Away from her he chilled and near her he burned.

But, Lord, what a delicious madness it was! To be near her, to watch her, to feel her softness molded beneath his hard body—it had become his consuming desire. His eyes darkened as he felt his control slipping another notch. Just standing here beside her, his blood was warming, his arms twitched to clasp her against him. Soon, soon she would be his, really his, he realized, trying to shake off this untimely arousal. He'd bed her and relish her charms . . . and invade her mysteries. And somewhere in the spending of this hoarded desire, he'd get it all out of his system. Then he'd get on with his life.

Her cold hand was slowly warming in his and he rubbed its softness with his thumb, back and forth, not realizing its reassuring power. She seemed so small, so feminine, so very young to be such a temptation. A foreign, protective impulse reared within him. He examined it warily, then allowed it. Whatever else she was, he reasoned while he still could, she was most certainly his . . . by the powers of the flesh and now by legal right. In moments she would be his wife, too. . . .

". . . honor and to cherish, in sickness and in health, in poverty and in plenty, all the days of our lives," he repeated, feeling himself becoming lost in the pulsing, dark centers of her eyes. There he glimpsed promise and passion and need. Something in his well-armored chest began to swell and he gave himself over to that budding

161

tightness. What did it matter how queer he felt? It was his wedding day. Tomorrow . . . tomorrow he would be back to normal.

Eden felt a sensual shiver as the cold metal of the wedding band slid up her finger and came to rest against her palm. Ram's hands closed over hers, swallowing them from sight, and for some reason she could not look at him.

The good Reverend pronounced them man and wife and then proffered a lengthy blessing on their love, their lifelong union, their Christian duty, their children and grandchildren, their material well-being, and their resistance to dread disease, including the gout. He made the married state sound a grave and serious business, so final and irrevocable that one had to die to be shed of it. And Eden's legs weakened at the impact of the words she'd just spoken.

"You may kiss the bride," the parson beamed, clutching his service book over his ample middle.

For a moment, nothing happened.

"Kiss 'er, Laird Ram," Arlo prodded with a sly grin.

Ram looked down into her darkened, expectant eyes and a spear of raw excitement shot through his loins. But as he straightened he caught a glimpse of James's angry glare over the rim of Eden's bonnet. He held Eden's head between his hands and tilted her upturned face to plant a circumspect kiss on her forehead.

Eden flushed crimson and lowered her face even further. He had scorned the offering of her lips and shamed her utterly . . . again.

"Yer not her uncle, man." Arlo appeared around Ram's elbow, scowling in mock horror. "Kiss 'er like a MacLean!" Ram shot a withering stare at his companion, then at James, and did exactly that.

But his kiss was tight and angry, deepening Eden's

162

humiliation. To think that moments before, her treacherous womanly heart was on the verge of surrendering! It was that awful carnal taint in her blood—

"That's more like it!" Arlor's unabashed humor uncorked a flurry of nervous talk and stiff congratulations.

Eden was kissed and hugged by her family and Arlo and the Reverend's wife, all while Ram's grasp on her hand held her prisoner at his side. She wouldn't raise her eyes from the floor except to manage a pitiful approximation of a smile at her family.

"We have the wedding dinner prepared . . . . and music . . . This way. . . ." Constance's voice strained above the tense buzz of the room and she leaned against Adam for support as she led the way to the dining room.

Ram pulled Eden's hand through his elbow and strode after them, leaving Arlo to follow. There was a scramble behind them and as they entered the flower-banked dining room, James's sneer was unmistakable.

"The first time I ever saw a wedding where the man wore the skirts."

Eden blanched as Ram halted, stonefaced, and turned slowly about to face a sullen wall of Marlow men.

"I cannot think what's gotten into me." Constance hurried between them with a frozen smile and a hand fluttering at her throat. "I'm so addlepated! Eden, your lordship, beside Adam at the head of the table." She gave Ram's coiled arm a pacifying pat and waved him to the far end of the long, linen-draped table. "Reverend and Mrs. Gilworthy, opposite them. Mrs. Skinner, Edward and Millicent Perkins beside them. Aunt Penelope across. . . ." She pointed, reaching for her closest son's arm. "Chase and Ethan next . . . and of course," she slipped her hand through James's stiff arm and discreetly hauled him along with her, "my dear right arm at my right hand."

Despite Constance's determined smile and strained cheeriness, her four children each wore an expression more fitting for a wake than a wedding. But of the four, Constance worried most about Eden's silence and the way she seemed to flinch and shrink from her new husband at each sudden movement or lurch of conversation. And more unnerving was the way she attempted to cover it with demure looks at Ram and tepid little smiles. Constance looked at her sons' darkening faces and knew they watched Eden, too.

Eden's modest behavior was in fact a triumph of Mistress Dunleavy's classes in deportment. Stubborn desire had rallied her senses in high treason against her will; strange fluid sensations ebbed and flowed alarmingly through her body, setting parts of her afire in response to his merest glance. It was all she could do to sit still in her high-backed mahogany chair, with him alongside, touching her.

She nodded at the Reverend's stories, accepted the many compliments paid her with all good grace, and generally seemed the refined young bride. But she knew what her new master planned to do to her in a few short hours. Ignorance was certainly bliss where brides were concerned. She tried in vain not to think about the discomfort, the crushing weight that would drive her down into the soft mattresses. Shame had long since purged the more pleasurable sensations from her mind and she refused to connect the strange excitations she was experiencing with what had happened in her bed.

Adam's maiden aunt, Penelope, was the first into her cups, as usual, and regaled those who would be regaled with snippets of remembrance of Eden's early years. Then eagle-eyed Millicent Perkins drew the carefully worded details of their "shipboard courtship" from a blushing Eden and a taciturn Ram. And conversation and humor windled downhill from there. When the silence became oo embarrassing, Constance would give Ethan's shin a motherly nudge and he would rise dutifully to propose another toast. Her game was up when Ethan jolted sharply at one of her intensifying kicks and slapped Chase across the shoulder, growling, *"your* turn."

It was the last toast.

"Millicent dear has agreed to play for us this evening, haven't you, Millie?" Constance sprung up like a loosed coil and quickly herded a relieved wedding party into the parlor once more for a bit of entertainment. After two renditions from Millie Perkins' thin, nasal voice, the good Reverend Gilworthy and his wife made excuses and departed; Aunt Penelope fell asleep in her chair and had to be carried up to a guest room; Ram was glowering deeper with each tick of the clock; and Eden's nerves were stretched till they burned. Eden nearly shouted with relief when Millie, miffed by their lack of musical acumen or any sense of appreciation, declared she had early obligations the next morning and dragged her long-suffering Edward home.

The minute Constance left the parlor to see them out, Ram rose and stretched his stiff legs, pulling Eden up beside him. "I expect we'll be goin' as well." He spoke to no one in particular, but the four Marlow men responded immediately.

"Tonight?" "Going?" "Where?" and "Like *hell* you are!" came the chorus.

This last came from Adam himself. All evening he'd watched with fatherly outrage the play of strain on Eden's face and read her reluctance for the night ahead. He jabbed his thumbs into his vest pockets and advanced on Ram with a stony jaw.

"Eden will spend her wedding night here," he pointed to the spot where they stood, "under *my* roof and *my* protection." Adam squared his shoulders with fatherl[y] fervor, unconsciously trying to match Ram's formidab[le] physique. "And if you wish to share it with her," h[e] growled, "you'll have to stay here tonight as well."

"I've made other arrangements," Ram uttered tightl[y] stepping between wide-eyed Eden and the hostile mal[e] contingent of her family.

"He's taken rooms at the Buxton Inn," Arlo interjected backing away as Ethan advanced to darem him to inte[r]fere.

"My daughter will *not* spend her first night of marrie[d] life in a public house!" Adam declared, his eyes narrowin[g] furiously. "I'll see she's safe and healthy, come morning with my own two eyes."

"She's safe with me now—I'm her husband!" Ra[m] jerked a furious thumb at his broad chest, livid at Adam['s] open scorn of his honor toward Eden. "And she'll slee[p] under—"

"This roof!" James stepped forward, white with ange[r.]

"There's no need for argument and ill feelings." Chas[e] stepped between the hot-tempered James and his brut[e] sized brother-in-law. He gazed meaningfully at Eden['s] pale face and huge, frightened eyes, causing Ram t[o] wheel around to look at her. They all looked at her, bu[t] she was deadened with mortification, incapable of mak[ing even the smallest response. "I'm sure we all wan[t] what's best for Eden. We're of the opinion she might fee[l] . . . more *comfortable* in familiar surroundings . . . to[night especially."

Ram stared down at her, taking in her trembling chin the rigidity of her slender shoulders, the tight stoicism o[f] her clasped hands. And he was overcome with a strange urge to heed Chase's reasonable words. He reached fo[r] Eden's hands and drew her toward him; she moved a[s] though made of wood.

166

"Eden—"

"Constance," Adam spoke to his wife as she entered, ignoring whatever Ram had in mind, "take Eden upstairs and . . . make her . . . comfortable."

And when Ram turned irritably toward Adam, Constance slipped her arm about Eden's shoulders and firmly ushered her out. By the time he turned back, his bride was gone; it was settled.

"Sit down, *son*," Adam ordered Ram through narrow eyes, "we have plenty of time for a brandy together."

When Ram was finally allowed to quit the parlor, it was late and his mood was as dark as the house. He was escorted to his bride's bed by her three hostile brothers, James leading the way through the candlelit hallways, Ethan and Chase flanking him. James turned curtly at the end of the hallway near Eden's room and came nose-to-nose with Ram.

"So you'll not be getting any ideas," James grabbed his arm, "the three of us will be passing the night just outside her door. The slightest cry, the merest sniffle, and we'll be through that door like a shot, if we have to tear it off its hinges!"

Ram was trembling with the effort needed to avoid lashing out at his onetime friend. His face matched his dark, burnished hair as he shot a furious glare at Ethan and Chase. They glared back and Ram realized that he faced a united front once again. God, how he longed to hear the crunch of bone and sinew!

Just outside the door, James halted him by the sleeve. His eyes were burning with the promise of retribution.

"Congratulations, man," he gritted out. "You're about to enter paradise."

\* \* \*

Eden sat before her vanity table, squeezing the handle of her brush as if she could force some courage from it. She tried to find comfort in the noble examples of history . . . the biblical Esther, Joan of Arc, the brave St. Catherine. Wait—St. Catherine had died rather than surrender her virtue . . . it was too late for that. She shuddered a sigh. If St. Catherine's pursuer had been Ramsay MacLean, she probably wouldn't have resisted him either. It was clear that nobility and Mistress Dunleavy would never get her through this night.

She thought of what lay ahead and stiffened, looking down at her thin, gauzy nightdress with its plunging neckline; it clung revealingly. Charity had laughed, *laughed,* when she dragged Eden's chemise from her and refused to give it back. Eden pulled the gown away from her and peeked at her own seldom-seen contours. A chill ran up her spine in the summer night and she snatched the thin fabric back against her, locking her trembling arms around her waist.

She looked about the darkened room and sighed. The shadows and exotic Chinese prints made it seem foreign, a little threatening. It reminded her so much of that night. . . . Voices floated from the hall, male voices, and Eden went rigid.

The door opened quickly and Ram lurched forward into the bedroom, whirling to stare at the door slamming behind him. His huge shoulders were braced beneath the tapered black coat and his legs spread defiantly as he glowered. He whirled back, raking the room with that fierce lightning-blue glare.

She wasn't hard to find, sitting on the bench in front of the candelabra. Her hair flowed over her shoulders and the light from behind sifted through the tissue-like fabric of her gown, outlining her body with titillating clarity. He sucked a hard breath as her beauty stunned him, rattling every nerve and tendon.

"You!" he charged, taken aback by the speed of his arousal. "You knew about this, didn't you?"

"What?" Eden blanched and her eyes jolted even wider. She pushed to her feet, completing the erotic silhouette that had already dealt his control a fatal blow. "Knew what?" she asked, her voice wavering.

Ram could scarcely swallow. It was as if someone had taken a drawknife to his guts and was hollowing him out bit by painful bit. His eyes burned; and he inhaled that hint of roses and lavender she always wore. A shaft of white-hot desire shot through his loins and he half-growled, "About this! Them makin' us stay here tonight."

"No, I didn't know. I honestly didn't—"

"Well, it won't make a whit of difference," his finger pounded the air between them, "not a whit! You're my wife tonight . . . and every other night, from now on!"

His words hung between them a moment before fading away. Eden covered her mouth with the back of her hand and her heart gave a lurch. He'd stormed into her bedroom on their wedding night, accusing her of plotting against him! He'd swept her denials aside without so much as a blink and in the same breath ordered she submit to him upon demand!

Eden's horror produced a corresponding shock in Ram. Why in heaven's name had he said those things? Listen to him, standing there, demanding she satisfy his lusts!

He stepped closer and when she saw that his fists were clenched, she couldn't have known it was to restrain his own unreliable impulses. She bolted and fled behind the vanity.

"Eden!" his voice had the grit of frustration in it.

"No—I had nothing to do with it!"

He lunged across the vanity and she ducked so that his

169

big fingers just brushed her gown. He glared at his handful of air and straightened, feeling a draft of belated reason swirling around him. She was running from him! He was actually chasing Eden Marlow around her bedroom on their wedding night!

"Stand still, for God's sake." He stopped dead and spoke through his teeth.

Eden shook her head, shifting her silky mane about her pale form. She backed warily toward the door and he set his hands at his waist, making his shoulders jut forward. *Stand . . . still."*

It came from deep in his chest and rumbled low and menacing all around her. The sound froze her in place. And when he sprang at her, she was unable to react quickly enough. His big hand clamped over her mouth as he dragged her against him and wrestled her across the room. With a hard glance at the door, he stared down into her frightened face. He groaned, seeing his fingers digging into her delicate skin. Stopping his bride's screams by brute force . . . how low could a man sink?

"Be quiet and I'll let you go." He spoke more angrily than he wished. She stiffened against him and he slowly relaxed his iron grip. After a moment he removed his hand from her mouth.

Eden sucked air quickly, preparing to scream Judgment Day itself down on him. Ram quickly realized his mistake, but this time covered her mouth with his. Her head thrashed and she wriggled and struggled against his overpowering body, but it was no use; he was massive and determined. And he was correct: he had the right now to take her however brutally and painfully he wished.

Whether it was the gentling warmth of his mouth or the heat of his body, something stormed and breached her will. Gradually, she slowed, coming to rest against his potent and dangerous body. She could hardly breathe,

170

had no strength in her legs, no power to fight him any more. She couldn't know her last refuge was indeed her most devastating weapon. Fear and humiliation set the tears welling in her copper-ringed eyes.

Eden strangled a sob against his mouth and he raised his head to stare down at the liquid crystal that clung to her eyes.

"P-please . . . don't hurt me," she gasped.

"Hurt you!" Ram recoiled as if he'd just been doused with icy water. "What are you talking about, woman? I'm going to bed you, not torture you!" he growled, realizing only after he had said it that somehow the two were equated in her mind. "What kind of monster do you think I am?" And he knew the answer to that, too, when she shrank from him again.

He released her and she stumbled slightly, covering her face with her hands. She collapsed on the vanity bench, her slender shoulders quaking. She could sense his hot gaze on her and hated herself for feeling like such a coward. But it was hard to take a stand when she couldn't even get her breath.

"Damn!" Ram watched her, his hands set on his waist, his brawny legs braced. *"Damn!"* He jerked away to pace and ran both hands through his hair; then he stopped and pointed at her.

"Even married to you, you're the damned hardest woman to bed I ever saw!"

Eden snubbed a breath and her head jerked as she swiped at her tears with wet hands. "Then f-find an honest tart an' l-leave me be."

"It would make my life simpler, to be sure!"

Her sobs renewed and began to escalate.

He stared at her in disbelief and paced away from her and back. A lump grew in his throat, refusing to be swallowed. Worse yet, he could still see her body through that devil's web of a nightgown she wore. His raw frustration only seemed to feed his ungodly arousal! A rut-maddened boar, that's what he was!

A surge of blood finally reached his starved brain and for a moment he considered that she might really be frightened of him. Had he hurt her somehow that first time in the garden? No one had ever complained of his loving before. But then, he didn't think he'd ever had a virgin before Eden: he was her very first. And at least in that way, the thought prodded him, she was his first, too. His chest wall suddenly became too tight for his ribs.

"It always hurts the first time." He spoke defensively, then immediately regretted it. Her shoulders sagged as if he'd struck her and she began to wail . . . really wail.

Ram stiffened, taking a nervous step toward the door. "The merest sniffle," James had said. And he could hear their muffled, angry tones outside.

"Eden," he crept back to her. "Eden, it's all right, really, lass. Honest, I wouldna hurt you for the world." He cast a worried glance back over his shoulder. She seemed to be gathering force instead of calming!

His hands reached for her and she shrank from his touch. But once his fingers felt her soft flesh, they refused to let go, and in a moment he was scooping her up into his arms, carrying her to the stuffed chaise. She wriggled in his arms, but her weakened resistance was testimony to the worn condition of her nerves.

He sat down with her on his lap and pressed her head against his chest to muffle her crying. Her hair was fragrant and so very soft. He wrapped her in his muscled arms, groaning internally at the feel of her curves pressed against his sensitive inner arms and chest. He glanced uneasily at the door. They wouldn't dare. . . .

"Shhh. You're all right, Eden: you're my wife now, I'll not let anythin' hurt you, I promise." She shuddered in his arms and he winced, despising himself. "Sweet Eden, don' cry. Shhh." He began to stiffly stroke her silky hair and the side of her face, finding a tender instinct that had been long buried surface. His words softened his tone and he began to feel what he spoke. "You're a lovely woman, Eden. And I guess if I were yer brothers, I'd feel the same as they do about you . . . wantin' to protect you."

She began to unwind on Ram's lap. His warmth, his murmured litany of comfort, and the magic of his hands on her liberally exposed skin reached the knots within her and began to loosen them.

The movement of his hard fingers over her hair and the skin of her temple bewildered her; it seemed tender. She heaved a jerky breath, waiting, refusing to believe her senses. His low murmurs began to register in her mind, adding fuel to her inner turmoil.

"Eden, be still now an' don't be afraid. Nothin's going to hurt you now, lass. I swear it. Don' cry anymore, Dede."

He actually seemed to be comforting her. She turned her head to rest her cheek against the damp wool of his coat. The scent of him permeated her puffy nose; soap and spicy brandy and warm wool — just like before. She heaved a sigh and relaxed a bit against him, still waiting. Then she realized he'd called her Dede. Another wave of tears coursed down her cheeks.

A strangely easy silence settled over them, Ram seated on the chaise, Eden curled on his lap. Each time she drew a shaky breath, he felt his own lungs being squeezed. Each time his arms tightened around her, she felt a bit of her distrust slide.

When she wiped at her nose and tears with the side of her hand, he rolled her slightly to one side and probed the side of his fitted coat for his pocket. A patch of white linen appeared and dabbed at her face, then was thrust into her hand.

Eden straightened, looking at the swatch of cloth that quietly demanded a response. She cast about and seized her most practiced and ingrained response.

"Thank you." Her voice was only a whisper as she dared a glance at his somber face from beneath a rim of wet lashes.

His carnal need suddenly died. When he gathered her into his arms this time, it was to assuage the pain he felt at her devastating attempt at a brave smile.

Eden felt his desperation as he held her tightly and she wondered at it. That sense of awe soon broaded to include her own unfathomable response. She drew comfort from his hard strength all about her and began to relax in his arms as though it were the one place in the world she truly belonged. She could tell his anger was past and knew, somehow, that her fear of him was mostly spent as well. From the safe corners of her crept a curious anticipation. Just what did it mean to be a wife to this man who both provoked and comforted her tears?

His heart thudded steadily beneath her cheek and she admitted more from her senses as the moments passed; the feel of his hard chest against her shoulder and side, the warmth seeping into her bottom from his hard lap, the soft rasp of his breathing, the rhythmic rise and fall of his chest. The tensions and crossed purposes of the day fell away as he continued to hold her carefully.

Eden felt his fingers rubbing little circles on her shoulders and back. The heat of his hand made her shiver and he stopped, lifting her chin to look at her face.

"Please . . ." her hands fluttered up to ward off his inspection, "I must look a mess."

"No." Ram brushed them away gently and took her oval face between his large hands. Her nose was puffy, her eyes glistened, and her lips were ripened to a luscious

174

red. He stared at her, absorbing every detail into his hungry heart. "You're beautiful, Eden, just as you are." His words echoed inside him, spoken once and for all time.

"No, really, I'm not. Just—" she made to squirm off his lap, but his arms refused to let her go.

"Not very politic of you, calling your husband a liar on your wedding night . . . especially when he's busy adoring you." She glanced warily at his face, to see it was lit with a wry grin that was four parts relief.

"Perhaps I'd best settle the matter with a closer inspection of this new wife of mine. Umm," he scowled as if considering where to start. Then his face brightened. "Your hair is like spun silk, lass, and has half the rainbow hidden in it." He crumpled a lock of it in his hand and held it to his nose, breathing deeply of it. The scent went straight to his brain and his voice dropped a full third.

"The sunsets in your eyes turn men's minds to the comforts of their beds, whatever the hour of day. You've a rosebud pout to your lips, you know, and a sweet lily softness to your skin." His finger hooked in the shoulder of her nightdress and eased it down to expose an expanse of soft shoulder and the top of a tempting breast.

"L-laird . . . Ramsay—"

"Ram."

"R-ramsay," she shivered, trying halfheartedly to counter the slow peel of her garment. He was teasing her and she couldn't keep the corners of her lips from turning up.

"No, please—"

" 'Please,' " he quoted her, his grin spreading. "Manners, too. I like that in a woman. But given a choice of good manners and good breedin', I'd take the breedin' part." His blue eyes crinkled at the corners and his grin curled another mischievous inch. He could see her fighting back a surprised smile and was seized with the desire to see it on her lovely features.

"What's this?!" he grabbed her bare shoulder and glared at it in horror. "You may have a freckle bloomin' there. God! That's grounds for annulment if anything is!"

"Ramsay!" Her mouth dropped open and shut immediately as she stifled a nervous giggle. "You're horrible!"

"And she's a fine judge o' character, too," he waggled one brow slightly and Eden couldn't resist. Her free laughter had a relieved quality that clutched at him even as he joined her.

"It bloody well sounds like laughter to me!" Chase pressed his ear closer to the door and glared at James's fevered countenance.

"I tell you, she was crying hard—I heard her!" James pulled Chase away and put his head to the door again, squeezing over to admit Ethan. The gloom of the hallway settled into the middle Marlow's face as his eyes narrowed at his older brother.

"This is disgusting," Ethan straightened, tugging his vest down and squaring his shoulders, "eavesdropping on a man's wedding night."

"It's Dede's wedding night," James shot back in a whisper. "Or have you already forgotten how her 'husband' forced his way into her bed—"

"Well, he ain't forcing his way now, is he?" Ethan glowered down at his older brother, then ran a weary hand down his face. "And maybe he never did. Give it a rest, James. You're not responsible for what happened."

"Ethan's right. What's done is done." Chase gripped his brother's arm. "It's between them now."

"Whatever's happening, she's havin' a better night than I am. I'm going to bed," Ethan snorted, turning on his heel to disappear down the dark hallway. Chase glanced at Eden's heavy door and sighed.

"Me, too."

But a minute later, he reappeared in the hall and shoved a new bottle of brandy into James's hands with an apologetic shrug. He stuffed his hands into his pockets and shuffled back to his room.

Laughter purged the last bit of strain between them and as they sobered, she relaxed completely on his lap. Of all the things she had anticipated this night, laughing was the least of them.

She watched at him with wide eyes and saw his gaze fix on her lips, his head bending. She lifted her face expectantly. The anticipation was excruciatingly sweet, but the fulfillment stunned her with its raw delight. His warm lips slanted across hers and his tongue traced their salty, sensitive contours. Melting under his kiss, Eden felt his hands slide down her neck to her shoulders, then descend her arms to wrap about her small waist, his long fingers nearly circling it.

Through her thin gown she could feel him exploring the curves of her waist and hip, even as his tongue opened and explored her mouth. She was turning liquid inside again, aching with shifting tides of new need.

Ram's hands paused at the edge of her breasts when he felt her intake of breath against his mouth. But her sudden tension was not caused by his quest over her body; it came from her own vivid response. Her breasts anticipated his touch with a tingling sensation that in her craving sharpened to near-torture. She lifted her arms and slid them about his neck, turning just enough for his hand to reach one full, satiny mound.

That movement was a subtle invitation to realms of

unexplored delight. His need flared anew as he pulled her to him and probed the depths of her kiss. She rubbed gently against the stern wool of his coat and her bottom on his lap wriggled closer to him. His arms twitched to crush her to him and relieve his need there and then, but a twinge of dying reason quivered through him. There were other things to consider. . . .

Ram raised his head. Her eyes were dark-centered rings of molten gold that echoed the new fire of her awakening passion. This time he would see them calm and blue with pleasure. This time there would be no qualms, no interrupting call, nothing to intervene. This time she would give herself to him and partake fully of what he had longed to give her since the first moment he had set eyes on her.

He kissed her lips, then her nose, then each eyelid. And he picked her up by the waist and set her from his lap.

# Chapter Ten

It took a minute for pleasure's mist to clear from Eden's mind. He had set her on the chaise and had risen, leaving her chilling with confusion. Her arms wrapped her half-bare chest and her face colored as she realized her body ached all over at his withdrawal. Every nerve clamored for his touch, every inch of skin remembered his caress and ached for it again.

Ram saw her shiver and stepped closer, running a work-toughened finger down the curve of her cheek. The corner of his lips curved gently at the doubt he read in her look. He bent to press a promise to her lips with his, then straightened, unfastening his coat from his shoulders.

Eden watched the pearl buttons of his shirt twirl and slide under his big, square fingers and her mouth went dry. His sun-darkened chest appeared beneath the white linen. Wisps of dark hair appeared at his throat, across his muscular chest, and down his stomach to disappear behind the bold tartan.

The familiarity of the sight was a mild surprise. Her knowledge of his anatomy should have appalled her ladylike sensibilities; instead, she found it a curious reassurance. She probably knew his body better than she

179

knew her own! So she watched, unable to tear her eyes from the play of muscle over muscle and the candlelit glow of his smooth, tight skin. He seemed even taller, more powerful, without his clothes. Yet in some ways, he seemed more human as well.

When his hands rested on the buckles of his kilt, her gaze fluttered to the floor and she found herself staring at his bare feet. Before tonight, she never would have thought of Laird Ramsay MacLean as having toes. Toes: of course he had them . . . and blisters that became calluses; and cuts that hurt, then healed; and illnesses that needed tending. How could she have forgotten those long hours aboard ship, those disturbing contacts. . . . He was a man, after all, and she was a woman. Men and women had managed to meet and mate for eons, and seldom was it fatal. Mistress Dunleavy couldn't help her in her marriage bed, but Mother Nature just might.

When Ram reached for her arms and drew her to her feet, her tousled brown head didn't quite reach his shoulders. He ran his knuckles up her throat and lifted her chin on them. Her eyes were clear, expectant. The frightened girl was gone, replaced by a woman with warmth in her breath and paradise beckoning in her eyes.

His hands caressed her shoulders, rubbing the loose fabric of her gown over her skin. Queer little trickles of heat slid down her breasts and over her belly to lodge in the sensitive hollow between her legs. Responding to the invitation in her eyes, Ram slid his hands under the shoulders of her gown and then down her arms, carrying that bewitching garment down with them.

"Wait—" She tried to hold her sliding drape in place.

"I've waited, Eden—" He tugged harder and stitches popped as the string at the top of the gown slid open. "How I've waited for you!"

The fabric caught between her full breasts but soon surrendered to his relentless downward pull. It caught again below her waist, but he let it rest there as his fingers trailed up her waist to cup her full, rose-tipped breasts.

Eden's little gasp brought a curl to his lips and he released those treasures to scoop her up and deposit her on the canopied bed. Her arms were crossed over her breasts, but a taut nipple winked from its imprisonment and he soon set it free, pushing her arms aside as he stretched out on the bed beside her. Uncertainty caused tension to bloom in her face and body again as she glanced at her wrist, captive in his bronzed hand.

"Eden, I won' hurt you," He released her and dropped a kiss on her forehead and the tip of her nose before claiming her lips. His warm skin spread against her side, inch by tantalizing inch, as he slipped his arms beneath her and cradled her head in one hand. "I only want to love you."

"Love you . . . love you . . . love you . . ." His words rumbled through her and sent a fever through her skin. Her senses surrendered unconditionally to the wanton flow of her body's desires. He loved her!

She drank in his kiss and folded her arms around his hard shoulders, pulling him tighter against her aching breasts. Instinctively, she wriggled her hip against him and he covered more of her soft body with his. He nibbled her jaw, the hollow of her throat, the creamy skin of her chest, then her tight, eager nipples. He caressed and teased her skin lightly, making her burn and press against his palm.

"Oh Ramsay . . ." She arched against his mouth and her eyes closed, savoring these raw new sensations. "What are you doing . . . to me? Oh, Ram—"

"Loving you, Eden . . . just loving and touching you."

Each stroke of his hand, each gentle nuzzle of his face at her breast turned that wheel inside her a bit faster, tightening a spiral of tension that built in her loins. A hot wind seemed to rush through her, robbing her of breath, lifting her higher and higher on its sultry wings. Soaring gliding on pleasure's updraft, she had to give back, t share this joy or she would burst.

Her hands hesitated over the heavy muscles of his bac and then followed the taper of his waist, massaging kneading, exploring once-forbidden realms. And at th sign, Ram eased his weight above her and focused on th velvety treasure of her mouth and its lush response Instinct arched her burning pelvis against him and h drew back to read her passion-glazed eyes. His nail fluttered down her belly and paused before continuin down her hip and the front of a thigh.

"Open for me, love," he murmured against her lips shaking with the effort needed to control his strainin muscles. He felt her tense and ran his hand quickly u her body to cradle her face and kiss her deeply. "Ope yourself to me, Eden. I want to love you. . . ."

The sense of his hoarse whisper finally settled in he mind and she realized what he wanted. It was anothe unnamed sense that made her understand this was n demand, but rather an entreaty. Her fingers threade through his thick hair and she pulled his head to hers joining their lips eagerly.

This time when his weight pressed her down into th bed, her legs shifted slowly, opening her soft, woman' flesh to him, yielding him her most secret self. Th burning, aching she had felt in that part of her flesh nov affirmed and encouraged her response. And when Ran pressed his swollen need against her, she shivered with memory.

"Eden, love . . . you are so beautiful. . . ." His finger tips stroked her face. He clasped her shoulders to him grazing her throat, her jaw, her shoulder with his lips Sparks from that contact showered through her, settlin hot and glowing in her loins.

Ram's muscles strained against the need for release a

e sank into her soft flesh by agonizing degrees. It was all
e could do to keep from plunging, losing himself in the
enter of her flesh. But he watched the awesome effects
f their joining in her face and knew he must control his
eed. He never wanted to see any fear of him in her face
gain.

Eden gasped as he surged higher within her, invading
er with his need, stretching and molding her to his
desires. He filled her and drove still further inside her, as
f reaching for her heart. There was heat and a throbbing,
urning fullness in her loins that both aggravated and
elieved the strange tightness in her. But the awareness
lowly surfaced, then burst like a bright rocket within her
. . there was no pain, no discomfort, only pleasure.

Her arms tightened about him and her hips began to
move beneath this, relishing each new sensation, discover-
ng the pure pleasure in motion. She moaned softly and
er head arched back as she rubbed her aching breasts
gainst his manly chest. Waves of stunning pleasure
rashed over her.

Twice Ram paused, resting against her as he fought for
ontrol. Eden felt his ragged breath moving her hair and
vas awed by the effort this marvelous pleasure cost. His
oody wore a satiny sheen, his muscles were hardened like
teel and trembled under her hands. His eyes were closed,
is jaw was set like dark granite. All she wanted was to be
loser to that fierce hardness that seemed joined to her
orever.

Her hips squirmed beneath him and he braced himself
bove her on his elbows, stroking her hair back from her
ace. Her eyes were feathery crescents, her lips swollen
nd stung crimson by his demanding kisses, her skin
lushed and moist with their combined heat. She was
Pleasure disguised as Woman, stealing his senses, beguil-
ng his soul.

He moved slowly between her silky thighs, seeking her

lips as he clasped her to him fiercely. Her breathy whimper trilled through him and spurred him to stronger, faster rhythm. Suddenly passion's vortex claimed him, spinnin him into ever-focusing circles of raw pleasure. Then a erupted in a scalding, transforming blast of heat and ligh that melted the barrier between self and other.

Eden met him as he plunged into her depths, feeling strange and marvelous surge in her body that propelle her to the brink of an unknown chasm. And at tha dangerous edge, all of reality slowed and she tumble over into a sensual storm that sent sweet flashes o pleasure jolting through her like lightning. Her sense were numbed and her being was suspended while sh thrilled and quivered under Ram's driving passion. Then beautiful floating calm infused her, a little like death, lot like paradise. Maybe minutes, maybe hours, late Ram flexed and rose, coming to rest beside her. The damp skin touched at shoulder, hip, and thigh.

It was some time before Eden's mind resumed t function through satisfaction's lovely steam. So this wa carnal pleasure . . . another little tremor skittered throug her and she wriggled with lazy approval. How utterl divine it was, how completely captivating. And what relief!

She managed a heavy-lidded look at him and knew instinctively what he felt. The same blissful exhaustio she sensed softened his features and relaxed his formida ble Scottish guard. He lay on his side with one heavy arm draped across her waist and his square face nuzzled into her hair on the pillow. Her gaze flitted secretively down his body and caught on his fully extended manhood. He eyes fled, but soon returned and shyly inspected this las secret part of him. Somehow it was not half so fearful a she had imagined . . . not that a properly brought-up lady would actually dare to imagine. . . . Then her eye drifted over to her own naked body and she felt a twing of discomfort, gazing down at the erotic contrast of her smooth, white body and the furred muscularity of his belly and legs.

Sighing shakily, she untangled the soft sheet from her other side and beneath her legs and drew it up over her to hide that disturbing sight. Her movement brought his head up.

"Are . . . you all right?" When she hesitated, wondering how to answer, he glanced down her now-hidden form and turned her face to his on the pivot of his knuckles. "I wasn't too . . . heavy for you, was I?" His chest and face flushed with chagrin when he realized how completely he'd abandoned all restraint with her. He'd promised to not hurt her and he'd meant to be gentle—but now he felt so drained and sated, he wasn't sure he'd been successful in the effort.

"No." She focused a sleepy look on the open concern in his face. It surprised her at first, then pleased her.

"No, what?" he demanded, relaxing only slightly at her peaceful expression. "Not all right or not too heavy?"

"Yes." Her eyes drifted closed and his concern grew.

"Yes, what?" His hand slid up her body to rock her shoulder insistently; her senses rippled under his hand. A tiny smile curled the ends of her lips. She opened her eyes.

"It wasn't . . ." she shifted her head to better view his rugged face and was capable of speaking only the topmost layer of truth, "half so bad as . . . that other time." Ram looked like he'd been slapped in the face.

"Half so bad—" He pushed up, bracing himself on an arm. His dark, burnished hair waved in disarray about his angular face and his blue eyes crackled with confusion. Conscience shook him and he twitched defensively, but her hand came up to stop his words.

"Very nice, Ramsay," she sighed contentedly, feeling color blooming under her skin. "It was really *very* nice."

Her dreamy lashes lowered and he felt them sweeping the excitable skin of his belly. "Thank you."

His chin drew back as he stared at her, his eyes filling with her alluring glow. He'd never seen a woman look like this after loving before. *Thank you, Ramsay.* He twitched again. God . . . she'd *thanked* him.

"My pleasure," he retorted dryly, feeling a guilty sense of relief.

"And mine," she murmured so softly he wondered if he'd imagined it.

So much for his concern about her fearing him. He punched the bolsters and pillows up behind him and dragged himself back against them, pulling the coverlet over his bare lap. Now he had a whole new set of things to think about . . . and he wasn't really in the mood for thinking at all. It was his wedding night, dammit! A man was supposed to enjoy it!

Eden's darkened eyes opened briefly as he lifted her into his arms, beside him on the pillows. But they soon closed as she curled against him like a sleepy kitten, needing warmth. His smile was tender as he watched her and he tucked a final corner of the sheet about her. Her cheek nestled against a hard mound on his chest and he watched her snuggle one knee atop his and insert her toes between his calves. He wanted nothing more than to be here, with Eden Marlow MacLean pressed provocatively against him.

Some time later Eden was awakened by the sensation of something sliding over her and she startled awake to find the sheet deserting her: Ram's hands were luring it away. She snatched at it and pulled it back as she sat up, her heart thumping queerly. Ram sat on the edge of the bed, watching her with a hint of amusement.

"Didn' mean to wake you." His voice was husky.

"I'm sure not." Eden colored; she had trouble meeting his too-handsome face.

"I wanted . . . to look at you," he admitted, his eyes straying down her silken shoulder to her bare side. His mouth was going dry.

"I'd rather you didn't."

The droopy line of the sheet against her ripe breasts magnetized his gaze. An unconscious hand pushed her enchantingly tangled hair back over her shoulder and she wetted her lips with as little thought.

"It's a bit late for modesty, darlin'." His grin had a boyish taunt to it. "I'm your husband, after all. What I haven't already inspected, I plan to get to verra soon." The burr of his speech was magnified, rolling sensually over her. The sheet began to move again.

"Really, Ramsay, it's not . . . it's just . . . *Oh!*"

The sheet fled with a sharp pop and her startled hands flew up to cover her shrinking frame. Gooseflesh rose along her arms and legs and she snatched her long tresses over one shoulder to help conceal her nakedness.

"Nay, woman, you've nothin' on yer person that's not purely enchantin'. And I mean to see th' full worth of my fortune." He rose and propped a knee on the soft mattress, reaching for her.

She squirmed away, but he caught her and dragged her from the bed to stand her between his bare knees as he sat on the edge of the bed. Every inch of her naked skin was scarlet with embarrassment and her chin seemed bolted to her chest.

"Let me see you, darlin'." He pulled her small wrists away and held them with gentle firmness. He watched her struggle with his command and began to realize that her reluctance was genuine. He frowned at yet another twang of guilt.

"You're such a beauty, Eden. You're not afraid of me still? Surely now you know I won' hurt you." He forced

187

her face up as gently as he could.

"It's . . . not proper, looking at . . . naked bodies." She choked on the word "naked."

"It'd be a sin of omission *not* to look at yours, darlin'." He grinned, letting his eyes have their fill of her before making a show of turning his chin away. "But I'll risk eternal punishment if it'll make you feel better." His eyes closed.

Suspicion narrowed her look.

"Oh . . ." She flinched at his bold grasp of her buttocks. "You said—"

"I wouldn't look. But I *won't* abstain from touching." One smooth movement pulled her against him and sent them both rolling back onto the bed. Trapped on her back and with her legs between his knees, she could only surrender her bareness to his marauding touch. His closed eyes made it even more embarrassing because she was piqued to wonder at what he was feeling. But his sensation flowed from his fingertips into his face. How expressive his strong, well-chiseled features became . . . and how closely they mirrored her own interior warming. Sensations's seductive tide began lapping over her again.

"Eden," he groaned, planting a lusty kiss on the corner of her mouth.

She turned her head so that his next attempt found its mark. Her hands traveled up his neck to toy with his ears and twirl lazy circles in his hair. She knew where he was leading and her eagerness to repeat that blissful experience shamed her . . . but only briefly. Her capitulating reason finally caught up with her passion. He was her husband: it was her duty to please him, and if she took some joy in the doing of it, so much the better.

"Oh, Ramsay," she managed as his hands slid along her curves. She shivered and wriggled under his masterful caress. And soon her breasts and her woman's hollow were burning for him again, only more intensely and hotter than before.

"What is it, darlin'?" he whispered hoarsely between nibbles at her breasts.

"I never . . ." her tongue stole over her dry lips, "guessed it would be like this."

"I'm afraid that's the very first thing I guessed." Ram moved on to nuzzle the skin of her belly. She arched her back to allow his hands passage beneath her and he rolled onto his back, carrying her above him.

"Ramsay!" She flushed and tried to squirm away, but he chuckled and held her in place effortlessly.

"I can't look," his sightless grin was pure lechery, "but this way I can enjoy more of you with the powers I have left." Heedless of her protest, he proceeded to caress her back and buttocks until he felt her relax above him. Then in a swift move, he grasped the backs of her thighs and pulled them over the sides of his hips, opening her to his heat.

"No . . . Ramsay!" She pushed up and found herself sitting astride his pelvis, his iron-clad arms holding her bottom tightly in place against him. "Please don't—"

"You don't like it?" He risked moving a hand up her waist to brush one tight, erect nipple. "You feel like you like it."

Embarrassment mingled with the heat flooding through her to vault her excitement onto a whole new plane. His hard body against her buttocks and between her thighs shocked her, but the shock ebbed into wonderful eddies of fluid delight.

"It doesn't seem very . . . proper." The huskiness of her whisper betrayed her body's eagerness.

He laughed and felt for her hands, placing them palm-down on his chest. "It's not proper unless you do your part, darlin'. Love me, Eden."

Looking down at his powerful body beneath her, seeing her fingers splayed over the muscle of his breast, feeling

189

his heat pouring through her bare thighs, she thrust aside everything but Ramsay MacLean. The man who had shamed and claimed her now pleasured her and tutored her splendidly in the art of loving . . . and of being loved. She wanted to give him everything.

Her hands moved over him, teasing, exploring, consuming the boundaries of his masculine shape. He twitched and encouraged her exploration with moans and throaty whispers that set fire to her nerves. Seeing him wince and writhe beneath her added to her excitement and somehow she knew that this must be what it was like when he watched her.

"Look at me, Ramsay," she commanded, trying to keep from wriggling above him.

His eyes squeezed tighter.

"Look at me . . . love me with your eyes, too!"

Ram looked up at his wife, now astride him, passion flickering through her voluptuous body, and he couldn't breathe. He watched his dark fingers slide over the newly learned globes of her breasts and felt he experienced them for the first time again. Her eyes were glowing coals of red and black and her unconscious undulations promised joys to come.

He rolled to one side and took her beneath him, knowing exactly what would satisfy them both. He slid between her legs and began a slow descent into her lush body.

Eden folded around him as he joined his flesh to hers, her arms lapping about his wide back and her legs weaving through his. She wanted to draw more of him into her, to capture and hold him there always. It was a woman's primal desire for completion, for union, that pulsed in her veins and made her body strain to absorb him. But in this age-old quest, her body was the hireling of her ruling heart.

Together they climbed bright highlands of delight and

pressed and loved and joined, holding nothing back. Ram's sturdy body brought her time and again to the edge of that precipice of pleasure, then stopped short, leaving her need to lurch higher each time. Her body wriggled in invitation, then entreaty; she rippled beneath him and murmured his name over and over, making it an incantation whose magic he couldn't defy.

The sight of her twisting and arching beneath him, the feel of her reaching for him and meeting his powerful thrusts, obliterated everything in his mind but her searing response. His own need faded into the background and he lost himself in the shifting nuances of her unleashed passion.

Then suddenly a hundred rockets exploded in the center of her and white-hot sparks sizzled through her loins and muscles, making them contract around Ram's hot body. She shook with the force of it and writhed against him in pleasure's highest and deepest throes at once.

Ram had erupted inside her with a flash of blinding intensity that shook the foundations of his being. And for a brief time, they were joined and floating free on rapture's brightest plane.

Eden couldn't move, couldn't think, couldn't even open her eyes. Her heart had nearly exploded in her chest, fire had scorched every nerve, and her insides felt like a cyclone's aftermath. She was drained of all but the very spark of life itself. And it was *wonderful*.

When Ram's weight left her body, she floated somewhere near heaven's gate, she was certain. She wanted to carry him with her and managed to turn onto her side to rest her head on his muscular arm. She had the oddly comforting feeling of being joined to him still, even though their bodies barely touched. And after the blinding silver brightness of moments before, a seeping blue peace invaded her. Her last jumbled thought was that peace seemed the same color as her husband's marvelous eyes.

Cool and gray, the dawn crept in, relieving the candelabra of its lonely vigil. Eden woke in the same position, her head on Ram's upper arm, one hand propped against his side. Instantly she was wide awake, her heart drumming. An earthy smile transformed her features into a study of total satisfaction. She moved and her body mewed small complaints that were ignored as she sat up and looked at Ram's peaceful form beside her. She watched the rise and fall of his chest, the untroubled ease of his powerful body, the sleep-softened beauty of his rugged face. Her smile reached her eyes and she was soaring. Energy pulsed through her limbs and she slipped from the bed to pad across the carpet, looking for her nightgown.

She found it in a heap by the chaise and picked it up, thinking that if last night were any standard by which to judge, that garment might prove the most unnecessary in her wardrobe. She started to put it on, but caught a reflected glint of light from the long cheval mirror near her open trunk and changed her mind.

She edged closer to the silvered glass and ran a smoothing hand down her hair before tossing it back over her shoulder. She chewed her lip uncertainly as she stepped before the glass. The sight of her own body shocked her, but she made herself stay and inspect her image. Her gaze flitted downward over her breasts, her slim waist, her nicely rounded hips. It caught on one feature after another as she recalled Ram's thoroughly sensual inventory of her physical charms.

She had endured his descriptions as purposeful flattery, but now she wondered if he really meant them. Her breasts were full, her waist narrow, her legs well-tapered and smooth. She turned and cast an appraising eye over her derrière, her shoulders, her hair as she shook it about her. There was nothing particularly shameful about the image she beheld. In fact, it seemed in her mind to compliment Ram's larger, stronger frame nicely. She was soft where he was hard, she curved where he was straight, she fit under his arm as if just made to nestle at his side. Her conclusion delighted her and made her twirl about before the mirror, hugging herself, accepting herself at last.

Through sleepy lids, Ram watched her curious behavior before the glass and wondered at it. He sensed it was not mere vanity that spread such joy in her face and flushed her lovely body with excitement. Silently he drew himself up against the bolsters to watch her pleasure. She was indeed more beautiful, more tempting, more enjoyable than he had dreamed in his feverish bachelor's bed.

She stopped and made a final face at herself in the glass before whiffing away to the washstand and pouring some water. She washed her face, her throat, her breasts, stiffening self-consciously as old patterns of propriety threatened to intrude. But quickly she was done and she arranged the wet toweling neatly on its rack before reaching for her nightgown. It wasn't on the chair where she'd left it and she turned quickly around to find Ram holding it in his hand.

"Are you sure you want it?" He stood by the bed and held it out to her, watching the uncertainty in her eyes.

"I think I'd better," she answered truthfully, embarassed by their nakedness now that he was awake.

"I can cover you as fully and keep you warmer."

"That you can, Ramsay MacLean," she answered to his honesty, but had to drop her eyes to do it. She blushed, pleased with the admiration she'd seen in his sky-blue gaze.

He laughed in a charming rumble and caught her up in his arms, striding for the bed. He grinned down into her

193

surprise as he installed her in the middle of the bolster and joined her there at the head of the bed.

Eden thought she knew what to expect next, but he surprised her by drawing her into his arms and jus holding her. Her eyes searched the dim space under the canopy as she waited, listening to his heart against he ear, savoring this bit of sharing. His fingertips left he arm to trail down her side and she wriggled under them For the first time in hours, she began to think.

"Why?" she asked quietly, turning her face up to him Her lips felt swollen and extraordinarily sensitive as she wetted them, watching his. In the silence, she reframed her question. "Why did you come to my room tha night?"

He watched the tip of her tongue disappear back int her mouth and something slid the length of him to lodge in his loins. He swallowed.

"I wanted you, Eden . . . I had to have you."

"You mean . . . like this?" She nudged the tip of one breast against his ribs and nodded toward their entwined feet.

"Exactly like this." His voice lowered as his eyes roamed her shoulders and the tantalizing skin the covers did no conceal at her side. "Not the most noble act, I admit. But you'd rejected my more honorable efforts an' I'd become a desperate man." That description became more apt with each shortening breath.

"What honorable efforts?" she puzzled, gazing up into the graying smoke of his eyes. He winced at her unwitting jibe.

"I would have asked for your hand that night in the garden if . . . if you hadn't been so damned appealing. I was leadin' up to it," his tone grew silky, "before I touched you. There's somethin' about you, Eden Marlow MacLean, that makes me forget everythin' I've been raised to. I see you and all I can think about is how your skin

194

will taste, how your body feels pressed against me. I have to sink my hands in your hair and feel your softness under me or I go mad."

He groaned inwardly at his blunt declaration and stiffened at the rousing effects of her sweetly exposed body and his own reckless honesty. He wanted her again . . . already!

"God help me, Eden, I can't stop it—"

Eden saw the strange look in his face and knew she had to kiss those firm, salty lips to make it go away. At the instant of contact, it was decided. His arms crushed her against him and pulled her across his chest. Their kisses deepened and soon those potent streams of shifting lava were moving through her again.

They entwined and caressed and slowly joined in a new and different rhythm. Fevered heat traded places with achingly sweet looks and caresses, the way strands in a braid each claim prominence briefly, then surrender it. And when their passions exploded together, it was as though existence itself was torn apart to be laid down anew.

Eden curled on her side exhausted and slept. Ram was near, not quite touching and far from the peace that had brought her sleep. His body was drained, sated, but his thoughts were churning.

His confession to Eden replayed itself over and over in his head. All he had to do was see her and his senses were disrupted; touching her set his blood afire; bedding her drove him to the brink of paradise . . . or oblivion.

He propped his cheek on the heel of one palm and studied her with aching eyes. Her face was dream-flushed, her hair tangled and curled about her sweet shoulders, her lips swollen slightly and bruised to the color of cherries. His other hand followed the dip of her slender waist and spread a caress along the rise of her hip. He examined the taper of her arm and curled his big, hard fingers through her soft, slender ones. She was a marvel of nature, a gift of rare and magical delights.

Her sleep was so deep that not even the rhythm of her breathing changed. He smiled wistfully and bent his head to press a kiss on her wrist. The faint scent of her filled his head and he straightened, confused by the new flood of warmth in him. As he watched her, the warmth began to focus into more familiar channels. Sly tendrils of need wound about his stomach and loins, calling through his blood. His breath came faster and his skin clamored for contact with hers. Oblivious to all but that need, he slid down beside her and pulled her back against his body, curling around her, spoon-fashion, and letting his heavy arm drape over her side. She stirred slightly, then settled again into dreamless rest.

He relaxed, puzzled by his sleeplessness. By all accounts he should be exhausted, nearly unconscious. And here he was, holding Eden again, enjoying the feel of her softness against him. His hand went questing and caressed the perfect mounds of her breasts, feeling them tighten slowly under his attentions. Suddenly, he was rising against her, roused to full need by these delicious toyings.

Ram stiffened all over, alarmed without knowing why. Then an awful insight crowded into his fast-narrowing thoughts: his words to Eden were more than an explanation, they were a condemnation! He truly did abandon everything—even simple decency—whenever she was near. His mind refused to function anywhere but in his loins, and he thought of nothing but bedding her. She made him forget civility, morality, humanity, and above all, moderation.

It was the lure of forbidden fruit, he'd succeeded in convincing himself. When he'd bedded her fully, the mystery, the anticipation would be gone. He'd be back to normal quickly enough. But now he couldn't stop himself

. . . he no sooner finished loving her than he wanted her again.

The fullness of her breast in his palm jolted both his eyes and his thoughts. *Look at him!* He'd found release in her tantalizing body more than once already this night . . . more than twice. God, *three times!* He'd never bedded a woman more than once a night, not in his whole life, not even if he wanted to . . . it was his iron-clad rule. And *never* more than once a week, no matter what.

But give him Eden Marlow in his bed and he behaved like a damned animal! Rutting and heaving and plunging . . . over and over. *Three times!* Lord, even old Haskell would be hard-pressed to match him there.

Ram jerked away from Eden's warm curves as though she'd bitten him. Randy as a beast he was, ready to take her again . . . and her practically dead from his demands as it was! Concern coursed through him and he touched the side of her throat, feeling for her pulse. It was strong but excruciatingly slow. He pulled his fingers away and stared at them, appalled.

Suddenly he was on his feet beside the bed, staring at her soft form with genuine horror. What was happening to him? He raked his hair back with trembling hands and glanced down at his swiftly dying passion. He was behaving just like his reprobate old sire . . . succumbing to the taint of his blood at last.

He wheeled away and snatched up his kilt, throwing it around him and buckling it with shaky fingers. Bare-chested and bare-legged, he paced furiously in the brightening room.

Lust had been the ruin of many a MacLean, he knew. And before now, he'd had no sympathy for his debauched forebears, whose stories of bastards and stolen brides and misdirected passions were rife with moral retribution. How easily he'd judged and condemned them for the sins of loving not wisely or too well. It was easy because he'd never felt such temptation himself.

Now the vengeance of his own harsh judgment was visited upon him. He'd unwittingly yoked himself to the one woman who could rouse his strongest, basest needs with her simple presence. Beautiful Eden Marlow was his one consuming desire, his penance . . . his punishment.

He stopped by the bed and stared stiff-faced at his young wife. She was beautiful and responsive and passionate . . . incredibly passionate. She met his need with one of her own and her body found the same release as his. He'd never seen a woman react to loving the way she did. . . .

His face darkened as he scoured her frame for some flaw. It darkened further when he found none. She was perfectly lovely, perfectly desirable, perfectly tempting. In point of fact, she was the only real temptation in his life. Wittingly or unwittingly, she robbed him of all rational thought and his legendary self-possession. In a while, he'd be exactly like old Haskell — slavering after every skirt that twitched by in hopes of satisfying this itch she bred inside him. *Three times* . . . and itchin' for *four!* That should be all the proof he needed!

## Chapter Eleven

Four hours later, bright sunbeams beat against the heavy tapestries at the window, some dodging successfully into the room. The air was still and heavy with expectation. Eden moved imperceptibly in her bed and a little sigh escaped her, but she slept on.

There was a light rapping at the door and Ram jolted up from the stuffed chaise. His jaw hardened as he glanced at the bed and strode to answer it. His shoulders braced and his muscles tensed as he worked the latch and pulled the heavy panel back a foot.

A graying servant woman in starched cap and apron stood there with a large, cloth-covered tray. Behind her stood James Marlow, stretching none too discreetly to see past Ram into the bedroom.

"Yer mornin' tray, sir," Charity bobbed, averting her eyes from the skin bared by his open shirt. Ram looked at her and raised his eyes to James's reddening face.

"I'll take it." He reached for the tray and Charity edged back an inch.

"It's my job, sir, seein' to Miss Eden of a morning."

"Not any more, woman." Ram's lips curled into a cool smile as he wrested the large tray from Charity's reluctant grip. He pulled it inside and gave James a spiteful glower as he slammed the door shut with his foot. He balanced the tray on one arm as he threw the latch, then carried it to the circular table near the cold fireplace.

He stalked to the bed with his hands at his waist and stared down at his sleeping bride, feeling condemned by the sheer length of her sleep. He shook it off and returned to the tray, lifting the cloth and finding tea, chocolate, scones, and sweet butter. His stomach rumbled as the smells wafted up; and he poured himself a cup of tea, snatched a crusty scone, and sat down to wait again.

James entered the dining room, where his family anxiously awaited the appearance of the newlyweds and met their inquiries with an angry shrug.

"I don't know what's going on. He wouldn't let Charity in . . . I couldn't see her. . . ." He plopped his unopened bottle of brandy on the snowy table linen and slid down into his chair.

"You suppose she's all right?" Constance raised a trembling chin to Adam, who patted her hand reassuringly, but looked away.

"We'll wait and see, Connie . . . wait and see."

Twice more that soft rapping came to Eden's door, and the second time Ram admitted Charity with a huge kettle of hot water. He glanced briefly about the hall and, finding it empty, smiled his cool smile again.

"Miss Eden's usually up an' about by now," the serving woman ventured, drawing his attention, if not his gaze. "The family's up an' been waiting breakfast on ye for some time now. Shall I wake her up, sir?"

Ram's gaze narrowed with a vision of the Marlows, crowded around the dining table and scandalized by the lateness of their rising, and positive he'd abused her in some crude, nefarious manner. A twinge went through him at how close their suspicions were to the truth.

"What hour is it?" Ram pursed a corner of his mouth and stroked his stubbled chin.

"About a quarter past eleven, sir."

"Then come back in half an hour to help your mistress dress and finish packing."

Thirty minutes later, Ram was fully dressed and standing beside the bed, fighting back his raw impulses with fists that refused to unclench. Eden stirred beneath his intensifying stare; her eyelids fluttered in the bright light. Charity's knock came again and he answered it.

She rolled onto her back and put an arm over her eyes, moving experimentally. She felt as if she'd been punched and pummeled, especially in her back and abdomen. She sent a hand to rub her sore belly and her nakedness beneath the sheet surprised her. A sudden blush of remembrance made her sit up quickly and look around. Ram was seated on the chaise, staring at her. She flushed deeper and clutched the sheet around her.

"Good morning—" Her voice was husky with sleep and her hair was tossed alluringly about her bare shoulders. The dark look on Ram's face stopped her and she frowned, confused.

"You've been abed late today," his gruffness assaulted her. "Rise and dress quickly. Your family awaits."

Her mouth dropped open and she stared at him, blinking away the last vestiges of sleep. She managed to wriggle to the edge of the bed and stand on the floor, jerking the sheet free and wrapping it around her. Her mind and body screamed a protest. Where was that tender, mesmerizing man who had initiated her into the joys of married life just hours before? She flushed deeply as memories collided with the cool proprieties of morning and planted the seeds of shame.

"Here, Miss Eden." Charity slipped an arm about her

waist and hurried her over to the corner, where a hip bath was waiting. "I think the water's hot enough, yet." She scurried to pour the hot and cool kettles into the lopsided copper vessel and then held the sheet for Eden as she slipped into the water.

"Is this strictly necessary?" Ram's hardened face appeared over Charity's shoulder. "I've said it's late already—"

Eden covered her breasts with her arms and Charity raised the sheet to block his view.

"It's only right Missy have a soothing bath after . . . yesterday." Charity shot an eloquently reproachful glare at him. He steamed quietly and paced back to the chaise.

Eden felt his eyes on her every minute as she bathed and dressed. He searched and assessed her with an air of male disdain that mocked everything she felt inside. The warmth with which she had awakened was chilled by this new reality. Her mind flew back over what was said and done between them and the remembrance shocked her. She'd kissed and wriggled and touched and . . . behaved like a pure wanton. But she also recalled *his* actions . . . kissing and caressing and commanding . . . he'd seemed to want her to behave that way. And it had been shockingly easy to abandon five years of training; he'd tamed her willful nature the moment he touched her. Where was Eden Marlow the lady on the most important night of her marriage?

Her heart lurched; her breast was empty and aching. Tears threatened, but she rubbed the cloth vigorously over her face to prevent them. Had her regrettably eager responses displeased him . . . or had he expected something more from her? Was she supposed to have done things she didn't know to do? Or was he still angry that her family had made them spend their wedding night under the Marlow roof? Oh, why did she have to feel so crushed and small inside?

Tense silence reigned as Charity helped her to dry and pulled a thin summer chemise over her head. Eden stole confused glimpses of his darkening mood as she rolled her silk stockings up her legs and twisted and tucked her garters. She climbed into her coral silk gown with shaky hands and jumped skittishly as Charity lifted the double ruffles around her neckline with exacting hands.

"Can you just hurry, please, Charity?" she pleaded softly as she was pushed down onto her vanity bench. In the mirror, she saw the servant's eyes flit to Ram's unchecked impatience and narrow disapprovingly.

"By all means, woman, do hurry." Ram slouched sullenly in his seat and his mood went from dark to black. "This is a fascinating show, but the *family* awaits."

"See that her packing is finished quickly," Ram urged, his hand clamped about Eden's upper arm. He gave Charity one last order: "I'll send a carriage for her trunks later this afternoon." Then he urged Eden none too gently toward the open door and ignored her attempts to free her arm from his viselike grip.

"*What* is the matter with you?" Eden whispered loudly, digging her heels in and making him pause, however briefly, in the hall. "Take your hand off—you're hurting me!" His face tightened and his color heightened, but his hand did gentle on her arm.

"We're late. I don' like being late . . . any more than I like layin' abed half the day."

Eden winced as if struck and Ram shuddered through another douse of self-loathing. "Come on, let's get this over with."

He half-pushed, half-dragged her down the stairs, then jerked her along toward the dining room. They paused in the doorway and Eden was surprised to find her entire family gathered, sprawled in varying states of agitation and despondence. At their sudden appearance, every head in the room snapped up. Adam jumped to his feet,

Constance raised puffy, red-rimmed eyes, Chase jerked about in his chair, and James was on his feet in a flash, upsetting the brandy bottle on the table before him.

"Glad to see you all assembled," Ram said with a taunting lightness. "Sorry we won't be staying for breakfast; we've imposed long enough on your hospitality."

"Not staying for your wedding breakfast?" Constance rose, dabbing at her nose, and appealed to Adam with a stricken look.

"Now see here, MacLean—" Adam tucked his chin and scowled his most formidable expression.

"My *bride* and I are leavin' shortly." Ram pulled Eden further into the room and released her arm to take her hand in a warning grip. "But we have time sufficient for you to verify her well-being firsthand. If you doubt my word, feel free to inspect for yourself." He pulled her forward and raised her hand high in the air, over her gasps of protest. She tried to pull it down, but he used it to leverage her into turning so that all sides of her were visible, one after the another.

"Ramsay—stop this—what are you—?"

"Notice, there are no bruises, no rope marks or abrasions." He pulled her dress down from one shoulder to reveal the smooth white skin. "Her flesh is not mauled nor tortured in any conceivable manner." He lifted the hem of her skirt to reveal a startling bit of ankle, and she fought it down furiously. "She is as hale an' healthy as the hour she was handed over to my disreputable care."

Eden's pale face turned scarlet and she stopped stock-still to stare at him in disbelief. "Ramsay!"

*"See here, MacLean!"*

"Damn your filthy hide—" James jolted forward, but was stopped by Ethan's chair as it pushed back abruptly into his path.

"But I can assure you, yer daughter's marriage has been *thoroughly* consummated." He reeled her to him and

204

clamped her to his side. "No takers? Well, let it never be said you weren't given the chance."

He bent and wrapped his muscular arms about Eden's hips, jerking her off her feet and slinging her over his broad shoulder. Oblivious to her flailing feet and her fists pounding on his back, he made the door in a split second. He paused and looked back, making a show of steadying Eden's rump on his shoulder with a brawny, possessive hand.

"Get some sleep, James. You look like hell."

Ram carried Eden straight out the front door of the stately Marlow House and into a hired coach waiting at the bottom of the marble steps. He dumped her unceremoniously on the floor of the conveyance and climbed up onto the iron step to fling an order at the gaping driver. *"Move!"*

Behind them, Marlows were spilling down the stately steps in various stages of rage and disbelief. Ram just had time to step over her and slam the wooden door shut before being thrown backward into the seat.

When the coach lurched into motion, Eden was tossed back against the edge of the seat, banging her shoulder. That pain and the combined shock of the morning robbed her of any response for the moment as she grappled to right herself. Arms and hands seemed to be snatching at her from every direction as Ram and Arlo, who had been waiting in the coach, contested to give her assistance up onto the bench.

*"Let go of me!"* she screeched, trying to shove their hands away.

"I'll do it." Ram glowered at Arlo and the loyal servant withdrew with a huff, leaving Ram to struggle with his bride himself. He grasped her about the waist, dodging her pounding fists, and lifted her onto the seat beside him.

"Don't ever touch me again!" She gave him a final shove with an ineffectual fist and stiffened back against the wall of the coach as far as she could go. "You vile, despicable. . . . How dare you treat me like that in front of my family!"

"How dare they treat me like a bloody criminal and sneer at my good offices toward my own wife?" he countered, his face stony as he jerked an outraged thumb at himself. "I'm good enough to give their daughter my name and save her from a life of spinsterhood, but not good enough to bed her an' provide decently for her. They've insulted my family pride, woman, an' I'll see they don' make that mistake again!"

"That's what this was about? Your insufferable pride?" Hurt mingled with disbelief in her voice. She sat up suddenly, jerking the twisted folds of her high-waisted dress into submission. For a moment her eyes dipped, seemingly to check the disarray of her garments, but actually to conceal the flare of scorching fire in them. When her chin raised, her nostrils were flared and her eyes blazed with an eternal fury. Her arm was arcing toward him before he had a chance to react and his head snapped to the side with the impulse of her unexpected blow.

"Don't *you* make the same mistake again, Ramsay MacLean. You'll wish you'd never set eyes on me."

Arlo's start and sharp intake of breath made her wince, but she held her ground as Ram turned on her, livid and shaking with sudden anger. His arm was back, his massive shoulders coiled for attack, and Eden held her breath, bracing for retribution.

"I already wish that." His graveled words were worse than any fist. His muscles had frozen against retaliation and began to thaw only after she jerked her trembling chin away from him. The silence crackled with unspent anger for a long while before Ram's ragged voice ended it.

"Tell the driver we're goin' straight to the *Effingham*," he ordered Arlo.

"But—"

"The *Effingham!*" Ram repeated with angry emphasis.

"Aye, Laird Ram." Arlo couldn't hide his disapproval, but he was up and opening the door of the coach and calling those very instructions to the driver before Ram had need to ask again.

Eden's face was as pale as the ruffled frills about her bodice, and her bare hands clasped and unclasped whitely in her lap. Her mind raced in dizzying circles. How could that tender man of only hours ago be the same arrogant brute who had paraded her before her family like a heifer on the block and then carried her out, rump-first, into married life? It confounded her. Then she'd *hit* him . . . *hit him*. . . . Lord, that was taking a chance! She'd never hit anybody before in her life, with the possible exception of James. And this churl had very nearly bashed her right back!

She swallowed hard to relieve the choking in her throat and found it only forced her inner tumult up into her eyes. Tears welled in them and she blinked repeatedly to keep from crying. What had happened during the hours she slept? And what could she have done to infuriate him so? Why were they going someplace other than the Buxton Inn? She'd never even heard of the Effingham. And what in heaven's name was she doing married to a man who had consistently misjudged and mistreated her since the moment they met?

Her stiff-faced sniff caught Ram's ear and he turned a stony face toward her just as the first tear escaped to roll down her pale cheek. Something in his chest caught; he tried to counter it by sitting straighter. She was going to cry again. He looked out the coach window and a muscle in his jaw jumped irritably. When he looked at her from

207

the corner of his eye, later, she was still sitting rigidly against the far wall, but her cheeks were wet. One slender hand came up in a secretive swipe and she sniffed very quietly. Ram scowled angrily, but delved into the pocket of his coat. It was empty.

He gave Arlo's foot a sharp nudge and motioned toward Eden. Arlo's blank look became earnest attention when Ram snarled silently at him and motioned to his pocket. Arlo fumbled and fished out a handkerchief, rumpled but clean, and Ram's message finally got through.

Now, why hadn't he just said something, Arlo wondered irritably. When he leaned over to press it into Eden's hand, she started at his touch and he drew back, scowling at his laird. It wasn't right, the way Laird Ram had treated the lass. No right and proper marriage, this.

Some minutes later the coach rumbled to a stop in a narrow crowded street and Eden's attention was caught by the familiar, salty twang in the air. Out the window she glimpsed a dingy gin shop; several apparent patrons were sprawled unceremoniously in the narrow street in front. The view from the other window was just as disturbing in its own way: rising above a row of squalid tenements were tall, bare masts that beckoned like bony fingers. They were at the docks!

She turned to Ram and started to speak, but he was up and swinging through the door, closing it after him, drowning out her question.

"Take it on down to the *Effingham,* then send the coach back for her things. I'll be along as soon as I attend to a minor detail." He swung away and the coach lurched, then balked, and started again soon after. Her last glimpse of him was as he was entering that foul little tavern.

"Probably going to get drunk!" she whispered hatefully, wringing Arlo's handkerchief savagely.

"Oh, not Laird Ram, Miss—M'lady." Arlo, unused to witnessing a lady's private thoughts, answered soberly, "Would take half the brew in Boston to make him a tootfull. So he ne'er bothers; one tilt to be sociable an' that's it. Right fastidious about that, he is."

"Well, maybe he's planning to start," Eden snapped, her eyes blazing.

Arlo had no response to that and jerked his chin down to stare uncomfortably at the berthed ships they passed. Suddenly the coach stopped and he unwrapped his arms from across his chest and opened the door. He smiled nervously and craned his head, looking for something. Relief filled his blunt features when he found it.

"Here we are, m'lady." He reached a substantial hand toward her inside the coach and she gave it a mistrustful glance before looking out the window to try to spot the Effingham Inn. Nothing on her side of the coach qualified even marginally as a decent inn. And on the other side were docks and ships. . . .

"Where is it, this 'Effingham Inn'?"

"It's . . . ah . . . right ahead, m'lady. You just can't see it from where you are. Come now, I'll see you down an' safe inside." He seemed to be pleading, for some reason; it gave Eden a cold shiver of alarm.

"I'm going *home*." She looked about wildly and jumped up, shoving her shoulder through the window and shouting up to the driver, "Take me back to the Marlow house and there's a tenner in it for you!" The man gathered up the reins instantly, only to put them down when Arlo sprang up on the hub of the wheel and countered, "Fifteen to stay, man."

"Twenty to take me back!" She wrestled through the window again and stayed there this time.

"Twenty-five!" Arlo declared desperately.

"Thirty! And another five if you leave now!" she pleaded.

"Fifty!" Arlo grabbed the driver's dusty, black-clad arm and squeezed.

*"A hundred!"* Eden shouted, "but only if we leave this second!"

"Name yer price, dammit, an' I'll pay!" Arlo was pushed to a last bit of bidding frenzy. The driver smiled toothlessly and pushed the wooden brake on, wrapping the reins around the top rail.

Eden snarled with impotent anger as she drew inside. Of course he'd listen to Arlo, she muttered nastily to herself. All men were in league together, remember? Let them sniff a profit and they abandoned everything for greed and glory . . . or lust.

Arlo jumped off the wheel, finding his knees weak under him. That was altogether too close, he groaned, and much too expensive. "Wait here!" he commanded, running down the narrow street toward the dirty tavern where his laird had disappeared.

But halfway there, he met Ram coming toward him with a small cask under one arm, and between gasps, he managed to get out, ". . . the driver, she offered to get back to 'er house . . . and I offered more . . . and more. . . ." His hand mimed the escalating bidding like a clockface gone wild, and Ram suddenly got the full meaning, including the word "expensive." They both began to run.

Eden was steaming, huddled in one corner of the coach, when Ram jerked the far door open and glowered at her dangerously. Above the sound of Arlo's settling the finer points of what "name your price" meant, he ordered her to get out in a very ugly tone.

"I can't," she glared back spitefully, feeling like a child caught playing in the dirt under the back porch.

"Oh, you can and you will," he uttered ominously.

"I have no bonnet and no gloves." She lifted her chin imperiously, feeling a little foolish with her last ladylike excuse. There was clearly no gentleman around to heed it. "I can't be seen in a public house without them. It just isn't done."

"No bonnet —" His face became a surprised blank for a second, then the absurdity of it hit him and a spear of raw, strangling frustration exploded in his head. He charged into the coach and his weight rolled it savagely to that side, sending her sliding within his reach.

She kicked and thrashed and fought with full Marlow passion. But he still dragged her from the coach, hauled her over his shoulder, and carried her down the dock. His purposeful stomping made her humiliating ride more torturous as they careened through a world of shins, ruined paving stone, and horse residue. She gasped and pounded and threatened, alternating between proclaiming her abuse to the whole world and trying to draw as little notice as possible. But even end-over-end, drowning in her own blood, she knew a lady in a fine, coral-red silk gown being carried rump-up, thrashing and screaming, over a man's shoulder would be a hard thing not to notice.

Ram shifted her slightly and she tried to brace against his back and raise her head, but a sudden turn defeated her and she dangled free from his shoulder again, feeling like she was being squeezed in two. Beneath her were aged wooden planks . . . and at the sides, foul, black water . . . then the wooden clapboards of a ship . . . as they rose higher . . . then a ship's polished deck. The blood seemed to pool in her eyes and she saw everything through its alarming red.

Ram carried her straight to the hatchway and struggled down the narrow passage to push through a cabin door. Between the low ceiling and the thrashing of his lopsided burden, he just managed to maintain his balance across the floor where he dumped her unceremoniously onto a wide bunk.

She saw stars as she fought to a sitting position and held her pounding head between her hands. Each movement was an exercise in self-abuse and she stopped, sitting still until her faculties cleared and she could make out that she was in a ship's cabin, a large one. And she sat on a high bunk nearly as wide as a regular bed and nearly as soft. Ram stood over her, his hands on his hips, determination etched in his stony features.

"The *Effingham* is a ship!" she charged angrily, finding it less difficult to focus her fury than to focus her eyes.

"A nimble wit," his anger wore sarcasm's mask, "I knew there had to be *one* in the Marlow family. It's your home, woman, for as long as it takes to get to Scotland." His hand swept the spacious, well-lit cabin behind him.

*"Home?* But we're to stay at the Buxton Inn at least a month. We have obligations—dinners and parties."

"I made no such plans." His mouth curled disagreeably. "And no one saw fit to consult me, interloper, molester, and rogue that I am. It was your beloved family concocted the mess, let them sort it out."

"You lied to us, to my family and me!" She brought up a fist aimed straight for his nose, but found it suddenly captive in his hand. His blue eyes flashed as he jerked her wrist toward him and felt her rigid body slide with it.

"I know well what was said, and in good faith," he bit out, "but my own word has been met with treacheries, woman. I'll not give your clan a chance to renege again. I was taking you home to Skyelt, anyway. They just set the date forward a bit with their underhanded dealings."

"You can't just steal me from under my family's nose!" She gritted her teeth as she finally slid from the bunk to stand beside him. Her knees were weak, but she managed a defiant thrust of the chin. "They'll look for me—"

"First, woman, *I'm* your family now." He jerked a thumb at his chest and the muscles in his jaw jumped as he shoved his face closer to hers. "I don't have to stoop to

212

stealing you . . . you're *my* woman now, and nobody else's. I've had enough of your precious brothers and their highly selective standards. I've not maltreated you, nor will I, but I'll not answer to anyone for the keepin' of my woman!" He loomed huge and wrathful above her, and when his hands closed harshly on her shoulders and pulled her close, her vision swam. Deep, penetrating tones invaded her skin and set her whole body ajangle with confused heat.

"You're *my* woman now." He felt the softness of her shoulders under his hard fingers, felt the tantalizing warmth of her form near his, and his whole body responded at once: it was like being doused with hot oil. He stiffened and thrust her back an arm's length. "You'll go where I go. An' you'll stay where I put you to stay. The captain has nearly finished loadin'. He was to have held the *Effingham* several days for us, but now there's no need. We'll sail with the first tide."

"You mean it!" Her horrifying conclusion finally made full sense. "You're going to keep me here? You won't even let me see them . . . to say good-bye?" Her shimmering eyes seemed torn from her bright dress, with centers that were well-deep with shock. She didn't know whether to scream, to laugh, or to cry.

"I'd not trust them to say mere farewells," he spoke through lips that scarcely moved. "And I've no stomach for tears — more than I've had already. This way is best."

She nearly staggered from his unmistakable reference to her tears in the night just past . . . her wedding night. She blinked to forbid the tears now pricking the corners of her eyes.

This was too much to bear! He was taking her to Scotland on the very day after their vows, yanking her from hearth and family, demanding she obey him like a good little wife, a possession . . . and forbidding her even to shed a tear through it all! This was the man who had sought her love in the heat of summer's night, in spite of personal hazard and society's censure? The man she had promised with eternal vows to love and to honor? The man who had comforted her tears on her wedding night, then taught her to revel in the eager secrets of her body? He seemed to have forgotten all that and a great deal more upon the mere act of rising. He was a different man entirely. . . .

Shame crashed down upon her as she wrenched away from his hands and backed around the end of the bunk, putting it between them. It was her own shameful desires that made her remember that tender lover; for another, harder man wore that face, that frame now. This man she knew too well: he was the one who had called her a trollop and assaulted her in her cabin aboard *Gideon's Lamp*. He had pursued her from the moment they met, with taunts and temptations and cunning. Undaunted by rejection, knowing they might be found together, he'd crawled into her bed and taken what he wanted. Cold fingers seized her lungs and she stopped, clamping her hands up over her upper arms to quell their shivering.

"Why did you force me to marry you?" Her hoarse whisper had an edge of loathing to it.

"You have that wrong, I believe." His gaze narrowed at the rigid white calm of her delicate features. "You agreed to marry me just as I offered freely for you."

"No! You took all choice from me the night you wormed your way into my bed. I see now, that was your intent all along—to be found in my bed, to be persuaded to lend me your name in a marriage meant to rectify my *dishonor.*" Her knees buckled beneath her and she had to steady herself on the end of the bunk. It was true! "You forced me to marry you." She felt rooted to the spot and frighteningly vulnerable. "Why? Why have you done this to me?"

"I've told you why. We'll not discuss it further." He

turned to go, his shoulders rigid, his fingers curling into fists at his sides.

*"Liar."* She hurled it softly but it struck him like a javelin between his shoulder blades. "You told me what you thought would flatter and pacify me to your own carnal ends. Now I want the truth, if you're capable of it." She was wound tight as a top as he turned back.

"You're penniless," she charged, seizing the most obvious possibility to prod the truth from him. "My father is not the richest man in Boston. You must have been disappointed in the settlement — mostly land, I believe. You should have found a fatter pheasant to pluck." She watched him take a step toward her and growl.

"I'm . . . not . . . penniless."

"Then a callous and arrogant bully who'd molest, then marry, a girl rather than let her reject you!" The blood coursed hot in Eden's veins as her taunts vented the deep anger that had been building in her since the night of her disgrace. "Then you'll find your power lust stretched perilously thin in this marriage, laird."

"I'll warn you, woman, I'm not a man to trifle with. An' I'll not hear more of this nonsense!" He took a step closer and Eden could see that his muscles were drawn hard with restraint.

"The truth stings, does it?" A gleam shot into her eye as she swayed around the bunk toward him. "What other revolting possibilities might yet be uncovered? Are you already married, then, and aiming to sell me to some exotic potentate for his harem?"

"Stop it!" he growled, advancing a step, his jaw clenching under eyes like blue lightning.

"Then *tell me the truth!*" she yelled, shocking both of them with her sheer volume. He sprang at her and snatched her off her feet, against him. He wrestled her stiff, thrashing form to the bunk, tossing her down on it and falling on her with his full ten-stone weight.

215

*"Stop it—let me up!"* She wedged her arms against hi chest and pushing with all her might.

"You want to know why I married you?" He tried t shake her savagely, but the results were oddly feeble. " had to . . . to save my inheritance . . . my land, m home!" he thundered, succeeding in halting her struggles if not her resistance. "It's a condition of my title that plant my seed in one Eden Marlow, of Boston, Massachu setts, and produce a child as heir before I inherit what is by law and right already mine. You wouldna be my mistress, so I had to make you marry me. And I have t make you pregnant, if the job's not already done!"

Eden couldn't breathe or blink or swallow. Her eyes glazed over from lack of air and he shook her again.

"Did you hear me, woman? I married you to get you with child, to make good my inheritance." Never, not in all his plotting and scheming and positioning, had he ever thought it or stated it so bluntly. The degraded sense of it turned his stomach and he felt a bitter taste rise in the back of his throat.

Eden shook her head, trying to comprehend what he'd said. His weight pressed her curving body down into the bed beneath it, robbing her of breath and concentration. She rocked and gasped and twisted until his body relented and allowed her room enough to draw air.

"Why would your inheritance," she managed, "be tied to marrying me? That's . . . absurd! You'd never set eyes on me until two months ago!"

"It's my father, Haskell MacLean, High Laird of Sky-elt," Ram bit out, bracing himself above her on his elbows and forcing her face up to his with his muscular fingers. "He was furious I wouldn't marry and produce him an heir. He went an' changed the assigns an' portions this spring. I am to produce a bairn on you within two years or forfeit my lands, my home, my title—everythin'." His gaze crackled with such intense heat that, for a moment, every objection evaporated from her mind.

"You're daft!" she finally rasped. "I've never even heard of your father! What reason would he have to make *me* a condition of his will?"

"He's heard of you, all right, but it was yer mother, Constance, that started it all. He *knew* your mother, in the biblical sense, years ago in London, and it seems th' experience left 'im marked for life. He never forgot 'is itch for her."

"He *what?* I won't listen to any more—" Eden yelled, trying to clamp her hands over her horrified ears.

"I said, Yer mother and my sire, old Haskell, were lovers in their younger days, and old Haskell never forgot her." He pried her fingers from her ears and wrapped his big hands around her wrists tightly. "When he found Constance had a daughter, he thought, *like mother, like daughter.* Blood bein' what it is, he assumed you would be as tempting as your mother . . . and as accommodatin'. And so he decreed the youngest filly of the line must do to breed his heir. An' he left it to me to get a child from you however I could."

"I don't believe a single word of it—you're sick in the mind—rambling on—this disgusting claptrap about horses and your father—"

"Listen to me!" He gave her a warning shake and she bit her lip as she stiffened, fully expecting a blow. He ground his teeth in frustration and his next words came in hot blasts.

"I married you because I *have to have* your child as heir to save my home. Believe me—nothin' less could have forced me to actions so reckless and so personally revoltin'! It's a bad lot for you, havin' to bear a man's seed unwillingly. But sooner or later, you'd have had to marry and bear heirs for somebody . . . and I'm no worse than the next. As soon as the deed's done, I'll not trouble you further, you may depend on that, woman!"

217

Beneath Ram, Eden lay staring, unseeing, up at him. Her heart and breath had stopped, her senses were stunned and reeling under their last staggering load. "Have to have your child—revolting to me—bear a man's seed—as soon as the deed's done—" She couldn't respond on any meaningful level, the horror of it had cut so deep.

The loathing in his granite-hard features was for himself, but no power in heaven or earth would have convinced Eden of it at that moment. When her eyes began to refocus, she saw his disgust, his professed revulsion as a condemnation of all that had passed between them . . . a rejection of her as woman, wife, and mate. His disgust at having to marry against his desires had eclipsed the tenderness that had awakened in their marriage bed. Now in the clear light of day, both she and this forced marriage sickened him.

"Get off me." Her voice was flat, and the angry lights were doused in her eyes, leaving them large and vacant. "Get away from me," she shuddered.

Ram scowled hotly at her limp withdrawal. The lifelessness in her face and voice dealt him a savage blow. He rose above her and slid to the floor by the bunk, finding his legs weak beneath him. She lay there, the delicate coral silk twisted about her sweet body, her lush brown curls atangle about her pale face, her beautiful eyes bereft of even the comfort of tears. God, what had he done?

A sneer from inside responded: he'd told her that her mother was a whore, and that he and his father had expected the same of her. He'd revealed that he'd forced her into a marriage, in which his only interest was using her body to produce him a bairn. He'd shown contempt and disgust for their union and indicated his eagerness to be shed of its tawdry carnal connections at the earliest opportunity. He'd stolen her from her family to keep her prisoner on a ship until they were at sea and she had no place to run. Short of beating her black and blue, how

218

much worse could he possibly behave to her on the very day after her wedding?

"I'll see you're cared for, woman?" His big arms hung useless at his sides. "I'll see you have a place at Skyelt." His tongue was thick and he choked on the words. Her crumped image swam before his eyes and he stiffened, stepping back. After this, she'd despise the very ground he trod. He shook his auburn head and sent a trembling hand back through his hair. Perhaps it was just as well she hate him. It would make their necessary contacts brief and unpleasant enough to combat the temptations he might otherwise feel toward her. It was a high price to pay, but, damn him, he deserved no better.

The door closed and a metal key clanked in the lock, penetrating Eden's anguished stupor. She jerked up in the middle of the bunk and felt sparks of anger showering through her as she glared at the door. He was deranged; she'd married a madman!

He expected her to believe her mother had taken a lover before she married Adam Marlow. Her eyes narrowed to blazing slits. And that the lover was still so besotted with her after twenty-eight years that he'd entail his own son's inheritance to her daughter's fertility!

She ground her teeth; she wanted to purge the chagrin she felt for her gullibility during the night gone by. She'd actually believed he wanted to marry her, had been so caught up by passion for her that his judgment had temporarily failed his honor. She had condemned his lusts for overtaking and humiliating them both, but at some deeper level, she knew the licentious taint in her blood had clamored for his touch, his caresses, the feel of his body against hers. She suspected his uncontrollable passion only answered the stirring in her own restless Marlow blood.

Then last night, he'd whispered love into her ear, over and over, and she had believed that, too. His potent

219

sensuality had taken her into realms of pleasure she had never dreamed existed. She felt such breathtaking tenderness for him, from him.

And it was all a lie . . . *a tawdry, disgusting lie.*

Tears scalded her cheeks at that most personal betrayal. She was furious at being abducted from her family, at being packed off like a bag of wheat for storage, at being forced by his dishonorable connivings to marry to save her "honor." But in truth, all those things seemed paltry beside the deeper humiliation of his dismissal of her as a woman of flesh and spirit. In her deepest heart, she had wanted to believe he touched her from need, from caring, perhaps from love itself. Every caress, every kiss, awakened a part of her she had never known existed . . . and banished her priggish, over-taught notions of what it was to be feminine. The resonance of their mutual response convinced her that he wanted her and that it was right to be a woman to him in that mesmerizing way.

But by his own word, he'd been performing a distasteful duty . . . making her pregnant. All the while, it wasn't her he wanted, it was a bairn—a baby. He had to have a child from her to buy back his inheritance. Was this Fate's punishment for her having abandoned the lady's role she'd been taught to accomplish?

The cruel bastard! She heard his words to her again and again. She was legally and physically at the mercy of a man whose arrogance and stupidity appalled her. She was a brood animal to him, not a wife. She was a hunk of flesh without soul or feelings to whom one rutting male should be as endurable as any other slavering mate. The thought sent a shiver of resistance up her spine.

Well, until heaven decreed otherwise, he'd not get a child by himself. Whatever the truth about his father and his inheritance, he claimed to need a baby from her. She walked defiantly to the middle of the cabin. She'd molder and rot before she let him use her as his brood mare. He'd never touch her like that again, not as long as she lived!

She ran to the leaded windows and stared down a sheer drop into the murky water of the harbor. Turning back, she searched the shelves and corners of the cabin for some means of working the lock. There was nothing. She slipped to the door and leaned her ear against it, making out a scuffling, settling sound and what might be Arlo's cough. Arlo . . . there was a brief ray of hope. The man might be loyal in the extreme—but he also seemed a man of conscience.

She applied the heel of her fist to the sturdy planks several times in succession.

"Arlo—" she took the chance it was him, "please, let me out of here! You're a decent, godfearing man. You can't keep me prisoner here against my will! Please, in heaven's name, let me out!" She listened, her ear against the door; the silence echoed back, making her imagine him either cowering under Ram's imagined wrath or laughing at her girlish plea. Stung, she pounded harder and summoned her direst-sounding threat.

"If you *don't* let me out, I'll see you boiled in oil—I swear I will!" Did they still boil people in oil? Her chin began to tremble and her voice cracked miserably.

"Let me *out!*"

She closed her eyes and wilted against the unyielding planks. No threat she could make would strike fear into the heart of anybody with good sense. She was a lone, defenseless young woman, schooled in nothing more intimidating than drawing room innuendo, capable of controlling nothing more ferocious than menus and guest lists. Mistress Dunleavy's tidy little summaries of the world had left her completely unprepared to deal with the likes of abduction and forced marriages and compulsive liars.

Slumping into a chair, she hid her face in her hands and tried not to hear the echo of his horrible words in her

mind. She'd been duped and degraded and manipulated
. . . and hadn't pride enough or sense enough to try to
see it until it was too late! Her lofty standards of
refinement, honor, and deportment had betrayed her as
surely as the treacherous desires of her tainted blood.
There was no escaping it: Mistress Dunleavy had failed
her as much as she had failed Mistress Dunleavy. What
was there left to trust?

She pushed her knuckles into the corners of her eyes to
staunch the tears . . . crying again! It seemed all she'd
done in the past twenty-four hours was cry! Her shoulders rounded miserably as that sardonic little maven of
truth that lived at the edge of her consciousness corrected
her; she had managed one other thing . . . three times.


The long afternoon hours progressed slowly and Eden
inspected the spacious cabin, hoping against hope to find
some means of escape. The walls were painted, not just
whitewashed, and were fitted with polished mahogany
moldings trimmed in brass. The floor was waxed to a
high sheen; evening light would be provided by two
polished brass lanterns that hung overhead. There were
three barrel-backed chairs and matching table, a desk, a
copper-lined washstand, and a small metal brazier installed over a metal skirt at one end of the cabin. Then
there was the mahogany bunk, built high to accommodate
several drawers beneath and built wide enough to accommodate at least two sleeping people—

Eden's lip curled nastily. *Let him just try it.*

At dusk, Arlo admitted her trunks and a supper tray to
her cabin, avoiding her gaze. She should have been
starved, but the food appealed little to her. She lit one of
the large brass lanterns, sponged herself clean, and
changed into her heaviest nightdress. Over and over her
eyes went to the door, and each time she rehearsed the

words she'd greet him with when he deigned show his wretched face again.

But he didn't come that night, nor the next day. It was on toward evening of her second day of imprisonment aboard the *Effingham* that she felt the boards shift and tilt beneath her feet; her sewing basket slid the length of the polished mahogany table and just managed to halt at the edge. She jumped up and snatched it against her, listening to the groan and shudder of rope and timbers and the distant shouts and flurry of bare feet on the deck above. She ran to the windows and stared disbelieving at the swaying vessels berthed nearby, knowing they were moored fast; their motion was actually the *Effingham*'s transfered.

Moving . . . they were leaving! She dropped the basket into a chair and ran to the door, pounding on it with her open palm and demanding to be released and set back on the dock. But tears soon clogged her throat and blurred her gaze, and she slumped weakly against the door and gave in to the need for release she'd forbidden these last two days. Clinging to the door for support, she murmured her plea over and over.

Arlo stood his post outside her door and wished whoever was twisting that knife in his gut would have at it and finish him off quick and smart. He listened in spite of himself and her desperate little sobs wrenched the deepest and most decent parts of him in the most painful way. They were underway . . . what could it hurt if he unlocked the door now and freed the little lass?

Eden jolted back, one hand over her mouth and the other swiping at her tears. The sight of Arlo standing there, key in hand, shoulders drooping, made her pause a moment before she ran out into the passage and climbed the steep stairs of the hatchway. The cool, salty air filled her head even before she stepped onto the deck, shading her eyes with her hands. Immediately she had her bearings and was running for the open railing. Near the edge, a pair of burly arms snatched her back and she tussled against them briefly before she saw the broad gulf of brackish water that separated the *Effingham* from the dock, a hundred feet of it or more.

"Sorry, Missy—cain't let ye go off in th' water now, can we?" The seaman's rough arms released her as she backed from the yawning crevasse.

"No—I didn't realize," she choked, "I didn't know." She backed to the safety of the railing and watched the distance between herself and her home and family grow.

She was oblivious to the dozen pairs of eyes that read her distress, but Ram MacLean certainly was not. He stood on the quarterdeck, reassuring the captain that the reluctance of his bride was a result of her unusual closeness to her family and that she'd adjust. The captain was scowling uncertainly, remembering the effect of her earnest wails and pleas on his hardy crew; her reluctance didn't sound very temporary to him.

The sight of Eden at the railing with her appealing figure and her girlishly wet face sent a bolt of ire through Ram, despite the reassurances of the dark, widening span of water between her and the dock. He wheeled and flew down the steps to send her below.

"Eden!" he barked, slowing and grappling with frustration as he approached. She didn't turn to face him, but stood gripping the polished rail with white hands, tears of pure misery burning paths down her fair cheeks.

"This is no place for you." Ram's tone bore traces of anger that shamed him minutes later. "Go below, woman."

"Would you deny me even a last glimpse of my homeland, your lordship? You are too cruel." She sliced him with a wet-lashed look of contempt.

Ram felt remorse and grabbed her arm to relieve his idiotic fear that she might somehow be able to fly across

224

the water and escape him. Though she did not resist, he found himself incapable of tearing her away, as he knew he ought to do. He leaned a hip against the railing and waited, feeling each of a dozen pairs of eyes turned on him in resentment.

They stood watching the busy dock grow smaller and the light of the lowering sun grow rosier. When distance and darkness forbade recognition of all but the merest outlines of Boston's busy port, Eden finally admitted there would be no last-minute glimpse of her family and turned, humbled, to make her way to her cabin. Only then did she feel Ram's possessive hand tight on her arm and only then did her spirit rise to do battle.

225

## Chapter Twelve

Eden was propelled through the doorway from behind and the none-too-gentle prodding affected more than just her momentum.

"I'm not a dullard nor a sack of grain . . . and I'll not be treated like such!" She raised her chin and her eyes glowed hotly in the semidarkness of the cabin.

"Behave like a lady, then, and I'll have no cause to correct you," he growled, feeling somehow at a disadvantage, having to bend his head to stand in the same room with her.

"As if you knew the first thing about ladies!"

"I know one when I see one, woman!" Ram bumped his head on the ceiling when he stiffened. His ire was close to escaping his control and, in spite of himself, he stared at her.

She stood in front of the bunk, her arms crossed beneath her breasts, emphasizing the enticing scoop of her neckline and the clinging drape of her polished cotton print gown over her ripe young curves. Her hair tangled in a cascade of lush curls flowing over her shoulder, emphasizing the contrast it made with her creamy skin. Her lips were reddened and moist and her eyes danced with angry lights. And suddenly a show of authority was no longer uppermost in his mind.

"Where's my trunk?" he growled, furious with those sly fingers twiddling away at the underside of his skin.

"It's not—"

"There it is." Dismissing her purposefully, he cast about for a splint and lit one of the lanterns swinging beside his head. A brass-bound leather trunk nestled at the far end of the cabin between Eden's much larger ones. Two strides and he was there, stooping on his heels before it and producing a key from his coat pocket.

"What's *that* doing here?" The mere presence of his possessions in her cabin seemed furtive and encroaching. "Get it out of here."

"A man puts his belongings in his cabin." He paused, raising the lid, and pivoted to cast her a thoroughly insulting look that included her in that category.

"This is *my* cabin." Eden's arms locked at her sides and her hands clenched as she stepped closer and flung a righteous finger toward the door. "Take that out of here and stay out!"

"We're married now, and much as it pains me, we must share these costly confines for the voyage—"

"We may have spoken vows, but we're not husband and wife," Eden simmered, determined to aggravate his pain a bit. "I'll not be forced—"

"Your marriage, woman, is as legal and binding a union as can be made on this earth."

"A union based on misrepresentation and fraud. I don't believe a word you've said, Ramsay MacLean, if that's who you truly are. You schemed to marry me for some nefarious purpose and you've abducted and degraded me, keeping me under lock and key like a prisoner—"

"I've told you the truth," he shot up, narrowly missing another nasty bump on the ceiling.

"And I don't believe it!" She drew back, finding him towering over her, and took a few steps backward. He

227

followed. "That disgusting lie about my mother . . . she did have a lover before she was married—it was my father!"

*"And* mine!" Ram countered hotly. "I'm not proud of my sire's ruttings, woman. I'd not speak about such unless it were true and necessary to relate. It's a painful thing all round, but I'll not be made out a liar because of my father's and your mother's perfidy."

*"Perfidy?"* She was seized by the urge to scratch his eyes out. "You've schemed and lied and mistreated me since the moment we met. You accused me of bedding my own brother, then offered for me like some cheap dockside trollop. More than once you forced yourself on me— including that night you crawled into my bed like a thief. Then you professed all manner of tender affection for me to lure my family into thinking a match between us was desirable. The only perfidy here is *yours!* And I'm not bound to honor any vow made to you while suffering a state of delusion."

"I'll not listen to more of your ravings." His jaw flexed dangerously and his eyes snapped angrily as he closed on her. "For better or worse, you are my woman."

"But not your *wife!"* she rasped, backing toward the door.

"I've told you the truth, Eden Marlow MacLean, and like it or not you'll have to abide by it until we reach Scotland and it can be settled in yer fevered little mind. And we'll share this cabin as man and *woman* and present a proper face to the passengers and crew."

"Never!" Her eyes blazed fiercely as her creamy breast heaved with escaping emotion.

Ram snapped inside, lunging for her and wrapping his heavy arms around her like chains, binding her to his exploding heat. She pushed and twisted against him, demanding release and calling him every low, degrading thing she could bring to mind.

". . . depraved monster . . . you'll have to force me . . ." she panted, "I'll never let you touch m—"

Ram's mouth crushed hers with a force meant to obliterate all resistance. It seemed the only way to stop her tirade and demonstrate his power over her. But the feel of her wriggling body, the heat of her in his arms, the lush warmth of her mouth under his pulled at his self-possession by the rots. His entire body caught fire with a burning that could only be extinguished by the charms of Eden Marlow MacLean. He groaned and crushed all but the sheerest breath from her as passion roared through him like fire through a dry forest.

Sparks from his heat caught in Eden, in her hair, her throat, her loins. Reason, resistance, and pride—all were consumed in the jumbled heat that flared within her. Her hands ceased pushing and began to clutch at his coat. Her arms escaped only to wind about his narrow waist and pull him closer. Her mouth slanted under his and yielded to his demands, then returned his ardor fully.

The harsh pressure eased about her and his hands began to run up and down her back and over her buttocks, lifting her to him as he rubbed his burning pelvis against her. She moaned against his kiss and her hips undulated in his hands, seeking him. Her toes left the floor and he moved both of them toward the broad bunk. His mouth never left the moist satin of hers when he lowered her and his own aching body at the same time.

Ram's weight crushed Eden, making her want to take more of him, all of him, inside her. Their deep kisses surfaced and Ram nibbled her throat, her chest, and one cool breast he freed from her accommodating gown. His hot mouth at her nipple drew tight some invisible string in her, bringing her taut against his bulging manhood and making her yield to him. Her hands flew over his broad body, reveling in its varied textures; rough woolens, silky hair, bristled cheek. The distinctive male scents of him washed over her, completing the bombardment of her will.

Rash hands raised her skirts, seeking the skin of her thighs and the moist velvet of her woman's flesh. Eden shuddered with need and arched against his hard palm. Ram groaned her name softly and pulled the last barrier of heavy wool tartan from between them, aching for completion, oblivious to all else.

Or nearly oblivious—a rapping at the door and the calling of his name interrupted the intense alignment of his senses. His fierce concentration was unsettled for a fraction of a second. But at such a fevered pitch, that was all it took: the blood pounding in his head abated just enough and his mouth stilled over Eden's creamy breast. He suddenly felt her fingers on his neck and back in a different way and his swollen flesh, poised at the verge of her womanly softness, shocked him.

Attuned to every nuance of his passion, Eden felt the change in him and struggled to understand what was happening. And in one chilling instant, she realized both where she was and what she was doing. A wave of disbelief washed over her, bringing her up on the bunk in the same motion that peeled him from her exposed body.

Her bare legs shocked her and her damp breast chilled noticeably, jolting her to cover herself. Bulging, the burnt-red tartan pressed against the edge of the bunk, and she lifted her eyes to escape it.

Ram was staring down at her, the grimness of his soul stamped on his handsome features. His dark face mirrored the shock and self-loathing Eden felt. "Hold yer fist, man!" he snarled over his shoulder at Arlo's insistent pounding. Then he returned to her.

"You . . . it's *you* that does this to me. Well, I'll not have my soul beguiled from me for a few minutes in Satan's paradise . . . no pleasure is worth that." He whirled on shaking legs and strode for the door, slamming it hard enough to shake the four walls.

Horror filled Eden's heart: not only had she succumbed to his male power; she'd responded to his touch like a wanton . . . a shameless hoyden . . . an insatiable jezebel! One kiss and she was writhing against him, craving those delights he'd proven existed inside her own body. And only seconds before, she'd forbidden him ever to touch her again! Where was her anger, her sense of right and wrong, her pride?

Shame weighed down her limbs as she tussled off that tainted bed and stared at it. Her cheeks burned from eager contact with his bristled face and she tried to hide them with her hands. He said it was her; she was to blame, somehow. He called what happened between them "Satan's paradise" and blamed her for tempting him. He wanted her and hated wanting her at the same time. What had she done to make him loathe her so? But then, what had she ever done to make him desire her?

She crumpled into a chair, unable to bear her own weight any longer. Her eyes ached with dryness and her shoulders were racked with sobs.

"*I'm* not responsible for his miserable lusts." She fought an unwelcome sense of guilt to defend herself to the hushed cabin. "I've done nothing, *nothing* to tempt or coerce him. He's the one began it all. It's his own flaws he puts off on me, and I'll not stand for it. Satan's paradise!" She jumped up and snarled at the door. "As if his black soul was worth coveting in the first place!"

But by the time Arlo brought her a tray of food an hour later, Eden's ladylike mien was restored. The tray was duly deposited on the table near her chair and Arlo hitched about uncomfortably and cleared his throat twice under her frosty gaze. Her head tilted and she refolded her hands in her lap.

"Is there something else?"

"There be, m'lady. I brung you a tray tonight, but yer

to join th'other passengers in the common room, if you expect t'eat tomorrow."

"*His* command, I suppose." Eden studied Arlo narrowly and noted the increased ruddiness of his square, guileless face.

"Aye, m'lady." He chewed his lip, clearly more willing to brave her ire than his laird's. He turned away, but then turned back.

"Laird Ram said ye had . . . doubts, m'lady. Well, I can testify he be the rightful son o' Laird Haskell MacLean. An' he be heir to all of Skyelt. It's a right bonnie place, miss, the old castle an' the dells and fields. They be men o' wealth, it's true. But not a bit purse-proud, neither the laird nor his son. Not fancy . . . but fine, strong lairds, miss."

That strain of pride in his apologetic voice moved something in Eden. For some reason she was willing to admit the best of this man while believing the worst of his master. Her starched posture wilted.

"Thank you, Arlo MacCrenna. I'll . . . think on it."
Relieved, the burly Scot turned toward his laird's trunk and knelt before it. He pulled out a clean shirt, a heavy wool blanket, and some shaving articles, tucking them into an awkward bundle. He paused with his hand on the door and glanced at her before fastening his eyes on his shoe buckles.

"Uh . . . Laird Ram will be . . . sleepin' up on deck, m'lady." His voice trailed to a rasp, then he jerked the latch and was gone.


The next two days tried both Eden's self-possession and her Christianity. She did appear in the commons to take meals and found that the only other passengers, Mr. and Mrs. Rochefort Tarkingham, were a cool and irksome pair of English near-peers with suffocating affectations and an annoying interest in her recent marriage. But then, they could scarcely be blamed. Not many bridegrooms preferred sleeping on the cold, wooden deck of a ship to bedding in warm comfort with their brides. Impervious to their curiosity, Ram was always there, polite and taciturn and watching her with a hint of disapproval. She couldn't wait to end those interminable episodes under the Tarkinghams' sly, probing questions and Ram's hostile scrutiny.

The only enjoyable moments of the day came in mid-afternoon and again after supper when she went on deck for fresh air. The sun was warm on her face, the breeze cool and fresh; and the ship's officers never failed to pay her a pleasant compliment. But Ram was there, too, with his sky-blue stare and his wretched kilt flapping in the breeze, calling attention to his half-naked legs. Ignoring him took an appalling amount of effort and she always left the deck with weakened knees, her heart thumping in her throat. What a base and easily tempted creature she was!

Twice they met in the passage and the close quarters required that they press either the walls or each other to pass. Eden's back brushed the wall, Ram's front brushed Eden . . . very slowly. She held her breath each time, feeling puddly inside, and fury engulfed her the next instant. Why couldn't she have been born anything but a Marlow, and worse, a female Marlow?

Ram appeared in her doorway the second evening. She turned from her trunk with a shawl in her hands and a defiant angle to her chin.

"You're not going on deck?"

"Perhaps it will be too crowded." She set her shawl aside and stared at him meaningfully.

"The weather is worsening. It may be your last turn on deck for some time." He stepped closer and Eden could feel the irritable heat from his eyes.

Her heart picked up its pace, confusing her. This didn't feel very much like righteous anger.

"If you insist," she snapped, jerking up her shawl and heading for the passage. He brushed past her at the foot of the steps, touching her nowhere and everywhere at the same time. She was trembling as he held out a hand to assist her up the steps behind her.

Her "No, thank you," was regrettably breathless and he seized her hand anyway. Goosebumps stole up her arm and she blamed it on the chill sea air . . . that and her complete lack of pride, decorum, and fortitude. It was him, she thought.

And it was her, he realized, that caused this tightness in his throat, this unreliable heartbeat, this flush of heat. No matter how stern his self-reproach or how determined his control, his hands still twitched to touch her, to draw her against him so he could lose himself in her kiss. Her contemptuous glare, her vehement denunciations, her hatred of him—none of them mattered to his stubborn desires.

Their shoulders touched as she stepped on deck. When she jerked her hand from his, he felt a shaft of heat run up the front of his body. His face darkened and he stalked to the railing where Arlo stood watching the swirling clouds.

A cold rain began to fall, sending the Tarkinghams scurrying below deck. At the far end of the ship talking with the captain, Eden covered her head with her shawl and hurried toward the hatchway. A gusty torrent of water descended before she was halfway there and she found herself being lifted by the waist and carried to the passage against her husband's side. Ram's strong arms thrust her ahead of him into the dryness and tightened as he struggled to keep his balance in the close quarters. She was already carried to her cabin door before her aching ribs permitted a breath.

"I'm perfectly capable of walking—"

He lowered her to the floor even as she spoke, but his arms refused to leave her waist. Dangerously close in the dim passage, he raised a hand to brush water from the shawl that covered her hair. His darkening eyes stared down at her wet face and he wiped rain from her cheek.

Eden's protest was lost in the scramble of her senses. Ram's auburn hair was wet and a shortened lock hung over his forehead; water glistened on his tanned cheekbones. He felt warm and hard and sheltering. He was so close . . . those full, generous lips that often tasted salty. . . .

She saw him swallow and felt him draw away.

"Go to bed," he ordered gruffly, then strode down the passage to the commons.

She lit one of the big lanterns, musing nastily that Ram deserved cold water for a bedmate. The ship began to roll harder and the rain knocked, then pounded at her windows. By the time she was ready for sleep, the ship rode alarming swells that were visible as white-capped mountains out her windows. She stood in her heavy robe watching them, feeling very small and very alone. She gave herself a stern talking-to and crawled under the heavy comforter to fall into a troubled sleep.

Near dawn a heavy fist pounded at her latched door, growing more insistent as the minutes passed. Eden bolted up in her tangled covers and blinked in the gray morning light. The ship was tossing, but not as wickedly, and the thunder and lightning seemed to have stopped. She gathered her wits and her robe about her and answered the muffled calls.

Arlo and a bull-necked seaman stood braced in the wet passage, soaked to the skin and struggling to support Ram's drenched form between them.

"Help 'im m'lady," Arlo entreated from behind miserably dark-circled eyes. "It's the seasickness again, bad. An'

235

he's drunk half a keg of black brandy in the boot . . . yer brother's remedy, he said."

Eden went white with fury. How dare he get seasick and drunk on her and expect her to nurse his miserable hide back to health? After accusing her of being the devil's tool and saying he wished he'd never set eyes on her. . . .

"Then let him stew in his own juice," she snapped, cringing at the way his arrogant head lolled helplessly to one side. The seaman abandoned his grip on Ram and barked something about having to get topside, then stalked off.

"Please, m'lady." Arlo grappled with his laird's crumpled form and the urgency in his face was too wrenching to refuse.

She throttled them both mentally, then stepped out into the wet passage, bundling her nightgown and robe about her knees. She jerked up an arm and grasped Ram around the waist. Together they managed to get him partway up and to drag him through the cabin door. As soon as they were well inside, Eden dropped him and straightened with a disgusted sneer.

"Up . . . onto the bed, m'lady." Arlo gestured her to take up his arm again and he urged his burden toward the tall bunk.

"He's wet clear through," Eden refused with a heated gleam in her eye.

Arlo paused to look at her, taken aback by her reluctance to see to his laird in such time of need. Eden straightened, annoyed by Arlo's expectation of generosity.

"You know what he's like." She swept a hand at him and defended her refusal to put him in her bed. "He'll thrash. And the ship will roll and he'll be on the floor anyway. It's dry and clean. He'll find it at least as comfortable as the deck above." Her last charge struck home and Arlo surrended his laird to the floor, straightening and rubbing his face wearily.

"You'd best get him some dry clothes." Her nose wrinkled at the smell of strong spirits and wet wool. Arlo nodded and turned to Ram's trunk, tripping slightly over his own feet. He took one step, handing the stack of linen and tartan toward her before going down on one knee, his face draining to a sickly green.

"Arlo!" She reached him just as he toppled over, groaning in misery. Growling, she shut the cabin door and bit her fingernails as she stared at the two sick men thrust into her care a second time.

Hurriedly she lit the swinging lamp and dressed beneath her nightgown. She took a dry quilt from one of her trunks and peeled Arlo's coat and shirt from him with his semi-cooperation, wrapping him warmly. Then she was forced to turn to Ram.

Gritting her teeth, she unbuttoned his black coat and his pearl-buttoned shirt, fighting back memories of the last time she saw those buttons give. She rolled him from side to side to remove his garments and swiped at this clammy skin with a bit of toweling before wrestling a dry shirt onto him. She paused over his wet kilt, hating the thought of such intimate duty but taking some comfort from the fact that he'd be properly humiliated by being so completely at her mercy. She undid the buckles and slid the waterlogged wool away, covering him hastily with the dry tartan and congratulating herself on her efficiency. But some minutes later it was still hard for her to swallow.

The storm was mercifully brief. By the following morning patches of sun had broken through the clouds and the ship rode calmer seas. Eden had spent the day before tending Arlo and overseeing the purging of her husband's system. She rendered Ram the least aid humanity would allow but found that even that weakened her anger dangerously. Bathing his face and administering watered draughts from his nearly demolished keg of brandy took little time, but it required touching his body and cradling his head against her breast. She made herself remember his callous schemes, his blaming and shunning and deceit. But the brief warmth of him against her breast recalled tender moments, too, and sweet looks and bold pleasures. More than once she turned from him with angry tears in her eyes.

Ram woke a day later with a surprisingly clear head and no recollection of the recent past. He sat up and stared into the bunk above him. It was empty and he scowled, rubbing a hand over his face as he pulled himself together. His joints demanded movement, then screamed whenever it occurred. It felt as if moss grew on his tongue and he had a thirst the Black Sea couldn't quench. Worse, his head pounded dully and the brightening light pierced his eyes like needles. He'd never in all his life felt more wretched.

"You're finally awake."

Eden's voice came from behind him. He propped an elbow on one raised knee and cradled his head on his hand. He didn't want to look but couldn't help himself. She sat at the table, her hands around a crockery mug, a serene expression on her face. She wore a green woolen gown over a chemise gathered to a band and ruffle at the neck. Her dark hair framed her ivory skin and her eyes were bright as fire.

"The storm was really rather brief. It's the drink you're paying for now."

"I'm paying for more than just a head of grog," he snapped, irritated by her assessment and by his position on the hard floor. He pushed to a squat, then strained upward. Everything swam and he fell back to sit on the edge of the bunk, his head in his hands. "Where's Arlo?" He rolled his shoulders and grimaced at the aches and slivers of pain that shot through him.

"Bringing you some nourishment, I expect." An impulse to help him had brought her to her feet, but she snatched herself back after one step.

"About time . . . I'm half-starved." His hand went to his lean belly and massaged it through his shirt.

"And fortunate to be alive," she retorted, irritated by his surly attitude. Had she actually expected him to be any different? "The state you were in, you might have died of exposure . . . or been washed overboard."

"Not with Arlo about." Ram's burning eyes narrowed. "He's loyal."

"Of course . . . faithful Arlo. You can always count on him to see to your every need." She grabbed her shawl from the chair behind her and paused, white-faced, in the doorway. "Too bad you couldn't make a bairn on him!"

The sound of the door slamming reverberated in Ram's head for a full minute. He clamped his hands over his eyes and temples and sagged, waiting for the racket to subside. His already burdened conscience groaned as he realized he was in her cabin. With no recollection of the previous . . . how many days? Faithful Arlo appeared moments later with a heaping plate of fried ham, potatoes, and biscuits and a small tin pot of coffee.

"Yer up and at it a'ready, I see." Disgust was written large in his blunt face as he deposited the fare on the table and looked his laird over critically. "Couldna wait to be insultin' her agin, could ye?"

"It's not your concern, Arlo; leave it." Ram stalked gingerly to Eden's chair and eased himself into it, folding his legs to fit them under the table. He picked up her mug and paused before setting it firmly aside and drawing the plate before him.

"She's a goodly lass, Ramsay MacLean, an' she's had a bad time of it wi' you." Arlo frowned and crossed his arms over his chest as he watched Ram attack and devour the food.

"She's no lass, Arlo." Ram glared from the corner of his eye as he chewed the salty meat. Arlo's shoulders seemed to grow a bit and a fraction of his stout neck disappeared into his coat.

"A lady, then."

"Hmph. *Not a lady,* Arlo." Ram tilted the tin pot of coffee and drank from it. He scowled at his long-time friend's resentful look. "An' if you're not careful, I'll tell you exactly how I know." He returned to his food with a dampened but determined appetite and Arlo's agitation was soon full blown.

"Twice now she's nursed ye like an angel o' mercy when she coulda left ye to stew in yer own juice . . . an ye dare talk so about her? Yer own wife? You make me ashamed I asked her to take ye in."

"Asked her to take me in . . . to my own cabin?" Ram's head came up, his eyes narrowed and wary. "It was my coin paid for the passage—"

"And her what tended ye and held yer head when ye were pukin' and ravin'." Arlo's jaw was set and his stocky legs were spread.

"*She* tended me?" Ram snarled. "And where were you, MacCrenna?"

"On the floor b'side you, weak as a kitten. It was her what tended ye an' held yer head and stroked ye. The Laird A'mighty knows why." His burly arms jerked apart and he strode away. "Th' air in here seems mighty foul, of a sudden." The door rumbled a second time and Ram tightened as if it slammed on him.

Her again. Arlo insisted *she* had nursed and tended him . . . he still didn't know how long, but it was probably too long. He stared at his half-demolished plate and wrapped his fingers around the cooling pot of coffee. He swallowed to ward off the tightness in his throat. Lord, he had a knack for digging himself a hole where she was concerned. She already despised him for a black-hearted fraud. Now after nursing him back from a drunken stupor, her opinion of his character would be sunk even lower.

Squeezing his eyes shut, he tossed down some of the strong, black brew and shuddered as it seared his abused stomach. The worst was, she was just coming to share his opinion of himself.

Eden spent the morning and most of the afternoon on deck, strolling or sitting on a small crate, leaning against the rail and watching the sea. In the bright sun, with the waves glistening and dancing all around her, she tried to forget her loneliness, her sham of a marriage, and Ram's irascible nature. She wanted nothing more complicated than to feel the breeze on her face.

It was late before her lagging steps carried her to her now-empty cabin. She shed her shawl and looked around, relieved to be alone. The blankets and comforter were folded and stacked neatly on the foot of the bunk, the table had been cleared and wiped, and fresh toweling had been hung on the washstand: Arlo. She smiled.

Supper would be ready before long and she sent one hand to smooth her supple gown and the other up over the outline of her hair. The wind had teased her locks from their assigned places and her nose wrinkled. She'd have to remedy that before braving the Tarkinghams again. She sighed; why did refinement and proper manners seem positively stultifying in those two? Collecting her hand glass and brushes from the tray of her chest, she climbed up on the bunk and began to take the pins from her hair.

There she sat, her mirror propped between her knees and her hair half-tamed, when the door opened and Ram stepped inside. He straightened and looked at her a long moment before turning to close off the passage behind him. When he turned back, Eden collected every detail of him in a blink. His face was more starkly sculpted, his eyes seemed darker, brighter. He was freshly shaven and wore a clean shirt, a green-and-gray kilt, and gray woolen hose. His hair was brushed back from his face and caught in a knitted gray cord. A blanket of control covered his broad shoulders and his features exuded a determined calm.

"If you don't mind." She jerked the mirror aside and flattened her knees to slide and stand beside the bunk.

"If you don't mind," he echoed her, "I've come to have a word with you."

"I'm not in a state to receive visitors." She caught his gaze fixed on her exposed ankles and calves and jerked her gown down to cover them.

"I've seen you less . . . presentable." His concentration narrowed alarmingly to that soft, brownish cloud lapping over her shoulders and curling down her back.

*Go in, speak your piece, then get out!* he'd warned himself, and now he repeated it in his head like a charm. But in two steps he was halfway across the cabin; he couldn't halt himself.

"Go on . . . with . . . what you were doing."

At first she resisted his command, but then she resumed brushing her hair with quick strokes. The sooner she was done, the less exposed she would feel.

"Arlo tells me you cared for us both, durin' the storm. *In, speak your piece, then get out!* he remembered.

Her brush paused mid-stroke and she looked at him, meeting his eyes unexpectedly, then tearing hers away. A warm flush burst against her skin from the inside, setting off an alarm. She backed away.

"I'm bound to offer my gratitude. It was . . . more than some would've done." He ground his teeth, feeling his resistance giving way. *You spoke your peace—now get out quick.*

But he couldn't make his feet move. His gaze tugged at hers and she finally succumbed, lifting her face to him. His look had an uncertain quality that seemed foreign on his bold features. It sent her stomach sliding.

"It was a Christian duty . . . performed at Arlo Mac-Crenna's request." She sounded slightly out of breath and realized her heart was thumping as if she'd just run, or was preparing to.

"Still, you had cause to refuse and did not." His feet moved at last and with dismay he realized he was now three-quarters of the way to the bunk. His muscular arms hung at his sides and his hands felt heavy and empty. The brush gliding through her hair hypnotized him. He suddenly burned to replace it with his fingers.

"It's best forgotten." She lowered her hands to conceal their trembling. She saw his throat flex as he swallowed hard . . . then he swallowed again.

"I can't forget, Eden . . . I can't." His husky tones vibrated through her seductively. Somehow they both knew he was speaking of more than an act of mercy. And somehow she knew he was going to touch her.

Luxuriant strands like raw silk wound through his fingers and curled around his wrist. He rubbed the locks of her hair between his thumb and fingers, losing himself in their texture. A hint of lavender and roses teased his breath and made his strong legs weak. The ivory oval of her face was raised, expectant, and the dark centers of her eyes grew larger. He took that last, fatal step and was beside her. Somehow he had known this would happen from the moment he opened the door. It was inevitable . . . predestined.

Eden saw his intent and, much as she feared, she could not move. He bent lower, heat seeking heat, desire searching for response. His lips covered hers with a summons more ancient than human memory.

243

They stood barely touching, fused by a single bolt of heat that defied logic. Ram's hands lurched to encompass her waist and she molded tightly against him. Her arms opened to clasp his broad back and her head tilted to fit her mouth closer to the velvety warmth of his. Hunger met hunger and exploded between them, blurring both past and future.

Ram engulfed her, lifting her against him and drinking in the soft, curving essence of her. It was a small move to the bunk and she was light in his arms as he lifted and lowered her, following her body down with his. She arched over his arms and he traced her jaw and throat with hungry kisses. The fine voile ruffles at her neck halted his downward path briefly. He felt for the tiny buttons, then peeled her gown and chemise from her with shaking hands.

"Oh, Ramsay. . . ." His hot skin spread over her bare breasts, and she nibbled at his lips and tugged at the cord that restrained his thick hair. Her fingers threaded possessively through his mane and she pulled his mouth up to hers, blistering it with unleashed desire.

Ram's eager hands reclaimed every part of her revealed beauty, rousing and mastering her passions. This once — he had to have her once more. He had to feel that shattering conclusion in her soft flesh again to free himself of this merciless need. She was his; it was his right to take her. His intensity eased at that unconscious claim and he rose above her to watch unearthly delights flickering in her face and rippling through her lush body. Her breasts arched into his hands and her eyelids fluttered with tiny shocks of pleasure.

Desire welled in him, demanding to be released in her depths. She welcomed his hard body and shuddered as he parted her legs and entered her. Each completing stroke made her wriggle closer to that hard, marvelous frame, seeking even more of him. This was what she wanted . . .

to capture and hold him inside her always, to feel this divine sense of union stretching through their days and nights together.

They moved in urgent heat, caressing and straining, eager to spend the passion they had hoarded during these last days. Their rhythm rode passion's steepest spiral, compelled to spin faster, higher, to the very limits of being. Breath, pulse, life—all was one. Together, they crashed through that last brittle barrier into flashing waves of pure light and pleasure.

# Chapter Thirteen

Bathed in warmth and quivering with ebbing satisfaction, Eden stroked Ram's damp shoulders and ran her hands down his ribs. The steam of quenched fires seeped through her, leaving a glow to trace its path. Her hair was damp around her face and her eyes were lidded with contentment. It didn't matter that she could scarcely breathe, that Ram's size and weight obliterated everything else from her senses. In that moment, her whole universe was contained in his frame, within the loving circle of her arms.

Ram flexed and rose, settling on the bunk beside her and pulling her tight against his strong body. One hand snagged the comforter and pulled it over them, tucking it around her gently. She nuzzled her face against the hair of his chest and showered little kisses over the area she could reach. His eyes squeezed shut and his breath stopped. The smoothness of her skin, the rounded curve of her hip pressing him, the tenderness her touch conveyed, together they carved an aching void in his middle. But the hurting was strangely sweet, even enjoyable. He pressed his lips against her temple and nosed her hair aside to kiss her ear softly. A wry smile stole over his face.

Eden snuggled her breasts and hips against him once more before giving in to the swirling mists of sleep. Ram watched her, his lids heavy, then sank slowly into that same realm, thinking that he had not felt so warm, so contented, in weeks. And his last tilting thought was that it was sweet, sensual Eden Marlow that brought him such feelings.

The cabin was dim with the last traces of the sunset's rosy cast when Ram's hands lost the struggle and began to wander purposefully over her sleeping form again. She was his . . . to have and to hold. And his urge to have and hold her finally supplanted everything else in his consciousness. His fingers slid over her waist and brushed her nipples, bringing them to attention. His palms massaged her back and the steep curve of her waist, then traveled downward to her hip and thighs. He clasped her buttocks with both hands, groaning silently as he pressed her against his swollen need. He grazed her shoulder with his lips and buried his face in her neck. Stirring, she rolled to her back and Ram's mouth slid unerringly to her breast.

The lovely warmth of sleep gave way to delicious tuggings at her nipples and hot caresses of her inner thighs and hips and belly. Her eyes fluttered just enough to glimpse Ram's head at her breast and she flushed with pleasure. He was loving her again and she was responding, even from the depths of sleep. She locked her fingers in his dark hair and pulled his face up to hers.

"Again, Ramsay?" she murmured, seeking his lips and opening herself to his hot demand. "You're insatiable. . . ." she charged huskily, pulling his chest over her and moving seductively beneath it.

Again : . . . *again*. That word he might have withstood, but then she used the other with it . . . *insatiable* . . . a word he'd always heard and used only in relation to his reprobate sire. *Insatiable* — it clamored in his head. Was that him, too? It was like a plunge into an icy river.

Ram drew back, raking a look over Eden's passion-blushed breasts, her swollen lips, her wide, dark-centered eyes. Her crossed arms tugged about his neck and she beckoned through her parted lips with a moistening dart of her tongue. A shaft of desire tore through his loins, setting his big frame trembling. Need pounded in his head and tension tightened every muscle. He was frozen above her, quivering and growing more horrified by the second.

What was he doing? Bedding her . . . taking her a second time? Lord . . . it was happening again! When he finished, he'd want her again . . . and again. Soon he'd not be able to think of anything else. He'd already been perilously close to that madness without even laying a hand on her. Soon he'd be nothing more than a panting, slavering animal . . . dangerous around any female . . . just like old Haskell!

He sprang from the bunk, muscles twitching, his desire dying.

"Ramsay?" Eden jerked up in the bunk, snatching the comforter over her aching breasts. "What are you doing? What's wrong?" A steamy sense of frustration filled her and she frowned, holding out a hand to him.

He glared at her gesture, his face chilling and hardening, and she pulled her hand back to clasp the cover tightly. The silence thundered around them.

"No!" Ram finally moved to snatch up his kilt and throw it around him. He jerked the buckles savagely. "Ye've done it to me again! You—with yer soft hair and yer perfumed flesh and yer beguilin' ways—pushin' me to the limits of endurance!"

Eden's mouth dropped open and her eyes glared over. Gooseflesh rose on her bare back and shoulders and she shuddered as if his burst of loathing had doused her physically.

"Ye've turned me into a randy beastie!"

248

"I — *I've* turned you . . . ?" she croaked in utter shock.

"I ne'er felt such bedevilment over any other woman. It's only you, Eden Marlow, that sends all my blood to my parts an' starves my head so I canna think nor resist th'evils of temptation. Yer Constance's daughter, all right — a livin', breathin' peril to a man's sanity an' salvation. And Haskell's the sickenin' proof of the degradation that awaits a fool who surrenders to ye!"

"What?" Eden's voice was shrill with disbelief as shame assaulted her naked skin. But her bare body humiliated her less than the treacherous warmth of her rejected feelings for him. "I . . . I've done nothing to tempt or debase you . . . *ever!*"

Ram stalked toward the bunk, eyes like quicksilver, chest heaving. "I've seen you — callin' me with your eyes and wigglin' your hips to entice me when you know I can see. No proper, God-fearin' woman behaves like that toward a man! And no *lady* moans an' thrashes under a man the way you do."

"But you're my husb —" Eden stopped her anguished protest with her hand and stared at him in horror. She'd given herself to him in innocence, following his passionate lead and believing it must be so between a husband and a wife. Had the taint of her own blood and his unchecked lust deluded her into mistaking low, carnal pleasures for proper wifely service? Despite her protests, she had begun to hope she could be his wife, at least in that mesmerizing way. Curse her miserable, craven heart for betraying her!

"It was as you observed — we spoke the vows, but were not made man and *wife,*" Ram spat, giving his disgust with himself free rein.

"How *dare* you stand there dark as King David's soul and disclaim the very vows you forced me to!" she rasped, bolting from the bunk, the comforter clutched against her front with whitened hands. "Your lust for mammon forced me to marry you . . . now you make me out a whore for allowing you to bed me!" She stomped closer, her eyes blazing and her nostrils flared. "You insufferable hypocrite! You base, lecherous, lying *Lucifer*! Marry me for a brood mare, then despise me for standing for you—"

Her arm was back and carried all the force of her whirling body as her hand smashed into his hard cheek. His head snapped back ànd his body after it.

"Don't you ever lay a hand on me again," she screamed, shaking with outrage.

Ram bashed the ceiling with his head and the added pain spurred him to grab her bare shoulders with cruel fingers. His eyes burned and his face contorted into a frightening mask of fury.

"I'll never bed you again, woman—not if I have to keep you imprisoned under lock an' key! Better to lose Skyelt than to lose my soul!" He gave her a vicious shake and left her staggering back onto the bunk as he half-tore the door from its hinges and fled the cabin.

Eden sank to the floor beside the bunk, her face buried in her hands. Emotion burned so hot in her that she felt charred and numb, unable even to release a cleansing flood of tears.

The depth of his loathing sliced her to the very core. He despised her . . . decreed her an unfit influence, a carnal and immoral temptress who wove a net of wiles to ensnare a man's soul. He declared she wasn't his wife, but a piece of property acquired in a tawdry deal, now to be disposed of as defiled. She began to shake violently, chilling with the anguish of her situation. She pulled the comforter tight around her, feeling like she'd never be truly warm again.

The vile cur! He accused her of lying in wait to lure men to their doom in her bed when he *knew* he was the only man who'd ever touched her! She'd never even kissed another man. Perhaps if she'd had more experience with men, she might have seen what he was up to and protected herself. And she'd have realized that Ramsay MacLean roused an uncommon and unholy response from her tainted and vulnerable flesh.

A horrible thought intruded: was it only Ramsay MacLean who commanded that shameful desire in her? Perhaps she would be vulnerable to all men in that shamelessly carnal way. He said she was Constance's daughter in every respect . . . especially that respect. Heat washed through her as she recalled the fevered exchange she had overheard in her father's study that day. Constance had initiated it! Those titillating whispers grated in her ears again and she shook her head. Very likely it was Constance's hot blood that had begun this sordid chain of events years ago, just as he'd said.

And Constance's hot blood pulsed in her veins as well! She shivered with fresh horror.

It was some time later that anger rose into the void in Eden's heart. The heat it generated evaporated her tears, sent blood back into her cold, lifeless limbs, and brought her to her feet.

She stuffed her crumpled green wool down into the bottom of her trunk and chose a high-necked challis gown with a starched muslin ruff and puffed sleeves that narrowed into a tight fit from elbow to wrist. It was as concealing and ladylike a dress as she owned, and she needed to feel like a lady to recoup some of the esteem that lay ashambles in Ramsay MacLean's turbulent wake.

Before Ramsay MacLean had barged into her life, she'd never seen a man's bare flesh, never screamed, never bashed anyone in the face, never had to defend her honor. She would have fainted dead away before calling anybody "Lucifer" or using the word "whore" aloud. Now her every other word seemed to be "lust" or "wretch" or some term for lovemaking. The slightest provocation sent her

251

either rubbing and slithering or railing and screeching. She couldn't count on her own responses from one minute to the next. She hardly recognized herself in the looking glass anymore!

She straightened, determined to take herself in hand, starting with supper. He'd see he hadn't bested her. The door handle wouldn't budge. She tried a second time, then pulled her hand away as if it were scorched. Disbelief widened her eyes and she backed away, staring at the unyielding planks.

The bastard! He'd locked her in. He'd said he would . . . and he did! Her chest heaved; her mouth worked soundlessly. Her hands doubled into furious fists; they attacked the door, to punish only themselves. A last savage kick vented her fury and sent a shooting pain up her leg. She bit her lip hard and hobbled across the cabin to hurl herself onto the bunk.

"Roast in sulphur!" she gritted out, mentally consigning him to the lowest regions of hell. Her chin quivered and her breath came in harsh spasms. "I'm troublesome baggage . . . locked up to save the world from seduction and depravity! I'm not even a fit receptacle for your precious seed! Well, I'll see you pay for this, Ramsay MacLean. You'll forfeit Skyelt, all right . . . and plenty more before I'm through with you!"

She strained and jerked at her back lacings, popping the stitching as she jerked the dress from her shoulders and shoved it from her hips. Her chemise came next, yanked roughly over her head and tossed halfway across the room.

Clad only in garters and stockings, she stood defiantly in the middle of the cabin and glared at the door. A wanton, was she? A slattern, a tool of degradation and moral pollution? She stared down at her satiny curves and long, tapered legs, curiously unshocked by the sight of them. A pang of remembrance pierced her chest, forcing

252

a tiny cry from her.

"You're a filthy hypocrite, Ramsay MacLean. Like it or not, *you* taught me this bit of shamelessness on my wedding night. And every night as I lie down, you'll bear the blame!" She crawled naked under the covers and lay rigid and defiant for a long while before sleep would dare approach.

Arlo came to her door long after sunrise the next morning. His calls went unanswered and he pounded a blocky fist against the door.

"Use your key if you want in!" she snapped, tucking her last garter and smoothing her challis skirts.

"Please," she made out, then came a mumbled something. A moment later she heard a heavy thump, then another, on the door.

"Go ahead — tear the dratted ship apart," she bit out, watching the door and wall trembled under increasing blows. The door swung open with a crash and Arlo rushed into the cabin, rubbing his shoulder.

"Be you all right, m'lady?" He hurried to her, clearly concerned.

"As well as can be expected." She drew herself up and stared at him. "Am I permitted breakfast this morning?"

"Oh," he frowned, seeing her dressed and apparently hale and fit, "that's what I come for, to see if yer up to a bit of food."

"After being starved last evening, I'll try to bear up." She lifted her chin angrily and strode into the passage.

Arlo stared after her and scratched his head, beginning to follow. But at the doorway he paused, his mouth pursed at one end as he ran a hand up the door frame. Rough fingers lingered over a worked metal hinge that was half-torn from the frame. He grabbed the handle and closed the door from the inside, finding it slightly swollen and too heavy to force into the frame against a broken hinge. Small wonder she was in a temper, unable to get her door open and her feelin' under the weather last night to boot. Well, he mused, he'd get a hammer from the ship's carpenter and make quick work of that.

The *Effingham* cut smoothly through the waves; sails billowed in the light wind. The sun was directly overhead, warming the deck and slowing the pace of the miscellaneous housekeeping chores in progress. Sail mending, deck scrubbing, cargo checks, and even a bit of personal laundering went on around Ram as he sat by the railing of the main deck, staring up into the flapping sails and trying not to think. The distinctive red-and-white stripes and the faint circle of stars on the flag above drew his eyes for a moment and he decided to try occupying his mind by thinking of the colonies, called "states" now.

He'd been impressed by much of what he saw, when not consumed by that infernal pursuit. . . . He stopped and shook his head, making himself recall the rolling hills, the fertile valleys, and the sheep . . . especially the sheep. And the space. As he'd ventured west to see the land he was about to . . . acquire, there had been untouched woods and valleys virtually unsettled. Those gentle hillsides were dark and thick with nourishing grasses . . . the kind that flatten flocks in a hurry. And there was water—clear, sweet water.

He scowled at his musings and jerked his thoughts back to the bustle of Boston. There were fine inns and elegant shops, and markets to rival the variety of London— without the stench. The streets were clean, mostly, and the folk industrious, mostly. And the people seemed welcoming and obliging. It was a thriving, energizing place—not like his Skyelt, with all her problems. It'd taken a journey halfway around the world to make him see what a burden his home had become to him.

Captain Wilcox strolled over and paused beside him, searching the riggings for whatever had captured the brawny Scot's attention. Ram pulled back from his reverie to acknowledge the captain with a terse nod and answer his inquiry.

"I was looking at your flag, sir, and thinkin' of my time in the colonies. It's an interestin' place, America."

"Aye, sir, it is that." The captain's stern Yankee face softened as he glanced at the colors, then back at Ram. He cocked his head and he shoved his thumbs in his vest pockets, appraising this odd and intriguing passenger. He spoke little, this surprising Scot, but what he said was always worth listening to.

"There's opportunity for a man there, sir. Good land, with folk pouring in, settling down and producing, and needin' goods and transport. My brother, sir, he's a landed man and done quite well for hisself. And him startin' out with little more'n a plow and the shirt on his back."

"Has he flocks, then?"

"And flax and barley and a variety of good feed crops—and a marvelous bog with the biggest, reddest cranberries." The stern captain suddenly looked transported.

*"Cranberries?"* Ram frowned. "What are cranberries?"

"Ah, sir, only the nearest thing to health and heaven in one. Red, crunchy berries so sour they damn near permanently pucker you!" Ram's nose wrinkled on one side and the captain laughed. "But then," his voice lowered and rolled like a gentle wave, "you put a bit of sugar on 'em and 'tis pure heaven in your very mouth." He sighed and leaned down to ensure confidentiality. "I got some sugared down, below in my cabin. I'm of a mind, they should have called 'em *eve*berries. Just like a woman, they are. Tart enough to jar your bones and set your teeth on

255

edge. Then you go and add a bit of sugar and they become a pure rapture for body and soul."

Captain Wilcox's long, weathered face broke into a rare grin and he ambled off toward the quarterdeck. Ram watched him go, wondering at the poetic turn of the seasoned seaman's mind ... comparing berries to women. *Women.* Eden's image flashed before his mind and his face was instantly stormy. There was no escaping her.

It could not have been more than minutes later, a cry came from above. A sail on the horizon sent every available man to the starboard railing. Captain Wilcox sent for his glass and searched for what seemed an eternity. Then he turned with a jerk and began barking orders to unfurl every inch of canvas the *Effingham* bore.

A bolt of energy burst through the deck and hands went clamoring up the rigging to release canvas as the wheel turned her hard into the wind. Up came the glass again, and Ram was on his feet, heading for the quarterdeck.

"She's flyin' a Union Jack." Captain Wilcox nodded grimly toward the growing speck of white. "We'll try to outrun her, but we're loaded heavy and she's lighter o'draft, with more canvas." His lined face turned to his crew, now scrambling with lines and craning over their shoulders to measure their peril.

"She's British." Ram squinted, trying to make out some feature of the other craft. "A war bucket or a trader?"

"The Good Lord knows," Wilcox gritted out. "An' I hope He keeps it to Hisself."

Helplessly they stood on the bridge and watched the gap between the charging British vessel and the *Effingham* narrow. The crew exchanged nervous glances and Wilcox sent two very British-sounding tars down into the hold.

"How can you be sure she's hostile?" Ram questioned, recalling the crew's earlier jokes about serving a hitch in the British navy if it weren't a "clear run."

"Look at the way she's runnin' at us full tilt. There's only one reason she'd charge us like that. They'll be tryin' to board and search . . . and seize what and who they can." Wilcox's face darkened even further and his voice hardened as if to settle his course in his own mind. "I won't heave to. If they want us, they'll have to scramble. If we're caught, there could be blood spilt."

Ram nodded somberly, only now realizing the hazard he had put them in by booking passage on an American vessel. But many American cargo vessels made safe passage and were welcomed in British ports for their raw materials, despite the well-publicized naval tensions between the two countries. He glanced at the captain's strained face and felt concern coil inside him.

The glass came up again and the captain lowered it almost immediately, his shoulders sagging fatalistically. "She's got a row of sixteen-pounders on each side . . . gunports open." He wheeled and began barking orders at the crew, who scrambled to execute them to the letter. The mate hurried up for a hushed conference and Ram made out the word "armory." Captain Wilcox paused; his lean jaw flexed and his brown eyes burned. But he shook his head and then delivered a terse order to the gaping mate.

Arlo came on deck just then and quickly encompassed the situation as Ram put it to him. He stood with arms crossed and neck shortened, glowering at the closing ship.

"Should I tell m'lady?" He glanced at Ram from the corner of his eye. By now he knew there'd been a row of some kind. Neither one had spoken ten words to him all day.

"She'll learn soon enough." Ram, leaning against the rail, closed the subject firmly.

The light frigate bore down on them and the open gunports became clearly visible to all. The captain sent a tar to suggest to the Tarkinghams and Mrs. MacLean that they stay in their cabins. The hatches were closed and padlocked, the ship's arms were removed from the armory and hidden away, and the ship's manifests and log were planted below floorboards in the tiny galley.

The pursuit narrowed. Signal flags became visible on the naval ship and Captain Wilcox snarled as he read them. His chin jutted a fraction more in defiance.

A resounding boom split the excruciating tension and a splash landed well short of the starboard bow. But she was gaining and all knew the next shot wouldn't fall so short. They were calling the *Effingham* to, first with flags, now with ball.

The second ball splashed critically close to the starboard hull and the third sheared a piece off the bowsprit. It was a delicate bit of gunnery, but Wilcox was in no mood to admire such finesse. Cursing stubbornly and shaking his fist at the bridge of the ship *Fierce Majestic*, he wavered and bitterly bowed to overwhelming force, ordering sail struck. Watching his crew scurry into the rigging again, he called for his sword and planted himself firmly on the bridge.

The *Fierce Majestic* drew alongside with ropes and hooks, her crew bristling with arms. Ram watched as planks were laid and the boarding party started across. He now recognized the captain's wisdom in not arming his smaller crew: blood would have flowed like the resentment that now crowded the *Effingham*'s deck.

A nattily uniformed young officer led the boarding party. He paused to station a contingent of men around the main deck and waved the rest of the party along after him. At the bottom of the steps to the quarterdeck, he glared up at the yankee captain's defiant posture. He mounted with increasingly loud steps, trailed by a surly quartet of armed sailors.

"First Officer Lieutenant Rupert Gladstone of *HMS Fierce Majestic*, sir," he saluted smartly. But only a second later an unmistakable sneer appeared. "In the name of His Majesty, King George, I order you to submit your vessel and its crew and contents to search and scrutiny," he intoned with practiced efficiency, resting a hand on the hilt of his blade and extending a rolled parchment toward Captain Wilcox.

"We've nothing of interest to the British Navy, sir." Wilcox found himself galled by this arrogant young wick's superior air. "Take yourself and your thugs off my ship and be gone!"

"I warn you, captain." The young man stiffened and determination aged his face remarkably. "I mean to search your vessel for deserters and contraband, with or without your cooperation. I should hate to have to forcibly remove you from your post and confine you to your quarters during my search." His tone conveyed that he would enjoy nothing more.

"You English peacock!" Wilcox thrust forward, his fists clenched at his sides. "You've no right to fire on a nonbelligerent vessel nor board a ship in the middle of the ocean. I'll not submit myself, my crew, nor my cargo to your indignities—"

The lieutenant was clearly prepared for such an eventuality and one hand movement sent the force behind him into action. A scuffle broke out as Arlo launched himself into the fray and Ram was forced to aid his rash friend. Tars swarmed over the *Effingham*'s rail and a general mélée ensued. The captain was wrestled to the deck, Arlo was cracked on the head and sank to a heap, and Ram was knocked, bludgeoned, and finally subdued by four of His Majesty's finest. Those of the *Effingham*'s crew that had joined the reckless fracas were bloodied and subdued. Those who had not chewed their anger silently.

"We were running from the Azores, already light on crew, when we ran into a severe storm a week back and lost three men." The lieutenant stared down at the lanky captain as if he positively enjoyed his futile straining. "By royal decree, we're empowered to search your vessel for deserters from the Royal Navy and return them to rightful service. Failing that, we're empowered to press into service British subjects of legal age and sound limb. Further, we shall seize contraband rum, all manufactured goods, and all other materials which might . . . pose any threat to the nation." He motioned to the sailors restraining Wilcox. "Take the good captain to his cabin and hold him there."

Some of the fight seemed to drain from the deck when the captain was removed to quarters below. The search progressed and contingents were sent to inspect the cargo and cabins. Ram's arms were bound at his sides and he was dragged and tethered to a lashing ring on the main deck. He shook his head, clearing it enough to think of Eden and what that scurvy lot might invent for her. His head was pounding and his jaw felt dislocated, but it was Eden's soft, defenseless image that gave him the most pain.

"A Scotsman," the officer paused above him, staring down with amusement at Ram's tartan and simple black coat, "how droll. Not likely that you're a deserter. Scots make notoriously poor sailors. In fact, they make notoriously poor anything."

Ram lifted a snarl to these cool taunts, but thought of unconscious Arlo and defenseless Eden and bit his tongue. His face reddened with restraint; the officer laughed shortly and strolled away.

The first contingent reported back from the cabins; there were three passengers below, one a fashionable lady, the others an English couple—cousins of Sir Ralph Edgerton, MP. No ship's log, no charts, no manifest could be found.

"The bastard's hidden it all," he snapped, sending them back for a closer look, with a caution to leave the passengers to him personally.

Then came the cargo contingent, with disappointing news; they'd found only bales of flax and cotton, some lumber, a bit of raw indigo, and only a crew's rum ration . . . nothing worth confiscating. And not an English-sounding sailor in the lot.

"Damn!" The lieutenant sent word to his captain and paced, jerkily, waiting for instructions. When they came, his mouth thinned and he stomped about the main deck, muttering and looking over the stony-eyed crew of the *Effingham*. "Him," he pointed to a muscular young sailor, "clearly a deserter. And him . . . him . . . and him." Each seaman he indicated was grabbed and throttled and dragged across to the *Majestic*, cursing and resisting.

Straightening, the lieutenant strode back to Ram and appraised the Scot's large, muscular frame and big hands. This one was no stranger to work, he mused, and clearly a British subject. Something about Ram's cool contempt goaded him into pointing his immaculately gloved hand again. "And him."

"Press me and you'll shorten your career to the length of this voyage." Ram struggled against the arms that tried to raise him to his feet.

"Brave threats from a man embarking on the low end of a naval career himself. Respect for rank is your first lesson, Scot." He drew back and smashed Ram across the mouth, bloodying his glove in the process.

Ram recovered swiftly. "I'm Laird Ramsay MacLean, son of the Earl of Skyelt, Scotland . . . a noble house of his *British* Majesty, King George. And I swear, you'll pay handsomely for the mistake of pressing me." The savage intensity of Ram's strong face made the officer step back and occupy himself with the irksome stain on his glove.

"You have no proof you're a nobleman, and therefore exempt."

"It's my man you've bashed on the quarterdeck." Ram saw his words take root.. Suddenly he wished he'd used his full title with the captain, instead of stubbornly traveling as plain Ramsay MacLean.

"I've no time to wait for his testimony . . . and no reason to believe it if I did."

"Then there's my wife."

"Wife?" the fair features sharpened with interest. "Your wife is on board? Where?"

"Below, in my cabin. Lady Eden MacLean . . . my bride. You may verify my identity with her."

"Indeed I shall." The officer regarded him with narrowed eyes and recalled that he'd not yet questioned the passengers . . . that "fashionable" lady. With a cold smile, he turned on his heel to make his way below.


Eden sat rigidly on the edge of a chair, watching the door and wringing her cold hands. They'd been boarded. She shivered and tried not to recall the stories she'd heard of privateers. The rangy seaman who had burst into her cabin earlier only asked questions; he didn't answer them. She had horrible visions of what might even now be happening on deck, and concern for Ram — and especially Arlo — coursed through her. They weren't men to suffer the will of others kindly. She could see the jut of Ram's square, stubborn chin in her mind's eye and could imagine all too well its potential for disaster. On the other hand, perhaps a little disaster. . . .

There were muffled voices from the passage and the door swung open. She lurched to her feet and suddenly faced a fair, slender young man in a dashing blue coat, cream-white breeches, and knee-high boots. He tucked his tricorn under one arm and paused to inspect her visually, bowing quite elegantly the next instant.

"Please forgive the intrusion." His face turned boyish with a charming smile.

"You're English!" Relief surged through her, weakening her legs, and she sat down abruptly, pressing her handkerchief to her temples and throat. "Thank God!"

"Royal Navy, madam." He took a step closer and extended his hand. "Permit me . . . First Officer Lieutenant Rupert Gladstone of the light frigate *HMS Fierce Majestic.*"

She wilted slightly and flushed at the worry caused by her overactive imagination. The lieutenant's pale eyes flew over her elegant blue challis dress and her ladylike form. He lingered over the unconscious allure of her fluttering lashes and blushing cheeks. He held her hand a moment before bending to apply to it a gentlemanly kiss.

"The seaman who came to my cabin hardly spoke, and after the cannonade I feared we were boarded by privateers. What a relief to find us in such safe hands."

"Unfortunately, your captain is not of like mind, madam. It took powder and ball to make him see the wisdom in laying to. But we have a mission to perform, searching for naval deserters and contraband." He smiled apologetically. "And I am bound to trouble you further, madam. One of the deserters claims to be a Scottish lord, naming you his wife and saying you will verify his identity."

"One of the Scots?" Eden's surprise was from hearing Ram labeled a "deserter," but she could see the lieutenant read it otherwise. "My *husband?*"

"I find it difficult to credit, madam, seeing you here. For such a lovely and refined gentlewoman to be wedded to a Scotsman . . . well! But I endeavor to be fair in these matters and must ask."

Eden straightened and felt heat spreading into her cold limbs. So she was asked to verify his identity, was she?

Now that it was convenient, she was his wife, was she?!

"I . . . am no man's wife, sir." She lifted a proud face to the lieutenant and straightened on the edge of her seat. "And I am surprised to hear that the gentleman in question would suggest such a thing. A Scottish lord, you say?"

"So he claims." The lieutenant relaxed on one leg and smiled his cool, captivating smile again. The defiant Scot hadn't been overly inventive in his ploy; perhaps he had flattered the lady and now hoped she might corroborate his story out of sympathy.

"Well, he certainly gave no evidence of nobility as far as I am concerned, lieutenant." Eden's serene expression hid a vengeful whim. "What will become of him, sir?"

"He'll be returned to sea duty aboard our ship."

"You're headed for England now, then?"

"Yes, miss. . . ."

"Marlow. Eden Marlow. I'm traveling home . . . after a visit with relations." Eden gave him her most dazzling smile, thinking that if he were given pause, he might realize that she seemed to be traveling unescorted. She rose and extended him her hand, allowing him to step nearer as he held it.

"I live with my . . . aunt, Mistress Prudence Dunleavy of Sherborne, Dorsetshire." She said it thinking only that Mistress Dunleavy would certainly be surprised to hear she had Eden Marlow for a niece.

"I am sometimes through Dorsetshire. What a lucky coincidence," he purred much too intimately, making Eden wonder if she'd done her work too well. But then he pressed her hand ardently and stepped away.

"Sorry to have troubled you, Miss Marlow. Duty calls . . . until we meet again." His bow was courtliness itself and Eden nodded sweetly to acknowledge it. He backed to the door and was gone.

Eden collapsed into the chair and tried to collect

264

herself as she listened for him to return. But all remained quiet and some minutes later she crept to the door and peered into the passage. It was empty and she sagged with vengeful relief. She'd just purchased Ramsay MacLean a separate passage to England . . . at His Majesty's expense.

Ram watched the irksome first officer donning his gloves once more as he stepped on deck. There was an irritating smugness to his hard, young mouth and Ram's ire rose as he swaggered over and paused.

"Stupid bastard . . . did you really expect she'd lie for you?" He turned to the crusty hands standing guard over Ram. "Take him."

"What?" Ram struggled in earnest as they dragged him to his feet. "What did she say? That's my *wife*, I tell you . . let me see her!"

"Get him across to the *Majestic*," the lieutenant barked, buttoning his stained gloves, "and be quick about it!"

"I'm so sorry, m'lady." Arlo's slope-shouldered misery struck a guilty chord in Eden as they sat on the deck the next morning. But the guilt was for provoking the faithful manservant's worry more than for her part in Ram's impressment. After all, he'd disclaimed her as his wife in all respects; it was only right she speak the truth when questioned. Ramsay MacLean was as much to blame for his fate as she was. But still, when she looked at Arlo's lined, haggard face, conscience nagged at her.

When the *Fierce Majestic* had broken off its raid and sailed away, Captain Wilcox had had Arlo carried to Eden's cabin and she had bandaged his head and tended him during the long night just past. Over and over he'd roused and asked about his laird, and each time Eden

responded with the meager report the captain had giv
her: Ramsay MacLean had been charged with deserti
and taken aboard the *Majestic* to serve his term at se

"If I just hadn'ta been so rash," Arlo now moane
wiping his blocky hands down over his face and squinti
to rid his vision of a double vision of everything. H
head ached from the effort. "I wouldn't have been layi
cold on the deck when they took Laird Ram. It's n
fault —

"No more than it's mine . . . or anyone else's." Th
she thought it best to show concern over Ram's fat
"What will they make him do as a sailor, do you think
It was the captain's voice that answered.

"They'll spend a few days teachin' him military disc
pline."

"Discipline?" Eden's eyes flew wide and the capta
nodded gravely.

"Then when they've had their fun, they'll work him t
he drops and then work him some more. They'll give 'r
every dangerous and dirty job there is on a ship . . .
hope to God he can swim."

Eden looked to Arlo, a horrified question in her eye

"Aye, he can swim, a'right. But he's not one for taki
abuse and turnin' the other cheek," Arlo answered, inte
sifying her concern in the process.

"No." A vision of Ram's stubborn jaw and the memo
of his inflexible resolve flashed through her mind. "He
certainly not one to forgive and forget." The conclusio
rattled her thoroughly. She'd imagined him swabbin
decks, hauling rope, being ordered about . . . forced t
hard manual labor. Her heart began to thud a bit harde
and her stomach tightened. She'd never thought of poss
ble dangers or of the military discipline meted out t
deserters . . . or worse. "Can they actually make hir
serve in the Royal Navy?"

"For the time he's on the *Majestic*, he's a seaman in Hi

Majesty's Navy—like it or not," the captain answered tersely.

"But he's a laird," Arlo declared pugnaciously. "They canna press a laird, can they?"

"A lord, you mean?" The captain was caught off guard. "Ramsay MacLean's a nobleman?" He looked from Arlo to Eden and back.

"Heir to the Earl of Skyelt, with estates near the Tay River in the midst of Scotland," Arlo supplied, his face growing hopeful. Eden nodded a reluctant verification when the startled captain looked at her.

"Well, that certainly changes things, at least in the long term. Once they make port in England he can slip off the ship and contact a magistrate . . . or the ministry itself— and have the lot of them up on charges." The captain's face went from dour to delighted. "Almighty heaven, what I'd give to be there when they find out they've pressed a peer of the realm and will pay for it with their commissions!"

"Thank God Almighty fer that." Arlo buried his aching face in his hands and propped his elbows on his knees. Then his head jerked up. "How long do ye think, a'fore they make port?"

The captain mulled it over. "Three—maybe four weeks yet at sea . . . possibly more with bad weather. Then there'll be time spent in holding and in the courts—or before a tribunal. Two or three months, I'd guess, and you'll have your husband back, mad—*my lady.*"

A weak smile was the best she could manage, hoping it passed for strained relief. Arlo brightened and boldly patted her hand.

"Don't trouble yer head, m'lady. He'll be back wi' ye before ye know it. And I'm sure 'tis only thoughts of you will comfort him in his trials."

That same evening, Eden again joined Arlo on deck. He was staring out over the railing as if trying to pierce the distance for some glimpse of his laird's fate. She respected his seeming need for silence and took a seat on a nearby crate. For a long while neither spoke.

"I expect you're a bit concerned, m'lady." He finally turned to her, his square face serious. "I'll see ye to Skyelt, m'lady, just like Laird Ram would'ave."

Eden didn't know what to say . . . she hadn't really thought that far ahead when she helped rid herself of the encumbrance of an unwilling husband. She would send word to her family as soon as they made landfall, letting them know she was safe . . . and then what? Go back to Boston, to the safety and the comfort of their protection? Images of her family's faces, sorrowful or horrified by her fate, paraded through her mind and she shuddered, aching at the shame she'd cause them. She'd be a disgrace or an object of pity, neither a very appealing prospect.

What else was there if she didn't go back to Boston? She'd have to earn her way, somehow . . . a teaching post with Mistress Dunleavy, perhaps, supervising hygiene deportment, and ritual high teas, and enduring overbearing parents. She felt suddenly claustrophobic at the idea. *Not* Mistress Dunleavy's. . . .

She sighed. What if she let Arlo take her on to Skyelt? How long would it be before his lordship came home, denounced her as the traitor she was, and turned her out? She had no delusions left about his harsh and self-righteous nature. Nothing in him had softened to her, not even when she'd given him all the willingness and tenderness she could. After this betrayal and the humiliation—and possible abuse—he suffered, he'd be lusting for vengeance, not for her.

But no matter where she went, no matter what course she chose, there would always be the threat that Ramsay MacLean would show up . . . and she'd have to face the consequences. Perhaps it was best to go on to Skyelt and have it out, right and proper, when he returned. Even if she were sent packing, at least it would be settled between them. An unwelcome lump came into her throat.

"Skyelt . . . tell me about it, Arlo." She was making her final decision.

He had grown progressively more troubled by her silence, but now brightened, eager to talk of his home.

"Ah it's a fair place, m'lady. Wide, rollin' hills an' green valleys. Half of th' old castle still stands, an' the house were build around it. Quarried the stone from nearby, so it's true Skyelt, it is. Half the folk of Skyelt live in or near the house . . . which is only proper, since half of them is kin to the laird in some way."

"And family—tell me about the family."

Here Arlo swallowed hard; his smile wavered before he bolstered it with his determination.

"There ain't much to tell. Laird Ram's mother died when he was young, and old Haskell, he never married again. The house is run by Mrs. McKay, the housekeeper. She's as much family as anyone, I guess. And there's Terrance, the steward, a fine man—honest an' hard workin'."

"And Ramsay's brothers and sisters?" Eden chose that moment to rearrange herself on her hard seat.

"He . . . don't have any." Arlo looked away briefly and muttered under his breath, "at least, none to speak of."

Eden settled and sighed. "Tell me about his father. I gather they don't get on very well. What is 'old Haskell' like? Is he really quite old?" She conjured pictures of a frail, bitter old man, desperately clinging to life in hopes of seeing his line continued in a grandchild.

"Now," Arlo fidgeted, "ye must understand, m'lady, old Haskell MacLean . . . he takes a bit of gettin' used to."

"So does Ramsay MacLean." Her eyes narrowed for emphasis. "*Like father, like son*, I suppose."

"Not *like father, like son*, milady. It be a shameful truth, they don't get on together an' ne'er have. But it's because Laird Ram ain't like old Haskell at all—"

Eden was thinking if it were the case, she and Ramsay's father might get on rather well, but kept it to herself.

"Old Haskell, he ain't got much head for workin' the land and Laird Ram, well, he's alwus thinkin' up some way to improve the flocks or the water or the crops. Laird Ram's a real man o' parts!"

Eden stiffened, shocked. "Really, Arlo. I'd rather not hear such unsavory details—"

Arlo scowled at her sudden withdrawal, then flushed violently as he caught the bend of her thoughts. "Oh, *no*, m'lady, not *them* parts! I meant he's a man o' learned parts . . . a 'man o' parts,' you know . . . been to the univer-sity in Edinburgh, he was. I were there with 'im a while, but I got to longin' for Skyelt and he sent me home."

"Ramsay at a university?" She sat back, astonished. "Do you mean to tell me he actually took a degree from the University of Edinburgh?"

"Oh, I'm sure he never took it unless he paid for it, m'lady. Laird Ram don't hold with stealin'. He's right fastidious about that, he is."

Eden had to chew her lip to keep a sober face, but her eyes began to water. She swallowed hard and took a deep breath before attempting to answer.

"Fastidious." It seemed to be one of Arlo's favorite words where Ram was concerned. "Indeed . . . tell me more."

# Chapter Fourteen

Eden arched her back and felt her spine groan. For four days since leaving the normal coach route, they'd labored through the rocky Scottish countryside aboard these swaying, plowfooted horses. Every night she'd massaged her sore rump and sworn she'd not climb back on the pathetic creature again. And every morning she had surrendered, putting her foot in Arlo's waiting hands and settled into the worn saddle.

The nearer they got, the more effusive Arlo's renderings of the place became. Exhaustion and tension combined to produce visions of a heavenly Skyelt with marble floors, down mattresses, stately beds awash in lush tapestries, and soothing hot baths. She'd never wanted anything more than she wanted to get to "grand" and "bonnie" Skyelt.

Ahead of her, Arlo suddenly straightened in the saddle and jerked off the path to head for a small creek overhung by jagged rock formations. Joy burst upon his face as he turned back and flung a stubby finger at the crest of a nearby rise.

"Up there!" He was racing hard for the grassy knoll, the pack horses following dutifully along behind him. At the top of the hill he stopped to wait for her and to stare down at his home with aching eyes.

Eden pulled back on the reins and halted beside him, resettling her riding bonnet on her head with one hand. Her eyes widened at the velvety panorama of the valley below. Never in her life had she seen such green—deep, translucent, mesmerizing green. Here and there were small stands of trees, but most of the lush valley was a carpet of verdant summer grasses that were interrupted only by an occasional rock wall or the cutting flow of a stream. Sheep were pastured about the valley in small flocks, giving the place a tranquil, timeless air. And from the distant center of this opulent tableau rose a gleaming pair of round white towers from a cluster of sprawling stone structures. It was the great hall of Skyelt; from Arlo's glowing description, it could be nothing else.

Eden's breath caught in her throat. She glanced at Arlo and found him transported to some fairer realm as he stared raptly at his home. But as she looked at the proud, sun-drenched spires, she couldn't help wondering what awaited her in their regal domain. She was a lady, she reminded herself, despite all that had had occurred. Her well-learned manners would do her credit before her husband's noble relations, no matter how exalted their standards.

"There she is, m'lady, Skyelt herself." He paused and the light in his face dimmed briefly. He'd intended to say more, but he shook off the urge and headed down the gentle slope for the grand castle.

Strangely, the white of the towers grayed as the two descended the hills, and patches of scraggly, overgrazed brown appeared on the lush green hillsides. Eden watched the splendor of her first vision of Skyelt fade. The structures that huddled around the old castle towers were indeed stone, but they were a higgledy-piggledy lot, thrown up without much forethought . . . nor afterthought, judging from their need of repair. Cows wandered freely about the land outside the complex, through what appeared to be kitchen gardens guarded halfheartedly by meagerly clad children.

The children gawked at Eden, and when they recognized Arlo they abandoned all pretense of their task to follow along, asking questions about his far journey that Arlo answered with generous humor. Soon tartan-clad adults joined them, waving and yelling greetings at Arlo, and staring at Eden to whisper amongst themselves. Eden summoned her most erect posture and tried to ignore their bold assessments.

Eventually they passed through a stone-and-timber gate that marked some division of the complex and all but a few of their followers turned away. Beyond was a wide expanse of bare dirt graced only by neglected and overgrown grass and unclipped bushes. The sloping area was ringed by a low stone wall; beyond it, Arlo pointed toward a fine view of the lower part of the valley. Pride swelled his chest and Eden forced a smile. When he shifted in his saddle and swept his other hand toward the entrance to the great hall of Skyelt, nothing could keep the smile on her face.

It looked like a ramshackle Norman fortress. The stonework needed mortar badly, and the huge iron-bound siege doors were weathered and splintered, leaving some cracks large enough to admit a man's hand. Far above were windows, little larger than old arrow slits, covered by faded shutters. All around, a plethora of weeds and dead vines clawed at the old walls, looking as if they might succeed in bringing them down at any moment. Arlo's face was beaming.

"Welcome—"

Eden was spared the trial of responding on a positive note.

Thrashing and grappling through the half-opened doors came three men clad in tartan—two in the familiar burnt-red, the third in a somber dark blue-and-green. The reds had the advantage, though not by much, and seemed to be ushering the furious blue kilt violently from the hall.

"Damn you, Terrance MacCrenna—I've a right—He's got to answer me!" The captive twisted and lunged furiously, trying to plant his heels and free his arms for a good swing.

"Ye'll get nowhere like this, Cavender!" Red-faced Terrance grappled awkwardly, trying to assure he found no foothold. "Go home, man . . . I'll send ye word when 'tis settled!"

*No!* I won' leave till I know what th' old bastard plans to do with 'er! I give my word in pledge!" Cavender wrested one arm free and managed a slow swing that Terrance was able to dodge.

A guttural, thunderous roar issued from inside the hall and the frantic scene froze momentarily. A storm of animal fury launched through the opening, banging both massive doors back against the stone and leaving them quivering in its wake. A massive human form charged across the dusty courtyard and Terrance MacCrenna and his helper abandoned their charge, scrambling back hastily. Flesh met flesh and a sickening thud resounded from the packed ground as the two men landed and wrestled briefly. The smacking of bone and muscle reverberated off the stone wall and echoed about the court.

Everything suddenly stilled. The hapless Cavender had all but disappeared beneath the crush of bulk and hair and burnt-red tartan. After a moment, the bearish, red-kilted victor rolled to one side and collapsed back in the dirt himself. And from his prostrate form came another howling roar that ended in something like: "—rance!"

"Yea, Laird Haskell—I'm here." Lanky Terrance hurried over, scowling, and offered him a hand up.

"Damn it! I'm no p-pulin' milksop!" Haskell MacLean smacked Terrance's hand away roughly and strained up to a weaving seat on the ground. "Put the cuddy on 'is horse and get 'im outta my sight—damn 'is hide!" he roared, grabbing his head between big, hard hands as if to hold it together. A second later he hitched his feet around and steadied himself before lurching up to stagger back toward the doors.

"Damn it all!" he snarled, pausing to glare at Terrance's dark face. "Can't a man have a s-scrap o' pleasure wi'out bein' hounded clear to hell to pay fer it?! My head—" His hands came up to keep it from rolling off his shoulders and he charged back into the hall roaring, "Ale! Where is that stupid cow—I want me ale *now!*"

Eden sat in shock, her jaw drooping, her eyes big as saucers. She saw Arlo look at her and managed to close her mouth.

"That . . . that. . . ." She couldn't seem to get it out.

". . . were old Laird Haskell MacLean . . . Laird Ram's pa." Arlo winced at the shock turning to horror in her face. "I said he'd take a bit o' gettin' used to." To escape the accusation of her shock, he dismounted jerkily. He was caught up immediately in Terrance's rough embrace.

"*Arlo!* Bless me—you're a sight for sore eyes!" Terrance whomped him wildly on the back and Arlo responded with a growling hug that lifted the slighter MacCrenna's feet just off the ground. When he was back on firm footing, Terrance craned his head, looking through Eden and around the pack horses for something. "And Laird Ram? Where's he? Did he not return wi' ye?"

"Nay, 'e's been . . . delayed. It's a story, Terrance. But I brought 'is bride. . . ." Arlo pulled away from Terrance's grasp and extended a hand to her, speaking with heavy emphasis, "Lady *Eden . . . Marlow . . . MacLean.*" It took a moment, but Terrance's eyes widened with recognition and shortly a grin spread across his features.

"Well . . . she's all that was said . . . an' a site more!" His lean face lit as he examined her quite openly. He

275

stared appreciatively at her velvet-clad bosom and nicely rounded bottom, then at her creamy skin, curving lips, and striking eyes. And a slow smile gave way to a faintly wicked grin of delight.

Eden stiffened and sent them both her most disapproving look, forcing Arlo to recall his manners.

"Ah . . . m'lady, this be Terrance MacCrenna, Steward o' Skyelt and me own father's brother's son. We was raised like brothers, Terrance an' me."

"Pleased to meet you, Mr. MacCrenna. I've heard much about you from Arlo." Eden felt her words leave her lips but could scarcely believe they stood there politely making introductions after what she'd just witnessed.

"Welcome, m'lady." Terrance drew a clenching breath and nodded.

"*—rance!*" An echoing bellow issued from the doors of the great hall and Terrance tossed a startled look over his shoulder.

"Ah, ye come at a bad time, Arlo. . . ." He wheeled and strode quickly to the doors.

"How long this time?" Arlo called after him.

"Two bloody long days!"

Arlo shuddered and made to follow, but Eden's furious glare pierced him halfway there and he turned back.

"Sorry, m'lady." He held his arms up to help her down. The minute her feet touched the ground, he abandoned her again, heading for the doors. She had no choice but to follow, her ire rising.

Inside, the great hall seemed in far better repair. Eden stood just inside the door, staring around her at the vaulting space that centered on a massive stone fireplace and a huge oak table and chairs. Faded tapestries hung about the walls and worn carpets covered the stone floor here and there. There was a huge wooden trunk against the far wall, a heavy, carved chest nearby, and miscellaneous stuffed heads of deer hung about the walls. The iron

276

torch brackets and chandelier had been refitted for candles, but for now the hall was as dark as the mood of its laird.

"*Dam-me* . . . what am I supposed to do wi' the little witch?" Haskell slouched drunkenly in a huge carved chair at the head of the table. Around him were emptied and overturned pitchers. He ran a big, tough hand down over his ruddy face and gray-speckled beard. "Damn th' woman! Sendin' me a bairn after all this time—"

"Laird Haskell." Terrance stood nearby, but not too near, trying to reason with him. "Come away to bed an' get some rest, now. Yer head'll be clearer in th' morn and ye can decide—"

"Coin—that's what she be wantin', Ter-rance . . . an' a bit o' revenge in th' bootle."

"Like enough." Terrance stepped closer and kicked a metal pitcher across the floor to where a gawking servant girl waited to snatch it up.

"She 'ad a nasty streak in 'er, that woman . . . alwus did. Don' know what I e'er saw in 'er, Ter-rance."

If Terrance was tempted to remind him, he thought better of it and tried again to persuade him. "This won' settle nothin', m'laird. Ye canna keep this up . . . day an' night, night an' day."

"I'll drink me own brew, man, how-ever, when-ever I please!" Haskell jutted forward and bellowed. But Terrance didn't flinch. "Jus' look at 'er!" Haskell flung a furious hand toward a nearby chair then scooped up a tankard and poured the contents down. The metal crashed against the table again and he glared at the form huddled defiantly in the big chair. "Wild as a mountain goat, wi' claws like a she-lion and a tongue like an adder! She bit me, Terrance . . . *bit me!*"

"Touch me agin an' I'll bite yer bloody hand off— *Father!*" a female voice growled.

"Carina, please!" Terrance pleaded, his arms open at

277

his sides.

Eden felt a nudge from behind and stepped further in, dimly aware of others pushing through in the doorway behind her. She stared in astonishment at a young girl in a dark tartan skirt and drawstring blouse, huddled so tight against a chair at the table that she hadn't been noticeable at first. Long, burnished hair swirled around her shoulders, and in profile the set of her jaw seemed vaguely familiar.

"I'll more'n touch you, girl, if you e'er bite me again!" He was on the edge of his seat now. "You'll keep a civil tongue an' do as yer told from now on."

"*If* it pleases me." The girl jumped to her feet and stood with petite shoulders back and eyes blazing. "Just like you, Laird Haskell . . . I won't do anythin' that don' please *me!*" She whirled and strode to the far door of the hall, pushing past a wad of gawking servants on her way out.

"Damn it!" Haskell swore, bouncing his already battered tankard on the stone floor and taking grim satisfaction from the way it jumped and clattered. At least something in this house behaved the way it should.

Arlo saw Eden's pale face from the corner of his eye and turned stealthily toward her. "M'lady . . . we come at a verra bad time. I'll show 'e up to Laird Ram's rooms and later ye can—"

"I'm sure I won't be staying." Eden turned to him with belated anger. "This place is fit for neither—"

"Who's that, Terrance?" Haskell demanded, pointing toward the entrance and weaving with the effort of forcing his eyes to the same place.

"Arlo," Both Terrance and Arlo answered at once.

"Arlo?" Haskell's body went taut. "An' where's my son? Ram, where's Ram?" He pushed to stand by his massive chair and swayed. Arlo hurried down the steps to meet the laird as he groped toward them, going from

278

chair to chair.

"Laird Ram was . . . delayed," Arlo answered carefully, and Eden made mental note. Even drunk as a skunk, the laird was not a man to be trifled with. Her nose curled as she caught a whiff of the stale-brew smell of him.

"But I brought 'is bride on ahead . . . Lady Eden." Arlo gestured to her just before Haskell engulfed him in a crushing embrace. It took a moment to register and Haskell raised a pair of red-rimmed eyes toward Eden, quickly finishing with Arlo to heave himself up the steps toward her.

*"Eden Marlow?"* he demanded. "This be Eden Marlow? My bonnie Con-stance's bonnie daugh-ter? Gawd! Who else? Look at 'er—the spittin' image of her ma." He stuck a bleary face near hers and ran his hand down the side of her face and across her shoulder with insulting familiarity, despite her shrinking. "Damme, if he hasn't gone an' done it! I told ye' Terrance . . . he'd do the job. He's gone an' got her . . . *married* her, Terrance!"

Euphoria temporarily robbed him of what little judgment was left to him by drink. He pulled the red-faced Eden into his arms and whirled her around.

"Set me down, you—you—" she sputtered, horrified and yet somehow unable to vent it fully.

He did set her on her feet, but only to free his hands for an even closer inspection of her. He felt her back, the snug fit of the velvet about her small waist, laughing delightedly despite her pushing and protests.

"Just like 'er ma, I tell ye!" Then came the final indignity: he grabbed her buttocks through her riding skirt and petticoats and slid his hands around her hips, examining them roughly. "An' built fer bearin'—just like 'er ma!"

He released her with a raucous laugh and pivoted toward Terrance just as Eden hauled back to knocked him silly. Arlo caught her arm and she jerked around, furious with humiliation. He was glad her virulent words were drowned out by Haskell's booming laughter.

"He's done it, Terrance! An' ye said it'd never work. Married her, he did . . . married!" He strode to his steward and clasped him in a hug so savage that the slighter Terrance staggered. Then something happened and Terrance braced and staggered again. In Terrance's protective grip, Haskell slid slowly to the floor and the steward lowered his laird's head to the stone gently. All was silent for a second as Terrance rose and gazed long-sufferingly at Haskell.

"Thank the Good Laird. I tho't he'd never go out."

A clamor of muffled laughter and voices broke out around the hall and Eden turned angrily, wrenching her arm from Arlo's apologetic grip. A score of Skyelt's residents had crept into the hall behind them and witnessed the entire degrading episode. From their comments and the good-natured shakes of their heads, they had witnessed such before with their laird.

"Sorry, m'lady—honest. He was drunk an' not thinkin' clear." Arlo tried to talk to her, blocking her attempt to reach the doors.

"Aye, m'lady." Terrance joined him, shoulder to shoulder, preventing her escape.

"I shan't stay in this. . . ." her eyes swept the aging hall with icy contempt, "*place* . . . another minute. I'll not be subjected to further mauling at that creature's will."

"M'lady." Terrance ventured a hand on her arm with raw pleading in his face, "He'll be purely mortified on the morrow." *That* was stretching things a bit, Terrance knew. But he was desperate to keep the daughter of the much-sung Constance under his laird's roof. "Please, m'lady, let me take you up to yer rooms an' we'll fetch in yer things. Ye mon give us a chance to show our best, now that ye seen our worst. An' I expect you could use a good rest—" What else did ladies fancy? "an' a warsh after yer hard journey."

A *warsh*. She didn't know whether it was the promise of a bath or the extraordinary plea in the lean steward's face, but something punctured her inflated ire. She glared from Terrance to Arlo and back. She was saddle-bruised, dirty, exhausted, probably not thinking clearly herself. In fact, the terms of her welcome to Skyelt were so bizarre, she could not help but think she must have only imagined part of it. She drew herself up with every scrap of refinement and dignity she could summon.

"Then I shall expect an apology tomorrow." She raised her chin and stared hard at Terrance. "And if it is not forthcoming, I shall be forced to leave immediately." He sighed and nodded, waving her toward the long flight of curving stone steps. But she hesitated, catching red-faced Arlo's gaze in an accusing glare.

"And you said they were nothing alike."

Terrance showed her up the stone steps and down a wide, plastered hallway to rooms that had obviously been added to Skyelt at a time when some laird was feeling unusually generous. Unfortunately, little had been done to change or improve the place since then. The furnishings were massive, ornately carved Jacobean pieces, the carpets of good quality but now quite faded, and most of the color had washed from the rich window and bed drapes as well.

Three enormous French leaded windows commanded a breathtaking view of the lower valley. While Eden approached to stare out, Terrance said something and withdrew, leaving her to her thoughts for a moment.

Her shoulders rounded; her rigid composure left her. This was Ramsay MacLean's home, his beloved Skyelt . . . his crazy father. Her hands were cold despite the temperate weather. She rubbed them together briskly and paced away, pausing by the massive bed. Her eyes lingered on the faded green and gold of the coverlet and a pang of longing caught her unexpectedly.

She turned sharply and found herself facing a large-boned woman with a softly aged face and lively brown eyes. Her first strong impressions were of strength and of feminine wisdom, and immediately she knew the woman's identity.

"Mrs. MacKay."

"That I am, Lady Eden." The woman stepped closer and Eden assessed her dignified gray woolen dress and immaculate white apron as Mrs. McKay took in Eden's fashionable green velvet riding habit, her impeccable carriage, her sun-blushed face and striking eyes.

"I am glad to meet you. Arlo has . . . spoken of you rather freely."

"He would. I assure you, Lady Eden, the only thing loose about Arlo MacCrenna is his tongue. Think none the less of him for it . . . he is a man, after all, and therefore subject to the errors of the flesh." And the staunch housekeeper smiled, which altered her sober face remarkably. "I expect he's worn your ears aplenty in bringin' you along."

"Well, he did try to inform me. . . ." Eden reddened as she thought of how little everything at Skyelt resembled Arlo's descriptions.

"An' made a peacock from a wren in the tellin'," Mrs. MacKay guessed from the look in Eden's eyes and her attempt to hide it by looking away. She sighed and crossed her arms about her waist. "There be no good in tryin' to conceal it from ye, m'lady," the pragmatist in Mrs. MacKay advised. "Ye come at a . . . difficult time. Haskell's in a stew, and when he gets like this, there's no reasonin' with 'im. An' if he takes to the keg. . . ." She threw up her hands and went to the bed, hauling back the coverlet to check the freshness of the bare ticking on mattress and bolsters.

"I'm afraid I don't understand what's happened."

Snatches of what she'd witnessed in the great hall came back to her. "Something about that young girl?"

"Carina Graham . . . aye." Mrs. MacKay folded one of the huge pillows against her and her face became pensive. "Her mother sent 'er to Haskell, sayin' he must do a father's duty by 'er and see to 'er future. Just packed her up an' sent her here wi'out a by-your-leave."

"A father's duty? I don't understand."

"Haskell's her father, of course." Mrs. MacKay's mouth tightened and she avoided Eden's puzzled look. "Now he's saddled with her, sixteen and a woman grown . . . and her wild as a mountain goat. Got his temper, she has, an' twice the devil on her tongue."

"Haskell's her father? But Ramsay has no brothers nor sisters. . . ."

Mrs. MacKay looked pained. "None by the same mother, 'tis true. Haskell's had but one wife and she give him but one bairn, Laird Ram. But Haskell's the lass's father, true enough." She bit back whatever else she meant to say, then hauled the other bolster up and carried both to the door.

Eden stood watching her go, absorbing the knowledge that Ram had a young sister . . . an illegitimate sister. Her eyes narrowed as she thought of Arlo's craftily vague responses to her questions about Ramsay's family. It was just one more thing she had been misled about!

"I'll send the girl up to make up the bed, m'lady. Will you be needin' anything else?" Mrs. MacKay paused by the door.

"A bit of water to wash? Is there a tub?" Anywhere else it would have been an insult to inquire whether there were a tub in the house. But Mrs. MacKay seemed to think it a natural question.

"Indeed. I'll see it's brought up and have the girl fetch water." And Mrs. MacKay left the room with a brisk nod.

The door closed. Eden made her way to a lion-footed

chair and settled on it gingerly. She'd been unwilling to believe her mother could have possibly known old Haskell in the biblical sense, as Ramsay put it. But from the way he acted, Ram's father must have known her mother in a very familiar way. And she'd pictured Ramsay's father as a wasting, desperate old man . . . he was more like a great, guzzling, graying bear. She'd thought Haskell was desperate for a grandchild because Ramsay was an only child . . . but he had a sister, albeit an illegitimate one. She'd thought Skyelt a rare and marvelous prize, one for which stern Ramsay MacLean was willing to debase and force a young girl. But Skyelt was far from Camelot. Nothing was as it was supposed to be!

What did any of it matter? She was staying just long enough to have it out with Ramsay MacLean, anyway. Then she'd never have to bother with him or his crazy family or his faded Skyelt again.

"Well, this hasn't been used in a long time." Eden stooped to swipe a finger through the dirt on the hip bath that was trundled in. "It shall have to be scrubbed thoroughly before it can be used." She looked purposefully at the dark-haired girl and it took a minute, but the girl blinked.

"Ye want me to do it?"

"Yes, I do." Eden nodded with an authoritative smile. "Reluctant servants" was a subject Mistress Dunleavy had covered in depth. "What is your name, girl?"

"Maisie, m'lady." And the girl went off, her lips moving silently.

Maisie returned with a brush and a basin and set to work on the hip bath. Soon it was clean, and by the time the sun was lowering on the far heath, it was filled with water and waiting. At Eden's request, Maisie undid her laces and then held a sheet of toweling up for a screen as Eden slipped from her clothes. Maisie's eyebrows rose higher with every garment Eden shed and she jerked her

284

face away from the sight of the lady's bare skin. Shivering, Eden grabbed the sides of the hip bath and sank into it wearily.

"Agh!" she shot up, "It's *freezing!*" She snatched the sheeting from the shocked servant girl and clamped it around her body. "That water's icy cold!"

"It be fresh — I swear! I brung it straight from the well meself!"

"With not a thought of heating it, I suppose," she growled. "The temperature shock could give a body heart failure. The standards in this place are appalling. A bath requires *hot* water, Maisie — heated in kettles and carried up!" She advanced on the tight-lipped maid with eyes snapping. "Fetch me some *hot* water, please!"

Maisie stiffened and ran from the chamber, slamming the heavy door behind her. Eden started after her, but was halted at the door: the sound of voices came from the hallway beyond, and she was still undressed.

". . . *hot water!*" Maisie was complaining to someone. "An' the hussy stripped off all her clothes — right down to the skin!"

"Apparently, ladies . . . English ones in particular . . . bathe more often than we do," Mrs. MacKay's low tones answered.

"Why? Because they be dirtier'n us?" Maisie demanded sullenly.

"It be just their way, girl. Like bathin' in a tub —"

"—instead o' the crick like honest folk."

"Maisie!" Mrs. MacKay lowered her voice, "She's Lady here now and howe'er queer her ways, ye'll do well to hold yer tongue and do as yer told. Now see if there be coals left in the kitchens and fetch some water to heat." If Maisie said more, it was swallowed by the clack of Mrs. MacKay's heels as they left her.

Eden fled, scarlet-faced, back to the tub and rearranged the sheet to conceal all but her head as the rapping came on the door.

"My apologies, m'lady. Maisie didn't know about the hot water. Ye must see, we're not used to havin' a proper lady in Skyelt. Hasn't been a mistress here since Laird Ram's mother died . . . and him a wee lad. It's been more'n a score of years . . . and things get . . . lax." Eden thought she saw a trace of color in the housekeeper's cheeks.

"It's . . . understandable." Something in the woman's manner made Eden want to soften her criticism of Skyelt's ways. And then another thought struck her. "Ramsay's mother died when he was quite young? And Laird Haskell never married again?"

"No, m'lady." Mrs. MacKay turned abruptly and started for the door.

"Not even Carina Graham's mother?"

"No, m'lady. He took a vow never to marry again." And she left briskly, leaving Eden's other questions unasked.

Eden climbed up on the edge of the bed to ponder this latest bit of Skyelt history. Haskell lost Ramsay's mother and vowed never to marry again. Well, it partly explained why Carina was born out of wedlock. But it seemed a hasty vow to make . . . and cruel indeed to keep. But then, perhaps his love for Ramsay's mother had eclipsed all else at the time. The MacLean men had a positive genius for acting in haste and repenting at leisure.

Her bath, when it finally arrived, proved more irritating than soothing, with Maisie in resentful attendance. The few words Eden managed to draw from her revealed that she'd been assigned as lady's maid and was anything but keen on it. Nor was she keen on the fact that Mrs. MacKay sent her up later with a tray for Eden's supper: it was more special treatment, Eden surmised from Maisie's sour looks. Eden bit her tongue and tried to act the true lady during Maisie's pouting service. If the girl didn't come 'round, she told herself sternly, she'd simply ask for someone else to be assigned. No sense in alienating the household over an uncooperative snit.

"Ye mon tell me all about it, Arlo . . . every bleedin' detail." Haskell sat forward in his great charved chair the very next afternoon and rubbed his hands together in anticipation. Without conscious thought, Terrance sat forward in his seat at the laird's right hand and Mrs. MacKay came closer and slid into a chair at one side of the massive table in the great hall. The laird of Skyelt possessed unearthly powers of recuperation and had risen about noon in a smart humor and with a monumental appetite.

"Come on, man!"

Arlo, seated at his laird's left hand, glanced about the hall at the suspicious timing of household tasks that brought half the staff into the hall just when that fateful command was given.

"Well, when we got to Dorset, she were leavin' for Boston an' we had to pay extra to book passage on th' same ship. Laird Ram—he don't do well at sea and milady nursed 'im back to health."

"I trow she did," Haskell licked his lips and his eyes glowed as he looked around. "Hot tatties, that one. I be a judge o' womanflesh an' I can tell."

"Well . . ." Arlo took a deep breath and forged ahead, "she didn' take to him right off. He done what he could, but she'd have none of him."

"Playin' coy, she was . . . ladies do." Haskell's grin faded a bit.

"But Laird Ram got right friendly wi' her brother, James," Arlo continued, beginning to worry as he mentally sorted through the details of how his laird had acquired Eden Marlow for a bride. "An' when we landed, this James invited m'laird to some fancy-dress ball her family give. Laird Ram, he spent a pretty coin on fancy clothes and went, thinkin' to warm 'er up a bit wi' his polished self. But it were for naught. She'd be havin' none of him, dressed up like a cock pheasant or not."

"What did he do to make her come 'round?" Haskell demanded, rubbing his hands together in anticipation and staring hard at Arlo.

"I was comin' to that." Arlo began to squirm, glancing around at their broadening audience. Word of Arlo's accounting was obviously spreading; Charlie, the iron-smith, just stepped in the door, leather apron, soot, and all.

"He . . . ah . . . convinced her and the vows was read before a parson in her father's parlor. Then straightaway we boarded the ship to come home. That was when th' English light frigate boarded us an' took Laird Ram for a sailor—whilst I was coldcocked and laying on the deck. The captain said they'd make him do a seaman's—"

"Not that!" Haskell swept his son's fate aside with a burly hand. "Ram'll give as good as he gets . . . an' they canna make him serve, he's a titled man. I want to know what he did to get her. There be a story here, MacCrenna, an' I mean to have all of it."

Arlo nodded with a sickly smile and studied his hands a minute before plunging ahead.

"Well, Laird Ram, he hit upon a plan . . . that if they were found together . . . well, she'd have a reputation t' uphold."

"And. . . ?" Haskell sat forward a bit more, growing suspicious of Arlo's reluctance.

"And she did have a reputation t' protect, and her family were generous with th' settlement—I brought the papers, Laird Haskell." Arlo made to rise and fetch them, but Haskell was on his feet in a flash, pushing Arlo back down into the chair, standing over him with a darkening

**ZEBRA HOME SUBSCRIPTION SERVICE, INC.**

120 BRIGHTON ROAD

P.O. BOX 5214

CLIFTON, NEW JERSEY 07015-5214

A $19.96
value.
*FREE!*

*No obligation
to buy
anything, ever.*

## Complete and mail this card to receive 4 Free books!

**Yes!** Please send me 4 Zebra Historical Romances without cost or obligation. I understand that each month thereafter I will be able to preview 4 new Zebra Historical Romances FREE for 10 days. Then, if I should decide to keep them, I will pay the money-saving preferred publisher's price of just $4.00 each...a total of $16. That's almost $4 less than the publisher's price. (A nominal shipping and handling charge of $1.50 per shipment will be added.) I may return any shipment within 10 days and owe nothing, and I may cancel this subscription at any time. The 4 FREE books will be mine to keep in any case.

Name _____

Address _____ Apt. _____

City _____ State _____ Zip _____

Telephone ( ___ ) _____

Signature _____
(If under 18, parent or guardian must sign.)

LP0295

These books worth almost $20, are yours without cost or obligation
when you fill out and mail this certificate.

# 4 FREE BOOKS
## YOU'RE GOING TO LOVE GETTING

face.

"Details, mah. What did the lad *do?*"

"He—" Arlo winced at parading the painful details of his laird's shady dealings before all Skyelt. But he was soon resigned to the fact that they'd all know about it before nightfall, whether from his lips or not. There was no such thing as a secret at Skyelt. "He climbed into her bed one night an' her brothers found 'em there together." He said it low and in a rush, but Haskell drank in every word.

"He climbed into her bed? Now, that's more like it! Ye hear that, Terrance? Climbed into her bed, he did!" Haskell resumed his seat with a flourish, looking positively vindicated. "And?"

"An' her brothers half killed 'im," Arlo added, more unhappy with these revelations with each passing minute. He could hear the indrawn breaths and the buzz at the fringe of the hall. "She didna exactly invite 'im in."

"He give a good account of himself, did he not?" Haskell demanded amicably, then stopped short. "What do you mean, she didna invite him?"

Arlo looked around and saw consternation on Terrance's face and dismay on Mrs. MacKay's and wished he could bite off his tongue.

"He went and climbed into her bed to . . . force her to marry 'im."

"That's a true MacLean," Haskell roared, relieved. "See what ye want and go after it!" A ripple of agreement went around the hall. "Hear that, Terrance, he's a man torn from me own flesh. I knew he'd do it once he set his mind to it!" And the ripple of laughter became a wave as Haskell's brows wiggled suggestively.

"One last thing . . . is she breedin' yet?" the laird demanded, leveling a look at Arlo that dared him to refuse.

"I don't know, m'laird," he answered truthfully, but his

289

face betrayed his doubt.

Haskell sat forward again and gave him a long, searching look, seeing there was much left unsaid. It unsettled him.

"It be a true union, don't it? He beds 'er, don't he?"

"I . . ." Arlo swallowed and tried to meet his laird's gaze, "I canna say." That sent a flurry through the assembly, and Arlo straightened, angry that he'd been required to betray his young laird's . . . and the lady's . . . secrets before the whole of Skyelt. "It be none o' my business where Laird Ram sleeps, or what he does." Another telling slip; he winced at his mistake.

"*Where* he sleeps! He sleeps wi' his wife, don't he?" Haskell read more in Arlo's stubborn silence than Arlo wished. "He *has* bedded the lass, hasn't he? On the wedding night, at least?"

"I wasn't there. They made him stay at the Marlow house for the night."

"Who made him stay?"

"Adam Marlow, he's her pa, and her three brothers. They wouldna' let him take her to the inn like he planned."

"And after?" Haskell prodded.

"On board ship, Laird Ram, he. . . ." Arlo swallowed and his neck disappeared stubbornly into his coat.

"He what? Where did he sleep on the ship?" Haskell was rising and leaning over Arlo again. Arlo's mouth drew into a tight, hard line, and Haskell pushed his face into Arlo's. "Did m' son bed with his wife or not?!"

"Not," the beleaguered Arlo whispered, out of range of all but Haskell. But Haskell's reaction broadcast the information as much as if Arlo had shouted it.

"*Damme!* He'll never get me an heir that way! What good is a wife you don't bed?" He paced away and back, glaring at Terrance's averted face and Mrs. MacKay's reproachful look. "Well, it canna be the lad's fault—God knows he tried. It shows he's got me own blood poundin' in his veins. It must be her what's at fault . . . it's her what canna keep a man's attention for a decent honeymoon!" He paced away and back again, his face growing darker with every step. "I'd have expected more from m' bonnie Constance's daughter. Her mother knew how to keep a man satisfied—an' bore *three* sons!"

He paced again until the strained silence seemed ready to snap. He set his hands at his waist, his broad, fleshy shoulders characteristically jutting forward.

"Cold porridge, that one. Knew it the minute I laid eyes on 'er."

"Haskell!" Mrs. MacKay stood and stepped forward. "You're to blame as much as her. It were a dark day you changed yer assigns to force yer son to somethin' he had no taste for."

"Are you sayin' my son has no yen for beddin' a woman?" Haskell roared, stomping back and punctuating it with a fist on the tabletop.

"I'm sayin' there's not a man here would like havin' a gun to 'is head while marryin' and beddin' a wife. Nor would you have stood for it yourself. And the lass is barely more'n a young girl, and a lady at that . . . used to refined ways and gentlefolk—"

"A cold stick," Haskell proclaimed, drawing a titter from the crowd.

"A lady, with manners and a bit o' refinement about her."

"Then *you* see to her milk an' water needs," Haskell charged. "And when Ram comes home, we'll see what's what!" He wheeled and barreled through the crowd at the back of the hall to escape outside.

Mrs. MacKay looked at Terrance, then at Arlo. Neither offered the support she felt she deserved, and she left to go upstairs, muttering about the low state of Scottish manhood. Terrance shrugged his shoulders and mumbled something about hoping Laird Ram didn't get to relish being a seaman. Arlo pushed up and ambled out toward the kitchens to rid himself of the foul taste the truth had left in his mouth. The drama was over and those gathered in the hall dispersed to their sundry tasks with enough to keep their tongues wagging for days.

Soon only Carina Graham was left in the great hall, leaning against the wall by the stairs with her arms crossed over her waist. She pushed off from the wall and let her tartan skirt sweep the ground as she swayed toward the door. Her long chestnut hair swirled about her delicate oval face and thick, lowered lashes obscured the stormy blue of her eyes. She could almost feel sorry for this "wife" of her elder half-brother. Forced into marriage by a man who crawled into her bed uninvited . . . such would have been her own fate many times over if she hadn't been wary. A woman who couldn't defend herself had to depend on the mercy (not to mention the needs) of men. Carina patted the slim, brass-handled dirk at her waist and smiled tightly as she stepped out into the dusty courtyard.

Several pairs of eyes followed her petite, womanly form and her stride lengthened purposefully, making her hips swing more. When she was ready, she'd see to it that some man's safety depended on her mercy and her needs.

## Chapter Fifteen

Eden stepped from the hall into a cool, gray afternoon, hoping the chill would dim the fire burning in the pit of her stomach. But the sight of the neglected courtyard only reinforced everything she hated about Ramsay MacLean's precious Skyelt. It was as arrogant as he was, and also slovenly, ignorant, and lacking in the commonest of civility and manners — yes, especially manners!

She shivered and rubbed her arms, glancing down at her green and gold printed dress, remembering how joyfully she'd chosen the fabric and the dreams she'd spun about when and where she'd wear it. Now it just seemed thin and inadequate against the dismal elements here. The moment they reached Skyelt, the sun hid its face and a damp chill invaded everything . . . even her bed these last two nights.

She kicked her way through the tall grasses to plop down on the stone wall and thought of her confrontations with Maisie. She'd asked to have her bed warmed last night and the chit had snipped that "m'lady" was responsible for her own cold bed and flounced out! It still made Eden's blood boil. She thought of disciplining the girl or reporting the incident to Mrs. MacKay, but a lady who couldn't cope with her own maid was doomed when it came to the larger duties of the house. For a moment it had escaped her that she wasn't planning to be there to accept any responsibilities.

She'd breakfasted, dined, and supped alone in her rooms yesterday. Maisie appeared all three times with an unsummoned tray, saying it was expected she'd need the rest. It was the closest thing to consideration she'd received thus far, and she spent the day in her rooms, unpacking and arranging and resting. And when another tray appeared this morning for her breakfast, she frowned and informed Maisie that she'd not need a dinner tray.

The great hall had been empty at noon and Eden thought about retreating to her rooms and calling for a tray after all. But her pride bristled at the shabby treatment she received from her father-in-law. Except for that bizarre incident when she arrived, he'd not shown his face to her . . . and she knew instinctively that no apology was forthcoming. As she stood in the archway at the bottom of the sweeping stairs, surveying the great hall, his gross neglect of even meager civility infuriated her. He hadn't shared a meal with her or made the slightest effort to get to know his son's new bride. She was living under his roof and they hadn't even been properly introduced!

She started for what she guessed must be the passage to the kitchens and was stopped just at the entrance by Maisie, bearing a tray that was bound for her rooms.

"That won't be necessary; I'll eat in the hall with the others."

"What others?" Maisie turned her face so that she looked at Eden from the corner of her eye.

"Lord Haskell . . . and whoever else takes nourishment at that table." She pointed at the huge table and reddened.

"The laird, he ain't here," Maisie said smugly, "and

there ain't no others." Eden felt the smack of her contempt and stiffened, clamping her hands together savagely.

"Go and tell the cook all the same, Maisie. I'll have my meals in the hall from now on."

Maisie hesitated long enough to let Eden know she complied only because she chose to do so. Eden stood rigid, fighting down a powerful urge to snatch Maisie's hair out by the roots. And her tongue grew salty with terms that would describe the chit appropriately. Never had she felt such violent urges come so close to her carefully polished surface. She was a hairsbreadth away from flailing and flogging!

She made herself turn and go to the table with a self-conscious attempt at grace. By the time Maisie returned, she'd seized control again and was able to rise above her circumstance, which was fortunate indeed. For Maisie carried the same tray and she smacked it down on the worn oak of the table before Eden and stalked out. Eden sat staring at the cloth covering the tray, her eyes burning with frustration.

A small sound from across the room brought her face up. Carina Graham rose from the shelter of a chair against the far wall and watched Eden openly for a moment. A cool, saucy smile curled her mouth, and contempt danced in her light-blue eyes. It was then that Eden noticed the brass-handled dagger at her narrow waist. She openly dismissed Eden from consideration and swayed to the great doors, then out.

Eden choked with anger and left the hall without touching the tray. The thought of retreating to her rooms galled her; it was exactly what Haskell and Maisie and even icy little Carina Graham expected. Instead, she wandered around the main house for a while, discovering a pleasant upstairs parlor that time hadn't dimmed; she made a mental map of the place. Three times she encountered servants going about their routine duties, and each time they looked at her with dull resentment before continuing with their work.

Now, sitting on the stone wall of the courtyard, she thought about it. They clearly resented her "English" ways every bit as much as she resented their mulish Scots manner. But she sensed it went deeper and was more personal than that. How could so many people take such an instant antipathy to a young woman they'd never even met? Did they resent her for being Ramsay's bride? If only they knew how little she relished the role herself . . . and how little she'd had to do with acquiring it.

Shivering, she rose some time later to make her way back to her rooms for a shawl. She'd calmed enough to decide on a walk around Skyelt, to meet some of those around the old castle first-hand. Somewhere there had to be a friendly face . . .

A flurry of running feet surged through the wooden gate and into the yard. A fellow in common brown woolens burst through the wooden gate, heading for the main doors. He nearly bowled Eden over as he barreled through the entrance and stopped just inside the great hall.

"Laird Has-kell!" he yelled, "M'laird, *hurry!* It's the Barclays!" He ran further in and yelled at the top of his lungs once more. Haskell emerged from a door near the far end of the hall, tucking his shirt into his belt and smoothing his kilt and his graying hair with brusque movements.

"The hell, you say. Barclays? You're sure, Amos?" His face was red and his breath was short.

"Yea, laird. I seen 'em ridin' this way."

"How many?"

"Only four, Laird. Looks like old Angus, the son, and

wo o' his men."

Haskell rubbed a massive hand back over his brow and
muttered something to himself. "Go, Amos, fetch me
Terrance an' Arlo and Tass MacCrenna . . . bring em'
fast. I'll not meet th' old goat wi'out an equal force at
m'back."

Amos raced off through the kitchens to do his laird's
bidding and Haskell turned back to the door, where a
half-clad blonde girl appeared, leaning against the moldings. Haskell's belt and black coat dangled from her
fingers and he paused, looking at her lustfully before
matching her against him and planting a hard kiss on her
upturned mouth. He released her with a whack on the
ear, then shoved into his coat.

"Go on, now, Annie . . . I'll see you later." He jerked
his head toward the kitchens and the girl hurried in that
direction, stopping to flick a teasing look over her bare
shoulder before she disappeared.

Eden flattened against the rough stone of the entryway,
stunned by what she'd just witnessed. Haskell and that
blonde serving girl . . . they'd been. . . . She blinked to
rid herself of the lingering image and the sound of
Haskell's approaching footsteps sent her flying into the
yard, her cheeks aflame.

Four horsemen came plunging through the gate and
Eden hurried to one side of the open doors, clasping her
shawl tighter and drawing herself up to her most ladylike
composure. She watched the kilt-clad horsemen rein up
and watched Haskell cross his arms slowly over his chest.
The only sounds were nervous snorts from the horses and
the creak of harness leather.

Two of the riders wore tams bearing clan badges; the
others were bareheaded. All wore the same dark-gray
tartan, woven with green and red, and the traditional
black coats. It was immediately clear who was the leader
of the contingent. A robust, graying man with a single

linen ruffle at this throat sat on his mount like a duke an
stared down at Haskell with an appraising gleam in hi
eyes.

"Angus Barclay." Haskell nodded, watching the leade
through narrowed eyes.

"Haskell MacLean." Angus Barclay responded with .
reciprocal nod, but made no move to dismount.

"What brings you here?" Haskell's question had th
unmistakable ring of challenge in it.

"I come . . . to pay respects. And to talk about th
water, north. I'll be makin' a well."

Haskell tilted his head and studied the tall, well-mus
cled form on the horse beside his old adversary. "Ian," h
nodded to the younger man.

"Haskell," came a like reply.

"If you come to talk water, we canna have dry throats,
Haskell pronounced, stepping back and lowering hi
arms. "Come inside." It signaled an end to the tensio
and immediately all four riders dismounted. But only tw
entered the hall behind Haskell, and Eden couldn't hel
noticing the disparity between the shorter, bandy-legge
Angus Barclay and tall, bearish Haskell. Ian Barclay wa
just short of Haskell in height, and between them Angu
seemed diminutive.

Eden frowned, unsure as to her own course, but in
trigued by the drama she'd just witnessed. She reentere
the hall and descended the steps to the main floor
lowering her shawl. Mrs. MacKay spoke with Haskell
nodding, and hurried out. Haskell waved the two men to
seats at the table and claimed the massive, carved chair a
the end for himself. Only then did Eden see Carina
Graham walking toward the threesome with a curious
light in her eyes.

Angus gave Carina an insulting visual inspection, the
turned to Haskell. "Isn't this one . . . ?"

"Carina Graham," she answered before Haskell could

giving her father an insolent look, "Haskell's bastard."

"Carina!" Haskell bellowed, his fists doubling on the arms of his chair. "Leave us!"

"Certainly, *Father*," she replied nastily, moving provocatively around Haskell's chair to pause beside Ian's broad-shouldered form. "Ian Barclay," her voice became softer as she looked him over boldly.

"Carina Graham," his deep tones responded. And as insolent, tantalizing little Carina swayed out of reach, Ian's dark head followed her . . . straight to Eden.

His dark eyes widened as they took in Eden's stylish gown and the curves it tried to hide; her soft, feminine coif; and the creamy smoothness of her skin. A smile tugged at his full, curving lips as he found her copper-ringed eyes and held them for an instant.

Eden flushed deeply and tore her gaze away as Carina swept by, a taunting glint in her eyes. And suddenly Eden was aware that Haskell, Angus, and Ian were all staring at her. She retrieved some semblance of composure, hoping Haskell was suitably chagrined at hardly knowing his daughter-in-law well enough to introduce her. She started toward them and saw Haskell's eyes narrow and his head turn to Angus.

"Well, now," his words were like a slap in the face, "let's move on to important matters. This well you want up north . . . where is it?"

Eden stopped short, blushing. He didn't intend to introduce her! He paraded his base-born daughter before his guests, but refused even to acknowledge her presence in the room! Her mouth opened and she sputtered and closed it, aware of one pair of eyes still fixed on her reaction. And she wheeled and strode angrily for the relative comfort of the cold and damp outside.

She stomped across the yard toward the gate and through it, oblivious to everything but the burning in her face and the dull thudding of her heart in her throat. She went by stone cottages, barns, stables, and finally the arch in the old outer wall of the fortress, seeing nothing but red.

How dare the old boar ignore and humiliate her like that! How dare he treat his own son's wife with so little regard! And like a thunderbolt it struck her—his attitude was no different from the rest of Skyelt's. In point of fact, it was exactly his boorish, overbearing atttitude that pervaded the place. It escaped her for the moment that she had referred to herself as Ramsay's wife . . . and insisted on being given place for it.

The dull thud of hooves and the creak of saddle leather made her look up, and she found herself on a half-barren path up a hill, heading away from Skyelt. Her chest was heaving with unspent emotion and the exertion of the climb. Her cheeks were tingling and her bottom lip was smashed between her teeth. Close behind her, a mounted rider slowed to a walk. She refused to look, continuing her angry flight.

"If you're lookin' for the road to London, it's that way," came a masculine voice that made her slow and finally stop. She paused, catching her breath, then turned to find tall, dark-haired Ian Barclay resting an elbow on his saddle, one finger indicating a clear road over the next hill.

"Thank you." Her eyes were fiery rings as she looked up into his square, sun-bronzed face, continuing, "But I'm only taking the air this afternoon." Her jaw tightened visibly and her arms crossed over her chest as if daring him to disagree.

"And takin' it very quickly, I see." His blue eyes lingered on the tantalizing rise and fall of the scoop of bare skin at her fashionable bosom. And while she decided whether to be irritated or not, a warm smile of admiration lit his finely chiseled face. That smile, genuine and freely offered, was not to be refused.

Color rushed into Eden's face as she realized she spoke with a very handsome man, and she lowered her eyes. She turned and began to walk more slowly toward the crest of the rise, hearing him dismount and feeling his eyes upon her.

"You musn't take Haskell too seriously m'lady. He's a great oaf at times, but he's not a bad man." He fell into step beside her, clasping the reins behind him.

"Only crude, loathsome, ill-mannered, and profane," Eden asserted with furious dignity, daring a glance at him from the corner of her eye. His almost black hair framed a finely sculpted face that tugged at her heart for some reason. Her head turned and she was staring at his square jaw when he stopped and reached for her hand, halting her. When he turned to face her full on, Eden was struck hard by the broadness of his shoulders and the intensity of his gray-blue eyes. A wave of memory combined with present sensation to weaken her knees.

"Allow me to introduce myself and to welcome you to Scotland, m'lady. Ian Barclay . . . My father's Angus Barclay. We hold the lands bordering east an' north of Skyelt." His bow was courtly, the pressure of his hand holding hers was perfectly calibrated—warm, but not overly familiar.

"How . . . do you know . . ." she flushed, thinking he couldn't possibly know who she was, "I'm a lady?"

"A man need not be rich to recognize a jewel." His smile was canted a few interesting degrees. "You're a lady, all right, and th' fairest I've ever set eyes upon."

Eden withdrew her hand and flushed like a giddy maid. Pleased and embarrassed by his praise, she began to walk again.

"Your name, m'lady? I'll be tortured if you refuse me." His muscular hand went to his wool-clad chest and his expression turned wistful.

"Eden . . . Marlow . . . MacLean." She ventured a cautious glance at him and caught the hitch in his easy stride as he took it in.

"Ramsay's bride." She thought his voice flattened a bit. "I should've known."

"You've heard of our marriage?" She stopped to look at him. His strong jaw was shadowed gray, his neck was muscular, his nose was finely arched between prominent, planed cheekbones, and his bowed lips were almost femininely expressive.

"I'd heard he was going to . . . marry. And it's like him to find the loveliest and sweetest lady in all England for his bride. He always did have the devil's own luck . . . from his very birth." He searched her delicate features and his face softened. "Eden . . . a garden of delights. It suits you, m'lady." His full, curving mouth drew up in an enchanting smile aimed at Eden's very center. And it found its mark.

She looked down at her hands clutching her shawl and she fidgeted in her shoes. The smell of warm wool reached her nose and she was suddenly aware of how close he stood and how strong he seemed. It was disturbingly familiar. A tingling wave of need washed over her. Why should she be assailed by thoughts of Ramsay MacLean just now?

"I . . . hope ye'll not condemn all Scotsmen from old Haskell's example."

"No," she swallowed and managed to make her feet move forward again, "the rest of Skyelt must share the blame for my opinions."

He laughed and the low rumble vibrated in her ears. "Ah, the warmth of a Scottish welcome. . . . You must see, fair Lady Eden, things are different here than in England—"

"Boston," she looked around at the countryside and

sighed heavily, "I'm actually from Boston, Massachusetts . . . in America."

"Ah . . . then likely it's a case of mistaken nationality. They've taken you for an English lady. You sound quite English." He was smiling when she glanced his way.

"I was schooled in England. But why should things like civility and humanity—even simple manners—depend on one's being born on th' plaid?" Her inner heat boiled over into her voice and she stopped, realizing they'd reached the crest of the hill. She turned to look over the mist-shrouded valley below and felt her cheeks burn from her unseenly outburst.

" 'Born on th' plaid'?" he echoed, laughing gently. "You're halfway to bein' a Scot already. You must see, Skyelt's not a grand house, like in England, with a laird and lady and servants. There's hardly a body on the place that can't claim kin to the laird in some way . . . and right or wrong, every one of them thinks he's entitled to a say."

"An arrangement that hardly makes for harmony . . . or efficiency."

This time his laugh tugged at the corners of her mouth and she couldn't resist the urge to smile at him. He engaged her eyes and his smile slowly faded. Eden felt a familiar tugging in her chest that sent flashes of warning through her. He was so male, so near, and making her feel like Ram did—

She tossed her head nervously and spotted a clutch of huge rocks not far away. She struck out for it and heard him draw a deep breath as he followed. Climbing up on one, she gazed out over the valley below, then turned to survey the high moors to her left. In the distance she saw trees, perhaps the woods that Arlo had spoken of so fondly.

"Is that part of Skyelt's lands? Those trees. . . ." she pointed and stepped aside as he climbed up on the rocks near her.

"Aye, that's the far north range o' Skyelt's lands. Beyond is Grenbruck, Barclay lands. I know it well, that wood. I know all of Skyelt . . . used to come here a lot as a lad."

"You and Ramsay . . . are friends?" It seemed an obvious conclusion, but when he mentioned Ramsay, something in his manner darkened, however briefly, and made her wonder.

"We're . . . friendly. There's always been a bit of combat betwixt us. But that's only natural, I suppose." He glanced at her and caught her looking at him. That charming smile reappeared and she felt its warmth wash her momentary confusion away. She smiled, relieved.

"Tell me about Skyelt and about Haskell . . . I'm afraid to trust most of what I've been told."

"Told by whom, Lady Eden?"

"Arlo MacCrenna. He escorted me from Bristol, after Ramsay—" She stopped and he scowled, nodding for her to continue. But she changed direction firmly and began to look for a seat on the rocks. Settling on the edge of a massive boulder with a view of the valley, she smoothed her skirts and ignored his expectation and his scrutiny.

"Ram isn't about? I didna see him in the hall. He didn't come with you?" Ian settled close to her on the huge rock and Eden's heart began to thud like she was climbing the hill again. His long, muscular legs and bare knees drew her gaze: they were long and muscular and. . . .

"No, he didn't return with us. I don't expect him for . . . a while yet." For some reason she withheld the news that Ramsay had been pressed into service in the British Navy. She thought it might please him to hear it, and for some reason, she didn't want to please him at Ramsay's expense. Her protective urge toward her arrogant, underhanded mate confused her for a moment. What was happening to her?

304

"He sent you on to Skyelt to confront old Haskell alone? God, what was the man thinkin' of? Where's that sense o' responsibility he wears like a thorny crown? It's a wonder you have any regard for Scottish manhood at all. Were you *my* bride, I'd not let you out of my sight, nor would I let old Haskell in the same county—" He stopped short, raising his brows briefly and pursing his lips as he looked away.

"You mean because he's an oaf and . . . a lecher?" Eden surprised herself with the conclusion but owned it immediately. Ramsay's references to old Haskell's ruin came crashing together with Arlo's cryptic comments and her recent observation . . . he was a randy old goat! A lecher deluxe.

Ian winced. "He's that, there's no denyin' it. Chases every skirt he sees. No decent woman will be left alone with 'im. Lord knows how the MacKay manages to fend 'im off."

*The* MacKay? *Mrs*. MacKay? The housekeeper?" Eden's eyes searched him.

" 'Tis common knowledge he's been after 'er for years. And 'tis also common talk that she's boxed his ears on occasion." He laughed a bit wickedly, "I'd ride bare as— I'd give a lot to see that." Noticing the consternation on Eden's face, he looked down at his lean, work-hardened hands and then at her trim ankles, exposed where the hem of her dress was turned up. He drew a quiet breath. "Now I see he's brought that little Graham spitfire into his house."

"She's his—" Eden stopped herself, frowning at this powerful urge to deride and condemn the lot of them.

"Yes, she is," Ian nodded, watching her internal struggle with a keen eye. "She's his bastard. And not the first."

"Not . . . ?" Eden looked up at his handsome face and found a strange light in his eyes. "Of course," she looked out over the valley to hide her reaction, "there could be others."

"There are indeed. I said most of the folk at Skyelt could rightly claim kin to the laird. . . ." He might have continued but her face had drained of all color and her golden-ringed eyes were so large, so shocked. He eased and smiled, holding her cold hand between his. "But you don't need to be hearin' such from one outside Skyelt. It's a fact, that's all. There's naught to be done about it. And he has his better side: he's generous to a fault with his people and a fierce fighter if it comes to that."

"It's really none of my concern." She managed to salvage some of her ladylike mien. "It doesn't affect me . . . or my marriage."

"Nay, Ram doesn't have old Haskell's taste for th'—" his short grin was apologetic. "He's not like his father in that respect, you may be sure, Lady Eden . . . Eden. In fact, it might be said he's just the opposi—" Her incredibly appealing eyes stopped him again. They were like the sun setting on the heath, rings of coral and gold in a field of azure, with sweet night calling in their centers. And Ian Barclay was seized by a desire to know just how Ram MacLean was with his new bride . . . a bride he'd sent ahead of him to brave old Haskell MacLean alone . . . a tantalizing beauty of a bride with sweet-scented lips and shining hair and soft skin.

"Just where is Ram, anyway?" He spoke softly, insistently.

"Somewhere in Portsmouth, no doubt, or on the way home. Perhaps we'd better be getting back." Eden felt his warming gaze tugging at her middle again and rose on shaky legs. Her head was spinning from his revelations and she didn't trust her own reactions to this rugged, gentlemanly fellow. "I must dress for supper soon. I'm positively starved."

He scrambled down the rocks first and held his arms up to assist her. She hesitated but finally made herself accept his big hands around her waist and he lifted her down. But as her feet settled under her, he refused to let her go, holding her close to him, staring down into her sweet face, losing himself in the glow of her extraordinary eyes.

Eden saw his head bending and felt her heart jerk queerly. He pulled her closer and pressed her lips with his, gently at first, then harder. Everything swirled around her. The hard muscles of his arms tensed more under her braced hands and she recognized the heat spreading from his hands into her waist. She tried not to react, but in spite of her, her head tilted a bit and she allowed him to kiss her, then explored the sensation of his lips against hers. It was more than pleasant; it was positively knee weakening. It was the same hard-soft wonder of Ramsay's kiss, but different in shape and pressure . . . and in her response. Something made her stiffen and he raised his head.

He looked away, grappling for control as she stepped back and hid the revealing glow in her eyes. He relinquished all but her hand, and soon raised it to his lips with a courtly nod.

"A kiss for the bride . . . it's tradition, it is not?" His voice was betrayingly husky, but when Eden looked up, that polished, gentlemanly attention was all that was visible.

She managed a relieved smile, hoping the stain in her cheeks would evaporate before the two of them reached the hall. Ian Barclay was the first person to treat her like a lady since she reached Skyelt, but it unnerved her that he'd treated her like a woman as well. Ian caught his grazing mount's reins and joined her, extending his arm to steady her as they made their way down the hill.

"Lovely Lady Eden, you must feel free to call on me if you ever need assistance." It was said with casual grace, but Eden sensed a genuine concern beneath it that

307

smoothed the wary edges of her thoughts. "Now, what can I tell you about Skyelt?" he mused, catching her eye and covering her hand on his arm reassuringly. "Ah—the old castle itself. . . ."

"M'lady . . ." The MacKay caught Eden halfway up the stairs to her rooms when she returned. The housekeeper lifted her gray skirts and hurried up the steps, her face flushed. "M'lady, there's to be a supper tonight . . . with guests . . . the Barclays. Yer to be present."

The MacKay's smile was apologetic and Eden realized it was not simply information; it was a command. The thought of its crude, churlish source darkened her eyes a moment.

"I had planned to eat tonight anyway," she answered in the oblique manner of a Scot without realizing it. "I'm going up to change for dinner. Would you send Maisie up to me . . . if she's nothin' better to do."

"Aye, m'lady." The MacKay caught her sarcasm and turned to descend the steps, frowning.

Eden heaved a deep sigh and closed her eyes briefly, trying to correct her unstable grip on her situation. She fingered her reddened lips and shivered. "Come home, Ramsay MacLean, so we get this over with and. . . ." And *what,* she didn't want to think.

The deep-green velvet complemented the ivory glow of Eden's breast in the cheval mirror Mrs. MacKay had rescued from some far corner of Skyelt and trundled into her rooms. She held up her hand glass and looked over the back of her gown, then turned to inspect the front. The starched linen frills around her bodice tempered the bold display of her breasts, but the cording wrapped about and hanging down her waist in classical style only accentuated her lush curves. The puffs at the tops of her snug-fitting sleeves emphasized the slenderness and grace of her arms. The tightly wrapped curls of her daytime coif were combed and loosened and lowered to an enchanting mass extending from the top of her head all the way down her back. It hinted at the tactile pleasures of those waves of brown and beckoned the viewer to get lost in them.

"It's quite lovely, Maisie." She smiled determinedly to the freckled serving girl, who stood nearby, eying her with equal parts of awe and suspicion. "You've a gift with a lady's coiffure." She chewed the inside of her lip, then made herself say it. "You'll soon be invaluable as a lady's maid."

"Hmph," came the low but audible reply as Maisie turned to go.

Eden went rigid with ire, but pretended not to have heard. The door closed a bit too loudly and she threw her hand glass down on the bed, trembling with anger. They resented her orders, they sneered at her compliments—the devil take the lot of them! She pulled her shoulders back and clamped her jaw as she strode to take one last look in the mirror. Her cheeks were stained, her lips were reddened . . . but otherwise, she was the cool, elegant image of a lady, well-placed in even the grandest house. Let old Haskell ignore her tonight, she growled mentally.

Haskell didn't see his daughter-in-law at first when she descended the stairs. But his were the only eyes she failed to draw at once. The hall was filled with men in tartan wearing sashes and bonnets with cock feathers and badges. And every one of them stopped to look at the young woman poised on the steps like the reigning queen of Skyelt. It was the precipitous drop in conversation that brought Haskell's head around. Standing near the fireplace, he turned to follow Angus Barclay's gaze to the broad stone steps and his fleshy face reddened at the sight

309

of her.

Arlo, in full Scots dress, moved toward the steps, but it was Ian Barclay who reached her first, extending his hand to lead her down into the hall. Haskell's burning stare pierced the room and settled to smoke at the sweetly feminine smile she turned on Angus's strapping son, then on the others assembled. His mood darkened as he took in the perfection of her skin, the ravishing fall of her hair, the grace of her carriage, the lush promise of her body. He'd never seen a woman to rival her—not even her mother, to the best of his dimming recollections.

And his manly son didn't bed her. Why didn't the young bull just insist on his rights like a real man? If she were his own woman, Haskell mused testily, she'd have nothin' to say in the matter . . . he'd take her and that would be that. And she'd be breedin' within the week. They always were. But she was Ram's woman . . . and he knew his son's Calvinist leanings well enough to imagine he'd never push this bit of icy perfection to the point of passion. The taste of defeat was made more bitter when witnessed by old Angus, who already had six grandchildren . . . *six* . . . and him with blood thin enough to do the wash in.

Haskell tossed back his last swallow of ale and strode toward his great carved chair at the end of the laden and groaning table. He extended a hand and waved Angus to a seat at his left, not trusting himself to speak just now. A din rose as the others seated themselves in random fashion, leaving a place at Haskell's right for the laird's son.

Ian held Eden's hand high and drew her around the end of the long table and past the somber black-and-gray coats that turned, to a man, as she passed. But at the head of the table, they found one chair. Ian cleared his throat discreetly twice before Arlo looked up from his customary second seat on the right, perplexed. Ian stared meaningfully at the lone chair, then at Eden, who was shrinking inside at this humiliating gaffe, and back at Arlo. Another age rolled by before Arlo caught his meaning and rose to give place to her.

But as she was seated, Arlo stood over the diner at his right and boldly cleared his throat. Having witnessed the process of the lady's seating, the man rose with tight lips and gave place to Arlo. The unseated fellow looked at the occupied chair to his right and it was soon vacated. And a ripple of bobbing and jostling went down the entire side of the table as the seating was readjusted to accommodate old Haskell's daughter-in-law.

Eden saw it from the corner of her eye and her face burned as she sat rigidly enduring the eyes of the table, some resentful, some—especially Angus—amused. When the commotion subsided and talk began again, she leaned back against her chair. Her hands were trembling as they reached for her pewter goblet and she drank deeply of the ruby wine. It would have calmed her greatly if she hadn't caught Haskell's gaze narrowed on her, obviously furious over the turmoil she'd caused at his table. Her face went crimson and she lowered it, feeling doubly condemned for having blundered at maintaining her own lofty standards of etiquette.

But Haskell's glare was witnessed. And handsome, gentlemanly Ian Barclay slipped a hand beneath the table to catch hers from her lap and give it a gentle squeeze. Soon she was able to serve herself from the dishes passing before her.

"Broth" was a thin, peppery soup with chopped carrots and barley. A "gigot" proved to be a savory roast leg of lamb, and "bridies" were pastries filled with onion-spiced meat. Biscuits, "baps," and "bannocks" were served with crocks of sweet butter and jam. "Tatties" and "bashed neeps" were in turn potatoes and mashed turnips, which were smothered by dark, rich gravy. And the most to-do came with the "haggis," which Ian explained was a delicacy so mystical that it was bad luck to speak of details of its composition. Eden pushed it about on her plate suspiciously, tried a mouthful, shuddered, and made herself swallow the pungent concoction quickly. Well, she was already full enough to waddle, and she made pretty apologies to Ian Barclay's twinkling eyes.

The gusty appetites and appreciative murmurs of the men around her made her realize the contrast between this feast and the plain fare she'd consumed these last days at Skyelt. The size and quality of the feed was undoubtedly a tribute to the importance of the guests. The conclusion stung: no one had bothered to so much as tilt a glass to welcome her. She straightened, reaching for her goblet and letting the rich wine seep hot into her blood.

Angus sat back and rubbed his rounding stomach with satisfaction. His eyes roamed to Eden and quickly assessed her abundant charms, noticing Ian's gentlemanly attention to her. Very little escaped shrewd Angus Barclay's notice, even pouch-full and lidded with wine. He glanced at Haskell, still swilling the repast with obvious pleasure. Anything that gave Haskell MacLean that much pleasure should be curtailed, he mused with a crafty light in his eyes.

"So, Haskell . . . this be the one?" Angus kicked back in his chair and pointed at Eden as though she were a stump. Haskell put down his knife and fork and swiped at the grease glistening in his gray-streaked beard. Angus smiled inscrutably.

Haskell stared first at Angus, then at Eden's braced surprise, then back at Angus. "Well, it took him long enough to get 'round to it," he thought. He had no delusions that Angus Barclay had braved the animosity of his house to discuss water rights, however important. Here was the bare truth of it: he'd come to look over the marital proceedin's firsthand.

312

"Aye . . . she be the one." Haskell reached for his goblet, watching Angus sharply over the rim of it.

"Yer a crafty devil, Haskell MacLean, I'll give ye that. She'd be hard for a man to refuse . . . even a man o' Ram's persuasions. So you've had yer way . . . is she breedin' yet?"

The great hall fell deathly silent, every eye trained on the paling lady with the huge, intriguing eyes; every ear itched to hear more. Ian stiffened beside her. Arlo dropped his face to spare her and thwapped the thigh of the fellow beside him, forcing his eyes away as well. But the chain reaction stopped abruptly; the drama was too high to give place to mere sensibilities.

"Nay, not yet," Haskell uttered with a devastating glare at Eden.

"Well," Angus wrested about in his chair to openly scrutinize her lusciously appealing breasts and creamy skin, "you'd best get the lad on her the minute he gets back. Allowin' time for the bearin' and birthin', he's only got the short side of a year to get the job done."

"Damn you, Angus!" Haskell's face flushed to near-purple and he thundered, trying to convince through sheer volume. "He'll see it through. He be a MacLean, true to the name an' the ways! He'll stoke her oven an' get his due—"

Eden rose sharply, sending her chair clunking back on the flagstone floor. Drained of color, she shook with humiliation and rage. One look around the sea of lurid, speculative male faces and she knew. *They knew.* They *all* knew. She threw a furious glance at Ian and found a guilty concern lining his handsome brow. They knew she was imported to stand for Haskell's prize stud. And they knew exactly the timetable for accomplishment of the task. They knew and they watched . . . d-damn the p-prying, voyeuristic l-lot!

She raised her chin and delivered a scathing glare at her

father-in-law. But the raw potency of her loathing only brought a mercenary glint to his steely-blue eyes. He was wondering if Ram might find a way to convert it to more useful passion when she turned and walked to the stairs with furious dignity. She turned on the steps and cast a damning look over the assembly. It was the final indignity she'd suffer in this wretched rathole of humanity!

## Chapter Sixteen

Sleep was unthinkable that night, and by the early light of another gray day, Eden had decided. She dragged two leather satchels from the wardrobes in the antechamber and carefully stuffed her most durable dresses and petticoats and chemises inside. She made a mental inventory, repeating it as a charm against the horrible waves of despair that threatened her. She had no emotional abundance to weep and rail against this awful place . . . she had just enough strength left to leave it.

She dressed carefully in her heavy velvet riding habit and met Maisie at the door to take her morning tray. The girl blinked sullenly and stared at her mistress, already risen and dressed in her fine riding apparel. She nodded reluctantly when told to return in a quarter of an hour.

When Maisie didn't return, Eden gave up waiting and went to look for her. She had rounded the steps in the hall and started for the archway leading to the newer part of the house when her heel caught in a thread at her hem and she stumbled against the wall. She closed her eyes and leaned heavily against the stone, trying to calm her wild fright. It was then she heard Maisie's voice, floating around the corner.

". . . I guess she about croaked, old Angus askin' if she

be bred yet and old Haskell roaring that Laird Ram'd get it done in due time."

There was a sly, derisive giggle and another, older female voice responded, "Sure he will. And I'm just as liable to spit pearls."

"Well, he cain't be blamed when the cradle's not filled . . . it's her an' her cold English ways . . . refusing 'im his manly due. No wonder he don't want to come home! Imagine refusin' our bonnie Laird Ram on his weddin' night! Half of Skelt achin' and eager to warm his knees any time he'd take the notion, and she that gets him legal is a cold, unfeelin' stick. Pox on her, she deserves to dry up an' wither like a juiceless hunk o' bone."

"Amen," came the response, and there was a shuffling that made Eden flatten back against the wall, her face and ears burning from the scorn.

"I'd best get up an' see what the fancy stick is wantin'." Maisie's voice seemed nearer.

"Afore she boxes yer ears . . ."

"Nah, she don't soil her lily-white hands with anythin' so low. If I don't want to do somethin', I just walk out . . . and she just gets stiff an' sucks in her cheeks and twitches. Bet that's just what she done in Laird Ram's bed." And the ugly laughter that this comment produced drained the blood from Eden's head.

Maisie passed by where Eden was huddled against the wall, turning white. Her anger at Maisie's insolence was supplanted by the revelation that the girl believed Ramsay had never even bedded her. The way gossip traveled here, all Skyelt probably believed it—Haskell, too. And worse, they thought it was her refusal, her coldness to him that had caused it . . . and even that it was her presence here that kept him away from his home.

But they were wrong! It was their precious Ram who'd shunned her bed . . . denied her a wife's respect . . . a wife's attentions. Everything was Ram's fault . . . every

316

bloody bit of it!

She staggered from the wall with tears welling in her eyes. Hang her bloody bags, she'd leave without them! And she turned on her heel toward the kitchen doors. Standing not ten feet away, directly in her path, was Carina Graham, hands on hips, challenge glittering in her usually cool eyes. Her pouty lips pursed tauntingly at one corner.

"So this is how English ladies pass their time . . . I alwus wondered. Eavesdroppin' on servant-gossip—how edifyin'."

A slap in the face would have produced less anger in Eden. She stood, trying to best the hurt and contain her escalating outrage, getting stiff, sucking in her cheeks, twitching. . . . Good Lord—Maisie was right!

Eden's eyes blazed and she started on a straight course for the kitchen passage, shoving Haskell's daughter aside savagely.

The kitchen folk stopped to stare as she stormed through, followed soon after by a curiously unsettled Carina. And Cook and The MacKay exchanged glances and hurried out the door to see where she was bound. She was striding hard for the stables, her riding hat bobbing precariously and her hastily done coif slipping.

"I want a horse, a good one," she demanded of the kilted stableman.

"Oh?" The rangy, flat-faced fellow looked her over carefully and scratched his head. "Nobody takes out Laird Haskell's mounts wi'out his say."

"Then bring me the hack I rode in on a few days back."

"That be the laird's now, same as th' others." His chin pulled in a fraction, seeing the lady's determination.

"I want a bloody ride!" she growled, savaging him with a firm look.

"Ye'll . . . have to ask Laird Haskell." The stableman took a step back into a horse pile. All trace of amusement

317

left him. "He be in the dairy, m'lady."

"Given his affinity for cows, I'd expect he spends most of his time there!" she snapped, pivoting a quarter-turn and stomping down the rise, sending geese and chickens flapping in her wake. She tore the bobbling hat from her head and gave it a contemptuous fling. Carina trailed behind at a safe distance, followed by Cook, The MacKay, and the stableman. Behind them, Maisie was stepping out the kitchen door, craning her neck to see what was going on before setting out after them.

In the whitewashed dairy, two older serving women plied large wooden churns filled with the morning's cream and they looked up in surprise to behold the English lady bride of their laird's son.

"Haskell?" she demanded with the economy of anger.

"In there." One of the gray heads tilted toward a planking door that led into the cow barn.

Eden jerked it back, and it slammed and trembled against the wall as she passed. Several men, some in tartan, some in brown working woolens, were gathered around a pen at the far end of the barn and Eden headed straight for them, down an alley of mostly empty stalls. Shortly, the churning women were entertained by a stream of Skyelt's luminaries passing on parade. They stared wide-eyed at each other and abandoned their task to venture into the barn as well.

Expectation hung on the air like morning fog and most of the men felt it even before Eden drew up beside the wooden pen. They turned one by one to see the brown-haired lady with the glowing eyes standing there, hands on hips, chin out.

"Laird Haskell." She managed to pare her contempt down to mere sarcasm for the moment. "I want a word with you."

Haskell was squatting down in the straw by a heifer, patting it blandly while watching the beast heave, trying to expel a calf. He looked up and stroked his beard, then returned to the sight of his herdsman scowling at the heifer's slow progress.

"Time for the rope, Feltie," he surmised, "she'll need a bit o' help with this one." And while Feltie and the other lads produced a rope and began to haul on the reluctant calf, Haskell straightened and crossed his arms over his chest, staring at her with lidded nonchalance.

"Haskell!" she commanded, losing what tenuous grip she retained on herself. "I said *I want a word with you!*"

"Yes . . . yes. . . ." he seemed patently more interested in the cow's difficulty than in his frosty daughter-in-law's.

"Tell your stableman to give me a horse . . . *now.*"

"Heave, lads," Haskell's face livened when the rope was strung between the whitewashed boards of the stall and hands inside and out began to pull, "Put yer backs into it . . . the lady needs yer assistance!"

Eden felt his words like a slap. And in a second, the rangy calf was sliding free of its mother and thrashing, wet and glistening, in the hay. Whatever she said was lost in a noisy cheer from the spectators and in Haskell's booming laugh. He knelt and picked up the wobbly new beast to set it by the weary mother's head for a good cleaning.

He raised a taunting leer to Eden's crimson face. "You got a good big heifer, you get a good, big calf."

"What?" her eyes rolled wild in her head, "what?"

"I said—" he stepped over the cow and into the alley, just feet from her.

"I *heard* what you said," she growled, letting her voice drop to its lowest possible register, "and they all heard it too!" She waved a furious arm at the growing ranks of spectators. Terrance had just arrived, big-eyed and panting. Word was spreading fast of a confrontation in the cow barn.

"Woman—" Haskell snugged his beard hard against his

chest and frowned.

"I want a horse and I'll have it—after I have a say!" she advanced on him and pushed a mutinous face up toward his.

"Haskell MacLean," her tone dripped finely distilled malice, "you're an unredeemable profligate; a lecherous buffoon; a brutish, offensive, and licentious old goat who inflicts his debasing lusts on those unfortunate enough to serve him. But I expect you already know that. *They* all do!" She flung a finger at the wary contingent that had followed her from the house. "But you're also crude . . . foul-mouthed . . . stingy . . . contemptibly ill-mannered . . . ignorant . . . and," she sniffed and curled her nose in disgust, "you stink like the bottom of an ale keg! And even if you don't already know that . . . *they* all do!"

"Hold yer tongue, silly woman, afore you make me angered!" Haskell reddened furiously, taken back at her virulent tongue and hot temper.

"Or you'll do what, father-in-law? Ignore and insult me? Treat me like a bloody stupid stump without pride nor feelings? Or assault and maltreat me like you did the minute I set foot inside your wretched house—you, stinkin' drunk and free with your hands on your own son's wife!"

"Maybe take a strong hand to you, wench—" he growled, starting forward and sending her skittering back. She nearly bowled saucy Carina Graham over, and in a flash of reckless ire, she snatched the sharp little dirk from Carina's belt. She straightened, her eyes blazing with crimson fires of warning.

"You won't touch me, again, Haskell—not without a price," she rasped, blandishing the wasplike steel instinctively. At the bottom of her feminine psyche was a refined lady in a pure, dead faint. "Not you nor any of the rest of your surly, suffocating house! This place is a sty, *my laird*, because its master is a swine. The servants have

320

insolent and spiteful tongues—they're sullen and contrary and ignorant of the most rudimentary rules of etiquette. Respect and civility are unheard of, Christian charity is abandoned, even food is rendered grudgingly—if at all!" Her voice had slowly risen and was close to vibrating the roof timbers.

"I've been leered at, sneered at, and affronted in every conceivable way! I've been ignored, avoided, and blamed for all manner of family evils—when the one injustice done was done to me! I'm Ramsay's wife . . . your only son's wife." She stabbed a finger at Haskell and then at red-faced Terrance and The Mackay and shrinking Maisie. "I'm their laird's chosen bride—however it came about! And I'll not be treated like a mongrel mistake in the lily-pure MacLean line . . . least of all by those who are!" She glared at Carina Graham and the girl surprised everyone by reddening and looking down.

Eden turned and advanced on Haskell, a hellish fire leaping in her eyes. The flames muted to satisfied, white-hot coals when he stepped back to avoid her as she approached.

"You're the one to blame for it all. You're the one who bedded my mother years ago—" she heard a sharp intake of breath from some of their audience, "and you're the only who decreed Ramsay must plant his seed in me, or forfeit Skyelt." The exhilarating release of fury insulated her against the fact that she was standing in the smelly barn, brandishing a knife at her husband's father and referring to herself as a plowed field. She'd never imagined the heady, almost sensual pleasures of abandoning all restraint. This was positively invigorating!

Haskell found himself against the back end of a cow, struck almost dumb in the face of her challenge. He'd written her off as a bad investment, a sorry milk-and-water pap, appetizing only until a man got a taste. . . .

"Now, woman—" he began in a warning tone, but his

321

face clearly showed a reassessment of his daughter-in-law and her situation in his household.

"That's right! I am a woman . . . and a *wife* . . . despite your tawdry little conclusions about my marriage. Your son bedded me on my wedding night . . ." and some shocking impulse made her add, *"thoroughly!"* A wave of reaction broke around her; she saw Haskell start and recklessly engaged his eye, repeating the word. *"Thoroughly!"*

Delicately fingering the blade in her hands, she turned and caught Maisie's shrinking look. There was one more thing to rebutt —

"And it was Ramsay's own choice to sleep on deck, aboard ship." Her head whipped back to Haskell, ". . . something about not wanting to suffer his father's pathetic fate . . . lumbering about like a great randy oaf —" She saw the cow's tail rise behind Haskell, but her ignorance of bovine habit sent her plunging forward. ". . . pawing and rutting after any wom —"

A powerful yellow stream caught Haskell squarely in the back, and the shock paralyzed him for a long moment. Surprise stopped Eden in mid-word and they both looked down to find a yellow puddle spreading as his kilt dropped the liquid overload. Muffled, nervous titters erupted all around them as Eden pulled herself together and raised a disdainful nose at her father-in-law's draining clothes.

"I couldn't have put it better myself!"

The dirk in her hand clattered on the bare stone at Carina's feet and she was halfway to the stable before huge, gulping breaths made her wobble on her legs. She was mad, they'd driven her mad in four short days!

But the blood pumping through her veins said otherwise, and for the first time in years, she knew the exhilaration of unfettered, uncensored reaction. Layers of restricting, mannerly varnish had splintered irretrievably;

now the ensuing upheaval left her shaking and uncertain, but strangely unfrightened.

She grabbed a dozing groom by the ear and ordered a saddle for one of Haskell's best mounts. He protested, she twisted, and he acquiesced, unwilling to sacrifice an ear to resist such a reasonable request. Eden struck out for the London road through a gaggle of gawking spectators.

Wind drained the heat from her face and cleared her head. By the time she crested the ridge at the edge of the valley, she reined up and stared at the panorama of Skyelt, once more made glorious by distance. A deep, ragged sigh released her tension; her head dropped back and her eyes closed. What was she doing?

A moment later, she urged the horse down the other slope of the hill and made for the stream under the rocks that she'd seen the day she arrived. Dismounting, she paced and finally climbed up the nearby boulders to sit and think a while.

What good would leaving now do? The damage was already done . . . they could hardly hate her more than they did already. Fleeing with nothing but the clothes on her back and a few gold sovereigns tucked into her bodice . . . why let them breathe a sigh of relief she was gone, when she'd be cold and hungry and in peril of life and limb, not to mention virtue, for whatever time it took to reach Mistress Dunleavy's?

And there was still the problem of Ramsay. A depressing chill settled on her shoulders. She always tried not to think of him, tried not to wonder if he was all right. But every night, lying there, naked in her bed, she felt an aching emptiness inside that she'd never felt before Ramsay MacLean had taken her into his arms and made her a woman. She pictured him tied to a post and flogged senseless, ill and wasting into nothingness for lack of tender nursing, or keel-hauled and bloody — with his stubborn jaw still clenched defiantly. And her heart always stopped at the thought.

Today was a day for raw, brutal truth. And the awful, bare-bones truth of it was that she wanted him, craved him, even if he didn't want her. It had been a terrible humiliation to learn she was only the purchase price of his inheritance. She should be shamed beyond living, should despise the very ground he walked on, should delight in every stab of pain he experienced at the hands of the British Navy. He deserved it all, the callous bastard. But here she sat, stopped in mid-flight, worrying about his tendency for seasickness and wishing he would hold her in his arms just once more before she expired of this terrible longing.

"What a sorry case you are, Eden Marlow . . . MacLean," she muttered aloud. Her life, her heart, her very soul had been turned inside out by Ramsey MacLean. There was hardly a shred of her hard-won polish left intact and she didn't even care. Moments later, she remounted and was riding over the hills toward Ramsay's favorite spot in all Skyelt, the woods.

"M'lady!" Terrance and The MacKay descended on her the instant she stepped into the great hall. "Oh, m'lady— are you all right?"

"I'm perfectly fine, Mrs. MacKay." She watched the housekeeper and the steward, wondering what they must think after her wild tantrum. "But I am quite hungry after my long ride."

"Laird Haskell was just about to ride out and search for you, m'lady." Terrance edged forward. "We were all . . . worried."

"About me?" Eden's unchecked surprise was some part revenge. "How novel."

"Laird Haskell invites you to eat with him, today at

noon . . . and every day, m'lady. His verra orders."
Terrance moved with her as she headed for the stairs.

Eden thought it over and nodded, slightly bewildered.

"I'll send Maisie up, if you like, m'lady," The MacKay
spoke up, "to help with . . . your bags." So they'd found
her things packed and knew she'd planned to leave. She
paused and nodded and climbed the stairs.

Maisie appeared minutes later in her rooms with red-
rimmed eyes, the unmistakable outline of a feminine hand
visible on her cheek. Eden watched how she unpacked the
bags with wary reverence and jumped skittishly whenever
Eden came near. Well, fear was one form of respect, Eden
decided, and she'd take their respect however she acquired
it. Maisie tidied up the washstand and curtsied awkwardly
when asking if there were anything else Eden wished. It
was fortunate indeed that Eden was sitting down at the
time.

This new spirit pervaded her leisurely dinner with
Haskell and a watchful, somewhat subdued Carina. The
table was set with linen napkins and Haskell held the
chair for her himself, giving her a strong whiff of soap
and sandalwood. Haskell asked politely, if rather stiffly,
about her family, and not once was the Deity's name
invoked inappropriately. His eyes seldom left her, but
Eden recognized a glint of hard-won admiration in them
and decided not to object. He answered her questions
about Skyelt amicably but she noted a mischievous twinkle in his eye when he volunteered a comment on his son.

"Named him after my favorite animal in the herd . . .
the ram."

"How like you," she smiled sardonically. "It certainly
suits him." She was devilishly pleased by the blatant itch
of Haskell's curiosity.

Carina watched her adroit use of knife and fork together and surreptitiously copied it. Haskell eyed her
every time his linen came up to dab at his beard. Eden

watched them, amused by their sudden conversion to the rigors of refinement. How strange that it took the volcanic disruption of her entire being to bring such changes about.

And her wonderment grew to include her own assertive manner through the afternoon and evening as she tested her new sense of freedom throughout Skyelt's main house. The servants invariably greeted her with nods of respect and wary sidelong glances, but they hurried to execute her crisp orders. She sensed none was eager to be the tripstone of her next explosion. By nightfall, they exchanged grins when they thought she couldn't see and "m'lady" had a new softness on their lips.

The sheets had been dutifully warmed when she crawled between them that night and she half-convinced herself it was all just a pleasant delusion . . . tomorrow Skyelt would revert to its surly, arrogant self and she'd find her bags still packed and awaiting action. At least it kept her from feeling the crispness of the clean sheets against her bare breasts and made her forget temporarily the need that lodged tenaciously in her loins.

The next morning, smells of chocolate and hot buttery scones and honey awakened her. She rose and stretched languidly with a wry tilt to her lips. Delusions seldom survived a good night's rest.

Arlo reappeared that morning, having visited relations in the next valley, and squired her about Skyelt. He noted the sparkle in her eyes and the new directness in her tone and grinned, thinking she was all the more enchanting for it. Everywhere they went, she had a quip, a throaty laugh, a question or compliment. The cool elegance of the young laird's wife was so thoroughly warmed, most of Skyelt swore she was a different woman altogether . . . and their laird likely a bigamist.

Their changed view of her matched hers of them. The wool house, the stables, the smithy, the cabinet shop, everywhere there seemed to be industry and energy and an acceptance of her that left her bemused. The place seemed so altered, she began to wonder if her first unflattering perceptions had been accurate after all. When she spoke her plain thoughts aloud, there were laughs, and she understood a bit better the brash, proud spirit of Skyelt's people . . . and their handsome young laird.

Arlo took great pains to point out the various improvements Ram had introduced since coming back to Skyelt from the university. Eden listened to the litany of agricultural and engineering feats and watched the eagerness of the folk to discuss their young laird's ingenuity and diligence. There was a light of pride in their eyes that brought Eden an excruciating pang of loneliness despite the surprising crush of people that inhabited Skyelt's complex. And she knew beyond a doubt it was the exasperating Ramsay MacLean she was missing.

That afternoon, they found Haskell in the lower valley on a hitherto undiscovered circle of the densest, greenest grass Eden had ever seen. It had been clipped by hand to carpet-like smoothness and at the center was a small hole into which Haskell was endeavoring to swat small white balls with a stick. Terrance stood nearby, leaning on a similar stick and concentrating mightily on the nuances of Haskell's movements and successes, while tactfully ignoring his failures. Arlo squatted and watched the alignment of ball and hole and nodded judiciously when everything seemed right.

Eden watched awhile, studying her father-in-law and recognizing some of Ram's gestures and movements in his broad shoulders and strong face. His big, toughened hands were surprisingly supple as they caressed the end of the club. A wave of unwelcome longing washed over her and withdrew, carrying some of her determination with it. Haskell felt her scrutiny and lifted blue eyes that were fierce with concentration.

"Galf," he explained, poising again over the ball. "A gentleman's game if ever there was one. Traipsin' around the hills in the brisk air, exertin' body and mind, testin' skill . . . and learnin' tolerance." He lifted one eye from his putting. "Yer husband's terrible at it."

"Probably the only thing he's not perfectly wonderful at," she mused tartly. Arlo's look of surprise made her cheeks pink.

"Nah," Haskell paused, staring at her shapely form and letting his eyes come to rest pointedly on her flat belly, "I can think of another."

Her arms crossed over her waist and she flushed. "Don't be too sure, my lord." She saw Arlo's and Haskell's eyes widen on her and turned back to Skyelt with burning cheeks. Now, whatever had made her say that?

## Chapter Seventeen

October's wane sent eddies of chill wind up the slopes of Skyelt's valley, and they fluttered the long grasses in waves of greeting for Skyelt's son. Ram sat atop the last crest of the London Road and felt the wind's sly fingers flirt with the hem of his kilt and dart away. It stirred an expectation in him that darkened his already somber countenance. His square face was sculpted lean and hard from days of grinding toil and wearing arguments, and his muscular body had a spare, angular look, enhanced by days of meager food and hard travel. He drew a ragged breath and felt the vibrating scrape of flint against honed steel all through his chest as he stared at the valley.

He'd ridden like a banshee for days to reach this point, spurred hard by conflicting desires. He wanted desperately to see his home, ached for the feel of the rocky slopes under his feet, for the smell of ripened grain in the low valley, and for the sound of his people's laughter. But Skyelt now beckoned to a confrontation as well. *She* was here; the closer he got, the more powerfully he felt it. Arlo had brought her, he was sure of it.

He didn't want to see her again, didn't even want to think of her. But fused to those feelings like the other side of a coin was the desire to confront her one last time and in the process disprove the haunting lure of his own memories. No single woman could possibly embody all the lavish, inexhaustible charms that teased and tortured his mind at night. Dread sat squarely on his broad shoulders. He'd have to see her to rid himself of this obsession. And the danger existed that his memories of her, like his memories of Skyelt, might be perfectly accurate. What would he do if that woman of passion and warmth stepped out of his fevered dreams and blended into the cold, vengeful bitch who had denied their marriage vows and sentenced him to grinding toil and degradation?

He shivered as the chilled wind caressed him like a faithless lover's touch. There was no hurry. He urged his tired horse forward with his knees and settled back in the saddle. The slow thud of the hooves echoed in his empty chest.

"Why do you still wear it . . . that dagger?" Eden pushed back the long tartan shawl that covered her head and draped about her shoulders. The sun and their brisk walk had warmed her and now that the hills broke the wind she uncovered her flowing hair to revel in the light breeze brushing her face. She'd been on the high moor with Carina most of the afternoon, picking late wild-flowers and looking for herbs. Her full basket dangled at her side and brushed her burnt-red plaid skirt.

Carina's hand went to the reassuring feel of the dirk's cool metal at her waist. A mischievous look darted from her blue eyes and she smiled.

"Protection," she declared. "A lass canna be without protection. I learned that early on. . . ."

"Really, Carina—who'd dare attack you here at Sky-elt?" It seemed a perfectly reasonable question in view of the fact that she was the laird's daughter. But Carina's look of suffering patience made her think again.

"Everett Blake, Hensley MacLean, Robert Mac-Crenna. . . ." Carina ticked off the list of Skyelt's eligible bachelors on her fingertips and then truly shocked Eden by adding the names of several married men.

"But you're Haskell's daughter."

"His bastard," Carina corrected with a surprising lack of malice. "An' don't think they don't know it. I be fair game in their eyes—bearin' Haskell's randy blood in me veins and born in sin . . . like comin' to like, they expect. An' the womenfolk keep a hawk's eye on my belly, watchin' for it to grow—the silly bitches. Ye canna grow oats in an unplowed field."

Eden stopped in her tracks and stared at her voluptuous little sister-in-law. "You mean you're . . . ?" Her jaw snapped shut. How unspeakably crass of her!

"A *virgin*?" Carina's laugh had a brittle edge that made Eden's heart sink guiltily. "See, even your ladyish sense finds it hard to believe. But it be no happenstance, I'm here to say. Stayin' pure is damn hard work! Just last spring," she raised a finger to wag, "I was in my bed in my mother's own house an' a neighbor's son crawled right in. I was near done afore I reached me dirk. He were a while recupperatin' and me stepfather was furious wi' me. We never got on, my stepfather an' me. 'Twas him, the old prune, insisted Ma send me to Haskell. He was alwus spoutin' scriptures on one hand, while jiggerin' his scales with the other." Carina roused from memory and looked at Eden squarely.

"High an' low, fancy and plain-spoken, they come. Even th' high an' mighty Ian Barclay tried me, at clan gatherin' last year."

"Ian Barclay?" Eden choked. "Carina, really. . . ." She couldn't imagine the handsome Ian as anything but kind and courtly. "He just . . . wouldn't."

Carina looked at Eden as though she were a bit daft and therefore to be pitied. "He's a man, Eden. All men grab an' growl for it, if th' chance betide. They're all like Haskell 'neath the plaid, even if they do behave different wi' a laidy."

Ramsay flashed unbidden into Eden's mind again. There was hardly a topic raised of late that didn't make her think of him. And she didn't care to think about why. For the first time it all began to fit into place. Ramsay was a man cut from Haskell's cloth, all right. She'd sampled only a tiny fraction of his needs . . . she dared not imagine the magnitude of the maelstrom raging beneath his very controlled surface. She shuddered, but it was clearly not from dread. Ramsay hated his own inclinations . . . he'd said so . . . even loathed his desire for his own lawful wife. The conflict he carried inside him must be enormous . . . and destructive.

"What did you do?" Eden became aware she was standing, silent, in the field just outside Skyelt's complex with Carina frowning at her. She'd felt the world tilting a bit underfoot and was scrambling to adjust.

"Do?"

"When Ian Barclay tried to bed you?" Eden was overcoming her last ladylike sensibilities rather quickly. Plain speaking got to the heart of any matter faster.

"Oh," Carina smiled rather tartly and her eyes twinkled, "I cut the bastard. He was mad as Old Scratch. Then I told him who I was and that he ought to be thankin' me for savin' him from the mortal sin of Amnon." She saw her allusion fall short and sighed at Eden's slowness. "In the Bible . . . he bedded his sister." She turned toward Skyelt and at her side her basket swung gently, moved by her hips.

Eden puzzled over that for a minute, then followed,

trying to figure it out. Ian Barclay was Carina's brother? Surely she meant in the metaphorical sense. . . .

Ram visually scoured the outer walls of Skyelt as he neared. His eyes narrowed at the ill-kept look of the place. It was overgrown and thatch and shingles everywhere were in need of repair. Sheep had been run right to the gate; he scowled at the brown, overgrazed patches littering the grounds near the stone wall. Just a few damn months away and Haskell had let the place go. . . .

His eye was caught by red tartan skirts caught moving through the lingering sheep at the corner of his vision. His head turned enough to absorb the sight: two women, young and unmarried, from the style of their hair. They strolled toward Skyelt, stopping to talk occasionally. He turned to inspect Skyelt's towers but some vague familiarity pulled his gaze back to them. He straightened in his saddle, staring at the swing of their baskets, the unhurried grace of their movements. His heart quickened and his thighs began to quiver, making his horse move faster.

He was crossing the stream at the vortex of the valley and starting up the rise to the hall when the wind tugged at one of the women's shawls and she pushed it from her shoulders completely. Her thick, dark hair was lifted and spread on the wind like strands of a spider's silken web. And Ram felt those sinuous strands sliding over him, wrapping about him, and a stab of panic pierced his gut. He went stiff all over as he watched Eden's features begin to focus in his eyes, not just his mind. He stiffled two urges — to race toward her, to run from her. And his horse plodded on, carrying him on a path bound to intercept her.

Just *when* he had surrendered to the urge to stare at her, he had no idea, but for some time, his eyes had devoured the delicacy of her cheek, the motion of her slender hands, the enticing sway of her bottom. And suddenly she was staring at him as well, her hair ruffling about her half-bare shoulders, her lips parted, her eyes luminous and shaded by that fringe of thick lashes. Ram heaved a sigh to combat the pull of her sultry, insolent look. The damned fool horse embarrassed him by slowing and stopping not ten feet from her.

She wore tartan, the fact rattled in his brain and refused to settle, and a common, drawstring blouse that bared her creamy shoulders to his hungry eyes. Her skin blushed in the cold and her breasts moved in a slow, mesmerizing rhythm. A faint smile curled her mouth and she tilted her head, her eyes glowing as they skimmed his rangy form with interest. He could feel her touching him, invading his skin, curling about his nerves and heating his loins. She was magnificent . . . and terrifying.

The sound of his name invaded his consciousness and his head jerked as he resurfaced in reality, shaking inside. The other girl had spoken. He forced his aching eyes from Eden to sweep a second, very appealing female with a thorough look. Recognition released his breath.

"Carina." Ram nodded to his half-sister and made himself think that she'd grown to be quite a handful of woman since he'd seen her last. What was she doing here? Carina smiled at him and her eyes sparkled with undiluted delight. His illegitimate sister was a creature of pleasure, he made himself recall, a tart-tongued temptress and a plague on the ranks of manhood. It was probably fitting that he'd find her in company with. . . .

He growled silently and gave his beast a knee. The contrary animal hesitated just long enough for Ram's eyes to defy him, too. Eden was watching him, her eyes glowing like the setting sun, his delicate chin lifted in challenge while her warm breath beckoned to him. Fortunately, he was some distance away before the shiver racked his broad shoulders. He'd managed passably well for a man whose entire being was aflame.

*"Ramsay . . . lad!"* Haskell embraced his son affably, alternating between clamping Ram to his barrel chest and thrusting him an arm's length away for inspection. "How the hell are you, lad?"

"Well enough," Ram managed to stay at arm's length long enough to say. A whiff of something akin to soap made his brow crease briefly as he returned his sire's raw appraisal. Haskell's skin was a full shade lighter, his wiry beard was trimmed, and he was dressed fit for burying.

"The bloody navy didna feed ya, I see." Haskell's broad grin dimmed as he took in the hawkish cast of Ram's features and the strange light in his eyes.

"It's not in their charter." Ram's voice was low and even as he stepped away and surveyed the hall and the tightly packed group of Skyelt's residents that had crowded just inside the door to welcome him.

"Damn the cuddy lot!" Haskell blustered uneasily, waving a brusque hand at The MacKay, who listened only a moment longer, then herded the kitchen staff back to their work. "We'll see ye fattened up. I hope ye give 'em what for, lad . . . pressin' a laird of me own plaid!"

"I did."

The understated finality of Ram's words added to his aura: he was fiercely controlling something volatile within him. He looked casually about him at the reassuring sameness of the faded tapestries and soot-darkened stone walls. The uncanny accuracy of his memories unnerved him and he suddenly wanted to lash out.

"You've let the place go to hell in a handcart, Haskell." He turned on his father with a fresh flame in his eyes.

335

Halfway to his chair, Haskell jerked around, his mercurial temper escaping. "So, that's how it's to be, is it? Not a minute inside the door an yer righteous as hell wi' me!"

"I expect a laird to see to his trust and accept his rightful duties wi' his land and his people. Ye fling it all aside the minute ye lay eye on a skirt or tankard!" Ram sneered with anger that was out of proportion to the offense. On second look Skyelt was, actually, somewhat better than he'd expected.

"From the mouth of a man wi' no taste for ale or women!" Haskell spread his feet and set his fists at his waist. "What say ye, Terrance . . . be a man wi'out fire in his gut alive or dead?" He swung his great bearded countenance around to glare at his steward. And in the same moment Ram shifted his javelin-sharp gaze to fix the same target.

"I ken . . ." Terrance answered with the aplomb of a man whose career was spent sandwiched between an immovable object and an irresistible force, "it's time to get on wi' the welcome, m'lairds. We all be parched to insensibility."

Haskell's nose curled in disgust and he harrumphed all the way to his chair. Ram's displeasure was no less subtle as he propped his foot on the chair at his father's right hand and leaned an elbow on his knee. Haskell stared at his son's fine, strong leg and bare knee and naturally thought of his daughter-in-law. And when Terrance's liquid peacemaker arrived, he quaffed a mighty chug and resumed the argument, though with noticeably less virulence.

"Ye married the lass; it be a start. It makes a man's heart glad to see his son accept a man's responsibility." The old laird's jutting chin was an invitation to a brawl, and Ram had to throttle himself to keep from accepting.

"Don't you be lecturin' me on the responsibilities o'

manhood, Haskell MacLean. Ye don't know the meanin' of the word," Ram growled.

"Of late, he's been learnin'.'" Terrance had meant to keep those words in his mind, but the sight of Carina Graham strolling into the great hall jolted them free. Ram followed his eyes to the girl's bewitching smile and absorbed the casual provocation of her movement.

A vengeful smirk appeared on Ram's lips. Haskell had his hands full there. It served him right. The smirk melted to raw glee at the thought of how often this little event would be repeated in the future, Haskell made to do right by his bairns. Haskell read his son's thoughts and was seized by the urge to retaliate.

"She's not breedin' yet." It was Haskell's turn to smirk when Ram's grin died. "Yer wife, lad . . . ye've not even asked about her. Ye canna still hold a grudge against me for forcin' ye to her. Ye've been more than compensated for yer troubles in acquirin' her, I understand. God! What I would've given to be a wee mousie in th' corner on the weddin' night!"

A ribald titter went through the crowd. Ram was suddenly incensed that his entire life had the tenor of a damned morality play, displayed in intimate detail before every soul on Skyelt and freely analyzed and judged. His foot hit the floor and he went crimson with rage as he faced Haskell's smug reprisal.

"Keep yer filthy mouth shut, Haskell," he spat menacingly above his father, his eyes molten silver and his fists clenched. A long, tense minute dragged breathlessly by before he jerked away and strode toward the stairs.

Halfway there he stopped dead. Eden was coming down the steps slowly, her shoulders back, her chin high, her Scottish garb swaying in a fetching rhythm. In a glance he saw her hair had been combed and tied over one shoulder in a thick, gleaming cord and that she'd added a tartan sash from shoulder to waist. The proud plaid invited the eye to fall to the one uncovered breast, clearly aroused and shockingly outlined under a soft cotton blouse. And at her small waist was a badge . . . the badge of his clan, nestled there against that tantalizing curve. His hungry senses flustered, then angered him. By the time she stood level with him and only a lunge away, he was wrestling with every carnal nerve in his body.

Eden looked at her husband, searching helplessly every detail of his leaner, harder frame. The simmering anger she'd confronted in the road, when he'd refused even to say her name, was a rolling boil now, perilously close to the surface. It had taken every ounce of courage she possessed to make herself presentable . . . and then to present herself before him in the great hall. She fully expected a diatribe against her betrayal and an order to begin packing. But somehow that all mattered less than her relief that he'd returned safely.

His darkening eyes pulled at hers until they were forced up and fused to his hot gaze. And in the seething cauldron of his emotion, she read his outrage and pain and her stormy future. Her proud stance began to melt under his heat; never mind that it was fueled by fury, it was still heat—raw and potent. Tongues of fire licked their way up into her breasts, tightening them visibly. Gooseflesh appeared on her shoulders and the bare lower halves of her arms. He was turning her inside out with that hard, dark-soul look of his circled eyes. When his gaze dipped to fix on her parted lips, Eden felt the blood rushing to them in futile eagerness for the feel of his against hers.

The passion that arced between them, like searing silver flashes of lightning, charged the entire hall. Not a breath was let in those spellbinding moments. The open fierceness of their laird's intensity shocked the assembly and the lady's smoldering passion titillated even those most immune to her charms. Mouths gaped, eyes burned dryly, pulses raced at this stunning confrontation. Gabriel's trumpet couldn't have torn them from the sight.

The rings of fire in her eyes muted to a white-hot glow that seared his brain. The muscles in his arms twitched, his lips throbbed, he was rousing to his woman—God! Here—in front of half the clan and his reprobate sire—he was ready to throw her down and mount her on the spot! Her potent magic had destroyed his anger and left his pride and his need for vengeance in tatters at their first meeting. With all the anger he'd hoarded, the need for retribution he'd nursed . . . he was reduced to a quivering, jerking mass of coiled nerves and heaving desires.

He tore his eyes from her and forced his face away. He paused, outwardly stolid, inwardly a molten mass. Then he stomped up the stairs toward his rooms, his face dark as Hades and still no word for her on his lips.

Eden stood there bearing the shock of the entire room, hot and shaking and drenched with humiliation. All eyes turned on her, some questioning, some lowering with sympathy, some squinting disappointment. But none had failed to absorb that it was their laird who drew away. With passion so high that it had come alive and pulsed on the air around them, he had stomped off, leaving his bride to stew in need and scorn.

She walked sightlessly toward the kitchens, her back straight, her face strained with control. And soon the gallery of Skyelt's notables and insignificants dispersed, clearly disappointed. Only Terrance and Carina were present when Haskell, who had drunk in the proceedings like a rare, potent liquor, threw back his head and laughed. They exchanged wondering looks as he began to convulse with mirth. He finally wiped his eyes and slowed to a weakened rumble.

"God! This'll be interestin'!" He heaved a deep breath of delight and roared, "Well, where's the food, MacKay?! I be starved!"

Eden had reached the stables before she stopped to look at where she was. She stood in the middle of the stone alley between the stalls, her anger bursting in her veins, her wrath blurring her vision. A long, quivering desire pulsed through her and she turned on her heel and strode back to the house. This desire she could deal with, the desire for revenge.

She was up the servants' stairs in a flash and striding toward Ramsay's rooms—her rooms! She drew a deep breath and jerked the handle, shoving the door out of the way viciously.

"Not a single word of civil greeting . . . nor a curse, nor a slap!" She planted herself inside the door with her fists on her hips and her eyes ablaze. "How dare you?"

Ram stood shirtless beside the washstand, drying his freshly shaved chin, and he strangled the towel in his hands as proxy for her neck. There she stood in the taunt of his family's plaid, pitching mad—changed in some palpable, unnerving way. And his long-stoked ire rose to her challenge. He stalked forward, clenching the linen in his fist, and stopped an arm's length away.

"And just what greetin' is suitable for a faithless bitch who'd deny her lawful husband and betray him to a bloody press gang?"

"I told naught but the truth when asked, Ramsay MacLean." A faithless bitch, was she? "It was you declared us mated, but not husband and wife. You denounced me and our vows and you got what you deserved!" His fury was so intense that the tendons stood out on his neck and arms. But he checked the tide of

340

violence that battered him from within and his forcible easing made Eden shudder. That damnable control of his! She was seized by the urge to push and pummel him past that limit he always drew with her.

"Yea, I was stupid enough to speak the vows with you," he declared nastily. "Perhaps I deserved such misery in punishment for my grand greed. The experience scored deep enough to last a lifetime . . . a lesson in the treacheries of women and lust. But I don' deserve to be mocked—nor my clan. Who the hell do ye think ye are, flautin' my plaid and debasin' my seal?" He pointed with contempt at her sash and badge.

This turn of events set Eden reeling; her mouth dropped open. He proclaimed her adoption of Scottish dress an act of insolence—offensive, mocking the manner and tradition of his family—the very people who had gifted her with it!

"Your father gave me this . . ." her hand went to the worked silver badge at her waist, then to the sash constraining her heaving breast, "and Arlo this . . . and Terrance this . . . and Carina . . . and The MacKay the slippers. . . ." she ground to a speechless end, choked by her own need to explain it to him. She wanted to bash him so badly her knuckles ached!

"If you don't want me tainting and meddling in your precious Scots ways, then you come and rip it off me! And I swear I'll never wear the plaid again as long as I breathe!" Temptation leaped into his eyes and Eden plunged recklessly ahead.

"And while you're at it, go ahead, give me your fist, damn you! Isn't that what you want? To beat me bloody and senseless and set me on a nag bound south?" She took a step closer, heedless of his size and his scarcely reined power.

"Well? What's stopping you?" she ground out, raw

341

defiance straining her every nerve. "Perhaps you haven't the stomach for a clean bit of vengeance any more than you have the stomach for making love to a woman!"

Steely fingers dug into her shoulder like a flash of lightning and his arm was raised and back before she could blink. At the last second she strained against him; her bravado fled as she awaited his blow. Eyes closed, she could still see the raw hatred in his face, feel his fury in his fingers digging into her tender flesh. She waited a breathless eternity.

Ram watched her twist in his punishing grip and a hot wave of other passion surged in him. He lowered his arm slowly, gritting his teeth and despising himself for not doing exactly what she had demanded. And he snatched her hard against him, her cool body searing its impression in his bare flesh like a brand. He couldn't breathe, couldn't move—could only let this agony pound through him as he held her against him. Her enchantress's eyes were squeezed shut, her face was strained, hurting . . . was he hurting her? Good Lord . . . he was mad!

Her eyes opened, dazed and mist-filled, but no longer frightened or defiant. Ram sucked breath and slowly went rigid. In one last frantic effort at control, he succeeded in shoving her away. She stumbled but caught herself against the door and straightened. She stared at him as he walked mechanically toward the bed and her heart dropped to her feet.

His broad, muscular back was lined and ridged with weals from a lash. Though healed, they were still red against the sun-bronzed smoothness of his skin. Eden's stomach surged.

He turned, shirt in hand, and strode to the door. Without looking at her, he paused and shrugged into the shirt. The loathing in his face was for his own mortal weakness, but it hit Eden with all the force he had just

342

withheld. And he stalked out.

Maisie slipped through Eden's door and thought the huge bedchamber was empty at first. She had turned to go when a slight movement on the big bed located her mistress. "M'lady? Be you all right?" She scowled through the growing darkness in the room to make out Eden's features and hurried to light the candles. "Will ye dress for supper, or do ye . . . need a tray?" It was the closest thing to tact Eden had witnessed in her stolid, sharp-tongued maid.

"I'm . . . fine, Maisie." Eden's voice was nasal as she shielded her eyes from the piercing light and slid from the bed. "I'll dress." Her face felt swollen and hot, especially about the eyes. She soothed her hair and lifted her hand glass from the dressing table to survey the damage. A sharp crease was imprinted across her cheek from a wrinkle in the damp pillow she'd fallen asleep on earlier; It betrayed how she'd spent the afternoon. She headed for the cold water at the washstand.

She had Maisie select one of her English gowns and pin up part of her hair. In truth, her appearance was the farthest thing from her mind just now.

Ram's reaction to her was nothing like those she had conjured up in order to prepare herself for their eventual confrontation. He was so hard and his hatred was so well mastered—controlled in the extreme. His azure eyes had pain's passage etched all around them. His square features had a hawkish, hungry look, and that chilled the core of her. And in those last horrible seconds in her rooms, every fear, every nightmare she'd harbored for him had been realized. She shuddered, feeling the tears rising in her eyes again. Her damaged pride, her missish ignorance of the real world had laid those awful stripes on

343

him. She knew her chest was empty, but she felt for her heartbeat anyway.

And her reaction to him couldn't have been more humiliating. Her whole body came alive at the sight of him, consuming every detail of his big, masculine frame, absorbing every nuance of his speech, his movement. For a moment in the hall, she'd thought he stirred to her as well; then he'd pulled away to leave her unacknowledged, announcing to all Skyelt that she was clearly unwanted.

He'd become untouchable . . . and Eden admitted miserably that she wanted nothing more than to be let inside that impregnable wall that defended him from all others, even from himself. There had been times when he made love to her that she'd felt his need and glimpsed a profound wellspring of tenderness inside him. Could it have been just his powerful heritage of sensual command she'd encountered? Perhaps inside that cruel wall, everything was cold and dead either from strangling control or neglect. It was all so confusing . . . so painful.


Supper was a somber affair, endured under Haskell's probing eye and Carina's characteristic mix of concern and curiosity. Arlo was notably absent from his chair at Haskell's right and it was certainly no surprise that Ram's chair was unfilled. Haskell stared darkly at the heavy wooden carvings that should have contained his manly son and finally demanded of Terrance Ram's whereabouts.

Terrance winced and drew a heavy breath as he put down his knife. "He was in th' stables or th' barns a bit ago. Him and Arlo and some of the lads had broke out a keg . . . to celebrate the homecomin'." He saw Eden's frown and shrugged apologetically.

Haskell watched Eden's angry attention to her food and

344

slammed his hands down on the table, pushing his great chair back as he rose. Rumbling irritably, he quit the hall and stalked off in the direction of the stables.

Later, much later, Eden walked the worn carpets in her bedchamber. A heart could only bear so much guilt before throwing over the traces, and this pall of unfinished business was growing unbearable. With every step she trod more blame underfoot and welcomed anger into its place. How dare he spurn the air-clearing that both she and Skyelt deserved, in favor of a drunken rout?

What a naive, ladyish twit she had been! She'd thought it would all be settled quickly once Ramsay returned. He'd rage and bellow and find some way to terminate their marriage, or at least toss her out. And one way or another, she'd be shed of these unsuitable and sometimes painful connections to him and to these crazy Scots.

But then everything had exploded inside her, unleashing the passionate part of her that lay deep within her strenuously purged and rearranged nature. A chain of events was set in motion that seemingly left both her and Skyelt changed. The reemergence of her unfettered and decidedly more enjoyable self had made it a different situation in just three short weeks. Skyelt had become her home.

Now Ramsay was here, refusing to confront her face to face, the coward. Her eyes narrowed as more complex possibilities insinuated themselves into her thoughts. Perhaps he hesitated to toss her out because of her growing bond with his people. Perhaps that was why seeing her in his tartan infuriated him so . . . it meant she'd be harder to get rid of. A Scottish man was considered laird of his home, in theory, anyway. And that expectation was pushed to reality for a Scottish laird. Laird Ram was expected to have his domestic life in hand—to serve as an example to his people, to provide a stabilizing influence in the life of Skyelt. He wouldn't throw her out, but he would use a more subtle, more humiliating tack . . . and make her flee of her own will. The sheer deceit of it seemed a stamp of veracity. What a labyrinthine mind the man possessed!

"Well," she declared nastily, "I'm not going anywhere, Ramsay MacLean. You just try and make me!" She doused the candles, stripped off her robe, and climbed into what had once been Ramsay MacLean's bed. "It's mine now," she muttered, pounding the bolsters into shape, "and I'll not be givin' it back. The best you can hope for, Ramsay MacLean, is to share it with me."

## Chapter Eighteen

One eye popped open, then the other, and Eden sprang up in the middle of her dark bed, disoriented. Her troubled sleep was disrupted by banging on the heavy door to her chambers. She rubbed her face with both hands and dragged her heavy robe over her shivering body. Only a fool slept naked in such cold. Sliding from her bed into the waning firelight, she fumbled with her slippers and called out, "Who's there?" Ram flashed into her mind and she was suddenly wide awake.

The handle screeched and the heavy door swung back to reveal it was indeed her husband—supported under each arm and around the waist by Arlo and two grooms. Ram's head lolled in a particularly familiar fashion and his long, bare legs were twisted under him like a pretzel. Terrance was propped against the door frame, looking ready to slide. The capable steward's gaze had an unfocused quality.

"What?" she snapped, feeling her pulse racing to catch up with her jolted heart.

" 'E's drunk . . . a b-bit, m-m'lady," Terrance acted as spokesman, since his tongue was the only one not pickled.

She hung one arm on the door frame and glared

straight into Terrance's face. The sour stench of spent ale rolled through the door.

"You've all drunk a bit. What reason is that to wake me from a sound sleep in the dead of night?!"

"Well . . . w-we brought 'im to 'is bed, m-m'lady." Terrance squinted, unsure he was getting her true reaction.

"You're mistaken, Terrance," she bit out, "these are my rooms. And I'll not share them with a rotting-drunk soak!"

"B-but . . . m-'m'lady," Terrance looked at his young laird, bewildered by her refusal and thinking of Haskell's order to dump him in her bed, " 'E's yer . . . h-husband."

"Like hell he is!" She was incensed beyond reasoning and pointed at Ram's limp form. "Do you honestly think he could *husband* me in that condition?" She saw the groom's bleary surprise and Terrance's drooping mouth and realized her ire truly shocked them.

"Ye . . . w-won't let 'im in?" Arlo spoke up, shifting and straining with Ram's lax body. Their drunken disbelief finally prodded her into saying it . . . hang the consequences!

"He preferred crawlin' into a jug to crawlin' into his wife's bed on his first night home. Go find him another bed to puke in and another nursemaid for his sore head tomorrow mornin'. I've got a golf lesson!" And she slammed the door.

The grooms were not half so drunk as Eden had assumed. They tumbled into the stables early the next morning and repeated the story of Eden's refusal to let Laird Ram into his own bed—*her* bed, she'd called it. The stableman raced to Charlie, the smith, whose eavesdropping wife told the tale to Cook and to everyone else who might lend an ear. Word spread like a brush fire and soon

The MacKay had the unvarnished details, the major interpretations, and the serious local commentary.

Lady Eden had barred Laird Ram from his own bed; the story ran scrupulously true to the actual happening. Him soaked tight, she'd sneered, and unable to function in a true husbandly capacity. She'd declared a man who preferred the comforts of John Barleycorn to the comforts of his wife of no use to her . . . sent him away saying not to bother her on the morrow, either. She'd be busy "golfin'!"

Predictably, opinion was divided along lines of gender—though men and women alike found it hard to fault her priorities where a good round of golf was concerned. Husbands spoke disparagingly of Laird Ram's laxness with his strong-willed wife, but were otherwise split on whether he should have sought the comforts of his bed before or after a toot with the lads. And many a wife cast a slant-eyed look at her husband that morning and silently applauded their lady's firmness in dealing with connubial error.

Ram was still asleep on a bench just outside the main doors, where Terrance and Arlo had dumped him, then joined him on the ground beside. None of them had thought clearly enough to find him another of Skyelt's several beds, and as a result, the snoring trio had become the object of expectant observation. Errands to The MacKay or requiring business in the great hall suddenly became quite pressing, and a steady stream of folk got a verifying look at their young laird's oblivion. The drama was piqued when Lady Eden, dressed in tartan and looking fit and fetching, came out the main doors, her caddy and clubs in tow, and paused to sniff with a rather pained expression.

Haskell was informed by The MacKay upon his late rising and it made his sore head all the meaner. Storming into the empty hall, he finally found Ram's hard bed outside and he roared for a pail of water.

Ram came up gasping, drenched and feeling squeezed all over, like his body was too tight for him. Moans and groans issued from the sprawled figures on the ground beside him and he shook his head to clear it. The sight of Haskell's florid face made him shut his eyes quickly. Surely he endured enough punishment within. . . .

"Up, Ramsay MacLean, an' see to yer duties, man." Such were an echo of Ram's own words to Haskell on many, many occasions, and they grated on his ears like a rusty hinge. "Ye've snorred more than half the day away—not to speak of drubbin' the renown of MacLean manhood through the mud. Get up and warsh and make yerself presentable before supper!"

Ram lurched and staggered through the courtyard gates to douse his head in a trough. It was some time before he could ease his way into the hall and drag himself up the stairs to his rooms. His head was splitting, his stomach was in revolt, and his temper was vile when The MacKay appeared with a foul-smelling brew she claimed would ease his distress. He had recovered enough to detect the firm note of disgust in her manner and he resented it thoroughly. After all, it wasn't as though he behaved so routinely . . . unlike Haskell and his cronies.

He washed and shaved, at some cost to his skin, and changed into a clean shirt from his still unpacked sea trunk. He took a minute to look about his chambers and found Eden's mark on every nook and cranny. Her dresses in his wardrobe, her lacy and frilly underclothes in his drawers, and her brushes and pots and vials on his dressing table. Her robe draped the foot of his bed and her small slippers were tucked neatly on the floor beneath. The sight tightened his throat; there was even that cursed lilt of lavender and roses on the bloody air! He'd see about rectifying this later, he decided tightly. He had an inspection to make before sunset.

350

Everywhere he went, people greeted him with excessive cheeriness and a new politeness. He went from grainery to smithy to carpenter, feeling a current of something disturbing on the air. His people smiled, but their eyes were full of assessment. They asked after his health, but nodded without genuine agreement when he replied. And more than once, he'd stopped and looked back to find two or more people huddled together, whispering feverishly until his eyes fell upon them.

In the stable, when he caught a groom's impudent eyes rolling, he boxed the youth's ears, but found it did little to relieve the strange feeling that was growing inside him. Something was wrong and he hadn't a clue as to what it was . . . except that it had to do with him. Eden's face and curvaceous form popped into his mind, and he scowled. Yes, likely it had something to do with her as well, since she was the only other change in Skyelt of late.

Haskell's blunt displeasure verified his suspicion.

"Soaked like a rag . . . on yer first night home," he sneered, "not a very appealin' bedmate, I'll give her that. Damn it, ye'll have to do better if you expect to sleep in yer own bed again!"

Ram swore softly and strode toward the well just outside the gate to wash before supper. Did Haskell think he had to apply to Eden Marlow to be allowed to sleep in his own bloody bed? His shoes crunched angrily in the gravel path and if the eruption of laughter hadn't occurred, he might have barged right though the tall wooden gate.

A knot of folk had collected about the well for evening water and a bit of gossip and his own name poured over him like an icy splash.

"Poor Laird Ram!" came a muffled male laugh. "He's got his hands full now. He'll have a devil of a time makin' a babe if she won't let him in his own bed!"

"Well," came a saucy female rejoinder, "him stewed

senseless, he wouldna be much use to her anyway, would he?"

"I say any man who'd rather drain a keg than tend a frisky wife, be askin' for the trouble he gets," agreed another man.

"No woman has the right to bar her man from his lawful bed, whatever his state!" came an irritable male assertion which was promptly booed and overwhelmed in a chaos of disagreement.

Ram heard no more. The little bitch had barred him from his bed last night! That was what had followed him about Skyelt this afternoon like a bloody spectre—making his people stare and whisper and make sly remarks behind their hands. It was the treatment they reserved for one whose behavior offended the social norm . . . like Haskell.

That's why he'd awakened on a cold bench in front of the hall . . . she'd refused him entry to his own rooms! She'd shamed him before his people, made him a laughingstock. Lord, how it heated his blood! He stomped into the great hall, his face dark, his eyes silver with ire. One look at this face and Haskell knew he'd finally learned it all.

The old laird was nursing a tankard on a bench near the fire and leaned back with grin of purposeful contempt.

"I say she was probably right. A game of golf would be a site more enjoyable than a night under the likes o' you."

Ram shook with tremors of volcanic rage. He pivoted and rushed to the stairs, fists clenched and face crimson. The magnitude of his fury brought Haskell a satisfied grin.

Ram reached his rooms just as Maisie was helping Eden into her dress for supper. He slammed back the door and spread himself in the wide doorway, fierce with the need for retribution. Two shocked faces greeted him and for a moment all was stunned silence. Eden pulled her dress up over her shoulders quickly and stiffened, bracing for whatever he'd come to do.

*"Out!"* Ram thundered at Maisie. His lightning gaze went to his unpredictable wife.

"S-stay, Mais—"

"Out!" he countermanded and started forward. Grim satisfaction settled over him as the girl jumped and gave him wide berth, fleeing the chamber and slamming the door shut after her.

"How dare you enter my rooms and order my maid about like a petty tyrant!" Eden drew herself up to meet him, sensing that this time his anger was different . . . deeper and not to be denied.

*"Your* rooms? You err seriously, woman. These are *my* rooms, my bed, my place at Skyelt. You're here only because it is mine. Everything here is my property to dispose of as I see fit. That includes you." He advanced and Eden took a step back in spite of herself. She'd never seen him exactly like this, so big, so determined, so . . . fierce. Her heart was throwing itself against her chest wall.

"There you're wrong, laird. You won't dispose of me at all! You and your underhanded tactics to force me to leave Skyelt . . . ignoring and shaming me before half the assembly . . . refusing to even speak my name. You're afraid to face me squarely and have it out."

"You overestimate my concern, *wife,*" he snarled. "It makes me no difference whether you stay or leave, as long as you stay out of my way from now on! These are my rooms and I'll have them back, now! But you needn't fear you'll be dumped helpless on the doorstep like some unfortunates—to freeze in the night air and catch death in the cold dew. We've plenty of other rooms." His cheek twitched angrily and Eden tried to swallow her heart. He'd drawn closer with each word and his darkened

353

features and lean heat assaulted her body in waves. "I want you out of this room tonight."

"And if I won't simper and grovel out of your way like a good little thrall? What will you do about it, laird?" She put her hands on her hips; her shoulders and head tilted with conscious provocation. "Are you up to having me flogged publicly? Or is private punishment more in line with your . . . tastes?"

Her eyes glowed with an angry allure, beckoning him, daring him to tame her. Her skin reddened, her parted lips felt swollen and bare. Heat poured through her loins like molten lead and he suddenly filled her senses, crowding out everything but his mesmerizing size and his coiled, explosive power. She wanted to feel that power, to direct it and revel in it. She wanted Ramsay MacLean over her, around her, inside her.

He'd never seen her like this. She was deliberately provoking him, daring him to exercise his manly prerogative. His body was churning with expectation as her defiant sensuality filled his head. Her words of a moment ago were already lost. Anger and passion overflowed their bounds, joining in flames of desire that exploded in the center of him . . . a fire that would consume him if it wasn't quenched in the moist heat of Eden Marlow's ripe, maddening body.

He stalked her slowly, letting his intent show in his hot gaze as it devoured her throat and breasts. This time he was in control—it was his need that drove events and for once his need fulfilled his will. The widening pulse of her eyes as she raised her chin sent a shaft of pleasure down the front of him and his arousal was complete. She was his and he'd take her on his terms—now.

Forced backward and caught between Ram and the bed, Eden made no move to escape. When his hands closed on her shoulders, she shuddered and braced her palms against the hardness of his chest. The resistance of her slender hands melted as his muscular arms clamped around her and his mouth swooped down to conquer hers. His tongue plundered the rich velvet of her mouth harshly, but she responded, tilting her head, fitting her melting frame under his arm and along his taut body. Her arms clasped his waist and slid up his broad back with possessive strokes.

Her response to his deliberate force unsettled him, and he pulled back to stare at her flushed face, the sultry fringe of lashes, the bruised and reddened lips. Ire stung him and he released her to grab the top of her gown and jerk it from her shoulders. Stitches popped as he shoved it from her hips and let it fall about her feet. She stood irresistibly still, hands clenched at her sides and shoulders trembling. His eyes flamed as his big hands came up to seize her thin chemise. He tore its pink ribbons to expose her full, taut-tipped breasts; but still she made no move, no protest.

His vengeance, confused and defeated by lack of resistance, fled him. When his sea-toughened hands finally reached for her soft breasts, it was pure need that moved them. The desire to humble and punish became simply the desire for complete mastery. He teased the tight, rosy nipples, then cupped and massaged the creamy globes that hardened under his touch. He watched her eyes close and her head sway to one side. She shivered and pressed against his hands, surprising him again. This was no longer a contest of wills; this was need and desire and perhaps. . . .

More, Eden thought, leaning against his hands, feeling them tug at those invisible strings that stirred her woman's flesh and set it afire. She wanted more. She wanted all of him. . . . everything. She felt his arms slide beneath her ruined chemise and she pressed silky breasts against the coarse wool upon his shoulders as they lifted her and moved her onto the bed. With surprising strength, her

355

arms refused to release him, pulling him down over her aching breasts. Soon, all of him covered her cool, naked skin and his kisses gave as much sweetness as they took.

He began with her mouth and worked his way down to her breasts and belly, kissing her, tormenting her with the hot tracings of his tongue. She burned under his hands and guiding them with gasps and wriggles of response. He encircled her small waist with his hands and buried his face in the smooth plane of her belly, licking and caressing it. She arched against him, wanting him to fill her, to bring her to that sharp precipice of pleasure that would launch her into paradise.

It seemed an eternity until he shed his clothes and spread over her welcoming warmth. Her legs closed around him eagerly, and he sank into her tight, satiny depths, dying a bit with each slow thrust.

"Eden, Eden, Eden." His hoarse whispers repeated her name over and over against her hair, her sensitive ears, her hot, quivering breasts. To Ram, Eden—the name and the woman—had come to mean paradise. It was an incantation of her sensual power and of his deepest need. And now he reveled in it, saying it into her eyes, whispering it along her throat, growling it along the dewy valley between her breasts.

She locked her fingers in his dark hair and stopped his throaty murmurs with her mouth. Surging upward, she met his thrusts and felt that jagged spiral pushing her higher, rushing her toward pleasure's boundary. And suddenly, without completing the journey, she arrived in hot, shuddering blasts of response. Time and being were suspended, irrelevant, in that breathtaking moment.

Ram halted, stunned: she tightened around him, arching, clinging to his hot body as aftershocks rumbled through her. Releasing his breath, he panted, watching satisfaction spread under her moist skin and a pleasurable fatigue relax her taut muscles. She was melting beneath him, absorbing him.

Moments later, her fingertips moved over the small of his back and crept over the tight mounds of his buttocks. She wriggled her pelvis against him lazily and pushed him deeper into her. When his delicious weight began to lift, her eyes flew open, seeking his, and her legs crossed over his buttocks, forbidding him to move away.

"Ramsay—Ram," she breathed, only now feeling the tension still coiled in his powerful body, seeing the unquenched fire in his eyes: it confused her. She might have asked what had happened, but the cluttered pathways of sensation were suddenly cleared and she felt his pulse drumming inside her, insistent and unsated. How could that be?

He waited, taut, disbelieving. What had happened was all too clear to him! No woman had ever found her pleasures before him . . . never. He was shaken and a little awed. He made to move away again and Eden's steamy eyes flew wide with alarm; her hands reached instinctively for his head.

Instinct told her she had to erase that strange look from his face and she knew only one way. Her fingers entwined in his hair and pulled him toward her waiting mouth. The deep luxury of her kiss, the eagerness of her hands on his back and buttocks were an opiate against his reeling thoughts. The fire stoked in his loins now seared paths down his legs and arms, making him clutch her tightly and thrust deeper inside her. He possessed her fully and he still wanted more.

*More* . . . it pounded like his blood in his brain . . . *more*. And suddenly he erupted into her sweet, straining depths. She contracted around him with a cry of surprise and together they soared, joined in breath and pulse and spirit.

Eden collapsed, unable to move, unable to realize what had just happened to her. Concentrating on his response, his powerful need had become her own desire, yet she had journeyed to yet another heaven on Ram's powerful drafts of passion. Each time it was a discovery, each time it was a little like dying.

"Ram," she felt him stir heavily and managed to catch his face between her hands. "I . . . missed you. . . ."

Ram withdrew and rolled from the bed abruptly, running shaky hands back through his burnished hair. A draft of air rushed in to replace him and raising gooseflesh with its chill. She pushed herself up and blinked in the fading light. He had thrown his kilt over his still swollen parts and his face was suddenly hard as granite as he fumbled with the buckles.

"Ram, what's the matter?" Her voice was thick and seductive, despite her heart sinking and her fear mounting. She'd seen this change before. "Ram—please!" She pulled the coverlet up over her breasts and scooted to the edge of the bed. Every garment he replaced was another barrier between them.

"Did I do something wrong?" she finally blurted out, ashamed seconds later when he stopped with his shirt in his hand to stare at her. Her hair tumbled over her like an erotic sable tide and her perfect skin was flushed from his chin's abrasion. Her lips were bruised by his force and her eyes were hung with liquid crystal.

He'd meant to punish her—to inflict himself on her. He'd meant to satisfy his basest cravings—lust and revenge all at once. But she'd opened herself to him, giving him whatever he wanted, yielding him all he would take. She'd responded the way no woman ever had; and when he might have withdrawn, overwhelmed, she drew him back into her arms and sought his pleasure as eagerly as she found her own. The beast conquered by the beauty, the rogue bested by the lady. God, how he loathed the animal he'd become!

"Ram, please . . . don't do this again—" She climbed

from the bed trying to drag the coverlet with her toward him, but she was stopped at its length and tugged futilely.

"Nay, woman, I'll not do it again." He flinched, misunderstanding her plea. The growl died in his throat as he stopped in the midst of shoving his shirt into his kilt. Standing there with her feet and legs bare and her hair tousled, she looked like a waif, vulnerable and confused . . . and so damned desirable. A wave of pure longing overcame him, and he had to flee in order to breathe again.

Eden stood shivering in the dim light, seeing Ram's face as it had looked in that last moment before he left. The image was burned into her eyes and heart forever . . . passion, longing, loathing, pride, disgust: all of a man's peaks and valleys compressed in one devastating look. And it was aimed at her . . . and her passion.

But it was a new Eden Marlow that absorbed the shock of her husband's carnal disgust and struggled with it.

"Damn it, Ramsay MacLean! I want you." Her arms cradled her waist as she stood wrapped in the bedclothes. "What's wrong with wanting you to warm my bed at night and wanting to wake up . . . in your . . ." the tears were starting to roll, "arms?"

She'd wanted him badly enough to seduce his anger and cheat his revenge. She'd wanted him enough to cast aside her own anger and pride, hoping to hold him, however briefly. But her longings were growing more complicated by the minute. A kiss, a moan, a glorious tumble were easy enough to provoke, as she'd just learned. But what good was all that ecstasy when he looked at her afterward as if she'd just crawled from under a rock?

Eden sighed and melted down onto her rumpled bed, rubbing her wet, sensitive cheek over the soft sheet where they'd entwined only minutes ago. She could hardly breathe; she wanted to lie safe in his arms and feel his chest rumbling as he whispered their future into her. She wanted to learn his cryptic, insightful kind of logic and talk with him about things that made her wonder. She wanted him to trust her with his thoughts, his dreams, his desires. She wanted to feel he cared about her, that maybe someday he could come to love her . . . just a little.

It hurt too much to think about and she made herself draw the curtain on those tender confusions. If he wanted her out of his bloody bed, he'd have to come and carry her out, naked as a jaybird. She snuggled determinedly into the tousled covers and dried her eyes. And they'd see whether he even made it to the door with her before. . . .

Her face began to glow with determination. In his sight, she might not be a wife, but tonight he'd made her his mistress, whether he intended to or not. And there was a long, cold winter ahead and the hot blood of a Marlow at his fingertips. . . .


That night, Eden had a fire laid in the seldom-used upstairs parlor and sent for Carina to join her. In recent weeks she'd come to treasure these relaxed moments in which she tutored her eager little sister-in-law in the refinements expected of a lady. Over a lesson in fine stitchery, Carina made tart observations on Ram's tardiness to supper and his agitation and poor appetite. It brought an enigmatic smile to Eden's lips. She confided that Ram had ordered her out of his chambers and that she had spent a good long while explaining that she had no intentions of turning them over to him.

Carina laughed heartily and commented that it was commonly held that, for all his learning, Ram had a lot to discover about women. Eden flicked a glance at the ceiling, and in spite of her attempts to hide it, the afternoon's tumult crept into her face.

"It's not his learning that's lacking." Eden's earthy flush made Carina's eyes narrow and her curiosity itch. "Ram's a man o' great parts, you know."

Carina went off in peals of girlish laughter and Eden added wickedly, ". . . if he'd only decide to use them."

When they sobered up, Carina wiped the moisture from the corners of her eyes and sighed heavily. "You be married and unbedded and I be wrestled to bed regular and still unwedded. There ain't no damned justice, you know."

Arlo came for Ram's trunk the next morning and Eden and Maisie watched as he and one of the grooms trundled it out and down the connecting hall to a modest room once reserved for strangers and visiting mothers-in-law. Eden raised her chin in forced triumph and smiled pleasantly at Maisie. Maisie smiled back and was soon off on an errand to the kitchens. And it wasn't long before the word spread that Laird Ram was moved out permanently.

An argument began among the folk over what was at fault; his insulting her the day he arrived or her barring him from his bed. But the end result was the same . . . the young laird wasn't doin' his duty, and the cradle would go empty indefinitely, at this rate. Laird Ram had never exactly set the place ablaze with his needs, unlike old Haskell. Too many local lasses and their mothers had been disappointed in their attempts to interest him in liaisons, permanent or otherwise. His dismal record there spoke for itself, some declared. And it looked ill to have him be the one to pack and leave. Too well they recalled that in that first electrifying confrontation, he'd been the one to withdraw, not her.

Haskell watched them at supper the next night, Ram avoiding her across the table and using stilted phrases and monosyllables when he was forced by circumstances to speak to her. The old laird's chin drew tight against his fleshy chest and he glowered, wondering if he'd done the right thing, trickin' the lad into gettin' soused and havin' him dumped in his wife's bed. He'd been sure that of a morn, nature would take its course . . . it always did with him. But this rare twinge of self-examination soon passed, and he determined to watch for a chance to give things a nudge again.

# Chapter Nineteen

Dry grass rustled under Eden's feet as she walked along the ridge above Skyelt and pulled the collar of her heavy fur-lined coat tighter against the damp, cutting wind. Pitch and dunk this wretched country—with its constant gray and damp—and its constant flapping tongues!

Never . . . never in her whole life had she struck a servant. *Never!* It had been drilled into her that ladies were far above such things. But Skyelt didn't recognize the distinction between ladylike restraint and lily-livered weakness. To be respected here, one had to take servants in hand, literally. Her face darkened like the swirling November clouds overhead.

The venomous old witch! "No use watching m'lady's belly," the old housewoman had sneered, not realizing the object of her conjecture sat mere feet away, just inside the upstairs parlor, trying to concentrate on reading one of the young laird's many books. "He ain't gone near her since he come home."

A nasty giggle that sounded suspiciously like Maisie's responded, "Not that she ain't tried." The giggle's ownership was confirmed. "The way she watches 'im when he ain't lookin' . . . she'd have 'im in her bed in a minute. It's 'im what's at fault."

"High an' mighty Laird Ram," the old witch had snorted. "Him with 'is fancy larnin' and righteous ways. Cook says he'd do well to larn a bit from his pa. I say he jus' ain't got the yen fer it. Belike, it's what the smithy said: 'We got one laird wi' too much juice, the other wi' none a-tall.' "

Eden had charged out of the parlor and very nearly laid the old crone flat on her rear. Her hand had stung for a quarter of an hour afterward. She stared at it now, flexing her fingers and curling them into a fist. She pressed it to her lips and her throat began to tighten.

This deep sense of humiliation confused her. Strangely, it had nothing to do with the way they'd spoken of her . . . of her looking at Ram, wanting him. Ram was their *laird*, and a good, fair man who had only their welfare at heart. They had his devotion and his care as she never would, and look how contemptuously they treated it . . . berating him, sniggering behind his back. She was beginning to boil again and walked faster, shedding her bonnet and turning her heated face into the light wind.

She walked the path toward the moors, reliving every miserable encounter of the past week . . . not that there were so many of them. If she'd thought to let time and proximity melt their icy relationship, she was miserably mistaken. He managed to be in the most inaccessible places, doing the hardest, most taxing work on all Skyelt. He never looked directly at her, spoke seldom, and suffered Haskell's thinly veiled taunts with a look that gave new vehemence to the appelation, "dour Scot."

Failing his company and desperate for another route to common ground, she recalled James's rakish assertion that began, "To know a man, one must read what he reads. . . ." And she'd begun to read books Arlo secreted for her from Ram's personal library. Her erstwhile husband's tastes ranged from Lord Byron to animal husbandry, from mathematics to Italian love sonnets. The latter heartened her briefly, until she paused to wonder who at Skyelt had been the recipient of their erotic cadences, murmured in his deep, resonant tones, in intimate postures. And immediately, she reverted to *The Principles of Roman Water Distribution*, wondering grimly how an appreciation of old aqueducts might be used to lure her husband into her bed again.

"Unescorted and abroad in this inhospitable weather—it must have been dire indeed to send you chargin' onto the moors this afternoon," came a deep, rolling voice that poured over Eden like a balm. She turned to find Ian Barclay staring down at her from horseback.

She'd been contemplating her problems and her feet so doggedly, she hadn't heard the animal's approach. Now she flushed with pleasure at the friendly warmth of the eyes trained on her . . . very blue eyes under thick, dark hair.

"Ian Barclay, you took me by surprise!"

"You were lost in another world—I hope it's not a disappointment to find yourself back in this one." He leaned on the pommel of his saddle and grinned meltingly. Eden wondered ruefully how the household of Grenbruck was able to function with him reducing the female contingent to mere puddles every time he smiled.

"Not at all disappointed," she replied. After the strain of the last ten days, she beamed both relief and pleasure.

"I've promised you my assistance . . . and the offer includes my ear." Ian smiled and dismounted, coming to stand in front of her, reminding her of his height and broad-shouldered grace. "Is it Skyelt still bedevilin' you? Or does this new furrow have to do with Ram's return?" One warm, square-tipped finger traced the expressive arches above her eyes, smoothing the frown from her face.

She shivered and had difficulty meeting both his gaze and his question. "I've learned to deal with Skyelt, mostly, but it's still learning to deal with me, I'm afraid."

"A pleasurable task, surely," he offered his arm and, in the grip of familiarity that went beyond their brief association, Eden accepted it. He smiled warmly and continued her on the walk he had interrupted.

"I doubt some at Skyelt would think so."

"Including Ram?"

His directness unnerved her briefly and the falter in her graceful stride betrayed it.

"Nay, Ram deals with me rather efficiently, I fear."

"But rather seldom."

Eden stopped, flustered, and tried unsuccessfully to remove her hand from his arm.

Ian's smile captured her eyes in spite of her. Its warmth and tacit understanding disarmed her completely. "I've known Ram all his life, Eden. I didna expect he'd have changed that much. He's got a king's finesse with mulish farmers an' herdsmen, the instincts of Solomon with feudin' neighbors, an' the shrewdness of Shylock when strikin' a bargain. But he's sadly lackin' in matters pertainin' to the distaff side." The look in his eyes said clearly that he had no such difficulty and Eden was piqued that she should agree with him on both counts. Why was she feeling this annoying need to defend her husband from his lifelong friend's candid assessment?

"He's angry with me." She turned to walk, slipping her hand free.

"A lover's quarrel. Tsk, tsk," he clucked with a teasing frown, "or has he ever been your lover? I wonder." She stopped to look at him and he shrugged with perfectly crafted charm and answered his own unthinkable question. "Of course, it would be too much to hope that he'd have abstained totally . . . I wonder that you're willing to remain at Skyelt at all, having tasted the best of both house and master. Not all upland houses are so poorly run, nor their masters so . . . lacking in the finer points of romance."

It sounded strikingly like an invitation to Eden and the dawn in her eyes began to heat.

"He has reason for his anger." She lifted her chin a fraction and watched him closely. "The reason he didn't accompany me to Skyelt was—"

"—an ill-timed appointment with an English press gang," Ian finished for her. "And he spent the better part of two months on a light frigate, learnin' the Royal Navy's brand of humility." He laughed at her surprise. "Skyelt's not an island, sweet lady. Despite the occasional ill breeze, there is regular commerce between Grenbruck and Haskell's estates. And you've observed how swiftly news flies." He held back the part about how he had cultivated any and all news of her since his brief visit to Skyelt some weeks before.

"It was my fault he was pressed," Eden blurted out, having nearly forgotten the protective urge that began this shocking conversation. Before now, this secret had lain between her and Ram alone, and only now she wondered why he hadn't declared it from Skyelt's sagging rooftops. If he really did hate her. . . . "I was asked to verify his identity and in a fit of pique, I . . . I didn't."

"You denied him? And sent him off into the navy's raw clutches?" The depth of Ian's surprise made her wince. "You betrayed the righteous Ramsay MacLean? God! I knew he had deficits, but the honeymoon must have been a regular disaster to merit that!"

"He was—it had nothing to do with—I was angry with him because—" She was suddenly sick of hearing of Ramsay's supposed deficiencies as a lover and husband! He certainly didn't seem "deficient" when he finally got around to it. It was just that damnable control of his, and his disgust afterward. What could have caused a brawny, red-blooded son of Haskell to hate his own natural feelings so? She was standing silently lost in thought, trouble creasing her satiny brow again. Was it her? Was there something about her he truly despised?

"You're a dangerous woman, Eden Marlow. Were I your man, I'd see your every wish fulfilled—and give you no chance to be angered with me." Ian's softly burred tones called her back and raised her attention to his strong, sculptured face. The glow in his blue eyes set her nerves trilling. He had moved closer, close enough to share his warmth with her, close enough to melt against.

Eden watched him and waited, knowing what he was going to do. Memory opened and flooded a need through her. She wanted to kiss firm lips, to feel strong arms around her. . . . It was her tainted Marlow blood rousing! The insight rattled through her. Ram knew her awful secret, her cravings, her unladylike responses to loving. And no doubt he guessed that sooner or later there'd be an Ian, or a somebody. Gripped by both horror and discovery, she could not avoid his arms as they moved about her. She was lost in the desire in his eyes and stood feeling utterly hopeless as his head lowered to hers.

That lovely pressure against her lips, massaging, entreating—it was all so beguiling, so terrible. Her hands went to his shoulders, but without enough force to push him away. Her fingertips touched his collarbones and her palms pressed against his hard chest. He felt so familiar, so sturdy, so. . . . Her eyes opened on dark hair, a sunbronzed cheek and temple, and she pulled back to look at him. The light that danced in those blue eyes was familiar too, missing something. It was almost . . . it was so close . . . it just wasn't . . . Ram.

Eden's eyes widened with new sight. It was the light of

Ram's eyes she craved and the feel of his strong arms. It was the touch of Ram's mouth that turned her into a wanton, the reluctant sweetness of his caresses that set her aflame. Ian's kisses were masterful and thrilling, but only when she closed her eyes . . . and experienced how very much like Ram he was. Her eyes flew wider.

"Ian," she murmured breathlessly, caught up in her shattering discovery, "do it again." Pleasure was born in his face and he obliged.

Every sensation filtered through Eden's new reality: the tilt of Ian's head was like Ram's, the line of his mouth similar but not quite perfect, his lean hands didn't seem to find that sensitive spot on her back the way Ram's always did. On and on, every bit of contact was scrutinized and Ramsay MacLean lurked in every hint of pleasure. In truth, Eden Marlow MacLean realized she was kissing her husband, or some of his better qualities, by proxy. It was a proxy that would have enraged Ram MacLean to the point of bloodletting.


Fortunately, at that moment Ram was far away, climbing down from a shed roof and brushing cobwebs and the dust of rotted wood from his heavy plaid. Carina had been watching him with the carpenters on the roofs and now strolled over to hand him a tin dipper of cool water from the well. He accepted with a searching glance around them and drank.

"She's gone for a walk," Carina read his questioning look and supplied an answer. When he tried to appear disinterested, she reiterated, "Yer wife, Ramsay, she's gone for a walk."

"She has that freedom. I place no restrictions on her." He handed her back the dipper and trudged to a nearby split-log bench. He settled down and ran his hands back through his thick, unbound hair.

"You place damn little on her," Carina observed, eying him with disgust. She settled beside him, still clutching the dipper. "You'd do well to see to your bride, brother."

"And you'd do well to temper that ragin' tongue, girl. Maybe then you'd find someone to take you off Haskell's hands." He looked at her petite, burnished beauty that shone even while swathed in a thick, concealing shawl and knew a wave of sympathy for Skyelt's hopelessly primed bachelors. The saucy tilt of her chin was a sensual ultimatum of itself. Two of them about the place—small wonder Skyelt wasn't the same anymore.

"There's no lack of applicants, brother—only acceptable ones."

"You've declined Tass MacCrenna's offer, then?"

"Haskell did—after I threatened to slash his fatherly throat in his sleep. He's fit to be tied." Ram couldn't help smiling at her, and her face softened to a mere sixteen years as she returned it.

"I expect he is. What is it you really want, Rina?" It surprised him to think that probably no one had bothered to ask her that before.

"What does any woman want, Ramsay? I want . . . a home . . . babes . . . a life." She swallowed hard and looked at her hands squeezing the cold metal handle on her lap. "Only I won't be packed off into a cold marriage because some man crooked his fat finger! All my life I've been somebody's problem. Just once I'd like to be . . ." her chin quivered unexpectedly, "somebody's . . . *joy.*" She sniffed, horrified, and uttered a startling string of expletives before getting herself in hand again.

"I want the right man, Ramsay MacLean." She grabbed his sleeve and he faced a wrenching blend of passion, desperation, and determination. "I want a man who won't paw and demand, but let me give him things on my own.

370

I want him to love me until I forget every swear word I ever learned. And I want to feel my toes curl and my stomach flip every time he smiles at me. I won't settle for less." She glanced defensively at Ram and found him looking at her with new understanding and a dawning brotherly affection.

"Any notions where we might find you such a paragon of manliness and endurance?" His gentle teasing brought the smile back to her lips and he felt oddly protective of his romantic little wildcat of a sister.

"There's you," she teased back. "But yer my brother and yer already taken, even if you haven't figured out what to do with yer wife yet. I'd tell ye exactly what she needs, but bein' the innocent you are, it'd make you blush." Her saucy tone was back and she gave him a scandalous wink as she rose and swayed back to the main house.

He laughed gently and leaned against the wall behind him, tucking his thumbs into his coat pockets. A shiver ran through him and Eden's lovely face suddenly emerged from an unexpected corner of his mind. Just what did Eden Marlow want? And why was he so afraid to ask her?

Ram saw Eden and Ian walking down the cart path together. Her hand nestled in the crook of his arm; they seemed content with the cozy picture they made. Warning tremors began to rumble inside him and he stiffened, scrutinizing their approach with harshly reined senses and harsher interpretation. It was Ian's bold admiration that reddened her cheeks, not the deepening cold. Her lashes fluttered because she played the coquette, not to veil her thoughts. It was the memory of more intimate communion that curved her lips upward when she spoke to Ian.

371

He could not have known that Eden's discovery of her feelings for her husband had inured her to all but Ian's physical presence.

". . . see to your bride, brother," he'd been warned. Trysting on the moors — he knew it with all the conviction that guilt and tight-fitting righteousness can wield. A panicky minute of indecision seized him: the urge to confront and lash out violently was strong, but years of ruthlessly practiced control finally proved stronger. His face set like mortar, his movements coiled and jerked as he made his way to the great hall to await them.

For their part, no two people had more separate thoughts than Eden and Ian Barclay. He was wondering about the current state of the annulment and divorce laws and lamenting the demise of the old custom of bride-stealing. Eden was wondering where her husband was and what intrigue she might employ to finagle him into her rooms that night. Failing that, she'd have to declare her love for him atop Skyelt's barn roofs, which had been his haunt of late. And she intended to do just that, declare her love for him, before another sunrise. Just how he would react, she couldn't imagine.

A strong clue to her reception lay in the way Ram's fists settled on his waist and his wide shoulders jutted forward when she and Ian entered the hall together. Ian assumed a slightly more subtle posture, his legs spread and braced and his thumbs tucked into his thick leather belt. Eden watched their exchange with wide eyes. These "life-long friends" had suddenly contracted lockjaw and spoke through clenched teeth. And Ram's glare at her had the subtlety of a dull claymore. Whirling, she stopped half-way to the stairs and turned to find them staring after her with equal lights of determination in their blue eyes.

* * *

In her bedchamber, she shed her damp cloak and picked up an iron to poke the dying coals in the grate. Her hillside resolve was tested the instant she stepped inside the great hall.

The door banged open and Ram stepped inside her chamber. He'd brought his combative posture with him.

"You've taken to trysting on th' moors, I see. You've learned Scots' habits, all right . . . a pity you chose to embrace the lowest and worst of my people's ways."

"Trysting on the moors?" Eden was surprised at the strange tenor of Ram's accusation.

"You canna deny what is plain to all with eyes to see. And Ian Barclay—of all men to flaunt in the face of your vows and my people! I'll not have it!"

"Flaunt in the. . . ." She echoed dumbly, only now realizing she was accused of blatant infidelity. "A low, filthy thing even to think, Ram MacLean. I took a walk to sort my thoughts and Ian Barclay came upon me," an unfortunate choice of words, she realized when his eyes narrowed further, "and escorted me back to the house! He's the soul of courtesy and friendliness—which is more than I can say for you or your shabby, evil-tongued household!"

"Ian Barclay doesn't excuse a belch without expectin' some gain, woman. And there's only one gain he would expect from you." His eyes raked her harshly, but with a deepening gleam.

"It irks you that he might find my company desirable when you've cast me off as unfit association, is that it?" She now stood an arm's length from him. His tight rein of control suddenly infuriated her and she twitched with the need to see it snap. "Perhaps it's your own desires you place in his heart. Perhaps it's *you* that can't look at me without wanting . . . and you're too fine and righteous to do anything about it!"

"Watch your tongue, woman!" He swelled and trembled with the effort of constraining his raw impulses.

"As for your people, I could hardly shame you more than you've done yourself." She choked it out. "They cluck their tongues and shake their heads and call you a juiceless old woman . . . for ignoring your duty to me—"

He grabbed her against him and the breath was slammed from her in the process. His mouth crushed hers with punishing desperation, ignoring her late resistance. Eden tried to resist him, knowing anger moved beneath his desire. A semblance of reason was salvaged, despite his overpowering force.

Her heart was thudding dully, hurting and blocking all other sensation. Grasping the sides of his coat for support, she quieted and stood perfectly still, allowing him to spend his anger in the crushing embrace.

Inescapably, his arms gentled, his lips softened over her yielding mouth. His kiss was not returned, but it was no longer denied. Surrender, it beat in his brain, it was only surrender. And the ache in her chest migrated into his. His point now moot, and shamed equally by his anger and his need, he ended the tender agony of his mouth on hers. He was shaking.

Dull pain burned in the coals of her eyes and her lips were swollen from her harshness.

"Why, Ram?" she whispered hoarsely up into his flinty features. "Why do you have to be angry to touch me? Once you held me with care. Is there no tenderness for me in you anymore?"

Each word sliced unerringly through his embattled heart and his hard arms slackened and released her. Her relentless yielding kicked the pieces of his fractured core into dark, numb corners, leaving him hollow.

The door slammed back as he strode out and Eden felt like he'd ripped her heart from her. She'd betrayed her longing for the tender and loving parts of him. But at least now she knew they existed. Twice they'd tamed his anger and gentled his touch. And it was all the harder to bear, knowing they existed yet were so far beyond her reach.

She settled numbly onto a chair and wrapped her arms around her, feeling small and wretched. She loved Ram MacLean, there was no denying it. He had conquered her body's desires, rearranged her priorities, and invaded her heart. There wasn't a part of her that was left untouched, not even her pride. She'd discovered powerful passions within her and learned to express them, she'd gained the maturity to see beyond the mincing manners of polite society and found the confidence to command her place in the world. Yet all her effects on him seemed negative. He hated himself for wanting her and she alternately enticed and disgusted him. She'd become a wedge driven between him and his one love, Skyelt and its people. She'd shamed him openly and betrayed him into pain and violence. It was a miracle he *hadn't* beaten her when she asked for it!

The tears clinging to her eyes froze in place. He had't beaten her . . . or disowned her . . . or even evicted her from *his* rightful place on Skyelt. And when he touched her, his anger drained and he grew gentle and passionate. . . . Eden's heart stopped and when it started again, hope surged in her.

He must care something for her . . . it couldn't be guilt or passion alone that melted his lips over hers and made his body tremble against her. What made him scorn his human feelings and count his tenderness and need for her as weakness? Why wouldn't he let himself love her . . . even a little?

"I want to know about my husband." Eden had stalked into the huge kitchen where the supper meal was in progress and ordered Cook and the entire scullery out in a tempest. She'd restrained the surprised MacKay and forced her gently down on a stool by the glowing cooking hearth. Now she stood in front of the housekeeper, her hands on her hips and her eyes crackling with determination.

"I want to know everything, every bloody detail."

The MacKay eased as she studied Eden, then nodded and waved her lady to a seat on a nearby bench. "I was wonderin' if you'd ask. Where shall I start?"

"At . . . the beginning. With Ram's mother and Haskell." It suddenly came to her that that would be the place. "He loved her a great deal, I take it."

The MacKay folded her hands and lowered her eyes. "Then you'd be takin' it wrong. As a young man, Haskell was much as you see him now . . . brash, lusty, if possible—even more arrogant. He married Ram's mother, Lady Edwina, because she was rich and from a family of males. He didn't know nor care she was forced to marry against her will, against her very nature. When he brought her to Skyelt, she found it much as you did, only she had no desire to claim her place here and for six years she suffered Haskell's indifference and the knowledge of his bastards. She had trouble birthin' Ram, an' Haskell was told she shouldna be brought to bed again."

"Ram was not yet five years when she died, birthin' a stillborn. She couldna stand Haskell's infidelities and had taken him to her bed again to keep him home. It took her death to make Haskell see she'd cared for him, in her own strange way. And he vowed ne'er to marry again . . . 'twas his way of honorin' her." The MacKay smiled wanly. "She'd have been pleased by the tribute."

"And Ram?" Eden scowled, feeling a melancholy kinship with Ram's abandoned mother. She shivered and crossed her arms over her waist. "What happened to Ram?"

"Lady Edwina had loved him dear and kept him close by her. He was purely lost after she died; Haskell ignored the lad mostly. Her brother, Uncle Fenrick, was an unmarried man of the cloth. He took the poor little lamb to raise, and Haskell was distracted and content to let him. When Haskell finally did come to his senses and send for his heir, Ram was seventeen, near fully grown. And they got on like oil and water; Ram filled with Uncle's sermon wrath an' Haskell abusin' the seventh commandment at every turn o' the hand."

"So Ram was raised by a bachelor uncle . . . and a minister. . . ." Eden's chest began to ache. The MacKay sniffed and her nose curled in distaste.

"Fenrick was more fire-eyed fanatic than minister . . . denounced his own bishop for tillin' his wife's field too often." She shook her head and sighed. "It were my idea to send Ram off somewhere that he didna have to battle neither the kirk nor his father. And with his knack for books and ciphers, the university in Edinburgh seemed the place . . . it done him a world of good! He learned and grew and began to make peace with himself. Except . . . in the matter of women."

Eden nodded, frowning as Ram's pain and conflict took shape in her heart's eye. It all began to make horrible sense.

"Haskell's lust was Lady Edwina's end and has been Ram's shame all his life. He's lived with Haskell's bastards on every hand, constant reminders of his own mother's fate. Ram determined never to marry, nor ever produce a bairn on any lass. But Haskell's a crafty devil and he knew Ram's care for Skyelt was uncommon strong. He's devoted his years since Edinburgh to improvin' the es-

377

tates. He's put his heart into it."

"And Haskell found out his old lover had a daughter. . . ."

"A bonnie daughter . . . and a true lady," The MacKay supplied. "He figured Ram's MacLean blood would have to warm to a daughter o' his fiery Constance. And he'd get a true son and a grandson in one fell swoop. It sounds selfish, but I honestly think . . . he meant well."

Eden squeezed her hands together between her knees and knew her last bit of anger at Ram's deceit and treatment of her was gone. He was no longer the cool, self-sufficient nobleman who had taunted her boldly on the deck of the *Gideon's Lamp* and forayed into her bed to force her into marriage. She knew him now as no other could. A battle raged inside him, pitting his morality and education against his startling inheritance of sensuality.

Thinking of him in those terms, she felt a kinship with his struggle. If it hadn't been for the persistence of his formidable passions, she might never have experienced the sensual joy that revealed the painful divisions in her own soul.

She sat before the fire, silent under The MacKay's soft gaze. She thought of the contrast between her parents' deep and passionate love and the rampaging lust that had filled old Haskell's life and went weak with pity. Ram thought that to succumb to desire was to become another Haskell . . . he'd *said* so. He didn't know other possibilities existed . . . wonderful, loving possibilities. Well, he'd just have to be taught—Eden straightened—even if it mean seducing him and his disgust over and over!

Her feelings paraded across her face, trailing resolve in their wake. The MacKay lent Eden's womanly heart all the support she could muster, knowing the decision must be Eden's alone and praying she would use the key she possessed to free Ram from the past.

Eden's breath filled her bodice and she rose, mouth firm and eyes alight. "Where is he?" The MacKay rose, relief erasing the frown of waiting.

"He's gone to check the flocks in th' western dales. Lord knows when he'll be back."

Eden smiled gently into the housekeeper's inquiring look as she recalled the desperate quiver of Ram's body against hers a short while ago. "I doubt he'll be gone too long."

# Chapter Twenty

"Please, m'laird." Lanky Terrance balanced his second youngest, wee Marilyn, on his hip and looked frazzled beyond bearing. "Come an' see, at least."

"That's Ram's work." Haskell huddled deeper into his chair near the fire and glowered at his beleaguered steward. "I be no engineer—nor a carpenter. Where in th' bloody hell is he, anyway?" He shot a meaning-filled glare at Eden, who sat in a chair near the hearth in the great hall, stitching. She looked up and sent him a stubbornly sweet smile.

"He's been in the runny dales, west, these two days. It's poutin' up to rain or snow an' we got to finish the roofs."

"Finish, then, an' let me be."

"Laird Haskell, ye mon come and give th' final word. Old Jacob says the rot's all through, but Tass MacCrenna vows it's sound enough to let till spring. Not *now*, Marilyn!" He gently removed the child's inquisitive hand from his nose. "The roof be half off and they'll not proceed till one or t'other is knocked senseless. Ye have to come."

"Damme, I *hate* this!" Haskell pushed up, his face dark and his mood blustery as he stormed out into the cold to settle the roofs over Skyelt.

Eden could almost muster a twinge of sympathy for her

conniving father-in-law as she rose and took little Marilyn from Terrance's grateful arms. It must be hard, learning to shoulder responsibility at Haskell's age.

Ram came through the door the next evening, tired, damp and dirty . . . and besieged by a clinging tumult of folk. Few trusted Haskell's decisions about the roofs, though they had dutifully set about tearing them off and rushing to replace them before the wet overtook. Some were outraged that their quarters were left exposed to the elements and some protested Haskell's dictatorial assignments of temporary quarters. Ram stopped inside the door, trying to listen to first one, then another, while the others railed. Each demanded his exhausted attention and they finally succeeded in dividing it so that no progress was possible.

Eden descended the steps in her fetching plaid and watched her beleaguered husband, warmth for him filling her senses. They looked to Ram to settle their quarrels and their lives like fractious children, heedless of his strained parental endurance.

"What's this?" She presented herself before the mob with her hands at her small waist, a determined light in her eye. "Have you no thought for anything but your own comfort?" she scolded. "Out, the lot of you! Give your laird a moment's peace in his own home!" When they hesitated, glancing at Ram, she began to shove them bodily. "Out! Take it up with Haskell . . . or come back tomorrow! *Out!*" She turned from pulling the inner door shut and found him staring at her.

Eden would have been pleased to know how much turmoil she fomented in his fatigue-softened control. Ram watched her glide down the steps and to the kitchen and the aching in his shoulders flooded through the rest of him. He'd been exhausted when he rode in and had braced and drawn on his deepest reserve of stamina to cope with the avalanche of Skyelt's renewed demands.

There were too many people in too little space, so much to manage to make everything work. . . .

Now in the silence of the great hall, he frowned, feeling the exhaustion taking hold with a vengeance. Looking down at his streaked leather jerkin, damp wool breeches, and muddy boots, he sniffed and winced at the aroma of pens and animals and fermented sweat. He'd spent his frustration in hard labor these last four days, trying not to think about her or his feelings. And what had it gained him except a sore body and a well-fermented desire to have her again? Too well, he recalled every word, every sensation of their last encounter; it was nothing to be proud of. And worse, the instant he stepped into the hall, he was itching to grab her again . . . even if it meant expiring of fatigue in her arms.

Eden found him with his head propped in his hands on the table when she returned to the hall with servants bearing a basin of heated water, linen toweling, and a heaping tray of food.

"Addie, you still look flushed." She turned to the elderly serving woman and took the carving knife from her gnarled hand. "Go on now, and send someone else back later to clear away."

Eden filled a plate and set it before Ram, brushing his shoulder slowly with her breast as she turned. She felt him tighten and search her, but her expression was businesslike. When she poured his drink, she had to reach across him for the tankard, and that was an opportunity to press against his muscular thigh and arm. She lingered long enough to let the heather-fresh scent of her invade his lungs.

"Where is Haskell?" Ram swallowed and shot a glance around the empty hall.

"In the stable . . . a foaling in progress," she managed a level tone, only inches from his burning ear.

"And Terrance?" He took a bite of food and felt his

skin tighten all over. What was she doing, standing so close?

"With his wife, I imagine. She was brought to bed two days ago . . . another girl." She moved away only to retrieve her sewing basket and seat herself opposite him at the table.

"Six daughters now?" Ram tallied them as his grip on his knife and fork became deadly.

"And three sons."

"I wonder that she'll speak to him at all." Ram shifted on his seat and gave into the compulsion to look at her. The nape of her neck was plainly visible to him under her half-lifted hair. He knew that tantalizing arch would smell like spring and would feel cool and sleek against his lips. His shoulder began to burn where she'd brushed it earlier and he stiffened, irritated.

"Was the conduit functioning smoothly at Claggett's Creek?" she raised a look at him from under sultry lashes.

"Fine . . . if they'll only remember to keep the iced chipped away from the slu —" He tightened further and frowned. "How do you know about the conduit?"

"I . . . learned. Clever, finding a way to divert the spring and dry up the boggy land, while providing a good source of water for the folk. An improvement on the classical Roman aqueduct, I understand. Old Marcus Agrippa would have been pleased." Ram stared at her, openmouthed, before retorting.

"If he hadn't died in 12 BC, you mean?"

And Eden smiled as she rose and sought the warmth of the fire.

As he left the hall for his room, Ram realized his fists were tensed and his shoulder muscles knotted hopelessly. How would she know about Roman civil engineering . . . and his own efforts here? More to the point, why would she care to learn? His heart beat a little faster. When he opened the door to his room, he was stopped by the sight of a huge wooden tub settled before a warm, welcoming fire. His whole body melted a few degrees toward horizontal.

"Ex-cuse, m'laird," came an old housewoman's voice from behind. She and two scullery maids carried big kettles of hot water past him and emptied them into the bath. They nodded as they exited and closed the door behind them. Ram was left staring at the hypnotizing coziness of the tub and the clean linen and fresh clothes spread neatly on his narrow bed. He rambled slowly toward the water and stooped to dabble his fingers in it. Nobody at Skyelt had ever heated a bath for him. The warmth flowed up his arm and Eden filled his mind even as an ache filled his heart.

The next afternoon was sunny and crisp on the hillsides above Skyelt and a much refreshed young laird sat on the ground in earnest conversation with his herdsmen and Skyelt's steward.

"Prissy, get over here and leave th' lamb alone!" Terrance frowned at his third youngest daughter and heaved a silent moan when the lamb reacted to her sharp tug on its wool and bolted, dragging her along unexpectedly. He thrust wee Marilyn from his lap into Ram's and lurched after his wailing daughter. He scooped her up into his arms and inspected her widespread fingers and dirty palms while she exorcised her hurt through her lungs.

"There . . . there's fine, daddy's lassie." He brushed her chubby hands and planted a pacifying kiss on each. "Just a little tumble's all. Don' cry, Prissy." He swept her light hair back from her teary eyes and carried her back to the meeting. "Shush, now."

Ram sat stiffly, holding wee Marilyn with delicate fingers and eying her uncertainly. The herdsmen were starting to rise and move about, drifting toward talk of hunger and the need to stretch. The most pressing business, winter pastures, was done, and they seized this latest interruption as an excuse to break off for a while. Soon Terrance sat down by Ram, sending his young laird a rueful smile of apology.

"Sorry, Laird Ram, but my Molly, she ain't back to full strength from the babe, and these two won't go with none but their pa." He saw Ram's flicker of irritation and immediately felt the folds of cloth beneath his wee Marilyn on the laird's lap. They were dry and he sighed, realizing Ram's displeasure had another source.

"Ye ought to be ashamed, Terrance MacCrenna, what you put your Molly through. Give th' woman a rest, man." It was out. He hadn't meant to be so blunt, but thinking of the fatigue in Molly's eyes and the wearing bustle of eight—now nine.—children around her plump form, it had just leaped onto his tongue.

"It's not like I haven't tried, laird." Terrance showed no indignation that his marital indulgence was called into question.

"Then try harder," Ram lowered his voice and glowered at staunch Terrance, who looked at him with some puzzlement.

"You don't know what it's like, laird. I give it my best. I'd ne'er hurt my Mol on purpose. But you don't know how it can be wi' a wife." Ram's glare sharpened and Terrance realized it was an unfortunate choice of words.

"After each bairn," he explained, "I swear to stay at the hall wi' Haskell, to spare her. And I do for a time. But I see her and my bairns ever day and sooner or later, I get the itch. And I make meself keep me hands off and begin to stay away a bit. She gets sad, thinkin' I got a doxy now an' don't love her any more. Then she comes to me crying and saying her and the bairns, they need me. It purely kills me to see sweet Mol so brokenhearted.

"So I take 'er in my arms and hold her . . . for comfort, y'understand. And she feels so soft and smells like sweet hay and warm milk. An' before I know it, I got the itch again. And a woman who really knows a man knows where to scratch. Laird Almighty," he swallowed with effort, "it ain't possible to think straight."

Ram sighed silently, feeling foolish for condemning good Terrance for something he was guilty of himself. Too often in the past fortnight, he'd felt his own control slipping, felt his own "itch" rising. Each day he was confronted by agonizing reminders that Eden knew exactly where to scratch. His face softened to sympathy, surprising Terrance. Marilyn was becoming fidgety and Ram absently cuddled her closer in the cool air.

"But the birthings? Doesn't she hate. . . ."

"Funny thing about it is, she don't seem to mind." Terrance read Ram's thoughts. "Says she loves th' bairns because they're mine an' hers. I saw her birthin' Jacob and—Gawd—I near fainted dead away. She just smiled and hugged me after." He shrugged, mystified anew. "I don't think a woman thinks about it the same as a man does."

Both sat quietly, wrapped in thought until wee Marilyn insisted on ousting her sister from her father's lap. Ram surrendered her cuddly softness with a light caress of her little shoulders.

Eden had watched him holding the toddler as she picked her way up the rocky hill and saw his face as he released her to her father. The sight plucked something near her heart and set it vibrating. She shivered in the cold breeze, quickening her step.

"I've brought your dinner," she called, bringing her husband and his steward around quickly.

Ram watched the way her curls swayed and the rising wind molded her English-style dress to her lovely curves. Unconsciously, he scratched the back of one hand, then his chin, and his belly.

Terrance knelt by the basket and lifted the napkin covering, emitting a low whistle. "Cottage pie, hot bannocks, butter-almond tarts, and two bottles of good wine." His face grew wistful and he grinned at Ram.

Ram looked at Eden and thought she reddened as she met his gaze full on. Her shiver brought him back after a moment.

"It's colder than I expected." She shivered again, running her hands up her arms and hugging them. "And 'twas a longer walk than I realized."

"You've no coat?" Ram frowned, unbuttoning his heavy wool coat and stripping it off. "Here, woman, put this on before you catch your death. You've no business running about in that flimsy garb." He settled the hardy garment over her shoulders firmly and his hands lingered a second as he pulled it together in front. She was smiling up at him with a glow that belied her chilled state.

"Thank you, Ramsay." Her sultry tones were enough to keep him warm the rest of the afternoon. He watched her turn back to the house and continued to watch until she was out of sight. When he turned back to his food, Terrance was grinning at him again.

Twice more in as many days, Eden found herself outside and inadequately clothed in disagreeable weather. And twice more she'd coaxed her husband's coat from his very back to warm her. The third time, Ram and a clutch of folk had gathered for the spectacle of doctoring an irate sow. Ram scowled deeply at the sight of her thin drawstring blouse and bare chest and throat. A suspicious glint wormed into his eyes as she swayed over to stand near him and ran a hand up and down one shapely arm.

"I never dreamed it would be so chilled out today." She had tossed it at his feet like a challenge — and a well-witnessed one. Many eyes awaited the outcome.

Three times in as many days was too much of a

coincidence. He looked at the laughing light in her face and felt drawn to go along with her game, wherever it led.

"Here, woman." He gave her a lidded look as he unbuttoned his coat and made to hand it over. But she turned and gave him her back, expecting him to put in on her. When he set it over her shoulders, she caught his hand between her shoulder and her cheek and held it a moment. There were multiple witnesses to the bold look of pleasure on her face.

"Thank you, my lord." The words lapped at him seductively, and he reddened as the twitch of her skirts held his gaze prisoner when she left. She was flirting with him openly, blatantly teasing. He looked around at the sidelong glances he was receiving and realized they knew it, too.

The next morning, when he left the hall, it was in a shirt and knitted vest. He had three coats, aside from his suit of English gentleman clothes. And Eden had every one of them. He saw her disappear into the dairy and followed, his jaw firmly set. He found her in a mixed company in the chilly milk room.

"It's cold this morn," he declared, setting his hands at his waist and looking heatedly at the warm knitted shawl she wore. His words became clouds on the frosty air.

"Why, so it is, my lord." She smiled sweetly and picked up a pail of milk, starting for the door.

"What are you doing here?" He grabbed the handle to prevent her leaving and brought every eye in the place on them.

"Addie's under the weather again." She turned to face him with eyes a bit too wide. "I thought to lend a hand."

"You've become uncommon helpful, of a sudden."

"Just repaying your generosity, my lord." She smiled into his eyes and a tremor went through him. He relinquished the pail and straightened.

"My coats, woman. I want them back."

"Of course, my lord." Her gaze swept their audience with flirtatious mischief. "Come by my room anytime and I'll be happy to . . . give them to you."

He stood, weathering muffled snorts and chuckles, and controlling his urge to . . . what? Storm and rant? More like to take her into his arms and give her exactly what she seemed to be asking for. He strode out into another cold day.

Early that evening, Eden found Ram and old Haskell in the loft of the large barn watching a wrestling match between two of Skyelt's strong young bucks. Carina Graham was there, sitting perched on a barrel, and she waved Eden to join her. She explained the ring, the rules, and the rivalry between stout Tass MacCrenna and leaner, taller Derek Ecklvie. They stripped off their shirts and began to circle each other, snatching for a hold here or there.

Eden watched Ram's deep concentration and her stomach slid toward her knees. When the grapplers went down, she saw his shoulders jerk and his arms and fists tighten under his shirtsleeves. He called advice to first one combatant, then the other, adding intense gestures of his brawny frame. Her mouth went dry and her eyes darkened.

". . . Eden . . . Eden!" Carina was shaking her shoulder and when she turned around, Carina let a low whistle that drowned in the raucous roar of the spectators. *"Damme!* It's like that, is it?" Carina stared at Eden's reddened face and glowing eyes. Eden nodded, desire squeezing her throat.

"He's that good?" Carina couldn't keep from asking.

This time Eden's nod was accompanied by the most longing-filled expression Carina had ever been privileged to witness.

*"Damme!"* Carina swore softly. "Somethin's got to be done!"

The match ended and Skyelt's sporting buffs descended on Ram to get him to take on the winner. They insisted and entreated, and in the end Ram decided the workout might take the edge off his nerves. He started for the straw-littered arena, stripping off his vest and shirt. Carina saw her chance.

"And M'lady Eden will give the winner . . . a kiss!"

Everything stopped dead. Only the sound of feet rustling the hay was heard. The whole assembly turned on Eden with drooping jaws and curious stares. Someone shouted, "Be that true, m'lady?!"

A kirklike silence reigned as Eden made her way to the edge of the ring, with a hard look at Carina's mischievous face. She lifted her chin and caught Ram's glare of disbelief.

"It's true," she declared, and a furor broke loose. Now *this* was a betting proposition! And all around the barn hands' bets were laid. Haskell was right in the thick of it, licking his lips with relish.

Eden perched on a barrel and watched her husband wrestle for her favor. Her heart was drumming a crescendo and she panicked briefly at the thought that he might lose just to avoid her. Her palms grew damp as she watched his broad shoulders work and her chest swelled at the sight of the fading lines on his back. Please, Ramsay, she thought, care enough to try, really try.

A kiss, he thought. Even if it hadn't been a draw in itself, it was a spur to think she could give it to Tass MacCrenna. No doubt she'd make it a ripe one, just to shame him, the hoyden! It was exactly the thing to shoot the deciding spurt of strength into his straining arms and legs. And Tass MacCrenna found himself on his back in an astonishingly short time.

Quiet settled over the spectators like a blanket. Someone helped Eden down from her perch and she swayed across the hay-strewn floor toward her husband's damp, glistening body. She walked into him and slid her arms around his waist, raising her eyes, her lips, her need to him.

Ram was panting, every nerve ablaze, every sense exploding. The fiery sunsets of Eden's eyes absorbed him. He bent his head and lifted her against him with the convulsive need of weeks of restraint. His mouth ground against hers, feeling it open and welcome him into its silky depths. He was molten, pouring over her and into her with volcanic intensity. And Eden gave him everything, her love, her passion, her heart. She molded against him as she might have in the privacy of their bed and his hand lowered to her buttocks, pressing her against him as he might have in the deepest throes of loving. In that moment, they were alone on earth, and they were one.

Their union was blinding. There had been a muffled snicker here and there when she started for him; now there was a tight, charged silence that almost precluded breathing. They watched as their "prudish," "juiceless" young laird eclipsed their collective passions as the searing sun does the cold moon.

It was only when Ram's legs began to tremble and he sought to relieve them that he recalled he was not in his bedchamber, nor even alone with her. He dragged his lips away and stared into her passion-lidded eyes, feeling an unreasoning disappointment at having to release her. Strangely, their audience was the farthest thing from his mind.

Haskell's roar ignited a wild flurry around them that made Eden's face burn. She managed a caressing stroke of Ram's waist as she drew away and started for the door. Her legs scarcely functioned, her lips throbbed, her body screamed a tantrum of need. It was a tribute to years of Mistress Dunleavy's discipline that she made it to the hall and then upstairs to her rooms. She sat in the gathering dark, hearing the beginnings of a true rout in the hall below. Haskell was roaring for ale and shrieks and laughter and abandonment grew by the second. There would be no supper in Skyelt hall this night, but none would go unfilled.

Some three hours later the noise had quieted markedly, though music from the pipes still whined occasionally in a disjointed way. Eden knew the time had come; she rose from the warm fire and rubbed her palms down her tartan skirt. She flicked a glance back at the fresh linen in the warmed, waiting bed, determined that she'd not crawl into it alone tonight.

There were drunken nudges and comments aplenty when she descended the stairs into the dissipated scene. Those who were alert on the benches around the hall and at the great table roused those who weren't, and many watched as Eden walked calmly to the head of the table.

"Ho, daughter—have a drink wi' me!" Haskell laughed and raised a tankard in her direction. She ignored him and settled her gaze on Ram, who sat with his head down on the table and his eyes closed. Arlo and Terrance managed to rise and greet her rather sheepishly.

"We . . . ah . . . drank a bit," Terrance provided. He wasn't stewed enough to have forgotten the last time he had announced this to her.

"So I see."

Everything seemed to have gotten very quiet. Eden looked at Haskell, who was leering at her reaction, and she smiled rather determinedly.

"Gentlemen, I think my lord Ramsay has had quite enough. Why don't you . . . carry him upstairs . . . to my rooms."

Arlo and Terrance stared at her retreating back and shook themselves sober enough to obey. They roused Ram and got him to his feet, but it took two more men to get him up the stairs. Lady Eden held the door for them, they would recall later, and turned back the soft, warm covers so they could dump him in her bed. Then she ushered them out firmly.

Ram managed to give her his arms and to roll to one side so she could peel his shirt from him before sinking back into darkness. Eden looked at his peaceful face in the candle's glow and sighed: it would have to wait till morning. She stripped off her clothes and crawled into bed to sleep with her husband for the first time since her wedding night.

The sun was well up the next day and there'd been no knock on Eden's door. It wasn't Skyelt's way to be thoughtful, so Eden decided it must have to do with the hung-over state of the kitchen staff. She smiled cozily and propped her head up on her hand to watch her husband sleep.

The morning light gave his hair a violet cast and his skin was hard and smooth, except where his beard was beginning to gray his face and throat. She couldn't resist the urge to kiss the wispy curls at the front of his ears, and her lips lingered to trace the strong line of his jaw. Then his shoulder beckoned, and then the mounds of his chest, and soon her nibblings had taken her to the edge of the covers and beyond. It was hard to swallow when she raised her tousled head to look at him. She was starving and he was a banquet for the taking.

She wriggled her pelvis against him and pressed one full breast against his side, releasing a moan. Her hands began to move like butterflies over his warm body, adoring him, stroking him, learning him anew. She wanted no more than to be with him like this every morning—well, perhaps she wanted just a *little* more.

Small flames ignited at the backs of her eyes and she licked her lips, looking at his. And she rose above him to press her mouth gently to his. Hot fluid was trickling through her limbs, pooling in her loins. Her stomach was empty and aching.

His arms startled her when they clamped around her bare waist and he returned her kiss. The fog in his senses, the pounding in his head were being purged by the need invading his blood. Her warm skin molded erotically against him, and he sent his hands to cover her and hold her as he shifted onto his side. And in one fluid movement she was on her back, staring up into Ram's darkening face. She shifted and urged him on top of her, reveling in his purposeful body as it leaned intimately against her. He was fully aroused and as his lips began to descent her throat, he made a simultaneous descent into her moist, eager body.

Her gasp brought his reddened eyes open and he froze; Eden felt his change and looked up into his sudden doubt.

"Love me, Ramsay, please . . . *love me.*" Her arms circled his neck and brought him back to her. And she knew the moment his decision was made: he placed his arms beneath her like a cradle and began to move inside her with long, satisfying strokes. Each movement lifted them higher, toward that bright, fragile barrier that separates spirit from flesh. And soon they crashed through it together, joined in loving and in the promise of love.

Eden was drained, shuddering, soaring. She whispered his name over and over, stroking his body and wanting to hold him like this forever. Her heart overflowed in her eyes. When he moved, she murmured, "You can stay."

But he moved over and collapsed beside her, staring at her beautiful hair and flushed body. She turned her head and stroked his troubled face with her fingertips.

"Ramsay—"

"I . . . don't know . . . how I got here." He was hoarse with confusion.

"What matters is that you're here." She smiled with perfect contentment. When he opened his lips, she put her fingers against them. "I want you here, Ram . . . I want to share your bed as well as your name. I can't stand being half a wife to you. I want you to love me."

He looked deep into those fiery windows on her soul and had to surrender, even knowing it was the path to misery for him. He loved her more than anything in his life, more than his Skyelt, more than his sanity. And since he loved her, he'd have to find a way to spare her. He'd have to control himself, to resist the temptation to drown himself in her pleasures. He'd have to be strong enough to protect her from the brunt of his seemingly endless need and to refrain from spending it elsewhere. Would he be strong enough to spare her the agony of the birthings his desire for her would undoubtedly cause?

Eden saw him wavering, thinking, and wished she could invade his thoughts as easily as she invaded his passions.

"Ram." She took his face between her hands to make him look at her. "Don't leave me. Stay and . . . be my husband." Glistening ribbons of tears wound from her eyes back into her hair and Ram crushed her against him and kissed them away.

"I will, Eden." The salt in her tears made his lips burn.

Relief filled her kiss as she wriggled against him, then relaxed in his strong arms. Then they were withdrawing and her eyes popped open. He was sitting up, holding his head, sliding his legs over the edge of the bed! In an instant she was up on her knees and holding his arm.

"Where are you going?"

"It's late . . . I've many things to do." He wouldn't turn to look at her.

It was dawning on her that things were far from being resolved . . . they had made love, but that damnable wall

395

was still there! A stone settled on her heart when he turned to look at her; his face was troubled. No clearer challenge had ever been set before a Marlow.

"Indeed. There *is* one thing you've been neglecting. . . ." She moved behind him on her knees and slid her arms around his waist, *"Me."* She pressed her ripe breasts against his smooth back and brushed her cheek against it. She felt his meaningful tugs and shifts and ignored them. She began to nibble at his shoulders and the sides of his back and was rewarded by stillness, then by little quakes running through him.

She nibbled her way around his side onto his stomach and added kisses to her bombardment as she wound her way up his chest and wriggled onto his lap. His eyes were closed and his jaw was rigid. She lay across him, feeling his arousal against her side and nuzzling the crisp hair on his chest. She glided upward against him to sit on his lap and his eyes came open.

"The first one was for need." She was aching suddenly. "Let this one be for joy." Her seductive smile was the ultimate temptation, and Ram's arms flew around her. His recent resolve buried itself somewhere in the middle of his wife's eager body, and he was compelled to seek it there.

His hands never left her as he installed her in the middle of the bed and covered her with his hot flesh. They kissed and touched until the fire between them threatened to consume both. Ram fitted himself into her body, feeling it was the only place he wanted to be, the only place in the whole world he really belonged. If he could just carry that feeling with him always! It was his last thought before his being erupted and he mingled with his love, his Eden, in another, sweeter existence.

Eden awoke an hour and a half later, exhausted and satisfied. She washed and called Maisie to help her dress, and immediately set the servants to moving Ram's things into her—*their*—rooms. And even before the news had been spread, all of Skyelt knew things had changed between them. Their young laird had appeared wearing a coat again.

But that evening, Ram came to bed just before midnight and climbed exhausted between the covers to fall asleep. Eden smiled, kissed his cheek, and snuggled against his side for warmth.

He was gone when she woke the next morning. She found him in Haskell's study at the edge of the hall, poring over ledgers with Terrance. He smiled at her and her heart nearly stopped; she hadn't realized until now just how rare his marvelous smiles were. She slipped to his side and ran a loving hand over the cap of muscle on his shoulder. She felt him shiver, and when his eyes rose from Terrance to her again, they were like the winter sky, blue and cold.

Eden was having none of it, his damnable restraint. Who'd ever heard of a predicament such as hers . . . having to seduce her own husband over and over?

Men, Carina had offered, had constitutions all joined and tied together in their bellies. To reach them, you had to reach their bellies first. Some you could feed, some you had to bed. And Eden concluded that Ram was one of the latter. And she was a woman who'd rise to just such a challenge.

That afternoon, Eden saw Ram enter the loft area of the large barn. He was wearing a kilt instead of his woolen working breeches. She felt a stab of kinship with all the men who'd ever lusted after the swing of a skirt and a pang of sympathy for all women whose men wore plain breeches.

Slipping through the door, she paused and found him kneeling on a stack of bags of oats, ledger in hand and head bent to avoid the crossed beams. It was dim, and the loft seemed warm and fragrant. The flame in her blood was fanned higher.

"Who's there?" Ram started and turned at the rustle of her feet.

"It's me"—Eden was scrambling to think of a reason—"I lost something the other day and came to see if I could find it." He frowned and she added, "A sash."

"Where did you lose it?"

"Up there, I think." She pointed to the far corner of the barn, at the highest mounds of the hay mow. Soon she was scrambling upward. "Perhaps you could help me look." Her heart was in her throat as he set down his book and made his way up the mounded bags of oats to the hay mow.

"What were you doing in here?" he scowled, looking at her suspiciously.

"Looking for—it has to be here somewhere—my red one with the raveled fringe—" She parted the soft hay in several places and Ram turned on his knees to do the same. Eden straightened and her gaze caught on the snug cling of the stitched pleats over his buttocks. She moved closer on her knees and her fingers ducked under that tantalizing edge and reached the back of a taut, hard thigh.

Ram froze and her hand quested higher, finding, teasing the tight fullness of his buttocks. She moved behind him and sent her other hand to join the exploration. Ram straightened slowly and Eden could just see that his eyes were closed. Her fingers moved around his loins, along his sensitive valleys, and down the sides of his thighs. When he began to tremble, she moved away briefly.

He turned, shaking mightily, trying to recall why he musn't succumb. Eden was there on her knees, her blouse untied to reveal her succulent breasts. She pulled the pins from her hair; it uncurled down her back and over her bare shoulders. His mouth had been cottony; now it began to water. He was roused and primed and all she'd done was touch him. Drawn by the glow in her eyes, he still hesitated until she uttered a throaty, irresistible plea.

"Love me, Ram. Please . . . come and love me."

He slid into her arms and into her body, loving her, completing her with aching tenderness. He was gentle, mesmerizing, loving. And Eden responded in kind, feeling in his manner a caring she had thought she'd only imagined on their wedding night. It sent her soaring into realms of pleasure.

Afterward they lay side by side in the hay on her shawl, bodies close, arms entwined. Ram kissed the top of her head and held her a long, agonizing minute before he moved away. His hand came back to stroke her face reassuringly, but his eyes were closed to her inquiry. She sighed and allowed him to help retie her blouse. Still it was not quite right.

## Chapter Twenty-one

The next evening after supper they gathered around the hearth for coffee and good Scotch whiskey. Arlo, like Ram, was subdued, and Terrance still held wee Marilyn on his narrow hip, which accounted for the occasional black looks he received from Haskell. Carina sat poised on the edge of her chair and managed to pour and serve with surprising grace. Haskell made a mental note that it was a stroke of true genius on his part, leaving his feisty daughter to his refined daughter-in-law's company. She was acquiring a more civil manner, if not a more civil tongue. He might honorably rid himself of her yet.

Then the old laird's attention returned to his son and he watched Eden's eyes drift like a compass needle toward Ram. It soothed his pride somewhat that Ram and his wife were at least sleeping in the same bed, no matter that his daughter-in-law had initiated it. Hot tatties, that one, he sighed. He'd known it the minute he'd set eyes on her.

Ram was late coming to bed again that night and Eden had passed through her hurt and fallen into unconsciousness. Ram stood holding the candle, gazing down on her lovely features, which seemed to make her frown in her sleep. He bent to press a kiss to her hair and tucked the cover tighter under her chin. She was making it very difficult for him; he felt his resolve slipping and darken, deciding another breath of cold night air was what he needed.

Eden learned of Ram's sudden trip to Skyelt's farthest pastureland from a terse, irritable Haskell.

"Just up and went," he grumped, wrestling about in a chair in his study. He made to get up, but Terrance's oddly parental glare made him settle back down. "Left a mess of things needin' doin', damn 'is hide!"

"And no word of when he'd return, I suppose." Eden's cheeks were flushed and her clasped fingers were white.

Haskell looked past her suddenly to the doorway where blonde Annie pressed her nubile body against the door frame, pouting. "Go on, Annie," Haskell growled, "Begone! I got no time today!" Annie's pout deepened and her steps dragged with disappointment back to the kitchen. Eden actually felt a bit of sympathy for Haskell's most recent "light o' love."

Before her mind was quite decided, she was striding for the stables. With a groom in tow, she struck out for the west and the Little Cotswold, as she learned the place was called. The stone cottage and pens of wooden rail and piled stone came into view more than two hours later.

It wasn't long before Eden found her husband, garbed in his green and brown woolens and his leather jerkin. She had formulated a plan but a fortuituously placed rock saved her the trouble of implementing it. Ram had left the group of crofters the moment he saw her. The groom helped her down, and with her eyes fixed on his stormy countenance, she started toward him and promptly found that stone and turned her ankle. He was first to her and angrily jerked up her skirt to assess the damage.

Her tears were real enough, but he eyed them suspiciously as he lifted and carried her into the cottage and set her on one of the several cots. He'd left the door wide open and for some reason that little inconvenience prodded her to feel true anger. When he knelt to examine her throbbing limb, she lost control and grabbed his head, surprising him and pulling him up to her easily.

Her hot, furious kiss burned through his entire body and in mere seconds he had to grip the edge of the rope-woven cot to remain upright. She pushed his jerkin back and over his shoulders and pulled his shirt from his breeches. Her cool hands slipped beneath to possess his chest and pull him closer. He was startled into compliance, overwhelmed by her aggressive need. She pulled back, her eyes burning furiously and her breath fast and hot.

"You'd better close the door," she rasped, "or I'll make you take me right here, on the floor, in front of God and your precious sheepherders!"

Unsteadily he made his way to the door, closed it, and drew the bar. He turned back; she'd removed her hat and unbuttoned the high-necked spencer of her riding habit. Beneath it she wore only a thin, French chemise that clung to her breasts. Her desire mesmerized him, pulling him forward as she lay back on the cot and held out her arms to him. When he hesitated, standing beside the cot, staring at her half-revealed beauty, she caught his hand the pulled him down.

"Love me, Ramsay MacLean."

Ram sank onto the cot and wrapped her half-revealed form in his own warm flesh. His hands invaded her clothes as hers had done to him. He kissed and nipped and devoured her creamy skin and full breasts. She winced when his leg touched her ankle and he paused to invade her skirt and massage and kiss the ache from her foot. And he stayed to nibble his way up to her thighs, kissing, caressing, until her hands pleaded with him to end her torture and take her fully.

It was like coming home, the perfection, the rightness of it. Eden absorbed all he could give and reveled in the way he filled her, body and soul. Together they clung and shivered and pulsed, exploring yet another unknown path to loving. And when their passion was drained and their hearts separated to beat as two again, Eden felt calmer, surer, somehow wiser. Ram, on the other hand, felt his grip on the situation slipping and his face strained to conceal this knowledge.

Eden left the bed first and tested her ankle as she smoothed her long skirts into place. The ankle was tender and Ram rose, pushing her to a seat while he searched a nearby trunk and came up with a strip of linen. He wrapped her ankle and, at her request, handed her coat to her.

Her dressing was businesslike and by the time she started for the door, Ram had rearranged his clothing.

"I have to be getting back."

"But you never said . . . what you came for." Ram's voice was thick and his skin a bit more bronzed.

"Didn't I?" She met his look. "Tomorrow night, Ramsay. I'll see you at home." She motioned to the groom to help her mount, but Ram waved him off.

"Are you sure you can ride?" He turned her around and his eyes clouded as he inspected her face for traces of discomfort. "Perhaps you should stay—"

"And interrupt your work again?" She softened visibly. "Is that an invitation, Ram?"

He stiffened and she could have bitten her tongue.

"Tomorrow night, then." She reached for her saddle with trembling hands.

Ram didn't come home for the following night and

Eden spent a good part of those long, predawn hours pacing and fuming. By sunrise she was in a full ripe snit and she dressed herself and went for a hard morning ride to work off the rage that had collected in her blood. "Better by far than sittin' in the corner an' greetin'," she mused, annoying herself with yet another Scottishism. Before long she'd be a dour Scot as well, with Ram to husband her.

Skyelt was abustle with morning chores and as she rode in, she noted a clutter of folk about one of the sheep pens. She directed her mount to it and stopped dead at the sight of her husband thigh-deep in woolies. By all appearances he was helping to corral and separate some ewes. In reality, he was avoiding her . . . and his husbandly responsibilities. How was she ever supposed to produce him an heir if he didn't plow her damned field?

She unhooked her leg and dismounted. She smoothed her skirts and felt the rush of steam in her veins hit her heart and set it pounding. Enough was enough. She stomped into the crowd of onlookers, drawing their widening gaze with her, and charged through the gate into the pen. The sheep bleated nervously and scattered. She set her hands on her cocked hips.

"Ramsay!"

He straightened, seeing her flushed countenance, her eyes aflame, and he knew a moment's dread. She'd become deucedly unpredictable and no doubt last night had stoked her ire aplenty. He'd had quite an argument with himself before deciding to ignore her little ultimatum. As her spell over his senses faded and his body quieted, his determination to avoid her had risen anew. Their marriage, his sanity, and her health depended on his control, he convinced himself once more, though the margin of victory was excruciatingly narrow. Now anger crept up his spine to replace that fleeting uneasiness.

"Where were you last night?" she demanded boldly, startling the onlookers into murmurs.

"Where I needed to be . . . at the Little Cotswold. I decided to wait and ride in early this morning." He turned back to examine a ewe one of the farmers was holding.

"Ramsay," she allowed her anger to boil over into her voice, "that wasn't what we agreed!" She was determined to shout it to the housetops if need be.

"You agreed; I didn't. I had better things to do—"

*"Than to bed your wife!"* she finished furiously.

That brought him fully around. He stalked in her direction, sending the sheep scattering and bleating.

"Hold your tongue, woman!" He glared at her, then at the lurid delight on the faces of their growing audience. Raised voices were always an invitation on Skyelt.

"I'll speak when and where I please, husband . . . and *what* I please. And it pleases me to speak the truth. Do you think they don't already know it?" She pointed savagely at the faces trained on them.

Ram was beyond ire; he just managed to make himself turn away. His body stood there, strung tight with seasoned anger, when her steely words sliced the cold air again.

"Ramsay. Your father named you *Ram*say. He should have named you *Ewe!*" She couldn't have known it was a taunt he'd heard before, a relic of older, more vulnerable days.

He was around in a flash, striding for her, sending her skittering back at the murderous look on his face. There were gasps and ohs and a few shrieks as he slammed into her, jerking her up and over his shoulder. He muscled his way through the animals with Eden thrashing and squealing and pounding at his back. The gate opened magically for him and he strode furiously for the hall, determined to lock her up.

But by the time they'd reached the great hall and he'd started up the steps with her, the exertion had spent enough of his anger to clear his brain a bit. Terrance and Arlo rose from the morning table to stare, their brows furrowed. Haskell emerged from his study, tucking in his shirt and waving Annie off him.

Eden called to each for help, but Ram countered with a glare that dared them to interfere.

*"Ale!"* Haskell roared, heedless of the hour. Of all men, the laird of Skyelt knew a climax when he saw it!

"I'm going to give you exactly what you've been askin' for, wife," Ram growled, dumping her none too gently on their bed. "But not before we get a few things straight! I'll not have that degradin' little scene repeated again or I'll take a lash to yer ripe little bottom myself—*be that clear?"*

Eden's growl matched his as her head swam and she fought through a maze of hair and clothes to glare at him. "How dare you manhandle—"

"You *like* bein' manhandled, darlin', else you wouldn't provoke me to it so often!" He shoved his granite face down over hers until she could feel its heat. "I've done everythin' in my power to spare you, to treat you wi' concern an' the dignity due a wife—"

*"Ha!"* She had to prop herself up on bent arms to face him. "Scorn and deprivation are expected treatment for a wife in Scotland, are they? You an' your righteous self-control—I *hate* it! You're the coldest, most . . ." her throat was squeezing off the flood of hurt-filled words, "unfeeling . . . bastard . . . ever . . . birthed."

"Unfeeling?" He pounced on her, knocking her back on the bed and straddling her on his hands and knees. His fingers dug into her frantic wrists and his hot eyes bored through her fury. *"Unfeeling,* am I?!" He dropped his full weight on her wriggling body, driving the breath and all motion from her in one fell swoop. Determined knees parted hers and he fitted himself against her.

"I can feel your body from clear across a field, darlin'," he said against her parted lips, savoring the hot little blasts of her breath. His deep voice gentled to spite him. "I hear your love moans on the wind day and night. My clothes have become your fingers on my body an' sleep makes me afraid of dyin' an' never seeing you again. I become the cup you drink from, just to touch your lips. I want to be the chair where you sit, just to feel your weight and hold you in my arms. I'm jealous of your damned coat, because it protects you the way you won't let me—"

His words had expressed her own torment with such feeling that she dared hope the same starved emotion was their source.

"Ramsay," she choked and blinked to clear the tears from her eyes, "do you love me . . . even a little?" He released her wrists and cradled her head in his hands.

"I believe that's what I was just saying . . ." His look was uncertain.

"You really do care for me?" Eden searched his face desperately, hardly able to breathe for the hope swelling within her. Her fingers fluttered over his features, her thumbs traced his lips. Then she knew where she'd find the reassurance she needed and pulled his head down to hers. His lips covered hers as his hoarded love poured into the rest of her wherever their bodies met. He groaned and kissed her nose, her cheeks, her wet eyes. She was like a drought-starved flower absorbing life-giving rain.

"Ram—" She kissed his face all over, then hugged his head to her tightly. "I've waited so long . . . you're the most frustrating man alive! I've wanted you so. . . ." She saw a shadow flicker across his face and vowed it would be the last. "Love me, Ram. Please . . . make love to me. . . ."

He was already fumbling with her buttons, devouring her warm skin as her dress and chemise surrendered to his determined assault. He undressed her and installed her under the bedclothes while he shed his shirt and kilt.

Ram slid into her arms, adoring her with his eyes and hands. He nuzzled and nibbled her breasts, her trim belly, her shoulders. She fitted so neatly against him, felt so soft, touched him so tenderly. He filled her and began to move, rocking her with a fierce and beautiful rhythm that carried her to the gates of paradise. Together they explored the bright shores of pleasure and together they settled firmly into a reality just as sweet.

Ram sat back against the pillows and pulled her close against him, feeling strange and full of energy. He looked down at her sleepy smile and knew the hard part was yet to come. If loving her was as natural as breathing, then stopping would be a lot like dying.

"I love you very much, Laird Ramsay MacLean," she murmured, tracing patterns on the bold muscles of his chest.

"I should have known," he rumbled with a mischevious smile, "when you braved my father an' Skyelt alone and were still here when I arrived. That took uncommon strong motivation."

"That and an uncommon strong stomach. But I'm not of particularly delicate constitution." She flirted with him from the corner of her eye. "You were right, you know. I'm not much of a lady."

"I said that?" He stared at her, reddening as he recalled it. Strange how he recalled nearly every word of every encounter between them when he couldn't recall what he'd had for supper the night before. He gave her one of those rare, rather sheepish smiles. "And to think . . . in biblical days they considered it a miracle when an ass spoke."

Eden giggled and then hugged him, luxuriating in the feel of his laughter vibrating through her.

"Well, it's not very ladylike of me to want you so badly and to respond to you with such . . . enthusiasm . . . . I think that's what you once called it."

"Umm. . . ." He nuzzled her hair aside, ringing her throat with kisses. He was losing himself in his need for her again.

"Love me again, Ram, now . . . please." Her hands slid up his thighs to his lean belly and she ran her splayed fingers over his middle. She surprised them both by moving up and sitting astride his lap. "And when you've finished I want you to love me some more."

In spite of himself, he was rousing to the feel of her sweet bottom on his bare lap and the sensual invitation of her taut, lovely breasts. She leaned closer and pressed her lips gently against his. That tender pressure was command and fulfillment all in one. It was love and caring and trust, given freely. And Ram's aching heart couldn't help but respond.

Ram slid down into the bed, carrying Eden with him, and she wriggled sensually over her big, warm mattress, teasing and kissing and laughing. And when he laughed at her tickling and made her stop, his eyes were moist and his heart was full. His kisses became determined and she let him master her slowly.

Some while later, Eden basked in warmth and satisfaction, watching her husband sleep and treasuring his hard-won love. He did love her and she was determined that her love would free him from the hurts and fears of the past, no matter how long it took. His strong face was younger, softer in satisfaction's sleep. She found herself wishing she could have been there for him when he was wee Ramsay, crying for his mother and feeling alone and frightened. Suddenly she wanted to give him that, to give him his childhood again in a bairn, a baby to love; it would salve those old hurts. The longing rose like a terrible ache in her.

"Ram, my bonnie husband," she kissed his ear and whispered into the side of his neck, "this time when you love me, give me a bairn."

His eyes opened and he rolled onto his back to look up at her. His frown made her know that he'd heard what she said. And seriousness aged his face before her eyes.

"Eden . . . don't . . . we shouldn't be. . . ."

"Shouldn't we?" She stopped his protest with her hand and made him stare into the certainty of her face and heart. "Ram, I want a bairn . . . it has nothing to do with your bloody inheritance. It confounds me that you actually want this crazy place. I want your bairn because I love you and I'd be carrying part of you under my heart in a special way. And I'd be giving you something no one else could."

"Eden. . . ." His face drained and his tongue swelled.

"Ramsay MacLean," she spoke his fears right out loud, "I'll not die a'birthing and leave you alone. I'm Constance's daughter, remember," she smiled impishly, "and enough of a peasant to bear easily. And then there's the pleasant business of plantin' your seed to start. You're a born farmer, I know. . . ."

"Gawd, woman," he unstuck his tongue, "the things you say to me!" Eden could see he was deciding whether or not to be outraged.

"Love me, Ramsay." Her eyes burst into glowing flame and she ran a purposeful hand up his thigh and brought it to rest on his hardening parts. She stroked him and felt him throbbing under her hand. "You can love me till you drop . . . and I really wish you would."

410

"Eden!" He seemed genuinely horrified by her bold proposal—or by his obvious reaction to it. "You don't know what you're . . . asking."

"I'm asking you to love me, Ramsay. It's not very ladylike, I know, but. . . ." Her eyes widened and her humor faded into a perfect look of chagrin. "I'm sorry . . . I thought. . . ." she drew her hand away, clasping it harshly in its mate. "On our wedding night, you seemed to want quite a bit of me.. . . You must think—" She moved away, praying his rising need would halt her.

When he grabbed her arm, she steadfastly refused to meet his gaze and he had to gather her into his arms to soothe her humiliation. He looked at her as though he'd never really seen her before. "What manner of woman are you, Eden MacLean, to serve a man's heart so well! To answer every question, to meet every need. . . ." She began to melt against him in strategic spots, surprised at the real depth of her physical need for him. It was no longer just a determined wife's ploy . . . she really did want him again.

"I'm your true mate, Ramsay MacLean." She could not look at him. "And I love you."

"So you do." He sounded a little wistful, but his strong fingers began playing a wanton melody along her spine and ended by covering her buttocks and drawing them over him. "You've asked for it, wife. Now I'm going to love you . . . thoroughly."

He began with her hands, licking and nibbling her fingertips and working his way up her arms to her sensitive elbows. She squirmed and he laughed, prolonging her torture, until she called him a deranged Frenchman and begged him to stop. He turned and dumped her on the bed, beginning with her toes and covering her all the way to her head, heedless of her fluttering hands, her indrawn breaths, and her last vestiges of maidenly mod-

411

esty. When he finished his exploration, he knew a bit more about Eden Marlow than she wished . . . and employed his husbandly knowledge in rapturous toyings and sweet, languorous caresses that left her gasping.

Just when she thought his exquisite torture would go on forever, he covered her burning body with his and completed their rapture. He arched and plunged into the center of her, even as she penetrated that last battered wall around his innermost self. And they lingered for some time on pleasure's brightest plane, reveling in the joy of true joining.

Exhausted, she curled onto her side with her head on Ram's arm. He curved beside her, close but not touching. His last coherent thought was that he felt joined to her still.

It was nearly dark in the bedchamber when Ram stirred again. His body was calm and at peace. He watched Eden sleeping and stroked her hair back from her face to kiss the sweet curve of her cheekbone. She tasted salty and sweet and warm. His head filled with the musky scents of loving and he sighed, aware of a growing fullness in him. He pulled her back against the front of his body, curling around her. Her breast snuggled into his hand and he smiled lazily at its soft weight in his palm. He enjoyed it, dropping a kiss onto the side of her neck and allowing himself a long, contented breath.

Her soft curves nestled intimately against him, filled his arms. The erotic scents of her filled his head; her womanly beauty absorbed his gaze. And he smiled from deep within: she was his wife. She pleased him willingly, she matched his strength and his strong passions . . . she *loved him*. His smile grew to a satisfied grin and he hugged her. There was nothing on earth more precious that what he felt right now. There was absolutely nothing he'd rather be doing than holding his wife in his arms.

*Nothing.* The word sobered him and brought his attention around smartly. He looked at her, searching himself suddenly. There were pleasant sensations of her closeness, there was a sweet fullness in his chest, near his heart. But nowhere was there an ache, a twinge of desire, a feeling of need. His eyes widened. He concentrated on the feel of her bottom against his loins and felt only pleasant pressure. Her breast in his hand was lovely, sweet, satinly. He was holding his beautiful, wanton of a wife in his arms and he felt . . . warm, satisfied. She'd loved him . . . and precious Lord, he'd loved her, over and over! And for the first time since he first set eyes upon Eden Marlow, his body wasn't burning for her.

She loved him; it made him shiver. She *loved* him; just saying it in his mind had a calming effect. Warmth spread from his heart outward and he was content in a way he'd never imagined. She loved him. Having her heart fulfilled part of that terrible, consuming urge to have her physically. She loved him!

He rose from the bed, staring at her with wonderment. He could love her until he dropped, she'd said. And now he no longer needed to. She loved him and he was . . . satisfied! A silly grin spread over him and he became positively euphoric.

"Eden!" He sprang back onto the bed and took her into his arms, shaking her gently. "Eden, my delight . . . my sweet hoyden . . ." She blinked and sat up, frowning sleepily into his joyful face.

"What's . . . happened?" She rubbed her eyes and sat up in his embrace, bewildered by his buoyance.

"I don't have to have you again!" he beamed.

It was a long moment before she managed to repeat what he'd said and in another moment it righted itself in her mind. Her jaw dropped. What fatal miscalculation had brought her to this? Ram was deliriously announcing

413

he didn't need to bed her anymore!

"Ramsay . . ." she grabbed his arm, "what are you talking about?"

"I'm satisfied, Dede. You've . . . satisfied me. I don't have to love you again and again and again until you're sick of me." He released her and rose, spreading his arms heavenward and stretching sinuously. "Isn't it wonderful?"

"Excuse me if I fail to appreciate your enthusiasm for not wanting me." Her shoulders rounded under their load of disbelief. She'd pushed him too far. "I was rather hoping we were beginning our marriage, not ending it."

"Eden," he turned back and his smile faded at the horror on her face, "I love you." He came back to the edge of the bed and reached for her. Her resistance was token and he pulled her against his hard, naked frame.

"I was afraid . . . once I started, I wouldn't be able to stop."

"Who's asking you to?" She was hoarse with horror.

"It's not you, Eden; it's me." He took her chin in his hand and looked into her dismay. "I was afraid I'd . . . harm you with my . . . needs. And that I'd not be able to be . . . faithful. Now I know I can stop . . . because your love and your loving satisfy me."

"They didn't before? Is that why you . . . hated me after? I didn't please you? And now that I do please you, you don't want me anymore?" Her eyes were huge and a little frightened. "Make sense, Ramsay, please." What had she done?

"I love you, wife." He crushed her against him and sighed deeply. Explaining one's deepest fears and doubts was deucedly difficult, even to one's true mate. "I hope that's enough for you. I've found it's enough for me. That's what I'm saying."

"That's better." Her arms closed around him, adopting his certainty, trusting his love. And in the silence, their contact grew sweeter.

"Am I really like Haskell, you think?" he finally spoke. It was *the* question to answer all her questions. He was beginning to know what she needed him to learn.

"In the very best ways." Eden rubbed her face against the hair of his chest, a little dazed, but feeling things were somehow right. "Only the very best ways."

## Chapter Twenty-two

Haskell celebrated his son's marriage for two very long days and then slept the sun around, recuperating. Skyelt had celebrated with him, as much as endurance would allow, and finally settled into dissipated torpor. Everything moved lethargically, even the news. Thus when Angus and Ian Barclay appeared at the door to the great hall with men at their backs soon after, Haskell was taken by surprise.

The Laird of Skyelt was of a mood to be generous and invite them inside, until he saw Robert Cavender and Edward Gunn in the company. Those two were minions of the Edinburgh courts, and the last time Cavender showed his face at Skyelt it had been to bring Carina Graham and a handful of legal writs. It boded ill for them to be in crafty old Angus' company. There were precious few civilities and Haskell planted himself before them like a bull with its horns down, daring them to so much as dismount. And shortly he heard the words that set his blood afire . . . when they began to mention the MacPherson will.

"Damn you for a scheming son o' perdition!" Haskell roared, jerking away from Terrance' restraint. "How *dare* you show yer damnable hide on my lands with such evil in yer black soul, Angus Barclay! Get off—afore I take a blade to you and send ye to yer devil master on th' spot!" He charged; several mounts rolled wild eyes and jerked and reared with their ears back, showing infinitely more sense than their riders.

"What's done is done, Haskell!" Red-faced Cavender struggled to contain his horse and his raw fury.

"It ain't done by a long ways." Haskell turned to stone before their eyes. His eyes hardened as they went from Cavender to Angus and came to rest on Ian. He searched the young man's squared, even features and the startling blue of his eyes. "Thinkin' of marryin', eh, lad?"

Ian's response was a slow spreading smile that did not reach his eyes. "Most men do, Haskell. Even you did . . . once."

Haskell met the thrust without flinching. He searched the set of Ian's jaw and the supple mastery of his lean hands on the reins, storing it away inside him.

"Damn you, Angus Barclay! Get off my lands!" He took one step and Angus' horse danced back nervously. But it was Ian who moved first. He set his mount to an easy, insolent walk and led the way from Skyelt's court.

Haskell stood a long time, watching them crest the northern slope of the valley; his face was troubled. He shook it off and reentered his hall, roaring for Annie.

It was well nigh noon before Ram and Eden emerged from their bedchamber that day, looking like they'd glimpsed paradise. Haskell watched the earthy sway of Eden's plaid skirts and the reluctance of Ram's hands to leave her and felt a peculiar swelling in his normally impervious chest. He sent a hand to massage the flesh above his heart and scowled, wondering if something was wrong with his health.

"Black Angus was here," he grumped, watching Ram seating Eden, then settling across from her for a bit of porridge and bannocks and hot tea. Ram paused halfway down in his chair, then sat down looking at his father.

"*Black* Angus, is he? What is it this time?"

"The MacPherson will." Haskell came right out with it.

"Ah." Ram nodded and set about filling his bowl while Eden poured tea.

"I said, the MacPherson will." Haskell looked at his son's broad shoulders and couldn't help but admire the young buck's appearance . . . and stamina — much like his own when he was younger.

"Not totally unexpected." Ram shrugged, watching Eden's supple fingers crumble brown sugar over her bowl of porridge and then smother the concoction with fresh cream. He grinned at her and she flushed prettily when she realized he was watching. "It comes up every generation or so . . . it's always wrestled to a standstill."

"Well, I don' like it. Ian's thinkin' of takin' a bride and Angus is castin' about to find him a home. A crafty old bugger is Angus. He's sent it to the Edinburgh courts . . . no mere local squall this time."

"Ian's getting married?" Eden looked at Haskell, surprised.

"Like enough." Haskell curled his nose.

"Grenbruck cannot be so small that there's not room for his wife," she declared airily, flirting with her husband's glance. "We wives don't take up much space."

"You don't take *up* space, you take it *over*," Ram retorted with a mischievous grin.

"But Ian don' get Grenbruck; it ain't his." Haskell burrowed back into his chair, feeling irritable and oddly left out.

"Oh?" Eden was merely being polite. She was watching the muscles of Ram's jaw work and felt herself sliding into the warm pools of his very blue eyes.

"Grenbruck goes to his blood son, Mattais." Haskell darkened further. "Ian don't have an inheritance wi' Angus."

"You Scottish lairds and your inheritances." Eden laughed softly. "What does he have to do to get his?" Ram's gaze withdrew slightly from hers.

"He made the fatal mistake of being sired by someone other than Angus," Ram said tartly. Then he glanced at Haskell. "It's a common enough affliction hereabouts."

Eden stared at Ram, then at Haskell, who actually seemed to redden. She startled herself. It wasn't proper for her to be thinking what she was thinking. It seemed a perfectly inescapable and completely appalling conclusion. Ram quickly relieved her consternation.

"Ian's my half-brother . . . and Haskell's first bairn . . . that we know of."

*Half brothers*, Eden mused, feeling a little strange. That explained why many things about Ian had seemed so familiar right away . . . why she was drawn to him so at first. There were so many similarities. . . . It seemed even more astonishing that she hadn't guessed.

"That explains why you and Ian seem so alike . . . in so many ways." She became aware they were both watching her; it was an unfortunate thing to say, she realized, when Ram's brow dented and he studied her a bit too intently. Their argument over Ian and "trystin' on the moors" came rushing back to her. "And that means . . . Carina. . . ."

"Is his half-sister, too," Ram supplied, watching the color heighten in her face.

"But he's a Barclay. . . ."

"Angus married his mother just before Ian were birthed an' gave the bairn his name straight away. But he be no blood kin an canna have Grenbruck. Now Angus is aimin' to get Skyelt for him wi' the MacPherson will." Haskell pulled deeper in thought and his face darkened. He let out a potent curse and strode from the hall. Haskell was actually upset, Eden realized, and she met Ram's odd look with questions.

"What is the MacPherson will?"

"An old bequest, worded oddly, from a hundred and fifty years ago, when old MacPherson held Skyelt and a good bit more around here. They . . . had a legitimacy problem in those days as well." His wary gaze seemed to warm. "Every so often, a Barclay drags it out as a bludgeon on a MacLean and they come to an impasse in the courts. There's only the sparse bit of wording . . . and it's so arguable that usually other things get dragged into it. It's a mess and always . . . expensive." A comic shudder ran through him and Eden laughed aloud. Ram was not a stingy man, but he was very careful with his resources. It was how Skyelt had managed to come back from the brink of oblivion . . . his careful husbandry. Now she knew now just how care-filled his husbandry could be and she would never object to it.

" 'Tis Haskell's own fault Angus is dredgin' it up now." Ram shot a resigned look toward the door through which Haskell had left. "He gave Angus ideas when he—" He stopped and turned his attention to his food with an enigmatic smile.

"When he what?"

"If I didna fulfill Haskell's conditions with you. . . ." He ground to a halt and made himself return to his food, which by now had lost its warmth and with that, much of it appeal.

"Then you wouldn't get Skyelt and . . . Ian would have?" Eden straightened, reading verification into Ram's silence.

"He's my *older* half-brother." Ram raised his head and his eyes searched her. "Angus loved Ian's mother, Helen, before Haskell took her, and in some crazy way, he always hated Haskell for not doin' right by her—even though it

420

would have meant losing her himself. And it always irked Haskell that Angus got Ian and a whole brood of others right and legal."

"Regrets about Helen, you mean?"

Ram smiled roguishly. "Romantic little darlin', aren't you? Can you honestly see Haskell moonin' over any woman?"

Eden spooned porridge into her mouth and made a face that summed up two separate reactions. "I suppose not."

"Finish," Ram pointed with his spoon, "every drop of that. You'll need the strength." To her inquiring tilt of head he responded, "Not that . . . yet. I'm takin' you riding . . . to my woods."

They did indeed ride that afternoon and to Ram's woods, as he called them. They walked through deep leaves, under a canopy of bare branches raised as if in tribute to the laird and his bride, and felt as though they were the only two people on earth.

"This is my favorite spot on all Skyelt," Ram announced, drawing her against his arm coat front. He nibbled the cold-polished apple of her cheek and then kissed her. "Want to help me make it the most memorable, too?"

Eden melted against him, all but inured to the impracticalities of making love in a cold, damp forest. "Umm." His kiss deepened and his hands invaded her ladies' coat, warming over her ripe curves. "Is it possible . . . here?" she murmured against his throat. "We might freeze. . . ."

"A good pupil of Marcus Agrippa should be able to engineer anything," he laughed, taking her hand and pulling her down into a sheltered spot and onto his lap as he sat on a huge log. He plunged into her kiss and shortly she forgot everything except his bare knees and her middle name. When he urged her around on his lap, she had a moment's pause and he teased her with how much she liked riding astride him. And in a few hot moments her fond regard for the kilt had risen to full reverence. It had to be the most convenient garment ever fashioned.

"Oh, Ramsay." She sat on the ground by the log, wrapped in his arms and blissfully ignoring the dampness invading her skirts from below, "This is a memorable place." She felt more than heard his gentle rumble. It drew over her heart like fingers on harpstrings. "No wonder you love it so." Her statement drew his thick brows down for some reason he couldn't explain.

"I've never had anything else to love but Skyelt . . . until you."

She stroked his chin with the top of her head and smiled wistfully. "We're too much alike, Skyelt and me. We both make demands on you."

"Do you hear me complaining?"

She cozied against his side and shook her head.

"You know, my trip to the colonies—"

"The *United States of America*," she corrected softly.

"—Yes, that. Well, I've never seen such land. Those western tracts your father gave . . . well, I saw part of them, and here they'd be worth a fortune."

"But land there, even good land, is not so dear."

"It should be . . . it will be, someday. One of our problems here is too many mouths, too many people on too little land. I can't help thinking that if some of our folk would be willing. . . ."

"You never stop thinking of it, do you? Skyelt and her people."

"My people." He ran a finger down the bridge of her nose and followed it with his lips.

"Can I be part of your people, too, so you'll never stop thinking of me?" She caught his lower lip between her teeth, holding it for the ransom of his kiss. And he gladly paid her price.

"Better than that," his palm slid to her tightening

breasts, "you're part of *me* now."

"Umm." That last part echoed in her own heart.

Cold November tumbled into a dreary, damp December. But it might have been balmy June for all that Eden and Ram noticed. They took long walks and talked and laughed, making love in irregular and sometimes shocking places. They watched each other over their food and were content to sit together before the fire of an evening. Their hands touched frequently, their lips often following. Haskell watched, fascinated if somewhat mystified. Terrance and The MacKay smiled and shook their heads fondly. Skyelt watched, subdued and content for now.

Carina caught herself staring wistfully after them, feeling an intolerable ache in her stomach that spread to her loins when she settled in her chaste bed at night. Worse yet, she found herself staring at hardened, muscular Tass MacCrenna and wondering if it would be so bad, married and bedded by such as him. Seconds later, she laid the air blue. Thinkin' with her loins, she was. She was near seventeen. She'd waited this long . . . she'd wait longer. But it was hard on her, seeing her brother and his wife so incomparably physical with each other—and so damned happy about it. Like the day she came upon them in the upper parlor. . . .

A hearty fire was built in the grate, the only light in the room. Near it, Eden sat on the floor beside Ram's chair with his bare feet in her lap. Her strong, supple fingers stroked and massaged his tired feet and his aching calves. His head lay back on the chair; his eyes were closed with private rapture. The scene was so charged with intimacy and sensuality that Carina turned to go, red-faced, for having stared.

Eden caught her movement and called her back. Carina swayed in and took a seat on a low stool nearby. Ram greeted her with a very relaxed smile.

"Take a lesson, Carina," he teased like a regular brother. "This is the way to treat a husband."

"Like bloody hell it is, Ramsay," she shot back. "You'll not catch me at some man's feet. More likely he'll be at mine."

"He might be, at that." Ram raised his head to peer at the shapely feet nestled before her. "But if he managed to get so far without losing blood, I doubt he'd stop with your feet, lass."

Eden laughed gently at Carina's uncharacteristic blushing and Ram chuckled wickedly.

"Two on one, is it now? Hell's fire!" Carina pushed up and stomped from the room.

# Chapter Twenty-three

It was the week before Christmas when a greater than usual confusion erupted in the great hall. It was a cold time when many folk came in to warm themselves and pass the cheer of the season. Haskell heard the scrambling and raised voices and was on his feet in a flash, his temper rising. Icy blasts from Odin's kitchen blew a strange set of figures through the main doors of the hall. A tall, booted figure, swathed in a huge camel-brown greatcoat that swirled and billowed about him, stood holding a groom in one hand and a stableboy in the other. Onlookers gathered in the doorway cowering as the wrathful English-garbed stranger bellowed:

*"MacLean!* Ramsay *MacLean . . . Where are you?"*

"What in the bloody hell?" Haskell set hands on the first thing he found, a dull, ancient claymore hanging on the wall, and barreled out into the hall. The stranger stood on the steps that led to the main floor, his legs spread and braced. His gray eyes burned brightly enough to start kindling and a furious voice demanded:

"I want Ramsay MacLean! Where the hell is he?!"

"Nobody lays hands on my folk and barges into me hall bellerin' rage at me own blood—" Haskell growled, advancing. "Show yer blade, varlet, an' say yer amens." In a breath, Haskell found himself staring down the nose of an elegant little pistol. He looked to the men in the doorway, but the stranger intercepted the glance and moved cautiously around so as to view all the room's occupants safely.

"My business is with Ramsay MacLean." The man's voice eased to mere hardness and he removed his fashionable high-topped beaver.

"He's not . . . here." Haskell lowered his blade.

"Then I'll see Eden Marlow," the brown-haired stranger snarled, "and don't try to tell me she's not here; *I* know she is!"

"Aye, she be here—but I'll not be parading her about for the likes of you," Haskell snapped, trying hard to think what possible interest a stranger might have in his toothsome daughter-in-law.

"Eden is my sister, and you'll fetch her here *now!*" James Marlow ran a furious hand back through his rumpled hair and ground his teeth together, appraising the shabby nobility and strength of the old hall and its grizzled master. His stomach turned at the thought of his little Dede caged up here . . . maltreated by that hulking husband of hers. . . .

"Yer *sister?*" Haskell was set back on his heels momentarily and searched the man's angular, patrician face for similarities to Eden Marlow MacLean. He squinted and glared and finally bellowed for The MacKay, still fingering the old claymore. The MacKay appeared and Haskell told her to ask his daughter-in-law to join him. It was the closest thing to a run that The MacKay had executed in years.

A hushed silence fell over the hall and the small figure that had slipped in from the kitchen behind The MacKay pressed against the wall behind the stranger unnoticed and moved closer with wide blue eyes fastened on him.

She pulled the sharp little dirk at her waist and set it carefully in her hand. Her soft leather slippers made not even a whisper on the stone floor.

James saw Haskell's eyes flicker and felt the pressure against the back of his coat in the same instant. He startled and Haskell laughed wickedly.

"Uncock yer piece, man. Ye've been had."

James felt an unmistakably sharp point in the center of his shoulders and cast an angry glance over one shoulder, seeing nothing. But it was there, more insistent than ever, and he uncocked his pistol. It was grabbed unceremoniously by the irate groom and brandished with comical menace before James's nose.

"Shall I bleed 'im for you a bit?" came a low, feminine purr that raked James's spine like cats' claws. The business end of the point had parted the threads in his greatcoat and now snuggled through the tight weave of his wool frock coat to nudge his skin. James flinched in spite of himself and turned his head just enough, aiming his gaze low enough to catch a half-bare shoulder and the side of a tartan skirt.

"Nah, lass, not yet." Haskell laughed and his old claymore clattered on the dining table. "Ye been had by a slip o' a lass." Never mind that Carina had held an astonishing number of Skyelt's males in a similar position over the last three months; she'd redeemed herself today in her father's jaded eye.

Eden flew down the stairs with mounting dread and halfway into the great hall she stopped dead. Every eye in the hall sought her, including two furious gray ones that widened in astonishment.

"James?" she breathed it in. *James!* And she was suddenly flying across the room and launching herself into her brother's stunned arms.

*"Dede!"* he grabbed her up against him, lifting her off

the floor and pressing his cheek against the top of her head, his eyes closed to stem the flow of relief in them. "Oh God, Dede, I've been worried sick about you — we all have," he moaned, reassuring himself with yet another crushing hug. "Are you all right?" He thrust her back an arm's length, but she dived into his embrace again, her face wet and her hair mussed irretrievably.

James finally managed to make her turn him loose long enough to look at her. Her face was flushed, her eyes glowing and luminous, her thick hair half-loose and mussed . . . there was an undimmed vitality about her that freed his heart to beat again. But then his gaze drifted downward and he startled at the simple drawstring blouse she wore and even more at what that garment revealed: for she was clearly naked beneath. And a skirt, a simple plaid skirt. She was dressed like a charwoman!

Anger bloomed again as her fingers fluttered over his face and he caught them, noting signs of wear that confirmed his suspicions. She threw her arms around his neck again and he glared above her around the gloomy hall and at the sullen faces turned on them.

"Come on, Dede, I'm taking you away from this pile of rubble. I'm taking you home!" She raised a surprised face to him and gulped for air, swiping at tears with her palms.

"But James —"

"No arguments, Dede. Get your things and —" he swept the hostile hall and Haskell's deepening glower, "on second thought, forget your things — we'll buy you some decent clothes in London." He had her halfway up the steps before she could plant her heels and halt him.

"James, what are you doing? You don't understand —"

"Eden!" Ram's voice boomed through the hall and everything halted as Ram strode quickly from the kitchens with Arlo in tow. The MacKay had reached him in time and gasped out her story.

"Ram!" Eden turned to him, tussling with James's viselike grip. "Look who's here!"

"James? What's going on?" Ram went rigid as he watched Eden's struggle against her brother.

"I'm taking my sister out of this . . . *sty*. I'll see you're repaid for what you've done to her, MacLean, I swear it!"

"James!" "What?" Eden and Ram answered his charge both at once. In a flash Ram was beside her, grabbing her frantic hand and leaping onto the step, even with James Marlow. Instinctively Eden wedged herself between them. Neither would relinquish her arm; then the charges began to fly.

"Damn you! And curse the day I extended my hand to you in friendship—"

"Hold, man! I'd not want to harm my wife's kin, but I'll hear naemore—"

"Just see how you've treated her . . . dressed in rags . . . and look at her hands—God! You're despicable!"

"She's *my wife*, James—

*"Stop it!"* Eden had managed to put her hands over her ears despite their collective grip on her and now screamed at the top of her lungs. Her husband and her brother were both shocked enough to recall that she stood between them. *"Stop it this minute!* And let me go—" She wrested both arms free with a growl. "What am I, a sausage?"

There was stunned silence in the hall as they both stared down at her. Her face was burning, her eyes rings of pure fire. "I am appalled!" she looked from one to the other and gave both a furious shove. She collected her wits with a breath and began issuing commands.

"Haskell, take your son outside to cool off! Mrs. MacKay, please order a fine welcoming supper laid and have Maisie bring the tub and plenty of hot water to the

429

corner guest chamber. Introductions will be made over supper. The rest of you," she turned to their audience with a stern glare, "are free to leave. You—" she grabbed James's sleeve and yanked him toward the stairs with her, "come with me!"

Shortly the hall was empty save for Carina, who was having difficulty getting the image of a pair of broad, graceful shoulders out of her eyes. Her gaze narrowed as she swayed toward the staircase, wondering what she might wear to supper that could be called "fetching."

"James Atherton Marlow, how dare you humiliate me so in front of my husband and his people?" She turned on him the minute the bedchamber door was closed.

"Dede. . . ." James's mouth opened and moved, but no sound came out, which was just as well. Eden had quite an earful for him. She'd picked up several new words from Carina, and every one of them loosened his jaw a bit more.

"You mean it?" he managed, staring at her ripe, tumultuous form and feeling utterly bewildered. "You want to stay here . . . in this . . . heap?"

"It's not a heap, James," she waved a hand about them, "Skyelt is a fine estate with good lands. It's lacked a woman's hand to see to the finer points, and I'm working on that. I'll not have you snarling and being surly, James—" Her throat tightened; her ultimatum would not come out.

James gathered her into his arms and sighed, stroking her hair. "We were just frantic, Dede, on discovering you'd never arrived at the Buxton Inn . . . we searched everywhere. We finally found someone on the docks who recalled seeing a woman being carried, kicking and screaming, onto a ship bound for the continent. I can't tell you what a miserable time we had. Then after weeks we got that damnable note—" He shoved her back to stare at her furiously. "You could have written more than 'I'm healthy and he's taken me to his home in Scotland'!"

"I wasn't sure it would . . . get through." It sounded lame, but she couldn't explain that she hadn't written more for fear of betraying the truth of her situation.

"Ethan and Chase were set to come with me, but it took weeks to get passage—with war about to be declared any minute. Had to come on a molasses run via Barbados as it was, and they had room for only one. It was delay after delay—and I was seasick. Then I had a devil of a time locating this place. Do you have any idea how many places in Scotland sound like *Skyelt*—especially the way they say it!"

"Oh, James, please . . ." she raised crystal-rimmed eyes to his strained face, "please don't be angry with me."

"I swore I'd kill the bastard, Dede." His throat tightened. "But I won't . . . if you don't want me to."

"No! Don't kill him." Her look softened girlishly. "I've come to . . . relish my husband." Her strange way of putting it made him frown.

"Relish? You make him sound like a dish of pudding."

"More like Colleen's shortbread, actually." She licked her lip impishly and laughed through teary eyes at the shock on his face.

A knock at the door saved him from a response and soon she was directing a hoard of serving women who busied themselves making up the bed, settling his bags, and preparing his bath—while giving the strapping American a thorough visual inspection.

Eden left him there and went in search of her husband. She found him in the dairy, still steaming.

"Come with me, husband." She winked at the old dairy women as she threaded her arm through his and drew him outside. "It wouldn't do to have you curdling the milk." Once outside, she pulled him around the corner of the

431

low stone building and slid her arms around his neck. His kiss was fierce and left her a little dizzy.

"I love you, Ramsay MacLean. Don't forget that when you face my brother again. I'm still here because I love you." Then she let him escort her to their bedchamber and proved it to him.

The mood in the hall was strained when Eden appeared that evening on James's arm. She'd groomed her hair and wore her elegant blue challis dress with the velvet cording and tambour-work frills. Arlo, Terrance, and Haskell were fully rigged out and stood solemnly with Ram. Eden introduced them gracefully, as though the afternoon's debacle had never occurred. James found himself feeling rather disconcerted, shaking hands and making pleasant talk about smooth sailing and dry roads for travel. Eden watched her tall, elegant brother struggle to adjust to Skyelt's caprices and smiled with quiet sympathy.

There was a sticky moment when Carina Graham entered and all stared at her most elegant plaid and the new way she'd done her hair: part of it was pinned up, curled in copper-kissed locks that trailed from her crown halfway down her back. She was introduced to James as Ramsay's sister and she swayed back and forth, her arms crossed casually under her voluptuous little breasts as she viewed him boldly from more than one direction. Her eyes lit at the snug fit of his chamois breeches over his lean, muscular legs and danced over the broad sweep of his square, impeccable shoulders. Her eyes came to rest on his clean, finely framed features and indignant gray eyes.

"Damme! Any more at home like him?"

"Two more—" Eden managed.

"*Lord!*" Carina grinned appreciatively. "They ought to

put yer pa out to stud!"

James stiffened, just containing his outrage when he realized they were actually laughing at the chit's unthinkable remark. What kind of madhouse was this?

"Come, James, be a gentlemen," Eden chided, giving his arm a nudge. Face reddening, he made to take the wench's hand and caught a glimpse of the dirk at her belt. He jerked up, stiff as a poker, feeling it against his spine again.

"You!" he charged, doubly chagrined by Carina's diminutive stature and very blue MacLean eyes. Carina drew back her hand and her eyes narrowed.

"Yes, me!" She was doubly defensive for wanting to feel his hand on hers and being denied it. "And it be a damn good lesson to remember, Mr. Marlow." She spat his name and turned with flushed cheeks toward the table.

James was seated by Eden and spoke little during the tasty meal. He was genuinely surprised by the magnificent wines served with supper and said so. Haskell was unaffronted and stated quite factually that his wine cellar, like many in Scotland, would rank him well even in France itself. When asked for his impressions of Scotland, James was miserably candid.

"Damp. Green and gray everywhere—like things are all moldering. The men are clannish and pinch-pennied and," he glanced meaningfully at Carina, "the women should be kept in chains." Arlo's hamlike hand restraining Carina was all that prevented bloodletting at the table.

"True, every word of it," Haskell nodded sagely, engulfing a mouthful of partridge.

Eden studied her older brother's stiff, exaggerated manners and the disapproving turn at the corners of his full lips. "Skyelt . . . takes a bit of gettin' use to, James." She put a tender hand on his arm. "But it's worth the effort.

433

Stay with us a while, until you're convinced that I'm happy here. I couldn't bear to have you leave without a visit, thinking—whatever terrible things you're thinking."

"Eden, not here." James looked at the faces staring at them.

"They all understand," Eden declared, reaching boldly across the table for her husband's big hand. "We're all . . . family."

Family. James came to learn just what she meant in the next week: no one had a problem that went unshared, but no one had any secrets, either. Everyone felt free to comment on everything, slowing the pace of work, but bringing solutions to problems from the most unlikely quarters. Argument was part of the normal daily routine, and work never seemed to cease . . . morning, noon, and night. And people—everywhere you moved in Skyelt's complex, there were people. But the volume of folk couldn't prevent frequent run-ins with those you chose to avoid . . . like Carina Graham.

He watched Eden and her husband and tried to decide if she were telling the truth about wanting to stay in this awful place. More than once she shocked him by settling herself on Ram's lap as they kept company around the huge fireplace. She touched and stroked him and rubbed against him like a pure wanton. It brought a shamed heat to his cheeks and made him stiffen and want to smack her hands. Where was the ladylike polish that had made him so proud of her when he'd come to collect her from Mistress Dunleavy's? Now she was bolder than all the Marlow men put together!

And Ramsay—he was changed. He smiled frequently; much of his dour mien was gone. But with it had gone a bit of his imperious dignity, and James wasn't sure he'd come out on the right end of that trade. A man, especially a lord, had standards to uphold. And how did one manage that while dropping everything at the flick of his wife's skirts? All Eden had to do was appear with that licentious light in her eyes and Ramsay was picking her up and striding for the bloody stairs. Eager was a ram-goat, his brother-in-law was — and his own sister was not much better.

Carina Graham was seated in the hall one morning as he strode in and she stared at his form-fitting breeches and long, tapered legs admiringly. "Maybe there's somethin' to be said for a pair of breeches after all." She turned to Eden with a raffish grin. "I don' suppose it would be proper to ask what they wear beneath. . . ."

Eden's burst of laughter appalled him and he colored and strode out into the cold air. The whole damn place was a nest of lechers!

Christmas Day, James put aside his quarrels with Skyelt and allowed himself to be drawn into the celebration. There was wine and ale aplenty and food to gorge an army of gluttons. Eden watched James dance with several lasses and noted that he refused all spirits except a sociable mug of negus for toasting. She really began to wonder when the mistletoe was trundled around the crowded hall and the most any sighing maiden got from him was a dry brotherly peck. That wasn't like him . . . was it? She whispered it to Ram and he laughed and shrugged, burying his face in her neck and suggesting she worry about her husband's needs, not her brother's lack of them.

Eden and Ram had retired long before James rose and stretched, ignoring Haskell's protests to make for his bed. As he rounded the top of the broad stairs, he heard muffled voices coming from a small alcove in the old stone wall and looked as he passed, in spite of himself.

Carina was flattened against the stone by a huge, muscular figure doggedly pursuing the neck of her blouse while straining to hold her there with his body. She was gasping and clutching at his shirt as her skin was quickly being devoured. Her eyes widened to true panic as Tass MacCrenna stopped her cry with his mouth and she glimpsed James's dark face in the same instant.

"Don't mind me," James's lip curled, "go right on with . . . whatever you're doing." Tass's head came around to blear at him.

"Damn you! Bloody, stinkin' sonofa—!" Carina squirmed and ranted as James strolled off down the hall, ignoring her insults. But it was Tass she was cursing, and his hold on her was loosened just enough for her to bring her knee up savagely. He stumbled back, howling. She ducked and ran for her room, slamming and locking her door with trembling hands.

Further down the hall, James slammed his door as well, staring at its dark outline and seeing Carina's wriggling body and lightning-blue eyes, glazed with passion under that barbarian. Coupling in the hall like bloody animals! Fire erupted in his veins and he found himself fully roused and completely bewildered by it. He wanted nothing more that to peel that crude lout from her delectable little frame . . . and take his place. The thought so appalled him that he threw open the window and stood in the invading cold for several long minutes. And for once he was glad to have a cold bed to crawl into.

The next day he was irked to see her looking so comely as he breakfasted with Eden and Ram. She gave him a cold, disdainful look and turned her chin away. James's skin began to heat as he stared at the luscious pout of her lips and the fiery fall of her thick, burnished hair against her creamy skin. His warming eyes trailed the half-revealed curve of her full young breasts and his fingers itched. Lowering further, his eyes caught on her dagger and he jerked his head around irritably.

"Well, James, did you enjoy our Skyelt Christmas?" Eden saw him watching Carina through narrowed eyes. "Your revelry was more restrained than I might have expected from a Marlow male."

"Because I declined to make a drunken, lecherous oaf of myself, you mean?" He leveled a disparaging look at Carina. "There were quite enough of them roaming about as it was."

"True. And not a single gentleman could be found to render assistance!" Carina's face flamed.

"It appeared you needed no assistance in becoming the proverbial 'good time had by all' . . . and in the hallway, yet." His taunt flayed Carina's pride and her dagger was out; she'd have climbed the table to get him if Ram hadn't sprung to his feet and snatched her back, holding her dangling above the ground.

"Rina! Stop it!" Ram growled, tossing a do-something-he's-*your*-brother look at Eden as he carried his sister out.

"James, I'm astonished at you!" Eden turned on him with real anger rising. "Carina is Haskell's daughter and my husband's sister, no matter what her birth. She's had a hard life for one so young — she's not yet seventeen!"

"Then she's merely taken to her profession early," he snapped.

"What?" Eden rose with a jerk, scarcely able to believe her ears. "She's a sweet, lovely child, James Marlow, and despite opportunity and appearances, she's still a maid. Why do you think she wears that bloody knife?" And she stalked out, leaving him to stew in his own guilty relief.

Eden entered Carina's rooms later and found her sister-in-law dry-eyed, seeming unusually small and almost defenseless. She took Carina's hands and made her reveal what had happened the night before.

"Damme!" Carina finished, "If I'd just worn my blade, Tass wouldn'ta dared."

"Why didn't you?" Eden frowned, seeking her downcast gaze.

"I thought if I didn't wear it, I might seem . . . more . . . a lady."

Eden might have laughed if she hadn't just realized why that was suddenly so important to Carina. She sucked in a sharp breath and had to confirm her insight. "It's James, isn't it?"

Carina nodded but wouldn't look at Eden. Her young face seemed hopeless and very wistful. "He's so handsome and elegant . . . and used to fine, beautiful ladies. . . ."

Eden's face and heart softened. She didn't want to hold out false hopes to Carina, but she recalled James's sidelong glances at her and couldn't imagine he'd be any more resistant to her enticements than the rest of Skyelt's bachelors. "Just be yourself, Carina," she offered as a bit of sound, if equivocal, advice, "and let what happens . . . happen."

A few days later, James dismounted from a brisk morning ride with Ram and stretched lazily, feeling his blood pumping hard through him. It was a twist of fate that his eyes fell on Carina at just that moment. She was slipping toward the main barn, furtively scouring the area immediately around her. James stopped in mid-stretch, and Tass MacCrenna's broad back muscled into his mind. Anger spurted into his racing blood.

"It's no business of mine if she ruts in the barn like a sow." But he was already halfway to the barn door where she had disappeared. Stepping inside, he heard her first, then as his eyes adjusted in the dimness, he made her out, climbing around over the stacks of hay tossed down onto

438

the barn floor.

"Where are you?" She climbed and poked, lifted hay and peered over the worn boards of the granery bins, searching. "I'll find ye, I swear I will—" Her voice dropped to a sultry, menacing rasp. "And I'll have you for supper!" There was a muffled noise and she whirled suddenly and charged a far pile of hay that now wiggled and squealed in terror. A rustle and a scuffle, and soon she had collared three squirming children and tripped another with her foot as he made to run for it.

"You're at me mercy now!" She grabbed two up in her arms and whirled them around while the other two climbed and hung on her. It was too much, and they all toppled into a pile of hay. She recovered first, setting her fingers to their ribs and warding off a barrage of hay. Soon they lay panting and laughing, a jumble of limbs and hay.

"Rina, play some more!" a five-year-old urchin gasped, sitting up.

"No," she joined him, trying to catch her breath, "you've chores . . . and I've duties. Enough for now."

Their collective wails and begging finally produced a low, sweet nursery song from her lips in compensation. Halfway through they joined her and James watched, feeling like he'd turned to soup inside and was draining into his own boots. What a miserable bastard he was. Children . . . she was singing to children. Her dulcet tones washed over him, reddening his skin. And when she finished, he stood a moment in the sweet silence before putting his palms together in gentle applause.

She startled and looked up to find James moving toward her out of the shadows. Shaken, she shooed the children up and out the door and started to rise.

"You sing very well." He bent to assist her and she pulled away, managing on her own. A minute before,

439

she'd radiated alluring warmth; now she was that defensive little she-cat again, claws ready. The speed of the transition unnerved him.

"It was just . . . a game we play. They work hard . . . they should get to play, too." She busied herself brushing hay from her woolen skirt and retrieving her thick knitted shawl. Her hands were trembling. It was the first compliment he'd paid her . . . *any* man had paid her.

She still had hay in her hair and it seemed the most natural thing in the world for him to help her remove it. She jumped noticeably at his touch and turned large, uncertain eyes on him as he produced a piece of straw.

"Hold still." Instinct made him move very slowly in reaching for another piece and then another. But when his hands moved again, it was to stroke that shining, burnished mass that had enclosed his dreams these last nights. It was thick and soft and fragrant.

Carina stood expectantly before him, her oval face tilted up to him. The rise and fall of her breasts under her blouse tortured his breathing. His hand trailed along her cheek; it was like fine Persian satin. His arms twitched and he stepped closer, cradling her face between his lean hands. His heart stopped when her eyes closed and she rubbed her cheek against his palm. His arms crushed about her small waist, lifting her against him as he dropped his head to cover her lips.

Carina was lost in the mesmerizing tenderness of his mouth. Her ripe young curves melted against him and her arms slid around his neck. She opened her mouth to his gentle probing, forgetting every rapacious kiss, every oral assault she'd suffered. This was so different, this was pleasure, gentle and tantalizing. This was James.

Shyly she began to return his ardor, making an exploration of her own . . . the silky, moist borders of his lips, the slight lapping of his front teeth, the raspy softness of his tongue. Then she was floating down and there was sweet hay around her and James above her. He kissed her deeply and trailed kisses down her chin and throat and across her bare chest. Her hands came up to explore his face, his crisp, wavy hair, the lean cording of his neck above his starched collar. She circled his hard shoulders with her slender arms and reveled in the difference in their bodies.

When James's hands tugged at her blouse, she made no move to object and soon her breasts were bare, warmed by the light of his gaze, then the rasp of his cheek over her tight, sensitive nipples.

His hands flew over her waist, her perfect breasts, her hair, and he shifted his body against her, feeling her quiver as he took one rosy nipple into his mouth. He was reeling. She was delicious . . . a perfect miniature . . . so small and yet so sensual . . . a vixen who sang to children, hardly larger than a child herself. . . .

Little more than a child. . . . The thought rumbled through him and the position of his mouth on hers sliced his consciousness like a knife. His head jerked up and he shuddered at the sight of her, warmed, open . . . abandoned into his lustful clutches. What in God's name was he doing to this child?

Carina felt him move and draw her blouse together. She was liquid inside, hot and dazed by her own desires.

"James?" She sat up, focusing her eyes with difficulty. He was sitting beside her, elbows on knees, face in hands. He turned to look at her and her breath caught at the tension in his face. Unconsciously she tried to cover her breasts and her gaping blouse with her arms.

He saw the bewildered hurt in her face and cringed at her feeble attempt to shield her sweet nakedness from him. His stomach was turning over. He stood and turned his back to her, running his hands back through his hair.

441

His tongue was thick and clumsy as he tried to find an apology for actions he knew to be unforgivable.

"James?" her voice wavered, cutting him.

"My behavior toward you was inexcusable," he ground out. "Please . . . find it in yourself to forget it and I *swear* it won't be repeated."

"You didn't . . . like it?" Her voice was so small, so devastated, he couldn't bear to look at her.

"That's hardly the point. If you were a lady, your brother would have to call me out—"

"If I were a . . . lady?"

What an incredibly stupid thing for him to say! Her father and brother were lords of a different name—what did that make her? His face was stern with misery when he glanced at her tousled beauty. She was a delectable child who had to wear a knife to protect herself . . . against men like him.

"I've behaved despicably, Carina." He clenched his hands and his eyes rolled heavenward. "I—I swear to God . . . it will *never* happen again!" And he strode out.

Carina sat on her knees in the hay, feeling his lips soft and coaxing on her body, his hands gentle in her hair. And his hard words slammed through her with fresh violence. She quivered, suspended between rage and collapse. Her eyes glistened with tears and she raised a feisty fist heavenward.

"Don't *You* be listenin' to a thing he says!"

All Skyelt had noted the tall American's elevated, gentlemanly manner and, with characteristic sagacity, concluded from their experience with their lady and her brother that Americans were far more civilized than Englishmen—nearly up to French and Scottish standards. And it was reinforced for them every time James encoun-

tered their tempestous little Carina Graham. His manner
with her was restrained in the extreme. He addressed her
as "Miss Graham," lent her an arm of assistance, and
seemed to appear magically whenever Tass MacCrenna or
another of Skyelt's bachelors ventured close. It couldn't
honestly be held against him that he blanched visibly
when the air around her occasionally sizzled with ire.

Eden noted his manner and the discreet distance he
maintained from Carina and wondered at it. Still more
surprising were his increasingly staid comments in mixed
company and his raised brows whenever he saw Eden
taking some small housekeeping task in hand. Ladies, he
observed pointedly, kept their hands lily-white and their
thoughts just as pure. And on the subject of Scottish
women's traditional dress he was adamant: they should be
ashamed to have more on their minds than they had on
their bodies. His stuffy moralisms began to grate on her
nerves and after supper one night she found her chance to
retaliate.

Standing before the hearth, James sipped a potent
French brandy and ventured the comment that, "If Scots
would control their women as closely as they controlled
their purses, the whole moral tone of the country would
be vastly improved."

"This," Eden turned to Carina and The MacKay, "is the
zeal of a recent convert to both morality and refinement."

"Dede." His face tightened gratifyingly.

"The true depth of his regard for the fairer sex is
revealed in his sage observation that—"

"Eden—!"

" 'To know a man one must read what he reads—' "
*"Eden Delight!"*

" '—but to know a woman, one need only be the chair
she sits upon.' "

"And he's volunteered to furnish quite a few parlors,

443

has he?" Carina mused, looking him over as if he should be plucked for supper.

"Fewer than you might think." Eden's eyes narrowed with an irrepressible triumph. "His vast knowledge of women was actually acquired beneath the knees of one 'Madame Rochelle.' "

"Take your wife in hand, Ramsay," James shook a furious finger, "*if* you're capable of it!"

Ram glanced at the savage gleam in his wife's eye and his feet hit the floor. In a flash he ducked a shoulder and pulled her out of her chair and across him, steadying her rear near his grin with a brawny hand.

"*In hand,* you said? Capital idea, James. But I don' think it's strictly American." And he strode for the stairs with Eden laughing and squealing outrage in the most insincere way.

## Chapter Twenty-four

"Eden," Carina put down her stitching and glanced around the sunny upstairs parlor, rolling her shoulders to dispel the ache of concentration. "How much would a lady's dress cost?" She said it so softly and avoided Eden's gaze to minimize the importance of her response.

"An English-style dress?" Eden scrutinized Carina's casual nod. "Well, I suppose it varies a great deal, depending on the fabric and trims and on the dressmaker's skills."

"Somethin' nice . . . to notice."

"Several guineas, perhaps. Why?" Eden watched her draw a deep breath and stab her needle into the soft cotton she was embroidering.

"I told Haskell today. . . I want a new dress."

Eden laughed, her eyes warming. "So that was what the roaring and stomping was all about this morn. And what did he say?"

"He flat refused, th' stingy old far—" Carina winced, "coot. He said me arse weren't bare and that was good enough."

Eden put down her embroidery and assessed Carina's unusually sober mood. "Why do you want a ladies' dress,

Rina?" The crackle of the fire burst around them in the silence.

"I want to show . . . I can be . . ." Carina's hands gestured her loss of words, palms up.

Eden frowned thoughtfully: James. Each day Carina affronted James's gentlemanly sensibilities in some new way while her longing for him grew ever sharper. The more restrained and gentlemanly he became, the more she was drawn to make him notice her, however outrageously. Their flaming encounters were becoming a chief source of entertainment on Skyelt, dealing a near-fatal blow to Carina's hopes. If there was one thing a gentleman wouldn't countenance, it was being made a source of entertainment — especially by a woman.

"Then perhaps I'll have a word with Ram."

That was how they came to be leaving a dressmaker's shop on the town square of nearby Aberfeldy two days later. The day was frigid but sunny, and they'd managed a smart bit of bargaining and were laughing at Arlo's good-natured grumping over having to stand for hours in a shop filled with feminine frippery.

"Good day, fair ladies!"

They turned and found Ian Barclay striding up, dressed like the English and to fit kill. With judiciously displayed charm, he entreated them to join him in the local inn for a warming bit of tea.

"I think not, Ian Barclay," Eden demurred with a perfect smile that reminded him why he wanted them to so badly. He made a disconsolate face and despite Arlo's glower, something made her add, "But you may walk with us a bit."

"There is no reason we canna be friends, dear ladies." He extended a dapper arm to Eden, then to his petite half-sister, sending Arlo a look that raised his hackles and sent him off in a huff.

"Except your attempt to take the food from our mouths

an' the roof from over our heads, you mean?" Carina clarified with a wicked glare.

"Surely you cannot think such of me, little sister." He looked at Eden, then back at Carina. "There will always be a place for you both at Skyelt."

"You seek the title of landlord, then?" Eden chided with her eyes.

"Not hardly." Carina watched him looking at Eden.

"I only seek to set a long-standing dispute at rest," he smiled dazzlingly. "But let us not speak of such dreary matters on such a fine day. Poor me, I don' often have Ramsay's luck when it comes to such delightful company."

They walked around the bustling marketplace and across the square without further reference to their legal differences. Ian was utterly charming and perfectly roguish in his banter. And in a short while it was deucedly hard to recall that he was suing to claim the MacLean inheritance.

"Eden! Miss Graham!" James bore down on them, his face heating at the cozy nestle of their arms on his. "Sir," he stared at Ian harshly, "you will please excuse my sister and her sister-in-law. We are preparing to depart."

"James." Eden flushed at his irate manner and started to protest. Then the absurdity of her own position struck her fully and she withdrew her hand from Ian in guilty haste. Whatever had come over her, allowing Ian to charm his way into their company? How could she ever explain? "This is Ian Barclay . . . a neighbor." James's eyes grew steely as he was forced to nod politely to Ian, though withholding his hand.

"It was a good thing Arlo found me first," James muttered angrily, ushering them along toward the stables where their small carriage waited. "Ramsay would have been compelled to save his honor. The blackguard is trying to steal your husband's inheritance—everyone

447

knows it." To underscore his point, he nodded pleasantly to two older ladies eying them speculatively. "In the future, try to spare some thought for your *husband,* Eden."

She stopped and jerked her hand from James's grasp, her face aflame; he was unforgivably right. She still felt a certain gratitude toward Ian for his kindness and comfort in her early days at Skyelt and she'd allowed it to overcome her judgment. She whirled to avoid James's piercing look, jamming her hands into her fur muff and walking quickly toward the carriage.

"And you, Miss Graham . . . a lady should beware her reputation around such scoundrels."

Carina pulled her hand away; it felt like her skin remained with him. "As you've been at pains to insist, Mr. Marlow, I'm no lady." Her flashing eyes filed with frustrated moisture. "And that *scoundrel* is not likely to damage m' reputation any more that I would his. He's my brother!"

Ram had watched it all as he was crossing the square—Eden's obvious enjoyment of Ian's company, James's approach, and their heated words later. Prickles traveled up and down his spine as the sight of Eden nestled at Ian's side continued to command his senses. Seeing her laughing and sparkling for another man's pleasure was a shock. These last two months at Skyelt, it had been easy to claim her caring, her passion for himself alone, to pretend there was no world outside their loving. Now, on their first venture out, he was reminded of what dangers the wider world contained and of just how vulnerable his new feelings for Eden had made him. His steps were heavy as he turned toward the horses and carriage.

It was a somber foursome that returned to Skyelt, each embroiled in private doubts and combating private miseries. James felt like a pompous, overbearing fool, and a jealous one at that. Carina was plunged into sullenness, convinced that James could never love her, she being one bastard among Haskell's many. Eden was deeply humiliated by her lapse where Ian Barclay was concerned, fearing she'd been away from society so long, she'd forgotten how decent women behaved. And Ram was watching his wife's troubled mood and wondering if their marriage could be enough to satisfy her the way it did him. Ian Barclay hung over the small party like a pall. It was only Arlo's determined conversation that made the tension bearable.

The atmosphere was ripe for a storm, and when they reached the stable yard of the hall of Skyelt, Haskell provided the lightning stroke that set it free. He came charging out of the stable, roaring at Ram, his jaw set for combat.

"Where've you been, boy?!"

"You know we went to Aberfeldy." Ram dismounted from his horse with a determined set to his shoulders. He reached a hand up to Eden and then helped Carina down while Haskell's stare all but set his back on fire.

"A fool's errand—diddlin' away precious time an' shirkin' yer rightful duties!" Haskell's huge fists went to his hips. Ram's eyes narrowed and a muscle in his jaw jumped, but otherwise his movements gave little evidence of the anger building inside him. "There's spring plantin' to plan, boy, and lambin' pens to build, and cows needin' breedin'!" Haskell declared.

"Clearly *your* area . . . breeding," Ram retorted, turning Eden around bodily and pushing her firmly toward the house in front of him.

"Well," Haskell raised his voice to a thunderous level, "it sure as hell *ain't yours!*"

Ram kept walking and Haskell was left stewing in his own bile in front of his bastard daughter and James

Marlow. That round had gone to his son. He stormed into the hall after Ram, spoiling for round two.

The long dining table was littered on one end with documents bearing seals and tomes of legal script. Ram paused to survey them, then turned away to usher Eden upstairs.

"Ye shoulda been here when they come!" Haskell succeeded in halting him. "It were yer duty!" Haskell was in another of his moods, Eden realized, and was determined to have his squall.

"Who came?" Ram was at the bottom of the stairs and turned back halfway.

"Cavender and Gunn. Servin' papers on us, orderin' us to Edinburgh an' into court as if we were common criminals. Them writs," he pointed heatedly at the parchments, "is signed by none other than Lawrence Bruce."

The name seemed to register with Ram and his face clouded. Eden watched irritably from the stairs as he went back to the table and picked up the documents, scouring them with a grim set to his mouth.

"So your sins are finally catching up with you, eh, Haskell?" Ram's smile was humorless.

"Angus finagled to get the case heard afore Bruce because—"

"Bruce hates you. Another of your ill-advised adulteries, of course. Is there anybody in Scotland who doesn't have reason to cut your throat? Damn you, Haskell." The air crackled as Haskell seemed to shrink under Ram's furious glare. "And double damn you for makin' me break the fifth commandment!" Ram was halfway to the door before Haskell recovered from his fleeting attack of conscience to take the offensive again.

"Ye can't blame me for it all, boy! If you'd done yer duty by me, and got me an heir, Ian's name wouldn't never have been mentioned in the same breath as Skyelt . . . an' Angus wouldn't have gotten ideas about the

450

MacPherson."

"You dare blame me for that?" Ram turned on him again, scarlet with disbelief. He moved slowly toward his father, both fists clenched and itching to crunch some bone. "You scheming, lying old reprobate!"

"Ram, please—" Eden flew down the steps, her anxiety and anger growing apace. She'd sworn bloody havoc on the very next person that cast aspersions on her husband's manhood. She hurried around the end of the table, barely containing herself. "Haskell, don'—"

"Who else if you're not to blame? E'en now when ye plow the wench's field nightly, ye come up fallow!"

*"Damn you, Haskell!* I've had enough—" Ram lunged for Haskell, hardly able to stop himself when Eden's body intervened as she launched herself at her startled father-in-law. And when flesh met flesh and Haskell stumbled back, it was Eden's arm that felt the searing pain and her fist that throbbed. Furious, she jammed her fist under her other arm to staunch the pain and advanced on Haskell, who was holding his nose and gasping and blearing at her through wide, watery eyes.

"Don't you ever, *ever* speak about my husband like that as long as you live! He's plowed my field all right . . . and planted! I'm breedin', Haskell! *Breedin'!*" She stepped closer, her eyes blazing with a preview of hellfire that her father-in-law would not soon forget. "So go shout it from the rooftops, you old wretch, and get drunk as a pig and brag about what a fine stud your son is! But all Skyelt knows that what makes Ramsay MacLean so special is the way he's *not* like you!"

She ended in a rasping shout, her chest heaving and tears welling in her eyes. Somehow she turned and made it to the stairs before the rockets went off in her vision and a wave of nausea overcame her. Distantly she heard Ram's voice and felt his arms around her. Then he was lifting her off her feet.

"If she's broke her hand, Haskell, I'll break your neck," Ram had uttered with deadly control. And he mounted the steps with Eden's limp form in his arms.

James, Ian, Arlo and The MacKay stood numbly, having watched the entire confrontation. Haskell roused slowly, testing his bloodied nose and wiping it. It was nothing too serious, he seemed to think, squaring his shoulders. He strode out past them and deep in his eye there was a glint as he passed.

"She's breedin'."


"Let me see it," Ram settled on the bed beside her and took her right hand. His face darkened at the swelling beginning on her knuckles. He flexed her fingers carefully and she bit her lip. "I don' think anything's broken." He left the bed to wet a cloth to wrap her hand.

Eden watched him with a sinking heart. He was so very controlled, she knew his anger was deep. Even so, his fingers were gentle on her when he returned.

"I'm sorry, Ram." She sounded small and felt even smaller. She could scarcely believe what she'd done. There wasn't any possible justification for her behavior . . . she'd interfered in her husband's rightful sphere, the defense of his own name and standards.

"If you ever do anything like that again, Eden," he was solemn and terse, "I'll lock you up, so help me God. I've been handlin' Haskell since I was a lad and I don't need a woman's help . . . not even one with a devilish strong right cross."

Tears began to drip in spite of her. "It won't happen again," her voice quivered. "It's just, I get so sick of his bullying and the way he talks about you like you're not . . . just because you don't . . ." The softening in his stern expression allowed her heart to beat again.

Her urge to protect him lodged in his chest and it was

impossible to be properly furious with her. He stroked a wisp of hair back from her face and caressed her cheek.

"I don' care what he says," Ram insisted softly, "nor should anyone with good sense. All Skyelt knows what he's like, and they know me as well. They'll think what they will." His eyes shadowed. "Are you really pregnant?"

Eden nodded, chewing her lip again. "I'm so sorry . . . I meant to tell you some night soon, in our bed . . . and now I've ruined that, too." Those wretched tears came again. "I'm really very happy about it," she sobbed as he gathered her into his arms.

"So I see." Ram's face was tight, his eyes moist above Eden's head.

"Really . . . I am. I want your bairn, Ramsay MacLean . . . my bairn, too. Please be happy about it." She turned her face up to his and the longing he saw there was not to be denied.

His mouth lowered onto hers and the comfort he intended bloomed unexpectedly into need for his extraordinary wife. His hands stroked her with tender restraint and it was a while before she realized what he was doing and why.

"Ramsay," she pushed him back and sat up, her fingers flying over the buttons of her coat, "I'm not suddenly made of glass." She pushed the coat from her shoulders and began immediately on the dress fastenings at the back of her neck. He would have risen, but she caught him back and determinedly undid her clothes before his burning eyes.

She sat with her dress around her lap, her chemise flung into some far corner. Her bare breasts were slightly fuller, otherwise there was no discernible difference in her irresistible body. She placed his hand on one warm, satiny globe and held it there.

"I'm your wife, Ramsay . . . and I'm made of flesh. I need you know more than ever."

Ram groaned and pulled her to him, losing himself in her thirsty kiss.

Skyelt celebrated the news of their young laird's triumph in a rather sedate fashion. Whether Eden's hot words to Haskell were the cause or not was anybody's guess, but there was no drunken rout in Skyelt's hall that night. Supper was served as usual, though the fare was exceedingly fine. Several of Skyelt's noteworthies were invited to the table, and The MacKay joined them, smiling.

James didn't know how to react to his sister's wild behavior or her shocking pronouncement of her maternal state. She was bolder than any woman he'd ever known, with the possible exception of Carina Graham. He found himself staring at Carina, feeling roused and deeply disturbed by it. He knew beyond a doubt that Carina Graham would be a wife like his sister was: passionate, loyal, and unpredictable. She'd make some man old before his time—and probably make him deliriously happy as well. And the thought of that nameless, faceless gent possessing and savoring her sweet, infuriating little person purely devastated him.

That Eden retired a bit early that night surprised no one. But their jaws dropped aplenty when Haskell called her name and took her hand with courtly reverence before she left. Nothing seemed to be the same at Skyelt anymore.

## Chapter Twenty-five

Word of Ram's marriage, if not of his fatherhood, had spread through the countryside like ripples on a pond, unsettling things and generating much curiosity. The main families had thought old Haskell mad when they learned what he'd done, entailing his son's inheritance in such a bizarre manner. They were more than surprised to learn the stern and manly Ramsay MacLean had actually complied with the requirements. There was generally a strong desire to see this lady-bride who would mother the future lairds of Skyelt. Her beauty was a foregone conclusion, Haskell's tastes being well known. But they'd heard rumblings of her rather unusual nature and of the way staunch, Presbyterian Ramsay was openly enamored of her. This marriage they had to see for themselves.

When the weather broke in early March, Skyelt's lairds were invited to a gathering at Laird Stewart Henderson's that promised to be part clan gathering and part society affair. It had been a while since Haskell had been invited into polite company, but he held no grudge and declared that a contingent from Skyelt would indeed make an appearance. A bit of gaiety was exactly what was needed to take his mind from the increasingly pressing concerns of Angus Barclay's suit.

Of late, it seemed to Haskell that he was the only one concerned with Skyelt's fate. Ram was too taken up with his wife and her obvious attractions, especially now that she was bred. Haskell couldn't see the sense in wasting such time on a project already completed. Irritation trickled into his veins when he referred a vital matter like hoof-trimming to his son only to have Terrance return minutes later, clearing his throat and saying Ram was otherwise engaged. The lad's sens of proportion clearly needed work.

Skyelt's contingent arrived at Henderson's craggy gray-stone Brantwyrd and it was evident that they were awaited. Nearly everything in progress ground to a halt at Ram and his bride were announced and shuttled around the elegant house for introductions.

There had been more that a few raised brows and impolite stares when Carina Graham was introduced just after them. Carina stood in the arched doorway to the crowded salon wearing a fashionable, high-waisted dress and a faintly uncertain look. Eden smiled and had Ram turn back, collecting Carina's arm in hers and drawing her around the room with them. The message was clear: to satisfy their curiosity about Ramsay's lady-wife, they'd have to receive his baseborn sister as well. And while they recovered from that shock, they were struck with the presence of a tall, striking colonial in their midst. James Marlow was an intriguing phenomenon, fine-looking, gentlemanly, and seemingly on friendly terms with old Haskell himself. Local society had seen enough in the first hour to keep them talking for weeks.

Ram smiled and greeted his neighbors with amusement, watching as Eden charmed them with her natural grace and understated refinements. He'd chuckled at her fussing and flurry over clothes and local etiquette, but could see now she was perfectly right . . . this was a test of sorts.

She'd wasted no opportunity to show her adoption of her husband's Scottish tradition, even to wearing a muted MacLean plaid made into a fetching, high-waisted gown. But she was still every inch the American-bred and English-educated lady, and proudly so. It was a judicious blend of pride and heritage the Tayside lairds found irresistible.

That first afternoon rolled onward, filled with games and horseraces, friendly wagers and genteel indulgence. Eden marveled at the swish and swirl of bold color in the men's highland dress and in the ladies's skirts, sashes, and bonnets. In the background, the whine and skirl of the bagpipes seemed ever-present, and from time to time a set of dancers would form to captivate the guests with graceful bobs and turns and leaps that everyone seemed eager to interpret for her.

Outside, in the cold, fresh air, they watched the young bucks of the country bare their sleeves and arm wrestle or battle with staffs while balancing on a log set above the ground. The ladies bowled and played at quoits and croquet. And later in the day, over tea and scones, the female contingent refreshed themselves and became better acquainted with Ramsay's lovely bride and the startlingly acceptable Carina Graham.

Eden colored abruptly when the servant announced the presence of Ian Barclay and in no time she found him bearing down on her from across the room. Her hostess leaned closer, her eyes wide.

"We had invited the Barclays, as a matter of form," the graying Leonora Henderson murmured apologetically, "coupled with the announcement that you'd already accepted. We certainly didn't expect . . ."

"Ladies." Ian made a fine leg to his hostess and took her hand, "My fair Lady Leonora. And Lady Eden, beautiful as the morning sun on the heath." He reached for Eden's hand next and would not be put by off the the telling wait caused by her shifting her teacup to the other hand. "So gratified to see you here, sweet lady." He lingered long enough over her hand to cause every feminine eye to notice his reluctance to let it go. "Regrettably, my father and family were unable to attend, Lady Leonora. They send their regards."

To her credit, the Lady of Brantwyrd rescued the situation by rising and trundling Ian off toward the men. She carefully shepherded him past Haskell and into her husband's sage clutches. Eden excused herself and drew Carina along with her to find Ram.

They arrived in the long, window-lined gallery in time to witness Ram's very controlled confrontation with Ian Barclay. Ram stood, hard-framed, returning his elder half-brother's scrutiny with a sardonic smile. Neither batted an eye, neither gave an inch. The air around them stilled and every man present froze with expectation. Time was beat out by Eden's thudding heart. She dared not intervene here, not after Ian's audacious behavior just minutes before.

James strode past her through the doorway and called Ram's name, cracking the dangerously escalating tension. He stopped at their side and greeted Ian civilly, extending his hand. Ian withdrew slowly from Ram's burning gaze to accept it and the whole gallery eased. With extraordinary coolness, James appropriated Ram for a hand of cards and the final wicket was negotiated with no apparent loss of face for either man.

For the rest of the evening, a palpable tension permeated the gathering. At supper and all during the dancing afterward, Eden was painfully ware of the way Ian's eyes drifted toward her whenever she'd taken refuge. She tried planting herself at Ram's side and found it made little difference; Ian still sought her with his eyes. Fearing Ram would notice, she pleaded fatigue and withdrew to a party of older women.

But it was already done: Ram knew exactly the way Ian Barclay had greeted his wife and then pursued her all evening. He pretended to ignore it for the sake of both Eden and the assembled company, but he knew sooner or later Ian's silent challenge would have to be met.

When Eden approached Ram with the intent of retiring early, he insisted on escorting her to their borrowed chamber. Once closeted inside, Eden leaned heavily against the bedpost and gave in to the little aches the evening's strain had produced in her. Ram's arms slid around her waist from behind and she melted back to revel in his strength around her.

"I'm sorry to be such a wilting lily," she murmured softly.

"Think nothing of it . . . you're probably settin' a new fashion: retiring early with one's husband in tow. Shocking actually." He nuzzled the side of her neck and rocked her gently.

"Did you see Carina . . . mobbed by eligible gentlemen?"

"And he without a blade in her hand," Ram rumbled.

"Don't be too sure about that," she laughed. "Will you keep an eye on her, Ram? I'd hate for her to misinterpret some young buck's intentions and carve him up on the drawing room floor. It'd be a century before she was invited anywhere else."

"I don't think my help is needed there. James hasn't let her out of his sight all evening. I think you're right about him . . . and about the effects of Carina's new clothes. She's been a perfect lady all evenin'."

Eden turned in his arms and embraced his neck, pulling him down. She teased his lips and felt him sigh against her mouth. He straightened determinedly and took her arms from his neck, kissing her hands warmly.

"I have to appear again for a while, so as not to scandalize Lady Leonora. I believe it's considered unfashionable, bein' besotted with one's own wife. Go to bed, love . . . and to sleep."

Eden sighed, watching Ram leave, then went to her leather valise and unpacked. She undressed before the fire and donned her robe. She'd just settled on the bed with her hand glass and pin box when there came a soft rap on the door and opened.

"So you decided to chan—" She stopped, half-risen on the bed, and stared into Ian Barclay's silvering eyes. "Ian! What are you doing here?" He stepped inside and closed the door a way that insured quiet. "This is most . . . improper."

"Improper, perhaps . . . but the only way I may have you alone for a few minutes. I came to Brantwyrd expressly to see you, Eden."

"Really, Ian. This must wait. If you've something to say—"

"But I do, sweet Eden." He was across the room quickly and settling on the edge of the bed before she could untangle her legs and remove herself. "I've somethin' to say to you . . . and I should have said it sooner, knowing how things were for you at Skyelt. Not a day has gone by since our first meeting that I haven't thought of you, wanted you." He captured her hands and ignored her tugs and breathy protests.

"I should have declared myself to you before Ram returned; then it might have been easier for all of us. I want you, sweet, enchanting Eden, more than—"

"No, Ian—" But he cut off her protest with a kiss that shocked her into momentary paralysis. By the time she emptied her hands and shoved him away, he was warming dangerously. "No!" She did manage to slide from the bed and jerk her robe down around her.

"I don't know what you think you're doing, Ian, but you'd better leave . . . now. Ram is due back any moment—"

"Eden, it's no good denying what you feel toward me. I've felt you respond in my arms, remember? I know what your marriage is like and I know we would be happy—"

"Ian!" She stopped him, her cheeks scarlet with humiliation, "you *don't* know about my marriage. It's true I was unhappy at first and I behaved toward you . . . unwisely. But things have changed . . . a great deal. I'm happy to be Ram's wife now, and I've made Skyelt my home. Ian, I'm carrying Ram's child."

Ian's face showed he hadn't yet learned that detail. He straightened and his eyes grew flinty with recalculation. "A minor detail, dearest. I'd be more that pleased to take the bairn and give it my name." His mouth curled with private amusement.

"You don't understand." Eden put a parlor chair between them and gripped its back with whitened hands. "Ian, I *love* my husband." She saw the angry chagrin in his dusky MacLean features and felt a shiver of horror run through her. "I never said anything to you about . . . I only let you kiss me. And I never meant you to think. . . ." What had she done? In a moment's loneliness and need she'd allowed herself to be swept, unprotesting, into another man's arms. And now her one indiscretion . . . a mere kiss . . . had become a threat to her marriage, and perhaps more. Her face drained and her legs trembled.

"Didn't you, Eden? Didn't you mean to make me want you?"

"I honestly didn't, Ian." Her head shook to echo it. "Please, don't make me say it any plainer. I'm Ram's true wife now, and I want to stay with him."

Ian stood very still, searching, analyzing. His MacLean eyes shone like clear, hard stones. "It can't be Ramsay . . . it must be Skyelt. For years they've talked of how old Haskell squirreled away his coin, refusing to spend it even to keep a roof over his head. I know he's got plenty . . .

and you've learned it, too." Ashes of anger dulled his hard cheeks.

"Who would've guessed the sweet-faced Lady of Skyelt has a strong-box for a heart? You're not in love with Ram, dearest Eden, any more than you're in love with me . . . yet." His laugh was self-deprecating. "I should've seen. It's Skyelt you want . . . and you have it for now. Well, Ram's position as laird is not as secure as you believe, lady. And when Skyelt is mine, we'll see where your high-priced affections will lead you." He made a sharp move toward her and she jerked away, her face filled with horror. He stopped, his fists clenched as he studied her rejection. Coldness frosted his eyes and pulled his mouth into a sneer.

"Another time, Eden . . . my *love*." He turned on his heel and left.

Eden crumpled onto the chair, quaking. She pulled her robe closer around her; she felt a chill despite the warm fire a few feet away. Ian thought she wanted him and actually seemed to think she'd leave Ram for him. Was it her fault? She'd allowed him to kiss her, even though she was a married woman who knew the unwritten rules. Still worse, she now knew Ian's suit to gain Skyelt was motivated by her. He'd planned to marry, all right . . . her! It *was* her fault . . . and especially after tonight, she'd be to blame if Ramsay lost his beloved Skyelt.

Some while later, the door opened and Eden started in her chair by the fire. Ram's familiar outline relaxed the convulsing of her heart and she reached out for him. She pulled the back of his hand against her face and closed her eyes, concentrating her love, her need for him into those few inches of contact.

"You're still awake." He stood watching the top of her head, resisting the urge to stroke her sinuous flood of hair. In his mind's eye, Ian was again leaving the hallway that led to their room and descending the stairs. Ram had sat a short hand at cards, then located Carina, who was safely ensconced on a sofa amid a trio of fascinated young males, with James hovering irritably nearby. He'd found himself measuring time as though it were the grating drip of a roof leak and finally flung convention away and started for his room. And he had just missed passing Ian on the steps.

Now he watched Eden's intensity with a dull, painful question clawing at him. Once before he'd confronted her with Ian, and he'd felt like a fool afterward. But there was no mistaking the promise of contact blatant in Ian's looks and movements this evening. And he felt doubly foolish for having been dissuaded from the plain evidence of his senses from the start. Ian wanted his wife . . . as Ian had always wanted everything that was Ram's, including his birthright.

Ian's pursuit was so bold, Ram had to wonder things it gave him pain to wonder. Ian behaved like a man who expected to be received. Lord knew, Eden was a passionate woman—who'd borne him little love those first weeks at Skyelt. Ian was handsome, with a glib way around women and an eye for the elegant. . . .

Eden felt his shudder and she rose, searching his strange, silent manner. When he peeled her from him and began to remove his coat with fluid, mechanical motions, Eden felt a moment's panic: he knew.

She backed away, feeling the heat of the glowing grate reaching through her robe, scorching the backs of her legs. He didn't look at her. His hands smoothed, folded his woolen coat, and set it aside. His strong fingers released the buttons of his ruffled linen shirt one by one and the silence came alive around them.

"When is the bairn due?" He turned to her with an unreadable face and slid the shirt from his bare shoulders.

"Due?" Eden's throat was tight, her mouth was going dry. Why would he ask? "Mid-summer—or later, I think.

463

Why?" Before he answered, she knew why and had to steady herself on the chair.

"You never said. I wondered."

"Wondered what, Ram?" she suddenly urged. This waiting through pinpoint eternities was unbearable . . . she had to have it out in the open.

"If . . . I am the father." When it left his mouth, it sounded foreign in his ears. Yet it was the thought that had been riding his mind these last minutes. She crumpled as if struck and turned away, her arms wrapping the small rounding of her belly.

"If . . . you're the father," she murmured, a spark striking at the backs of her pain-darkened eyes. "How could you even say that to me?" After a moment she straightened and looked at him with pain fueling a new flame in her. "Who else would be the father of my child?"

"Ian, perhaps."

She paled. "Or perhaps the Archbishop of Canterbury . . . or Julius Caesar! They're just as likely candidates for cuckolding you!"

"He was here tonight," Ram charged, feeling his control of himself and the situation slipping. He wanted to throttle her and also to hold her and burn all thoughts of other men from her with fierce kisses and his body's raging heat.

"Yes! He was here." Anger powered her limbs as she moved closer to his dark heat. "And he left soon after he came. He didn't ask who the father was!"

Ram sucked in his breath and lunged at her, grabbing her with furious hands. "Is it Ian's child? Did you lie with my brother?"

"You . . . unforgivable . . . bastard!" She twisted briefly in his hands and a fit of blind rage brought her knee up savagely between his braced legs. He doubled over, groaning and clutching at himself. It stunned Eden for a minute . . . she'd actually hurt him. She watched

464

him stumble back toward the bed, some of her own hurt neutralized by his pain.

"Ramsay—you made me furious!" Her voice was thick and she had to blink to see him. "I've never lain with Ian, nor any man but you. The bairn was gotten in November, about the time I . . . asked you for it." His face came up, tightened against her protests, and fought to stay that way. "If you'll recall, I was occupied in your bed at the time . . . and every night since."

"Then why was Ian here tonight?" he demanded hoarsely. "And why was he sniffing you out all evening like a bull in rut?"

Eden was stung and furious again. *"Sniffing* me? Lord, how flattering—being compared to a cow in heat! Well, women are a bit more discriminating than cows, Ramsay. We're actually capable of faithfulness! I've been true to you, laird, and it has nothing to do with morality or fear or lack of opportunity."

"He came here because he wants you." Ram's voice lowered as he rose. Eden's heart was thrashing around in her chest as he loomed above her.

She couldn't deny that; she pulled herself up as tall as she could muster. Nothing she'd said was penetrating that stubborn wall she'd thought had come down between them.

"I've never bedded Ian Barclay," she rasped, her heart in agony over one fatal kiss . . . one she'd asked for with Ram MacLean in her mind and heart. All the passion and love she'd given meant nothing if they'd failed to win his trust. Eden knew there was still a part of Ram MacLean she'd never touched.

"Carina's right . . . all men *do* think alike." She was writhing inside. "Ian assumed exactly what you have . . . that I'd have no pride nor integrity in my marriage. It was wishful thinking on his part, Ramsay. What's your reason?" She could see the turmoil, the struggle in his face.

"I've spent my days and nights with you, giving you everything I have to give. And I'm here, bearing your child, because I love you, Ramsay MacLean. I'd never bed with Ian Barclay, because . . . he's not you. I pledged you my faith . . . it's all I have. God, Ramsay, please let it be enough!" It came out in a rush that ended in a snubbing spasm and the damned-up tears began to pour down her cheeks.

When he reached for her, she shrank away, turning her face from his blurry image and muttering for him to leave her alone. His force pulled her against him and banded her struggling body with steely arms. Her shell of resistance was crumbling, weakened by her tears and her aching need for his trust.

He forced her face up and drank in the tears that rolled from eyes that refused to open to him. He had to have her; he couldn't live without her. His lips caressed hers, blending the salt of her tears with the liquid sweetness of her mouth. Need erupted in him, need for the strength, the honesty of her. His loins caught fire and ignited his heart. He pulled her harder against him, trying to assuage his physical pain, trying to take her inside him to extinguish that raging inferno.

"Eden . . . I love you. . . ."

Not "I trust you," or "I want you" or even "I need you," Eden realized through her own steam. It was *I love you* that ground from the center of him. It contained the essence of longing and determination.

"Oh, Ram. . . ." she rasped, working her trapped hands up his front and cupping the nape of his neck. "Please believe me," she managed against the fluid sensations his mouth was driving through her. "Believe I love you enough . . . to be trusted with your love." His determined response was the erotic rippling of his shoulder muscles under her searching fingers. And he was picking her up, carrying her to the bed, and then stripping off his plaid.

The darkness of the bed drapes shaded his face and hid his mood as he came to her. Her senses quivered with desire for him and with a new, intruding fear. She needed his trust, his faith as well as his love. And she knew her stubborn, complicated Ramsay well enough to realize that his acceptance of anything had many levels. Deep beneath the intensity of his mouth, gliding over her hot skin, was a chilled breath of something not yet thawed. She pushed at his chest until he stopped devouring her bare shoulder and paused above her.

"I want to know," she whispered against the choking in her throat, "what you're thinking." A muscle in his bare side tightened and a little voice in her murmured sagely. Mercifully, her reason was fighting the slide into oblivion the touch of his mouth always produced in her.

"I'm thinking," his voice was raw and hungry, "how I love your breasts, especially now, and how your nipples seem larger, darker—" His tongue followed the flow of his words. "And this hollow between your breasts is a cradle I want to climb into . . ." he nuzzled it hotly, "and pull your satiny skin over an' around me. God, you're so soft and rounded and silky all over." His hands caressed her intimately. "My parts are burnin' for you, Eden, and the only way to put out the fire is to plunge into your soft, wet body . . . I can feel you're ready—"

"No," she swallowed desperately, trying to salvage some last shard of reason, "please . . . not that. Deeper . . . more. . . ." Her tongue flicked out to wet her dry lips and he pounced on it, pulling it into his mouth with the same relentless slowness that was moving him over her body, wedging his heavy frame against her soft woman's mound.

". . . deeper," he echoed and parted her flesh with his in absolute obedience. He embedded himself in her, stopped by her moan and his own driving need for

467

release. He gripped her shoulders and buried his face in her breasts. He was floundering, losing something he mustn't give up . . . succumbing to the seductive waves of her body moving against him, enclosing him, drawing him from himself. It was slipping from him, his anger, his unconquered fear. She was beguiling it from him with the sweet, eager yielding of her love.

"I love you, Ram."

He surrendered to it without conscious thought. She'd fought and yielded; she'd resisted, then loved. She'd decided in her own, immutable Marlow way to have him as mate, as man, as friend. She'd pursued his demons, stalked and hunted down his heart with tender cunning. And in her moment of triumph she'd laid her own love at his feet. Where was there room for doubt, when she filled every crook and crevice of his being?

Eden felt him grow taut and still against her and opened her dark-adapted eyes on Ram's face. She searched his heartstopping expression, fearing to breathe.

"God knows I love you, wench."

"But do you *want* to love me, Ram?" Her body quivered with expectation, roused with painful hope. She watched the dim reddish glow of the firelight turn the rings of his eyes violet, unaware she was watching the remaking of a man as well.

"I want it," Ram rasped. "Oh Eden, I want it!" Everything in his nature was swept up in the cyclone inside him. He shuddered, feeling old patterns, old values, old needs blown away without a trace, leaving only the bare earth of his soul, fertile and hungry. And with every kiss, every caress, his new being was resown, renurtured. All that mattered was her and him, being here, loving.

Eden felt his desperate joy all around her and absorbed it like thirsty ground. She whispered her love into his ears in a warm litany that unknowingly celebrated his recreation. Then their bodies moved in the age-old rite of

468

continuance and renewal and their hands moved in tender exploration, relearning each other. The release of their bodies was consumed gloriously in the total joining of their beings. Never had there been such fulfillment in their physical loving. Never had Eden guessed the rich wonder of self, given selflessly and returning, enlarged by another's presence.

And when they nestled side by side, exhausted and exchanging sleepy, helpless smiles, they were not separated, though their bodies hardly touched.

The next morning, when Eden and Ram surrendered to a last tenacious shred of social conscience and descended from their borrowed chamber, it was already noon. Ian Barclay had given his regrets to his host first thing that morning and withdrawn to leave for home. Neither Ram nor Eden had thought of him until later in the day, when Lady Leonora mentioned his hasty departure. They were content to drift through leisurely pursuits, touching hands constantly and exchanging glazed and potent looks that titillated and scandalized Tayside society.

Haskell watched, torn between admiring his son's manly indulgence and worrying that so much of it should be invested in one woman, especially a wife. He shrugged his shoulders and determined to let his randy offspring get it out of his system. The boy had a lot to make up for, the Good Laird knew. And she didn't seem any worse for wear.

He turned his sights to his bastard daughter. To his befuddlement, he found himself both gratified and piqued by the steady stream of young bucks around her. Carina was his daughter, all right, and they all sensed it, the lecherous lot. But her virtue was an advertised fact — no easy handful there, he smirked righteously. Just as quickly, his grin faded; there was nothing more fascinating or more infuriating than a virtuous handful. He shuddered to think he'd had a hand in producing such a treacherous combination and rolled off toward the Henderson stables. Compared to women, horses were easy to understand and a lot more satisfyin'.

That afternoon, James drew a deep breath while holding his vest in place, then strode toward Carina with fresh resolve. Her soft, high-waisted satin shimmered in the gallery sunlight and her hair had become a burnished halo about her delicate face. By the time he reached her, he'd almost forgotten what he'd meant to say.

"I . . . you . . . would you join me for a ride, Carina?" he remembered after throttling himself mentally. "Henderson has a fine stable, I understand."

"James." His name on her lips made him shiver. "Yes, I'd be delighted . . . but I'll have to change." Her lashes fluttered as she indicated her seductively simple gown. His tongue cleaved to the roof of his mouth and he could only nod, enraptured by her sedate movement away from him. She turned and found his eyes aflame. "I'll see you by th' stables, then."

It took James a full ten minutes in the cool, sunny air to force his body into submission. And he was another ten trying to think of "safe" activities that might keep her at his side, but not within his reach. When she appeared, he was again the gentleman and behaved with admirable restraint.

They chatted pleasantly and James found himself staring at her small, gloved hands on the reins and roving over her tiny waist and ripe little breasts, all properly velvet-clad. He wasn't attending his mount properly, and it nudged sideways into hers. Sharp hoof met tender cannon and Carina's horse bucked. She was paying no better attention to her animal and was tossed askew in the saddle. Without firm control from the reins, the horse took its head and began a nervous run. She was jolted back and just grabbed the saddle in time to keep from being dumped.

James was after her in a flash, calling her name and cursing his own clumsiness. He swung low in his saddle and reached for the drooping reins, straining heroically as he pulled the mare to a halt. The animal laid its ears back and danced nervously. Carina unhooked her leg and slid down its trembling side to be away from it. But as she hit the ground, her ankle turned under her and she fell. In an instant, James was lifting her, carrying her away from the obstinate beast.

"Ow, oh—that was stupid of me!" She was biting her lower lip and clinging to James to blot out the pain in her foot.

"Rina, love, are you all right?" He set her down on a nearby boulder, but gathered her tight against his chest when her arms refused to leave his neck. He held her for a minute, feeling her softness, trying to make his mind function properly. When he looked down, her face tilted up to him, her lashes moist, her breath fragrant between her bite-reddened lips. He sucked a suffering breath and loosened his hold on her.

"Is it your foot?" His voice was betrayingly hoarse.

Her eyes dimmed with disappointment as much as discomfort and she nodded.

"Does it pain you a lot?"

"Some . . . oh James, you were wonderful." She spoke tightly to mask the pain in her ankle. "It all just got out of hand so fast—"

"I'm to blame, Rina, letting my mount drift into you like that. I don't know where my head was." He straightened and tried to summon a scrap of restraint once more, but shortly found himself saying, "Perhaps I'd best have a look at it."

She nodded and shortly he was on the ground before her, raising the hem of her skirt and drawing her slender foot into his hands. She blanched as he pulled the boot from her, and he apologized again. The intimate way he called her "Rina" made her heart beat a jerky refrain. She wouldn't have admitted it, but after the initial screech and throb of pain, it wasn't nearly so bad now. The feel of his long, supple fingers on her ankle, probing, testing, was more than a match for her discomfort.

"Oh," she groaned, closing her eyes.

"I'm so sorry, Rina," he communicated. "Does this hurt?" He flexed her ankle; and when she nodded and replied, "A little," it should have been his cue to release her foot. But her sky-blue eyes opened and her face was now flushed. His hands wouldn't leave her stockinged foot. He was suddenly trapped in the mesmerizing flecks of gold that caught in her hair. His gentle hands massaged and moved up her leg, exploring its contours, awakening a sensual promise Carina had never associated with that part of her. Her breath came faster as his hands quested higher, to her knees.

"James! Carina!" Eden's voice made him peel his hands from under Rina's skirt. As he reddened, he spotted Ram and his sister fast riding toward them. He managed a quick look at Carina's face and found no reproach there, and perhaps even a pang of disappointment. He wouldn't have had time to make his feet before they were upon him, so he remained where he was, with her stockinged toes cozily ensconced in his lap.

"Th' mare shied and bolted and when James stopped her, I made a bad dismount an' hurt me foot. It's what I get for not actin' more ladylike," Carina explained, very conscious of James's position at her feet.

"I . . . don't think it's broken." James surrendered her limb to Ram's brotherly inspection and tried not to meet Eden's questioning eye as he rose. When Ram agreed, James moved to lift and set her back on her mount and was glared aside by her brother. He stiffened and went to collect his horse under Eden's perceptive gaze.

The ladies rode and the gentlemen walked, leading their horses. Ram carried Carina from the stables into a veritable storm of concern. She was bandaged and cosseted and attended graciously. James was again crowded from her side and his one consolation was that she'd not be dancing or riding with anyone else for the rest of their stay.

Eden regarded her brother as he watched Carina and fell into a morose mood. She looked up at her doting husband.

"Well, she was right, you know . . . she did have him at her feet."

Ram laughed.

## Chapter Twenty-six

"Don' bother me wi' rats in the grain, man!" Haskell waved Terrance away from him and bellowed, "Get some damned cats and leave me be!" The steward still hurried toward him across the courtyard, and Haskell made a disgusted face and turned partway on his seat on the stone wall.

"It's not . . ." Terrance puffed, leaning on his ledger, "th' rats . . . it's poachers, m'laird."

"In the grain?" Haskell was distracted momentarily by the sight of blonde Annie heading toward the well with an empty bucket at her side, swaying an ancient invitation.

"Nay . . . in th' wood." Terrance took time to swallow. "You ken, we set out Tass and Robert MacGill to watch fer 'em. Well . . . early this morn they nabbed two MacLinty boys . . . an' them with the birds right on 'em. Ye mon come, m'laird."

"MacLintys? Let Ram see to it; I'm in no mood." Haskell was stroking his beard and getting a gleam in his eye.

"Laird Ram ain't here. He and m'lady, they rode out this morn wi' a basket an' bottle and didna say when they'd be back." Terrance braced himself, but when the oath came, he was still unstrung by its raw disgust.

"Again? God preserve us! Don' that boy do anything except that around here anymore?! Alwus mewlin' and cooin' . . . and ruttin' about like a bloody stag." The gleam in his eye died, and when Annie looked his way with a hopeful expression, he scowled at her darkly. She tucked her chin to her chest and headed quickly fro the kitchen. "It ain't natural, Terrance, to be randied up so by yer own wife . . . it ain't fittin'. A man's got other duties to see to—responsibilities. We got Edinburgh to think of . . . an he just buries 'is head in his wife's tits an' won' listen to a word of it. It bodes ill, Terrance. They got a sharpie for a barrister an th' magistrate in Angus's pocket. An' we only got a fortnight afore we come to hearin'."

"It'll be all right, m'laird." It came out rather lame, for Terrance was as worried as his master. "Laird Ram'll come through. He alwus does."

"But come through now, Terrance? I canna think what would happen to us all if Ian got his hands on Skyelt." He sighed heavily and stood, adjusting his wide leather belt about his waist firmly. "Now, where be these damned poachers?"


Edinburgh was enshrouded in a low cloud of mist . . . when Eden first glimpsed it from the small carriage. Ram had often spoken of "Auld Reekie," as the town was frequently called because of the infernal pall cast by ten thousand chimneys crowded into so small a space. But the sight of densely packed tenements rising several stories above the narrow streets, their tops lost in the gray, sunless haze, was astounding. Even more surprising was the way silk-slippered luxury and shoeless misery trod in and out the same gates and came to rest in lodgings side by side. Cowgate, once a section at the edge of the Old

Town where many wealthy families had concentrated, was seeing an influx of those with lesser fortunes and greater misfortunes. And the New Town, once shunned as a patch of drained swampland, now flourished as the seat of the new and thriving community of Edinburgh.

They wound through the noisy, bustling city, stopped and rerouted several times. When they finally reached their rented apartments in fashionable guest lodgings in the New Town, Ram lifted Eden and Carina down from the carriage with a terse apology for the delays.

"The city's changed since I was here last." He cast a troubled eye around him at the crowded street and the gray and damp and ushered them inside the busy, street-level common room of their lodgings. Eden recognized disappointment beneath his irritation.

"Cities do have a way of changing, Ram." She put a tired hand on his arm and smiled into his tight expression. "Boston had changed quite a lot for me in nearly six years."

"At least Boston was clean," he uttered quietly, closing the subject.

He and Haskell conferred with the landlord, then he carried Eden up three long flights of stairs to their comfortable apartments, which covered an entire floor of the building. He gave her stern orders not to attempt mounting the stairs by herself, owing to her condition. She sighed and looked at Carina and nodded. Sometimes Ram could act like such a "laird."

The next three days Ram and Haskell and Terrance spent in conference with their lawyers, returning each night to escort Eden and Carina and James to visit families Ram had come to know in his university days. Ram was greeted affectionately by these folk and they embraced Eden fully as Ramsay's wife. She began to see how precious his memories of Edinburgh were. It was among these generous, decent, and enlightened people that Ram had resolved many of the conflicts of his youth. Silently she said a prayer of thanks for their help in making him the man she'd come to love so well.

But at night, when they returned and Eden was trundled off to bed, she heard Ram's and Haskell's voices, low and angry as they wrangled over the details of the MacPherson will and the arguments to be made on either side. And on the last night before the hearings began, she waited up to talk with him about it.

"Is it so bad?" She sat up in the bed shadows.

"Is what so bad?" He turned to the bed, shirt in hand, surprised to find her awake.

"The suit. I heard you and Haskell arguing . . . he's very worried."

"A new wrinkle, isn't it?" He laughed with a harsh edge. "Haskell actually worried. Angus'd give the plaid off his arse to see it."

"And you?" Eden reached for his hand and drew him down onto the soft mattress beside her. "You don't want to show it, but you're worried, too.

"Angus has high cards this hand." He rubbed his thumb over her cheek and it began to glow. "But I'll work it out—I always do. If there was some way to do this wi'out having Haskell in the court, where Bruce can see 'im. . . ."

". . . and remember his sister's disgrace with a married man," Eden finished, snuggling against his chest. "It's not fair, Haskell's sins coming back to haunt you. With a little effort I could really hate your father."

"His 'sins' have haunted me from the day I was born, Eden. It's nothin' new. And much as I dislike him, he's a powerful hard man to actually *hate*. I don't think even Angus actually hates him." He leaned back against the bolsters and rested his chin on top of Eden's head. "Of late, Haskell has my pity more'n anything else." She raised a bewildered frown to him and he kissed her forehead. "He's never known the likes of what I have wi' you, Eden. I don' think he even guesses it exists. And even out of his selfishness and lechery came somethin' good." He patted her rounded belly and grinned a fierce little grin. "Somethin' very, very good, love."

His lips crushed hers and she lovingly yielded him the passion, the release he needed. His kisses and caresses had an intensity to them that clutched at her heart. It was as though he buried himself in her to forget the horrible quandary in which they were caught.

The first day at court, Ram, Haskell, and Terrance left their rooms early and joined their lawyers for a while before the hearing. Eden, Carina, and James settled into the gallery later amid a collection of Edinburgh note-worthies, many of whom had entertained Ram and Eden in their homes over the last week. And Eden realized that Ram's earlier social rounds had been judiciously charted to result in this very demonstration. It was a strategy that was suddenly very reassuring.

Arrayed in the gallery on one side of the court were the MacLeans and their host of Edinburgh supporters. On the other side sat some Tayside lairds Eden recognized from the Hendersons' gathering and several young men and women of impeccable fashion and unexceptional looks around a genteel, graying woman. The Barclays, she was informed by Arlo in a whisper, including the once-disputed Helen herself. They were two opposing camps, each with influence at its back.

Below them on the courtroom floor, Ram and Haskell occupied one long table, surrounded by a covey of bewigged, black-robed barristers. Directly across from them were Angus and Ian Barclay, similarly attended. Eden couldn't help but notice the glint in the Head

Magistrate's eyes whenever he gazed in Haskell's direction and the way Haskell burrowed deeper into his chair like a sulky, resentful boy.

Through the morning, Ian Barclay's eyes often strayed in Eden's direction, and each time they seemed to hold a private amusement. Eden straightened and saw only Ram, sending him smiles of encouragement whenever she caught his gaze. The legalisms droned on and on, and it seemed the same things were often quoted by both sides, only given different interpretations.

There was a tense moment indeed when interruption followed heated interruption and both ranks of lawyers emptied their benches in a chaotic shouting match. Never good at restraining an impulse, Haskell joined the mêlée, threatening to lambast both Angus and his chief counsel. Ram had to restrain him physically and with James's help held him while old Lawrence Bruce skinned him verbally and banned him from the courtroom.

By supper that evening, Haskell was properly soused and raving furiously. He stormed out of the rooms and Ram looked across the table at Eden.

"He may do damage, but now at least it won't be in court." He smiled.

Eden frowned, puzzled by her husband's lightened mood. "I don't see how you can joke about it. He was a disgrace today."

"There are some things you *can* count on Haskell for." he smiled.

"You . . . expected this to happen?" She was truly scandalized.

Ram shrewdly sipped his wine. "Now old Bruce will only see me . . . and my lovely wife, five months gone with child. Honest, upstanding me, saddled with a crazy father and still managing to bring my home back from the brink of ruin. Could improve our chances measurably." Ram's chuckle became tension-clearing laughter.

Arlo began to laugh, then Carina, and slowly Eden was drawn into it. It was a gambler's strategy, and all present realized it. But with Haskell removed from the picture, the odds did indeed improve.

It was a brief respite from worry, however; for the next day, the arguments again flew furiously and seemed as pointless. Birth records and baptisms and records of death and inheritance were duly presented, with both sides tracing present blood back to the MacPherson whose ambiguous will was at issue. The courtroom become hot and charged, and more than once shouting matches broke out. Head Magistrate Bruce noted that Ramsay MacLean did not take part, but it didn't seem to improve his judicial disposition. When they left the court at the end of the day, a desperate, sinking feeling overcame Eden as she watched the tense lines at the corners of Ram's mouth.

After supper Ram and James left for a meeting with the lawyers and she felt his worry in his perfunctory kiss. As she undressed and prepared for bed, she kept glimpsing Ram at his beloved Skyelt, walking the land, watching his flocks come to fold, hearing his people's complaints. The softness in his voice when he spoke of his home haunted her, and for the first time she let herself wonder what would happen if he lost. She kept remembering Ram's assertion that it was more than just the facts of the case that often decided the outcome, and her heartbeat dulled.

Carina was asleep in a room far down the hall, Arlo waited for Ram and James downstairs, and Haskell was sleeping off a monumental soak. Eden doused all but a single candle and sat brushing her hair, trying to make things normal by behaving routinely.

The door opened softly behind her and at first she

didn't hear it. A footstep on the wooden floor brought her around like a shot. But her shock only deepened as Ian Barclay slipped forward out of the shadows.

"You!" Eden managed only a ragged whisper as she gripped the back of her chair.

"Good evening, sweet Eden."

"How did you get in here?" Eden rose, checking her robe hastily. Her face reddened. "Leave at once!"

"You didn't leave the hallway window open just for me?" Ian asked and stepped closer, his eyes flitting appreciatively over her robe and loosened hair. "You know, every time we speak privately, I feel shamefully over-dressed."

"Out, Ian, and close the door behind you."

"I've gone to some lengths to talk with you, Eden, an' you show me so little courtesy," he chided. His voice lowered. "Have you any idea how difficult it is for me, watchin' you in court every day playin' the dutiful wife?"

"No more difficult than it is to be there enduring that farce. And I don't have to play at being a wife, I *am* Ram's wife."

"Does he lose himself in your hair, Eden? Lord, it's magnificent."

"This is intolerable." She darted around him toward the door, but he lunged and snatched her back, pulling her struggling form into his arms.

"Eden, my love, you weren't always so adamant in my arms." His strength rivaled Ram's, and he held her easily. "More than once you melted against me an' returned my kisses."

"Ian, I'm pregnant—with Ram's child." She pushed until he relented and allowed her an inch. "Let me go!"

He laughed and bent to kiss her. She avoided his mouth and maintained her stubborn pressure against him.

"I was wrong to ever let you kiss me, Ian, and I'll not

481

let you disgrace us both by repeating it!" Something in her words seeped through to him and his hold on her slackened. She waited, tensed, and after a long moment looked up at him. His handsome features were strong and his eyes burned with resentment. "Let me go." Slowly he released her, and she leaned against the bedpost for support.

"Why, Ian? Why are you doing this? You're a man of the world . . . you know when a woman wants you and when she doesn't." Ian turned on her, his eyes blazing.

"What matters, dear Eden, is what I want. And I want you."

"Why?" She shook her head, unable to fathom his motives.

"Does your vanity demand to be courted, m'lady? Shall I praise your beauty, your graces?" There was a faint tinge of the sardonic in his tone.

"Just the *truth*, Ian," she bit out. "Why do you want me so badly that even my own wishes are of no significance to you?"

"You're Ram's."

It was a flat declaration that hit her with the impact of a claymore. She swayed under waves of recognition. It was suddenly so clear; why hadn't she seen it before? Their paternity, their striking physical similarities, their ambition — all thrust them inescapably into rivalry. As they came of age, the stakes had grown until that rivalry extended to the deepest, most personal spheres of life. It was a rivalry in which firstborn Ian had always come out second.

"Ram has the devil's own luck. I laughed when I heard he was forced to get a bairn, knowin' his aversion to temptations of the flesh. I thought at last I'd have my way. Then he actually married, and a tempting peach of a lass — the kind a man dreams of. Even then, it was clear

482

to all he didna know what to do wi' a wife, and I thought I still had a chance. It was natural for me to try to remedy his failings . . . and claim Skyelt in the boodle."

"Ian, no—"

"I'm only a day or two away from being master of Skyelt. And my dear brother will be turned out on his righteous ear." The fiery light of certainty in his eyes made Eden think he knew something . . . more than what had been introduced in court . . . something that made the settlement of the suit in his favor a foregone conclusion. It was suddenly hard to breathe.

"Drop the suit, Ian, please." She moved toward him, her face draining, her eyes bright with new fear. "For God's sake, must this senseless rivalry go on and on?" When his hands closed on her shoulders, she stiffened, but would not quail.

He stared into her luminous eyes and felt his blood rising. Her fresh scent invaded his lungs and he rashly craved her. His fingers clutched the curve of her jaw and his attention fastened on the lush rose of her lips.

"I want you, Eden Marlow."

"You don't want me; you want Ram's wife, Ram's inheritance." Tears were streaming down her face. "To you Skyelt is property, a prize, a bit of revenge for the accident of your birth. But Ram loves Skyelt; it's his home, his people—it's part of him!" Her words drove into the center of him and his fingers tightened furiously on her.

"My noble, honorable brother." Anger smoldered silver in his narrow gaze and his mouth became drawn and cruel. "I'll not give Ram his beloved Skyelt, but your precious love can *buy* it for him. Leave Ram and come with me . . . and I'll drop the suit."

Her jaw loosened and she stared at him, stunned by his demand.

"Ram may have his precious Skyelt, or he may have you. He cannot have both."

"No! No. . . !" She shook her head and jerked from his grasp. "You're mad, Ian." She scrambled back until the bedpost stopped her.

"On the contrary, Eden . . . I'm only now coming to my senses." The horror in her face spurred him on. "Ram may have Skyelt only if you purchase it for him. You must come to me willingly and share my name and my bed. And as I was Haskell's, but born a Barclay, so your child will be Ram's, but born of my name."

"Never!" Loathing crystalized her shock. Her arms flew across her belly protectively.

"Never?" he returned caustically. "The die is cast, my sweet. Ram will have Skyelt only if I have you . . . and his bairn. Don't be so rash as to reject my generosity out of hand. You won't find my brother half so noble, or so loving, when he has nothing to his very *legitimate* name." Certain that his ultimatum had struck fertile ground, he smiled coldly and turned to go. At the door, he stopped and cast her a scathing look of triumph.

"What do you think? Does my noble brother love you as much as he loves his precious Skyelt?"

Eden lay in the darkness, sleepless and numbed by shock. She'd never imagined it might come to this. One short kiss and a lifetime of anguish to pay for it! If Ram lost Skyelt, it would be all her fault. How could she ever live with him, knowing that?

Ian's cruel words burned in her mind and left her heart a charred cinder. *"Does my noble brother love you as much as he loves his precious Skyelt?"* Ram had needed Skyelt so badly he had forced her to marry him to save it. She knew he loved her now, as much as any man might love a woman. But how did that love compare with his need for a home, for a heritage, for pride and accomplishment?

When Ram returned, quite late, he carried a single candle into their chamber and walked on his toes. When she called his name, he started and turned, searching the shadows for her. His face was lined, his shoulders were rounded with fatigue. He fumbled with his clothes and in the end, slid into her arms wearing the kilt and stockings. There was a strong taste of brandy upon his mouth.

"You've been drinking." She stroked his hair and held him tight against her chest.

"Not much . . . and you've not been asleep," he returned soberly. Then he buried his face in her neck and kissed her fiercely. The pressure of his hands surprised her as he began to stroke her intimately, insistently. Somehow she understood his urgency and met his need for comfort with one of her own. She welcomed his strength, his heat, and soon she shed her nightgown to yield him her softness, her love. Their bodies touched and joined, riding waves that formed a driving new rhythm.

Eden listened to the roar receding in her head and turned an expectant face to Ram's relaxed profile. "Is it so bad?" When his loving blue eyes opened on her in puzzlement, she clarified, "The lawyers' news." He sighed and turned his head to stare up at the canopy.

"Not good. It's hard to read, but I've had the feelin' we've been losing ground. And late today, after you left, Angus's counsel delivered a petition to Bruce. He looked it over and adjourned straightaway. Some of our counselors think it might be an old document just come to light, but I canna imagine they'd have held it this long into the arguments if it were. It could be a compromise, a splitting of the north and western land. Whatever it was, Angus was uncommonly pleased with it."

"Ram, what if—"

He shifted quickly onto his shoulder and stopped her words with his hand. "I will not think of it, Eden. Skyelt is mine—ours. And it always will be." Eden felt the middle of her going hollow. Moisture filled Ram's eyes, and in those azure depths Eden glimpsed his uncertainty and pain. She gathered his head against her breast and shed tears for him. After a long silence she drew back to look at him. He was dry-eyed and distant.

"There could be other places, Ram—"

"Skyelt," he spoke the word lovingly, "is my life, Eden. It's my birth, my family, my heritage. There is no other place for me."

She noticed her tears flowed once more. Ram held her as she cried, and in his soothing embrace she drifted into a troubled sleep.

The next morning, Eden sat in a straight-backed chair near the bed, watching Ram taking his much-needed rest. Skyelt was his life, he'd said. It was true. Now Ian's certainty made sense and brought the dreaded ultimatum back to her; Ram could have Skyelt of her and her babe—not both. It had to be one or the other.

The fluttering in her womb surprised her and her hands moved protectively over the rounded contours of her belly. This was Ram's child, and it was Ram's beautiful loving that had sown it in her. Suddenly she wanted to scratch Ian Barclay's eyes out. She should have taken a dagger to his black heart the minute he set foot inside her room! How dare he proclaim himself master of her fate . . . of Ram's fate! Where was her mind, her pride, her courage? She'd refused to allow Haskell to dictate to her; why was she allowing Ian Barclay to deliver his nasty ultimatums?

*Think, Eden!* She rose and began to pace. It wasn't that Ian wanted Skyelt so much; it was more that he didn't want Ram to have it. It wasn't that he loved Eden; he just couldn't bear to see Ram happy in his marriage. Skyelt or Eden, not both.

She stopped by the bed and stared down at Ram's handsome profile and sleep-softened face. Tears welled in her eyes and she wiped them away angrily. Skyelt was his life, but so was this babe. She could never ask him to choose between Skyelt and his wife and child. But she could do it for him. He could have Skyelt . . . if he didn't have her.

She paced back and forth, subduing her tender feelings. It was the most painful thing she'd ever done, but she steeled herself and drew on her deepest reserves of strength. If she left him, went away, Ram would have only Skyelt and not her. Ian's ruthless condition would be met. Perhaps it would be enough. And then perhaps someday after it was all settled, she could write him and explain. And perhaps he'd forgive her.

Ram awakened to find her calm but exhausted. He held her on his lap and put his hand on her belly to try to feel the babe move. There was a sad, lingering quality to her kiss and a tiredness about her eyes that alarmed him. When she suggested that she not attend the court session today, he kissed her and tucked her back into bed with a husbandly tenderness.

When she called him back to the bed for one last, lingering kiss, he thought he understood her mood. And he straightened with a confident smile, determined to put her mind at ease.

"You mustn't worry, Eden . . . everything will work out."

"I know. I love you, Ram."

And Eden watched her husband leave her bed for the last time.

The hired carriage arrived at the stroke of noon and the landlord obligingly trundled her trunk and cases down the stairs to stow them. Eden was dressed in her fine high-waisted tartan and wore a jaunty, plumed tam over her loose curls. She settled a warm coat about her shoulders and gave the landlord two letters to see delivered, one to Ian Barclay at the High Court and the other to Ram when he returned that evening. Soon she was installed in the carriage and it lurched into motion, heading south.

Unable to resist a last look back, she wondered if she'd turned to stone in the last day; everything inside her was numb. She forced her thoughts ahead of her to Newcastle and the difficult process of finding passage on a ship bound for Boston. There would be no time for sentimental mewling about; it was just as well she'd left her heart behind her.

The carriage disappeared from sight a few minutes before Arlo MacCrenna appeared in the common room of their lodgings and asked for the key to his laird's private rooms. The doors were locked and he was puzzled and a bit concerned that m'lady hadn't answered his knocks. The landlord responded that her ladyship couldn't have answered; she wasn't on the premises. She'd just left in a carriage, not more than five—ten minutes before, baggage and all.

Arlo startled. Baggage? In a moment, he was off and running down the street toward the livery. It took forever to get a mount and set off after her. The landlord indicated she'd traveled south. He had a terrible, sinking feeling in the pit of his stomach about this. M'lady had a temper, he knew, but nothing in his laird's mien indicated they'd had a falling-out. He wove his way through crowds of bustling vendors and the dense foot traffic of the Royal Mile, beginning near Edinburgh Castle and continuing down High Street and the Canongate. He went down the Southbridge then around through Cowgate, using up precious time. He considered going back to court for his laird, but quickly decided Ram had enough to contend with—and struck out for the London Road, pushing his mount hard.

In the evening, at a small stonework inn on the Tweed River, he finally located the carriage and muscled his way past a belligerent innkeeper to confront Eden in her rented room. After a day's grinding travel, her endurance and spirits were at low ebb and her dismay at being found so quickly was buried beneath the comforting sight of Arlo's stern, blocky countenance. She threw herself into his arms and hugged him with embarrassing vigor. The innkeeper scowled, but retreated downstairs, leaving them alone.

"If you'll be packin' your things, m'lady, I'll be takin' ye back at first light. Laird Ram'll be beside himself with fright for ye. And God knows, he has enough worries without this madness!" He glowered and set her down on the side of the bed.

"I'm not going back, Arlo. You know I love Ram and I'd do naught to hurt him . . ." she could barely finish for the choking in her throat, "but I'll hurt him less by leaving now, before he loses Skyelt." The story of Ian's night visit came tumbling out and Arlo tried to subdue his shock for her sake. When her tears rolled with quiet misery down her cheeks, he produced a handkerchief and patted her hands awkwardly. He began to see her predicament, to understand the reasoning behind her difficult decision. But he couldn't bring himself to approve her rash scheme, no matter how she justified it. Then she truly shocked him.

"I'm bound for Boston, Arlo." The determination in her quiet voice was like silk-clad steel.

"You'll do no such thing, m'lady!"

"Yes I shall. I'm going home . . . if they'll have me. If not, I'll settle on my dower lands. You canna stop me, Arlo MacCrenna. At best, you can come with me and help me." She stared at him meaningfully from under a rim of wet lashes and made the most of a trembling chin. "It will be difficult . . . this far gone with child, and traveling alone."

"God's teeth!" Arlo swore, "Ye shouldna be travelin' at all in your condition. God A'mighty knows what would'ave become of ye if I hadn'ta come after ye." He was sorely tempted to drag her back to Ram by the hair on her head, inheritance or none. But the painful, determined light in her eyes appealed to the sentimental side of him. "I brung ye to Scotland safe, m'lady, I'll take ye home. But I'll not like a minute of it."

In truth, Arlo meant to enhance the difficulties of the journey to imply that leaving Scotland, or England, would prove impossible. And in the process, he would wear her down with well-timed entreaties to return home. But everything went startlingly according to her will; for every small obstacle, she had an inventive solution. They had no funds; she produced a small casket of gold coins. She had no lady's maid; Arlo could serve with buttons and baggage and she'd abandon her lady dresses for the simpler Scot's dress of blouse and skirt. Her advancing state of pregnancy would slow them; she proved in astonishingly fine health and possessed of remarkable stamina. They'd never find a captain willing to take on a female so far advanced with child—and willing to run the British blockade to Boston to boot; now, that one would take a bit of work.

To save funds, Eden insisted they take rooms at a small inn called the Gull's Wing, near the waterfront at Newcastle. It was noisy and frequented by seamen and tarts, but the rooms were surprisingly clean and the food was good. Arlo fretted about the rough trade in the tavern downstairs and about leaving her periodically to scour the docks in search of a captain with a touch of larceny or colonial fervor in his soul. He didn't intend to find one. Eden smiled and patted the familiar dirk at her waist and sent him off again and again, knowing fully his intention.

The innkeeper was a curiously decent man with many dubious talents and connections. Eden quietly approached him with their problem, and the sturdy, scar-faced fellow scratched his head and agreed to make inquiries. And after nearly a week in his establishment, Eden found him at her door one morning with a bit of news. A certain Captain Buckley, of his old acquaintance, might be the one she sought, and at her request he arranged for the captain to meet her in the tap room that afternoon while Arlo was gone.

Eden was seated in the most secluded corner of the Gull's Wing nursing a mug of barley water when she saw the conversing with a tall, black-coated man wearing an outmoded tricorn and immaculately polished boots. When Captain Blade Buckley bore down on her, she felt her throat close up and lent Arlo's doubts about her sanity some credence. The dark man was the very picture of a seafaring rake or pirate, from the roguish scar slashing his left cheek, to his lean, hawkish features, to the hard light in his bold gray eyes. When he removed his hat, his black hair was overly long, but his movements were brisk and fluid. He stopped before the table and nodded as his bold gaze inspected this "lady" in need of transport. She was an eyeful; he was telling himself she could only mean trouble. He smiled a wry, roguish smile. A little trouble was the stuff life was made of.

"Captain Blade Buckley, at your service, ma'am." He nodded and didn't wait for her invitation to seat himself opposite her. She watched him make the first move and screwed up her courage.

"*Blade* Buckley?" she found herself as saying. "What Christian mother would name her son after an instrument of war?" Buckley stared at her, then honored her bold stroke with a narrowed eye.

"My mother was a Moor."

"Oh." Eden wilted inside. Arlo was right about her; she was daft. She swallowed her good sense and pushed on. "I need transport to New York or Boston, Captain Buckley. I can pay well, but I must be assured safe passage and . . . some protection. And my man and I must arrive no later than mid-June."

The captain stroked his chin and a light appeared in his eye as he tallied the lady's charms and spirit. He was well nigh forty, old enough to have refined his tastes in women and to appreciate a bit of challenge. His thoughts were not particularly difficult to read and Eden began to regret this interview.

"It could be arranged." Then the captain caught the glint of gold on her finger and inspected her wedding ring with a wary eye; there was more to be known here, and he didn't like the looks of it.

"I'm a fine sailor, Captain, and my man Arlo is equally capable. We'd be no bother to you. But we must have assurance we will arrive by mid-June."

"M'lady!" Arlo came rushing across the tavern toward them, his face aflame, his nostrils flaring. "This be most improper, you consortin' with the likes—"

Buckley rose and towered darkly above Arlo, trapping the last words in his throat.

"Is *this* your *man?*" the captain demanded incredulously.

"My companion and my . . . guardian," Eden asserted with an irritable look at Arlo.

492

"M'lady, this is unthinkable—ye canna be sailin' with his kind!"

"Well you won't get to Boston with any other kind, little man. There's a state of war on, declared or not," the Captain returned.

Eden watched their exchange grow hotter and saw their precious passage sailing away on the torrent of Arlo's pride.

"Arlo!' She interrupted another insult and scowled at him fiercely. "The captain is right. His vessel is tight and sturdy. He's accustomed to running blockades and is a fair, decent man." She prayed the innkeeper's summary of his old associate was accurate. "The only question remaining is one of timing!" She turned a crimson but composed face to the craggy captain. "Can you make the run before mid-June, sir?"

"It is possible, my lady," his eyes raked her, "if I decide it's worth it. What is your hurry?"

"I should think that would be obvious, sir." Eden rose and watched the captain's chin drop as her belly became quite visible. "I would prefer my bairn be birthed on dry land." There was a tense silence and, from Captain Buckley's darkening scowl, Eden gathered she'd lost her only real hope. Frustration and her own wavery, maternal emotions brought tears to her eyes despite her attempts to blink them away. How dare she mewl and cry now. . . ? She took the handkerchief Arlo had extended and sat down stiffly, dabbing at her eyes.

"Are you running to or from the father?" The Captain's eyes roamed her and the way her short, burly "guardian" cosseted her. More than once, the man had called her "m'lady."

Eden raised a patrician defiance to him and sniffed hard. "From. But do not misunderstand it, sir. He is my true husband and he has my affection . . . and my faithfulness. If you take me to my family in Boston, you must . . . abide with that knowledge."

"Then why—"

"M'lady does what she has to do." Arlo patted her shoulder protectively and wore his best bulldog-with-a-bone expression. "An' I'll do what I must to protect her."

Captain Buckley leaned back and appraised the pair: they belonged on the bloody stage, the two of 'em. He was growing soft in his advancing years to even consider taking them. But there was a story to be had here, and damned if he didn't enjoy a good story about as much as he enjoyed a good woman these days. There was an excruciating silence before he spoke again.

"We sail in three days' time. I'll draw up a contract for passage that spells out my rules and you'll agree to abide by 'em. My men aren't accustomed to . . . passengers, especially female ones. They'll have a few choice words to say, an' even big wi' child, ye'll have to keep away from 'em, my lady. Otherwise . . . I think we'll suit."

# Chapter Twenty-seven

Ram stared at the crumpled letter in his hand and heard the voice he loved most in the world repeating its few simple words in his head.

*"I love you, Ramsay MacLean."*

A shudder went through him and he wadded the letter in his fist, staring at the smooth oyster parchment that contained Eden's flowing, feminine hand. He stood in the center of their graying bedchamber, his broad shoulders slumped in fatigue. His eyes were ringed and his face gray and shadowed with growth. It was dawn, just past the longest night of his life, and the desolation inside him was unbearable.

He stared at the small lacquered vanity, now bare. Her brushes, her little boxes, her mirror. . . . He ran his fingers over the cold, smooth surface, thinking that must be what his heart would feel like if he could touch it — cold and empty. Eden was gone.

He sat down on the side of the bed with his head in his hands. He'd returned from the court in late afternoon to find their bedchamber empty. It had taken awhile to realize that both she and her things were gone. He quizzed James and Carina, and even Haskell, on her plans, her movements during the day — but no one seemed to know anything. Arlo hadn't returned to the court after noon and no one had seen him, either. Then the landlord had trundled up the three flights of stairs and delivered her letter: one sentence, five words. And his world was set on its edge.

He'd shouted, grilling the landlord like a madman, unwilling to believe the only conclusion possible; she'd left him. And in a near-rage, he'd stormed out to scour the city. Hours later, he'd returned to find James and Haskell gone, searching for her, and Carina awaiting their messages, beside herself with worry. She'd forced him to eat a bite and then watched him leave again with tears in her eyes.

All night they'd searched and come back empty-handed. By the first light Ram knew she'd quit the city, and not in the direction of Skyelt. He racked his brain trying to think of what could have caused her to leave. And the only thing that came to him was the suit and the prospect that he might lose Skyelt. As much as he tried to disavow it, he knew Eden was deeply disturbed by it. They'd spoken of it in their bed at night, and she'd comforted and reassured him as only she could. Yesterday morning there had been that strange, lingering sadness to her mood and the clinging of her kisses. She'd been bidding him farewell.

He wouldn't believe his own thoughts. Eden had endured Skyelt for his sake, had come to accept it, with its many problems and inconveniences . . . hadn't she? Or had it been her position as lady and mistress that had finally warmed her heart to his home . . . and him? The blood drained from his head, dizzying him. Did she find the prospect of life with him unbearable without title and estates?

He tried to squeeze those painful thoughts from his head and only succeeded in driving them down into his heart. The pain of losing her eclipsed everything else. He stumbled from the bed and went down into the street, shoving James and Haskell aside as they tried to reason with him. He fled into the gray, wakening city. But nothing would blunt his pain.

Hours later, Ram burst into the court, his hair and clothes in disarray, his face ashen and hard. He smelled of ale but was far from drunk. James rushed to the commotion at the back of the court and succeeded in bundling him outside while their lawyers begged a short recess. Haskell joined James in the lobby and together they subdued Ram's angry strength.

They tried to explain to him that judgment was near to being handed down and that they'd searched for him—he was needed desperately. The closed, bottled look in his face finally gave way to a semblance of understanding. When Haskell shook him and demanded he act like a laird and a MacLean, and see to his duty, it seemed to sink in. They took him to a nearby tavern and made him more presentable. By the time court reconvened, he could take his place at the table of lawyers feeling grindingly sober. Beneath the deadly control at his surface, he was roiling inside.

Summary arguments were being concluded and Ram felt old Lawrence Bruce's eyes narrowed on him, then on Angus and on a savagely smug Ian. As Ram watched, Ian removed a document from his coat and slowly unfolded it. He watched Ram's face with a knowing glint in his eyes, then turned to read the oyster-colored parchment. Just visible was the familiar flowing, feminine script, and Ram's attention slowly came alive. The paper, the woman's hand, and Ian's vengeful smirk smacked him awake and his legendary control erupted with a MacLean vengeance.

*"Damn you!"* Ram jumped to his feet, shouting. The

497

MacLean bench of robes sprung up and just managed to contain him as he raved, "You miserable bastard—what have you done with her? She's my wife and I'll not give her up—I'll see you dead first!"

The court was in turmoil—Bruce pounding his gavel, yelling for order; lawyers on both sides rushing to restrain each other; Angus straining to hold his adopted son, who was smirking and taunting Ram with Eden's abandonment.

"I did nothing, you righteous prick—except point out to her the certainty of your coming poverty," Ian shouted above the chaos around them. "I offered her a place with me, instead! And it seems she found neither of us worth her time!"

"You maggot by-blow!" Ram thundered. "Where is she?! I swear you'll tell me or I'll beat it out of you—" He knocked down two of his own in trying to get to Ian.

"How does it feel to be a loser, brother?" Ian shouted, scrambling toward Ram. "Your wife *and* your precious home!" And in his vengeful frenzy he spat one taunt too cutting: "Don't you want to know if the brat is yours or mine?"

Ram exploded, launching himself across the table and knocking Angus out of the way. Ian thudded back under his impact and they grappled over the benches and railings and onto the floor. They wrestled toward the back of the court, fists meeting bone and flesh time and time again. Haskell seized the chance to charge in and take a long-awaited swing at Angus, and Angus retaliated in kind. The gallery emptied and soon it was impossible to tell who was fighting and who was just screaming bloody encouragement. When Ram and Ian crashed through the doors into the lobby, even the magistrates abandoned their seats to follow.

Ram's fists connected with Ian's face over and over, and a blinding pain burst in Barclay's head. He stumbled and when Ram's shoulder smashed into his midsection, they fell onto the floor again. Ian's fingers were driven by pain around Ram's throat and Ram grappled between tearing Ian's fingers off and tightening his own hold on Ian's miserable throat.

"Where is she?" Ram rasped, freeing one hand enough to bash it against Ian's head, loosening his choke hold. But Ian squirmed and thrashed with his legs and managed to roll both of them over onto their sides, his fingers clawing at Ram's eyes, narrowly missing raking him blind.

"I . . . don't give . . . a damn," Ian growled through the blood running down his chin, "as long as she's not wi' *you!*"

Their savage thrashing slowly eclipsed all other grievances. Bailiffs and lawyers and Edinburgh's elite staggered to a halt and stared disbelieving as the young titans battled. Blood flowed fully down each face and splattered on the floor. Scratches and blows and crunching bone and sinew echoed eerily against the walls of this bastion of order and justice. In the end, it was Ram's sea-honed stamina that gave him a final spurt of strength and ended it: Ian's head was lifted and smacked against the gritty Italian marble of the lobby floor and he went slack. Ram lay across him, blind with pain and heaving. A stunned quiet reigned as James peeled his brother-in-law from Ian Barclay's inert form and supported Ram's bloodied, staggering bulk out the street doors.

It was Ram's last appearance before Head Magistrate Lawrence Bruce.

Captain Blade Buckley's crew were a scurvy, hardened lot, as heathen and larcenous as had ever sailed the seven seas. There was hardly a man amongst them not missing some extraneous part of his body: an ear, part of a hand, an eye, a few toes, quite a few teeth. Further, there wasn't a man amongst them who would not kill, or had not, for his shipmates. It was as confusing and treacherous a brotherhood ever assembled under a furl of canvas.

Eden and Arlo were installed aboard the *Sea Raven* in the dead of night and the crew had only heard rumors of the passengers until they were well underway. There were rumblings about a beautiful lady and the mates' curiosity thickened to a palpable stew on the decks of the ship as they negotiated southward to London and the Channel.

Arlo went on deck the first day out and returned white-faced. He gruffly demanded that Eden confine herself to their rather spartan quarters. He heartily regretted allowing things to go this far; he should have been more urgent in his secretive letter to Ram explaining where they were bound and what he knew of why. He was never good at taking women in hand and had hoped his laird would arrive before they found passage. But m'lady had outfoxed him, and he could only hope he was leaving a clear trail.

Eden discounted whatever Arlo had witnessed topside on the *Sea Raven,* putting it down to his oddly delicate sensibilities. But since there would be weeks ahead to encounter Blade Buckley's ship and crew, she contented herself with resting away the strain and fatigue of the first leg of her flight.

She thought of Ram constantly and never without a pang of uncertainty as to her course. Each day, as the babe moved stronger, it brought tears to her eyes. She recalled her husband's strong hand pressed against her belly in eager expectation of his child and died a little inside. She dined in her cabin from trays Arlo brought her and grew increasingly moody and maudlin.

They were charging out into the Atlantic, bearing south to catch the easterlies, when Eden finally couldn't bear the isolation any longer and ventured out on deck one sunny afternoon. Arlo was in the captain's cabin and didn't see her wrap her thick shawl around her shoulders and push her long, uncoiffed hair back carelessly over her shoulders. It would have given him palpitations to see her labor up the steps of the hatchway. The way she collected the leering stares of that crew would have brought on full apoplexy.

The brightness of the day and the startling beauty of the ship were a stark contrast to the marked and sly-eyed faces pressing in on her. Before long, she could barely swallow, her sunset eyes wide with what she read in their slow, menacing approach and predatory postures.

One by one they came to a stop between her and the hatch, sizing her up visually and clearly pleased with what they saw. She drew her heavy shawl tighter around her, still feeling as if they stripped her naked with their eyes. Her heart began to beat in her throat and her face reddened.

Their self-appointed leader, a man of middle years who was missing several teeth and two fingers of his left hand, had a bulging middle, but the leathery hardness of his bare arms and lower legs dispelled any notion of flabbiness. He, like the rest of the crew, was fighting fit and dangerous indeed. He took an ominous step closer and Eden felt herself cowering back against the rail, wondering if Arlo or Blade Buckley would hear her when she screamed.

He reached for a handful of her wind-whipped hair and Eden glared at him with as much indignation as she could muster while her legs caved in beneath her.

"Git 'er, Harry!" someone encouraged him.

"Ain't she a pretty li'l thing," Harry laughed nastily, drawing a hoot of lecherous observations from their audience. "I says ol' Blade be holdin' out on us here! She be spoils and we all get a share—startin' now—"

When he grabbed her against him, Eden thought she was likely dying anyway, and with a burst of fatal bravado, managed to bring her knee up with force that must have been aided by an unexpected upswell of the ship. Her tormentor groaned and stumbled back, clutching himself. Here and there came a howl of outraged sympathy for an injured mate, and they began to crowd closer, snarling.

Eden's arm raked Carina's dagger at her side and the adrenalin pumping through her set her bairn to kicking vigorously. How dare these wretches threaten a defenseless woman entrusted to their care—a woman so far gone with child! She clutched her belly and snarled back like a cornered she-lion.

She shed her concealing shawl and drew the wicked little blade in the same movement. "Get back, you mangy curs!" She brandished the dirk in an arc and there was a general distancing. "I'll split the spleen of the next bastard who lays a hand on me an' my bairn!" Carina's favorite threat was unconsciously appropriated.

"She's . . . stuffed!" came a shocked observation. ". . . Been mounted an' bred," and "A'ready got a belly full," and "Ain't enough room there for a pickle!"

"I am with child," Eden corrected, shielding her bulging middle with her other hand. "I am Lady MacLean of Skyelt, Scotland. And you'll keep your hands to yourselves or be prepared to pay for your sins with your own blood."

*"Damme* for a Sister o' Charity!" Harry swore, pushing upright with a tightened face. "She's a *mother.*" All eyes turned on him and witnessed the way his mood became grave. He crossed himself and reddened, pointing. "Look at her, ye randy, slobberin' pack o' wharf-rats! Cain't ye see she's a *mother?!*"

A new light dawned in their eyes as they watched their unelected leader and the little mother. There was nothing in the world that commanded jaded Harry's respect except his old mother. And because of her, he allowed no comment deriding a breeding female or a mother in his presence. So strong were his feelings and so potent his dealings that the crew had had to purge all derogatory terms containing the word "mother" from their vocabularies. And it was even risky to use terms referring to canine mothers in his presence.

"*Lady* MacLean, ye say?" Harry pulled his shoulders back with an air of dignity. "Then me and me mates here be at yer service, m'lady. We had no way o'knowin' that you was . . . a mother."

Eden felt as if she were going to faint. But instead she made a show of sheathing her knife and accepting her shawl from the hands of the mate who had picked it up. She settled it around her bloodless shoulders and nodded stiffly in Harry's direction. How she made it to the hatch, she wasn't sure, later. But strong pairs of hands gently assisted her down the steep, unwieldy steps and soon she was safely inside her cabin again.

In the warm June buzz of Boston's fashionable Beacon Hill, a hired coach wound through the brick-paved streets and stopped before the Adam Marlow house. Two barrel-chested seamen jumped down from coach to stand by the door, and another seaman and broad-bellied Harry emerged to join them. A splash of red tartan came next and Arlo MacCrenna stepped down into the balmy morning. The men jostled to lend assistance to a very pregnant and cumbersome Eden MacLean. Together they bore her down to the curb and fussed over her, Harry offering to carry her to the door and Arlo frowning him down.

She was ushered along to a pair of massive blue doors that enclosed an uncertain welcome. She drew a labored breath and managed a nervous little smile as she straightened her high-waisted dress over her middle and pulled her underblouse up higher over her rounded breasts. She fidgeted with the silk snood that held her heavy fall of hair and forced her chin an inch higher. Arlo squeezed her hand and she nodded for him to apply brass to brass at the knocker.

There was a long wait. They stared at each other uneasily, and Eden felt fear settling on her already crowded stomach like a stone. Arlo knocked several times and the tension spawned a bit of irritation in her. Lofton, their butler, always answered promptly and efficiently. Eden began to feel it was a terrible mistake coming here. Perhaps they'd been seen from above . . . and wouldn't be admitted.

From somewhere in the house came the rumble of a human voice, unintelligible but undoubtedly male. Scraping and dull stomping accompanied calls for the butler, and finally a tightly uttered oath was just audible from near the door.

*"Yes?"* Ethan jerked one of the double doors open angrily, his cravat half-wrapped and his hair wet. His eyes widened on the sight of his bulging sister, wrapped in a dizzying red plaid, flanked by a glowering Scot and a crew of nautical cutthroats. For a moment he was too stunned to respond, and his disbelief was easy for Eden to interpret as disgust.

"Well," she managed a defiant toss of her head while she subdued frantic misgivings, "will you let me come in, or must I birth this bairn right here on the doorstep?"

"Eden!" Ethan jolted back and numbly motioned her into the hall before him. He blinked as the whole unsavory crew crowded in after her and stood eying him with open hostility. "It was a shock, seeing you so. . . ." Words failed him. But a gesture explained that it was her very advanced pregnancy and unusual garb, her rough escort and salty greeting . . . *everything* shocked him.

"Dede?" He concentrated on her eyes, bewildered, and finally began to smile at the reassuring familiarity of them. "You've come home?" He lurched toward her, but was brought up short by the movement of one of the scowling crew.

"It's all right, Fast Ned." She laid a restraining hand on the arm that ended in a wickedly sharpened hook. "He's my brother Ethan." But the tension did not abate until she looked at her tall middle brother. "Am I welcome here, Ethan?"

"Well . . . of course, Dede." The flicker of doubt in her face clutched at him. "God! Of course you're welcome here . . . we're your family!" His arms dangled at his sides awkwardly.

"Then have you a welcoming hug for me?" She could not keep the quiver from her voice and before the echo of his name died in the hall he'd pulled her into his lanky arms and squeezed her tightly. She threw her arms round him and let a few silent tears of gratitude escape before she gained control of herself and pushed back.

She asked him to recall Arlo and then introduced the rest of her escort: Harry, Fast Ned, the Shark, Charleston Bill, and Old Dimmy, the ship's carpenter. They'd insisted on seeing her settled with her family and seemed a bit less ferocious, now that she was welcome. Ethan eyed them with wary respect and shook their hands, and hook, with incredible aplomb. Eden explained that they'd rather adopted her aboard ship and had taken excellent care of her.

"This be the one what gambles?" Harry sought clarification, looking Ethan over carefully. Eden nodded and Ethan reddened. Apparently she'd described her family in detail.

"I mustn't keep you standing in the hall! Mother and Father are out, and Lofton's off doing something or other. Come and sit, Dede." He took her arm to usher her into the main parlor and Harry cleared his throat loudly and said they'd have to be going, now that she was safely delivered.

"Now you be sure an' send us word when the bairn comes, lassie," Harry insisted and the others agreed. She smiled fondly and gave each a little kiss on the cheek as he left.

Ethan watched, thoroughly bewildered by her seeming affection for this grizzled and menacing lot. Then he settled her on the sofa in the parlor and rang for someone to see to her bags. When he turned to her again, he noted the pain etched in her eyes as she looked about the fashionable salon.

"Ramsay?" he asked, having already drawn his own conclusion. "He did not bring you." He tucked some pillows around her awkwardly and brought a stool for her feet.

"No," was all she would answer. And she would not meet Arlo's gaze.

"Does he know about the child?" Ethan sat down beside her and tried not to stare at her huge belly. Her cheeks were apple-red and her hair shone from attention. There was a moist glow to her slightly rounded face and he was relieved; it meant her health was probably good.

"He knows."

Eden was installed in her old room and Arlo was put nearby in a guest room, despite his protests. Charity hugged her and cried a little; Colleen came from the kitchen to see her all garbed in plaid and hugged her and cried a lot. At Arlo's insistence, they left her in her room to rest.

Ethan sent immediately for his father at their trading company offices and met his mother in the hallway the minute she returned from a morning call. He didn't know exactly how to describe what had happened and simply announced that Eden had come home and was resting in

506

her rooms above. No, she hadn't mentioned James, and yes, she seemed fit enough for a woman in a motherly way. It was a prodigious act of restraint that kept Constance Marlow from invading her daughter's room.

When Eden awoke in her blue-and-white papered bedroom, she was a bit confused, but she quickly recovered and slid gingerly from the bed and smoothed her soft tartan dress. The babe was awakening inside her and moving strongly, and she patted the plaid mound soothingly.

"I wonder if your grandma and grandpa are home yet."

She found them, with Ethan, Chase, and Arlo, in the parlor, pacing and fretting. When she appeared at the door, Constance stopped in the middle of the floor and clutched her chest, stumbling back toward the sofa.

"Dear God! She's . . . Oh! . . . Oh!"

Adam was torn briefly between rushing to his daughter and catching his swooning wife. He left Chase to see to his mother and bounded to Eden, engulfing her in a wet-eyed embrace.

"My Dede! My sweet little girl . . . come home at last." He gradually released her and wiped the tears from her cheeks with his thumbs. "You're so beautiful, Dede. We've worried so—" But Chase was muscling in to give her a hug and laughing at the way she had to turn sideways to reach him. Then it was time to face her mother and Eden approached the sofa, watching the way Constance's eyes widened on her belly.

"Hello, Mama." No *Mam-ma,* this time. Eden felt a dark swirl of emotions pushing to the surface. So much had happened, so much was revealed since they'd parted. She was no longer the innocent little daughter who had refused to believe her mother's passionate past. She was woman confronting woman. The experiences of loving and sacrificing had tempered her resentment of her mother's immoral conduct and now gentled her reactions.

"Ethan said you were . . . but I never imagined it was so. . . ." Constance pushed upright and struggled to rise.

"So far along?" Eden finished for her, feeling a bit condemned by her mother's shock. "If you'd rather I took other lodgings—"

"No! Don't be ridiculous. Of course you'll stay here!" Constance clasped and unclasped her hands frantically, then finally gave in to her overwhelming urge to clutch her daughter in her arms.

For a long time they embraced, and both faces were wet when they drew apart and Constance ushered her to the sofa. Eden was wiping at tears with her palms and Arlo offered her one of the several handkerchiefs he'd taken to carrying. Masculine throats cleared all around the room.

After assurances of her good health and denials of any and all complaints, they settled around her and listened as she told a somewhat censored account of her departure from Boston and her journey to Scotland. The part about Ram's impressment elicited outrage from the men and Constance fluttered distress. When Eden leveled a knowing gaze at her mother and described her first meeting with Haskell, sparing no outrageous detail, Constance swooned in earnest. Eden left no doubt in her mother's mind that she knew the whole story, then went on to describe Skyelt and her unique adjustment to it. She laughed when recounting James's arrival and his distaste for things Scottish. Then she described her sister-in-law, Carina, and laughed at their shock over the laird's bastard daughter.

Then came the part about the suit, and Eden had some difficulty as she drew toward the conclusion of it . . . the ultimatum that had sent her fleeing from her husband's side. It was still too painful to relate, and when she pleaded fatigue and retired upstairs, Arlo filled them in as best he could. They were suitably shocked and angered, and they vowed to see that the remainder of Eden's pregnancy and confinement would be free of care and trouble for her.

At supper that evening, Eden wore a comfortable tartan skirt and a blouse that boldly emphasized her motherly state. This had been her costume for many of the recent days and was *de rigueur* for Highland women in a family way. Her family's eyes upon her reminded her of the differences in cultures, but didn't concern her overmuch. She'd taken down her hair and allowed Charity to dress only half of it, leaving the rest in a liquid flow down her back.

Conversation was somewhat strained and Constance was driven to muse aloud, "I was to have had ladies in for coffee tomorrow morning . . . I'll send a message round and cancel."

"Oh, not on my account, please." Eden assessed the rueful expression on her mother's face and her eyes narrowed. "Do go ahead with your plans. In fact, it's been some time since I had the company of other women. I'd enjoy it immensely."

"But . . . in your advanced condition . . . it's not. . . ."

"Proper?" Eden laughed at the guilty stain that came to her mother's face. "I was quite legally and most properly bred, Mama. What shame is there in bearing the fruit of my husband's affections?"

"Eden, really!" Constance seemed a bit shocked and her brothers buried their noses in their custard. "Ladies . . . *do* retire from society when they reach such . . . an obvious stage."

"Well, I can't think why," Eden observed pointedly. "This last bit of waiting is so tedious, I should think some company would be a great relief. There are far enough inconveniences without being bored witless." She listed in her chair and resettled herself rather obviously.

Adam cleared his throat and Ethan and Chase decided they'd suddenly had enough custard and excused themselves. Constance's eyes narrowed on their retreating backs, the cowards.

"Perhaps you'll be too fatigued to join us." The faint knell of hope in Constance's tone rankled Eden thoroughly.

The way Eden saw it, her mother was a day late and a bushel short with this propriety nonsense. Where was all this delicacy and sensitivity when she was bedding boarish old Haskell?

"Me? Fatigued? Heaven forbid." She beamed in cheerful defiance. "I'm fit as an ox. Now if you'll excuse me, I think I'll have a turn around the gardens before retiring."

The next morning the ladies called promptly at ten o'clock and, precisely at ten-fifteen, Eden descended the stairs to join them. She wore a sky-blue, watered-silk dress with no waistline, one she'd ordered for their stay in Edinburgh. Charity had coiffed her hair into a flood of upswept ringlets, and her skin glowed with warmth and health. She floated into the parlor in a cloud of maternal elegance, surprising her mother's guests into speechlessness. Constance's relief at her sedate and fashionable appearance was a bit too obvious, and Eden smiled wryly.

"Eden, dear, you do remember Millie Perkins, Edna Carstens, and Charlotte Lloyd. . . ."

"Of course I do. How lovely to see you, ladies." Eden settled awkwardly on a roomy straight chair near the tea table and managed to look serene under their shocked scrutiny.

"Constance, you sly thing, you kept the reason for your little coffee a surprise. Sweet Eden's come for a visit." The gears in Millie Perkins's mind could be seen working.

"To be candid, it was a bit of a surprise to us at first." Constance sent Eden a glance that dared her to refute Millie's conclusion. "We're so delighted —"

"And where is that handsome husband of yours?" Millie crooned, her eyes dancing with the thought of being the first with such a juicy tidbit.

"He's—" Constance began, flustered.

"In Scotland, still," Eden finished, meeting Millie's curiosity head-on. "Family business. I came ahead for a visit."

"And at such an tumultuous time." Millie's eyes were riveted on Eden's belly and she added, "what with the declaration of war and all."

Constance was shrinking in her shoes at the light in the women's faces. She began to pour coffee with trembling hands.

"Well, our crossing was without incident . . . quite smooth, in fact," Eden felt a reckless urge as she watched her mother's mortification. "I've certainly found travel a . . . broadening experience." She looked down at her belly and chuckled at the appropriateness of her remark.

The three old cats burst into laughter and Constance purpled, sending Eden a furious look. It was all Eden could do to calm herself and accept the proffered cup with a bit of grace. They asked after her health and slyly probed the reasons for Eden's journey to Boston in such an advanced condition. Eden fielded the questions admirably, using a confidential tone to confide virtually nothing. She entertained them with vivid accounts of the people and places along her route and began to describe Blade Buckley and his disreputable crew in some detail.

"—and what he could do with that hook—"

"Dede!" Constance forbade another word with a scathing look at her daughter and stood up. "We mustn't tire you, dearest. Being mothers ourselves, we all understand that you need a great deal of rest."

It was a command Eden was tempted to refute, but she knew she trod a thin line with her mother and demurred gracefully. Constance ushered her out and turned an irritable eye on Eden's mischievous face.

"You'll have them wagging tongues all over Boston,

Eden Delight. Whatever were you thinking?"

"It's my Christian duty, Mama," Eden twinkled naughtily. "While they're prattling on about me, they're giving everyone else a much-needed rest." And she gave out a naughty laugh as she mounted the hall steps.

## Chapter Twenty-eight

"You look lovely this evening." Chase brushed Eden's forehead with a kiss and proceeded to a chair near the french doors that were opened to allow a sultry breeze through the parlor. He settled and opened a paper to read by the light of the lowering sun.

Eden sighed, sent sliding into memory by the little endearment, and suddenly full of longing. She wanted to feel Ram's strong arms about her, wanted to touch his skin with her own, wanted to trace his handsome features with her eyes instead of her memory. She was in desperate need of a good hugging and none seemed forthcoming from her staid and insufferably correct family. She wrapped her arms around her shifting belly and gave it a hug instead.

"Ow!" She drew a sharp breath. "You little dickens!" She stiffened and pressed on her side to dislodge something from under her ribs.

"Are you all right?" Chase was on his feet in a flash and hovering over her.

"It was just a kick," Eden smiled ruefully, then brightened. "And he's still at it. Want to feel?"

"Eden." Chase straightened, and his reddening face made him look a lot like Adam Marlow when he was trying to be stern. "Really . . . the things you say. . . ."

"Well, some of it I learned from you," she charged. "Who was it told me ladies had 'meadow muffins' for tea?"

*"Not* me." He shifted feet and reddened further.

"Yes it was, Chase Marlow." She suddenly looked like she was going to cry and swiped furiously at the tear in her eye. "And now you've turned into a stuffy, Back Bay snob. You're even stingy with your love."

"Dede, that's not true." A lump was rising in his throat as he watched her fighting waves of emotion.

"Yes, it is. You're all ashamed of me and my bairn. Everybody acts like it doesn't exist . . . or tries to keep me out of sight . . . except Arlo. Well, I'm damned happy about having this babe, even if everyone else seems to think it a disgrace." She began to cry in earnest, and Chase searched his gentlemanly pockets for a handkerchief. He held it out to her lamely and she shook her head and covered her splotchy face with her hands. Then he went down on one knee beside her chair and put his arms around her gently, drawing her shoulder against him.

"I had no idea it was so hard for you, Dede. It's just, you're a bit of a shock to us all. . . ." He let her cry for a while and finally dabbed at her face with his handkerchief. Her little smile of gratitude was pathetic.

"Want to feel him move?" Before he could object, she had his hand and was pressing it against the side of her belly. He protested, but she shushed him and held it there. The babe protested the pressure and began to squirm. Chase's face paled and his eyes widened. But slowly, under Eden's proud grin, he began to warm.

"Ram used to put his hand there and smile at m—" She swallowed the rest and made herself smile bravely at Chase.

Ethan found them there minutes later, laughing, Chase's hand on his sister's bulging middle while he babbled half-intelligibly to his new nephew.

"God." Ethan strode in, his face a mask of indignation. Under his glare, Chase sobered and straightened, then stood, flushing guiltily. "Have you no couth at all, the two of you?"

"Ethan Marlow," Eden struggled to her feet, "I'll have none of your righteous attitude. Chase was feeling my bairn move."

"That's . . . disgusting." Ethan sniffed and glared at his younger brother.

"Then I pity little Adelle Stockton, if she falls into your sterile clutches," she glared back at him, pleased by his jolted look. "What a proper stick of a husband you'll make. You'll pack her off to some dungeon when she'd breedin' and deny her the merest scrap of affection and consideration—just when she'll be needin' it most." Eden's eyes blazed. "Perhaps I ought to warn her; you'll be spendin' your nights with your hands filled with jacks and queens, instead of her!"

"Ramsay ought to have kept you locked up!" Ethan ground out.

"He tried," her eyes narrowed, "but bolts and bars only work from the inside. How do you think I got pregnant?"

Ethan's jaw dropped and he turned on his heel and left.

"You were a little hard on him, Dede," Chase reproved.

"I know. He deserved it."

Ethan avoided her for the next few days and she began to feel a bit guilty. He was heading for the door one evening after supper when she planted herself in his way and refused to give passage.

"I was hard on you, Ethan . . . I'm sorry. I canna expect you to live and love as I would."

Ethan watched the strain in her round, rosy face and felt an unexpected wave of warmth. "It's all right, Eden. I know it's hard for you."

"Then will you give me a game of cards to show there's no hard feelings?" She smiled wistfully and he was powerless to refuse. They rounded up Arlo and Chase and sat down in the parlor for a pleasant evening at the pasteboards.

Well into the evening, Eden suggested they increase their wagers, and when Ethan agreed with a twinkle in his eye, she announced her bet; if he won, she'd forebear saying a word to Adelle Stockton. If she won, he'd have to feel the babe move. He was a little put off, but in the end he had to be a sport and so agreed. Eden pulled out a few tricks taught her by Charleston Bill aboard the *Sea Raven* and won handily.

Ethan grumped and snorted that something under-handed had gone on and tried to wriggle out of the payoff. Eden was having none of it and enlisted Chase's support in collecting her winnings. Arlo stood by red-faced as Ethan knelt by her and allowed his hand to be forced against her belly.

"Wake up," Eden pressed the other side of her belly and got results, "and meet your Uncle Ethan. He's really a very nice man." She smiled at the widening of his eyes and patted his hand on her belly. And Ethan fought through his chagrin and was soon smiling, too.

That's how Adam and Constance found them upon returning from a dinner engagement; in the parlor, with several hands pressed against Eden's belly, laughing and making up nonsense words for her unborn babe. Constance melted weakly on Adam's arm and her face drained. Eden grinned when she saw them and invited them to come feel, too.

Adam declined rather tersely and led his wife upstairs.


Arrangements were made for Eden's confinement, and it was the greatest of fortune that Charity had all the requisite midwifery skills. Constance staunchly maintained she would assist, and small clothes for the babe and buntings and blankets were assembled. The room adjoining Eden's would become the nursery and was duly decorated and outfitted with frilly curtains and a rocking chair and a box of toys retrieved from the attic. In the center of it stood the handcarved cradle which Old Dimmy, the carpenter of the *Sea Raven,* had constructed for the babe. Increasingly, Eden migrated there and knelt by the cradle, running her fingers over the smooth, waxed boards. From the look on her face, it was not difficult to read her thoughts, her longings.

Constance stood in the doorway watching and felt a sympathetic pang for her daughter's lonely ordeal. Adam had comforted her greatly in the last days of her pregnancies, and she recalled those long-forgotten fears and misgivings with which she'd approached childbed. Her sweet, salty Dede had no husband to comfort her. And though Eden would never discuss it, Constance knew her daughter faced the possibility of never seeing her husband again. It was clear from heart-wrenching scenes like those as she knelt by her babe's cradle that Eden loved her brawny Scot with everything in her.

July first arrived, steamy and miserable. Eden grew cross and even saltier under her endless burden. By the second day of the month, even she was finding herself difficult to live with. And when she stood in the fragrant garden that very morning and felt that first dull contraction in her belly, she nearly leapt with joy.

The household flew into action and settled down to wait in the same instant. Below, in the parlor, Adam and Arlo and Ethan and Chase all paced and drank liberal shots of brandy. Upstairs, Eden exasperated Charity and her mother by refusing to take to bed until she could walk no longer. And when the waves of pain became hard to bear, it was Ram she wanted and Arlo she called for.

"No, Eden, it's not possible—" Constance tried to push her back against the damp pillows. "Men simply cannot be present—it's not decent!"

*"I want Arlo!"* Eden raged, her eyes wild with determination. "By God, I'll go and get him myself!" She struggled against her mother's arms and the pain spurred her to even greater strength. She very nearly made it out of the room with both women holding her back.

They wrestled her back into bed and her eyes glazed with tears of loneliness and desperation. She clutched her mother's arm. "Please, I canna have my Ramsay—let me have my Arlo!"

Constance felt Eden's clutching fingers as if they were on her heart instead of her arm.

"Go and get the damned Scot, and be quick about it," Constance snapped, and Charity fled the room. Arlo was dragged in minutes later, numbed slightly by brandy, but still horrified by the sight of Eden, her hair damp and tangled, propped up on pillows in her bed. When she held out her arms to him, he swallowed and shuffled toward the bed, his eyes averted. He stood and hugged her awkwardly, smoothing back her hair and shushing her. He smelled of that peculiar combination of warm wool and brandy that spoke comfort to Eden; the scent was so much like Ram's. She calmed markedly and seemed finally ready to face the entrance of her bairn into the.

world.

Constance instructed Arlo to sit by her head and let Eden squeeze his hands. They put a sheet up over her knees when the time arrived. Now that she was more relaxed, the end of it came quickly. Eden and Ramsay MacLean had a strapping son.

Eden named her son Andrew Arlan Adam MacLean, declaring that between his three namesakes, he ought to find plenty worth emulating, especially since one was the patron saint of Scotland. Adam was strutting, cock-proud of his grandson, and spent each morning after breakfast in the nursery, watching him and crooning to him. Afternoon was Grandma's time with little Andrew, and in the evening Ethan sometimes deserted the Rotterdam Club and Chase forsook Madame Rochelle to spend time with Eden and their nephew.

Eden's tenderness with her son and her love for him were sometimes nearly painful to watch. She stroked his little cheeks as he nursed and hummed lullabyes and told him how very much like his papa he was. And suddenly there would be a catch in her throat and she'd close her eyes briefly. Constance ached for her daughter's well-hidden unhappiness and prayed the mess would somehow work itself out. They had rallied round her for Andrew's birth and would see her through this as well.

The first three weeks of Eden's motherhood were a sweet lull between storms. But no sooner had Eden gained her feet than she insisted on caring for her babe herself and carried him all about the house with her. And, heaven help them all, she nursed him right before her parents' and brothers' horrified eyes. When Constance tried to speak to her about it, she laughed and said she knew Marlow men were well aquainted with the female breast, so they needn't pretend to be outraged. She did, however, promise to be more circumspect in public.

And a month after Andrew's birth, Constance returned from an afternoon's tea and found her drawing room filled to capacity with a frightening and grizzled crew of sea dogs. Eden was serving tea and sweets and entertaining them all in the grand style as they passed Andrew amongst them, cooing and chucking him beneath the chin. Eden introduced them to her white-faced mother individually and collectively as the crew of the *Sea Raven,* the ship that had brought her home to Boston. Constance endured as much of their leering and salty language as she could, then slipped out to warn Charity to count the silver spoons.

August crept into Boston on cooler ocean zephyrs and the mood of the city lifted. The seriousness of President Madison's June declaration of war had settled fully on the city and seemed to be having the predicted results on trade. The economy of Boston — indeed, much of new England — depended on trade with Britain, and despite impressment and interference with American shipping on the high seas, most merchants and commercial interests considered war with Britain the ultimate folly. Britain was still the most profitable market for many American commodities and was generally seen as the defender of stability and order against the excesses of Napoleonic France. Not the least of their reasons for opposing the war was their desire to avoid the inevitable taxes and loans and the loss of needed manpower to a "standing army." The American economy was too new, too volatile to withstand yet another long military involvement, they argued.

But the Federalists and the commercial interests of New England states had lost to the War Hawks, a combined force of southern and western interests that insisted on asserting American power and independence, on redressing wrongs, and on expanding American frontiers. Families like the Marlows were torn between the desire to support their fledgling nation and the need to maintain their own family fortunes. In the end, they paid their taxes and continued their risky shipments to and from England.

The British blockade, while far from perfect, had slowed shipping over the last two years, and word of incoming ships now spread quickly through the city. If more than one ship made it through, there was an air of celebration in the waterfront district that gradually permeated the shops and markets around.

One breezy morning, Constance prevailed upon Eden to leave Andrew in Charity's capable hands and to accompany her to the shops that had seen a recent influx of goods from the continent. Her ulterior motive of drawing Eden out into society, thus securing more conventional behavior, was not difficult to decipher. Eden grinned wryly and donned her green-print batiste dress with its hunter-green spencer and matching bonnet and looked very much the lady as they set out for the shops under Arlo's escort. They bargained over French stitched gloves, fine damascene, soft, pliant lawn, fine tatting, and laces from Belgium. They went from shop to shop, buying a few small things, but mostly just caught up in the bustle of the streets and in meeting friends and acquaintances.

When rumor spread of another ship coming in, Constance was heartened considerably by the news that it was flying Dutch colors and insisted on taking the carriage by Adam Marlow's offices. They met Adam and Chase coming out of their warehouse, heading for the nearby waterfront. Adam's face was flushed and animated. He had shipments due in on a Dutch packet and hope was renewed each time news of a successful crossing spread.

They walked the short distance to the docks, hearing

521

the growing rumble of voices and cheers and the drone of wheels. By the time they arrived at the docks, quite a boisterous crowd had gathered, waving and straining the dockside ropes to touch the ship as she nudged into berth. Through the crowd they could make out very little, and Adam left them a safe distance back and threaded through the crowd to get the name of the ship. It was the *Royal Bergen,* not the *Nord Zee,* he reported, a bit crestfallen but nonetheless relieved that ships were still getting through.

They watched the sailors in the riggings waving and heard the crowd's return greeting. Tarts and shopkeepers, sailors and longshoremen, tradesmen and shipping scions; all were there to enjoy the small triumph of a safe and successful run. There was a festive atmosphere that was hard to resist as they waited to learn what the ship carried. Flemish laces, Constance suggested; wire cables and seed, Adam surmised; good Dutch cheese, Arlo sighed, and they all laughed. Chase suggested they speak with the captain to see if he knew anything about other Dutch ships and their fortunes and Adam agreed.

As Chase wove through the thinning crowd, Constance turned to Eden and mentioned that it was nearing time for dinner. Eden nodded, but her eyes were riveted on the ship's rail. A flash of red had caught her eye and disappeared. She scoured the edge of the ship above the heads of the milling crowd and sternly ordered her heart to cease that queer thumping. She tore her gaze away, feeling her buoyant mood suddenly ruined by a mere glimpse of color: real or imagined, it was Ramsay's color. She shivered and cast an uncertain look toward Arlo's kilt. Its burnt-red background and crossthreads of gray and vivid greens and blues were somehow reassuring and melancholy at the same time. Arlo read her pensive look as he had so many times before and took her arm to turn her away toward the carriage.

Something made her take one final look over her shoulder toward the ship and she stopped dead; Chase was hurrying toward them with a burnt-red kilt in tow. For a long, heart-stopping moment, that was all Eden saw . . . red. Then, as it drew near, she made out the crossthreads of gray and green and blue: it was the MacLean plaid, and she could not lift her eyes from it.

Her heart stopped. She turned fully, feeling Arlo's hand release her. An irresistible force magnetized her gaze and pulled it upward, over a broad, black-clad chest to stern, finely sculptured features and a shaggy fall of hair that shone with a fiery cast in the midday sun. Eden's heartbeat quickened; the blue eyes she had seen every night in her dreams now silvered with hot emotion as they slid over her.

Her eyes burned dryly, but she refused to blink, fearing he'd disappear. Ramsay, her Ramsay . . . here! Fear and hope warred within her, blocking every word that sought her lips. Her perceptions widened by painful degrees. His jaw muscles were outlined beneath taut skin, his fists were clenched, his stance was braced. He was so controlled, so rigid; only his glowing eyes hinted at the tumult inside him.

"Look who I found," Chase uttered lamely, watching the powerful mixture of fear and joy in his sister's expression. Her body came alive, she quivered visibly. And when they just continued to stare at each other, Chase looked at his parents and shook his head uneasily.

"Ram, you came . . ." she rasped and her hand reached toward him, pulled back an instant later as if not daring his rejection. But that small gesture was enough.

"Eden—" Ram took a step closer, his face bronzing with surfacing emotion. Lord, how he wanted to thrash her—how he'd promised himself that luxury over and over in these last four months! He meant to punish her for running from him, for stealing his heart and his child and leaving him just when he needed her most. He'd strangled his passion for her a hundred nights, pacing, waiting, almost hating her. But now that she was within reach, looking at him with all the fear and longing and pain he felt himself, all he could think of was crushing her to him and burying his burning reason in the middle of her. His arms reflexed with the need to hold her; his throat rasped with unspoken contradictions; his lips burned for the feel of her skin; his chest ached with emptiness for the reassurance of her love.

The charged silence became unbearable. The unbidden memory of another reunion came into Eden's consciousness . . . that time he'd wanted her and hated her—and he'd turned away. She could feel his wanting, his unsated desire for her like a living thing reaching for her on the air they both breathed. She couldn't let him turn away again—

Ram's arm was like frozen steel when she touched it. She pulled and he resisted. Then she seized him with both hands and pulled, beseeching him. Once he was in motion, allowing himself to be tugged along with her, she turned and pulled him past her startled family and down the side street. The carriage . . . somehow she knew she had to get him home.

They moved faster and soon she was reaching for the carriage door. "Home, Martin . . ." she called to the startled driver, "and hurry!" When Ram hesitated, staring down at her with an angry light in his eyes, she listened to her heart and pushed him into the carriage so that he had to climb aboard. He reached back for her hands and fairly lifted her inside.

In those long, excruciating minutes, Eden couldn't look at anything but his strong, beautiful legs. She breathed in the salty, warm smell of him that heated her desires to a fluid state and she surrendered to the wisdom of her blood. Words were spineless, fickle things that allowed themselves to be used without conscience; any resentment or contrary emotion might snatch them up to wreak havoc at a time like this. It was better to save the words until the passions were subdued . . . or spent. When hearts and bodies were of one accord, then there would be time for minds to meet and speak and for love to guide the sorting of their words and lives.

Four times in as many miles, Eden's name had risen from his depths and been stopped on his tongue. She was trembling visibly, and Ram translated the tension of her posture and her avoidance of his body as fear. She was right to respect the anger that rode beneath his surface, for he was not yet sure he was fully in control of it himself. His hurt was deep, despite his certainty of her motives in leaving him. And deep hurts, like deep loves, did not resolve easily. He didn't trust himself; he didn't know where to begin to resolve the chaos of their marriage. He knew only that he wanted her and the love she had awakened in him more than anything in the world — even more than he had wanted his precious Skyelt.

And in that moment of their separate searching, his hand touched hers as it was braced on the seat between them. It was a small thing, his warm skin brushing hers, but it seemed an affirmation of her thoughts. He decided to let passion lead the way.

Ram was up and through the door the minute the carriage stopped before stately Marlow House. He reached up for Eden with gentle hands and a troubled, angry expression. They stood a moment on the street, by the brick pillars at the gate, searching each other, barely breathing. Eden seized the moment as she seized his big hand.

525

"Come on!"

She pulled him up the short stone walk, up the steps, threw open the heavy door and pulled him inside with her. Lofton was crossing the center hall and stopped with a puzzled frown on his face as she dragged Ram past him and up the stairs. By the time she'd turned down the hall toward her rooms, she didn't have to pull him any longer. He was beside her.

He stood in the middle of the bedroom where he had first awakened her love and watched her lock the door. She removed her bonnet and tossed it on the floor. She turned to him and released the buttons of her spencer, shrugging it from her shoulders. Part of his defenses fell at her feet with it.

"Eden—" He was quivering hot already, feeling things reeling further and further from his control.

She jerked the pins from her hair and shook it all around her, watching his eyes darkening and his face growing dusky. Her eyes locked into his as her fingers moved to the buttons at the back of her neck and she jerked her gown away from her. The dress had molded her thin chemise to her curves and she stood feeling his eyes searching, examining her. She realized there were changes in her body since Andrew's birth, and for a moment her heart stopped. There were no words to describe her turmoil; there was only her heart's plea.

"Love me, Ramsay . . . please—"

Before her words died in her throat, his arms closed around her and she was slammed against his hard body and lifted off the floor. He swung her in a dizzying circle before stopping to plunge into her breathless mouth. He was starving and she was sustenance, the stuff his life was made of. His kiss was fierce, commanding. Heady sensations of his hardness, his potent male certainty, weakened her legs and made her surrender her weight to him.

He dropped a muscled arm to the backs of her knees and lifted, carrying her to her bed and spreading himself over her like a heavy blanket. Eden reveled in his driving weight, responding to the sinuous velvet tongue that caressed hers and beckoned to her passions. Her fingers wove through his hair and traced his ears and the cording of his neck. His kisses devoured her throat and spread lower over her chest. It was a wonderful torture, this wanting he worked inside her. Her body began to move against him, seeking the contours she was fashioned to fill. When he left her to remove his clothes, his hands were shaking, his eyes were black and silver, burning.

He came to her boldly, sliding his hands up her tapered legs and lifting her long chemise with them. A draft of doubt sent her hands fluttering to hold it in place, but his deep, ragged laugh stilled them. And in seconds she was naked to the loving scrutiny of his eyes and hands and lips.

He began at her knees and trailed his tongue up her sensitive thighs until she squirmed and tried to force his head up. He resisted her easily and with animal pleasure nibbled the side of her hip and the satiny dent of her belly. Something about it was different, a subtle, interesting differences that caught in his brain. He nuzzled the dark curls at the base of her belly and worked his way up to her small waist and over her ribs to her breasts. They were fuller, their tight nipples darker, larger. He nuzzled and licked and kissed them, aware of a sweet, tantalizing smell he couldn't quite place.

Eden clasped his head and pulled his face to hers. She nibbled his lips, ran her tongue over his raspy chin, and gasped when her breasts began to tingle with familiar warning. The pressure of his chest against her released a small stream of milk from her breasts, and Ram was confused by its wet, silky warmth. He withdrew to look at her and his hot eyes silvered with understanding. That lovely, sweet smell was the scent of milk from her breasts.

Her face was crimson — anxious. But Ram plunged into the little cup formed between her lovely breasts and savored her bounty with languid strokes of his tongue, adoring the warmth and texture of her satiny skin beneath. Then he lifted his hungry lips to hers and tasted her with fresh desire. Her legs parted beneath him and he fitted himself against her softness without conscious will. Another moist warmth awaited him, and he sank inside her, feeling enveloped by her. She was invading him as surely as he was her.

Eden's hands traced the well-defined muscles of his broad back and her nails raked the sensitive skin under his flexed arms. She filled her hands with the tight mounds of his buttocks, urging him closer, higher. Her willowy legs entwined with his as she moved to meet his thrusts. Between them an urgent and mesmerizing cadence built, drawing them upward onto pleasure's highest plane. Between them passion beat higher and finally crested and crashed like mighty breakers, destined to wear away all obstacles with their faithful, relentless pounding.

Spent but far from exhausted, Ram slid part of his weight to the bed, lying diagonally across her. He felt the flickering pulse in her throat and smiled at the way its racing matched his. His big fingers traced the damp beauty of her profile and the graceful column of her neck. He rubbed her shoulder with his palm and let his fingers slide down onto her full, generous breasts. He cupped one and felt her shiver. Her head turned and her eyes glowed coral and golden.

"It's the babe," he whispered hoarsely, owning the cause of the intriging changes in her. His hand slid from her breast to the slight hollow of her lean belly. "The last time we made love, you had a sweet little mound growin' here."

He choked and his face was strained. "Do I have . . . a child?"

Eden nodded, unable to hold back the tears that came. "A son."

"A son," he repeated in a whisper, catching her salty liquid on his fingertips. He forced himself to swallow. "And do I have a wife?" He was asking, not demanding, though it was his right to demand it . . . and more. It warmed her heart and she brightened inside.

"You should know what happens to people who say you don't," her eyes glistened ferociously.

"Banished to the galleys?" His laugh was taut and deep. She felt its vibrations all through their still-joined bodies.

"Absolutely. Want me to prove I'm your wife?" She rose onto one elbow and leaned toward him, her eyes glowing. When he nodded, spellbound by her aggressive mood, she grabbed his head from behind and pulled it to her waiting lips. It was a brief, hard, sensual challenge of a kiss, and when she released him, he pulled her back to answer it masterfully.

"If you ever . . . *ever* do somethin' like this to me again . . ." he growled against her mouth afterward, "I'll hunt you down and I swear to God—you'll not see the light of day for the rest of your life! I'll keep you by me if it means locking you up."

"Ram, I had to—"

"You *had* to stand by your husband, Eden, and you left me. You *left* me there! I nearly went crazy when I found you gone. I tore Edinburgh apart trying to find you. I beat Ian senseless when I found out what had happened."

"If you know why I left, then you must know . . . it was the hardest thing I've ever done, Ram. *And the surest.*" He darkened and she cradled his heated face between her cool hands to try to make him understand. "Skyelt is so much a part of you—it's your life . . . you even said so. Ian said the decision was already determined, that Skyelt would be his. He thought I was enamored of the lady's role and would leave you for him once he had it. I couldn't bear it, thinking I might be the reason you'd lose Skyelt. He was determined to take everything you had. When I refused him, he said you could have Skyelt or me, not both. I decided . . . it was more important for you to have Skyelt."

"Just like that," a fire was lit at the backs of his eyes, *"you* decided what I needed. You and my precious bastard brother—deciding my fate! And you never thought to consult me, to let me do a man's duty, make a man's choices." His fingers dug into her bare shoulders and she bit her lip to keep from flinching. "You've interfered once too often in my duty, Eden MacLean!" He gave her a hard shake. And Eden knew the anger in him had to be spent, or it would lie hard and sullen between them always.

"Beat me, then!" she demanded, furious with the way her eyes filled and wetted her reddened face. "Just beat me good and get it out of your system!" He stiffened, and his muscles coiled. Hitting her went against his nature, but she felt him straining against the urge to do what she taunted him to do. And without thinking, she smacked his shoulder with her fist.

Ram pounced on her, driving her beneath him fiercely, snatching her wrists and pushing them above her head. The quick violence of his reaction drove the air from her. But with her eyes closed, trying not to cringe, she felt the heat, the intensity of his body coming to life inside her, where their bodies were still joined. And suddenly his lips were crushing hers, forcing them apart, devouring her surrender.

He shoved deep inside her, and released her wrists to clasp her shoulders and pull her tight against him. He devoured the skin of her shoulder and breast lightly then returned to her mouth, reaching for her soul with his penetrating tongue. He was moving inside her with strong, lifting strokes that excited her relentlessly.

"Dearest God, Eden, I love you more than anything in my life." He raked her bottom lip with his teeth, then kissed her fiercely. "Don't let me be angry with you . . ." he pleaded, half-coherent, "love it from me. Love me until I'm not angry any more—"

Eden heard with her heart, and her body and soul willed themselves to do his bidding. Her legs wrapped around him and she met his blinding need with one of her own. She was fierce, clawing and arching to demand more of him; then she submitted to his conquest, opening herself to him and giving him control of her. They strained and pressed until their damp bodies slid over each other and curled and writhed in the throes of white-hot ecstasy. Their heat was pure and burned away the last crusty remnants of anger's dross. And in that blistering forge, their love was refined yet again, then tempered to awesome strength in the slow cooling of afterlove.

This time, their intimate bodies parted; only their skin was shared. Wonder and exhaustion claimed them, and for a long while they slept, their fingers entwined, their sides touching.

More than an hour later, Ram awakened her with butterfly kisses from his lashes on her dream-blushed cheek. She watched the lidded contentment of his face and smiled, madonna-like. Her arms entwined around his neck and she wriggled lazily against his warmth.

"Are you still angry?"

"A little. It may take a while for you to make amends." His smile betrayed him and his hand swept her body adoringly.

"Well, you'll have to be patient," she murmured.

"There's another who has claim to me now. And he doesn't like to be kept waiting." She traced his frown with her fingertips and laughed. "Your son needs feeding." She glanced down at her full breasts and his gaze followed hers and he flushed.

"Oh."

He watched her rise and wash and don a robe, admiring the womanly ripeness of her body, the lush sway of her full breasts. He was heating again and felt a familiar remnant of forbidding tension. She approached the bed and kissed his forehead.

"I love you, Ramsay MacLean."

He relaxed all over as she swayed to the connecting door and disappeared. She returned shortly with a swathed bundle in her arms.

"Sit up, darlin', and meet your son . . . Andrew Arlan Adam MacLean." She placed the babe in Ram's big hands and smiled at the discomfort in her husband's face. Her laugh was low and musical. "Just pretend he's a newborn lamb, Ramsay. Handle him gently but firmly. He won' break, love. He's sturdy like you."

Ram relaxed some and she rounded the bed to crawl up beside him and rearrange the bolsters at his back. She stroked the fuzzy cap of burnished hair held safely in the crook of Ram's muscular arm and her heart filled. Ram lifted a little hand and it curled tightly around his toughened finger. He brightened and looked at Eden.

"I think he likes me."

Eden smiled as Ram nestled the babe against his chest and stared at him wonderingly. In the silence he brushed Andrew's cheek and the babe turned toward his bare chest and groped noisily toward Ram's hard, flat nipple. Ram held him away and sent Eden a stricken look. She laughed.

"I think it's me he wants now." And she took him from

Ram and put him to her full breast. She fed him and explained a few things to Ram as he watched, fascinated. For him, it was as if this were the first bairn on earth. And when she returned Andrew to the nursery, Ram sighed and closed his eyes. His lips moved in a prayer of thanks.

## Chapter Twenty-nine

It was late indeed when Eden and Ram finally rose from their bed to wash and dress. Ram sat on the edge of the bed with her between his knees and and traced the valley of her spine with his lips. This delicious love play meant they were taking forever to dress. And he knew it was also forestalling the inevitable.

"I would'ave been here sooner, love, but it took forever to get passage. Had to come by way of Amsterdam to find a captain willin' to run for Boston. And . . . I had some other things to settle. . . ."

Eden had felt it building inside him and pulled his arms around her waist and nestled her bare shoulders back against his bare chest.

"Tell me," she urged. "The suit." And suddenly she knew, from the way he hadn't mentioned it until now, it would be bad news.

"I lost . . . more or less."

She turned in his arms to search his pensive face. "Lost? *How?*" She shook her head in disbelief. Ram's expression held no anger, no blinding pain . . . only a rueful acceptance.

"Well, I said I battered Ian a bit . . . I'm afraid it was in the courtroom that it happened. Old Bruce wasn't favorably impressed."

"Dear God, Ram! I *did* cause you to lose Skyelt after all." She tried to pull away, but he trapped her against him with a harsh laugh.

"Not hardly, darlin'. Ian gave nearly as good as I did, and was just as eager to kill me as I was him." His voice lowered. "You didn't lose Skyelt for me . . . everyone did, includin' me. Old Bruce called court to order the next day and was fit to be tied. He declared if he could, he'd see neither family would have the title nor the lands. It seems old Angus wasn't overly skillful with his attempt to influence Bruce's decision with coin. And Bruce still hated Haskell's randy guts. Ian and I presented no decent choice after we tore his court apart. He said he was sick to death of the lot of us and we should all roast in sulphur." Ram's laugh was pained and tears sprang to his eyes. "Damme, he was right. There we stood; battered and bloody, covetous an' brawlin . . . a sorry lot, indeed."

"Ramsay! None of it was *your* doing! And after all the evidence of what you'd done at Skyelt —"

"No." He strangled a laugh and covered her lips with his fingers. "Old Bruce was right in the end. He awarded the estates to Angus and the title to Haskell, to spite them both. The provision was attached that Haskell would live on at Skyelt until his death. Angus had to agree to sign the estates over to Ian, him being a man claimed by both families. So you see, Bruce saddled Ian with Haskell for years to come." Ram's shoulders began to shake as the irony spawned a cleansing laughter in him.

"Now Ian has to put up with him. . . ." Eden felt a vengeful approval tickling the corners of her lips. Then she joined Ram in relieved laughter, amazed that he showed so little bitterness at what should have been a deadly blow. She sobered to stroke his face and pour deep into his gaze.

"It's not right, Ram. . . . They've taken everything from you."

"Not by far, love. When you left, I realized where my real riches were. I was wrong about Skyelt . . . about so many things. Skyelt's land, not life. And I have land here, remember? Good land. And here I have you and my bairn. *You're* my life. Haskell's title comes to me, but what does an empty title matter? I realize now: Bruce freed me, Eden. Skyelt's not my burden any longer. Let Ian wrestle with Haskell and the lot, an' welcome to it. You know, I'm not exactly beggared by it."

"You're not?" Eden hadn't even thought of what fortune might remain.

"The proceeds of my mother's unspent dowry and another healthy account have to come to me. I swear, old Bruce was softer on me than he knew . . . or maybe he did know. If you'll recall, I had thought of sending Skyelt folk here, to your dower lands . . . that bonnie rich valley. I just never expected some of that folk would be you an' me."

"You're really not disappointed?" Eden traced his jaw lovingly.

"I've had solitary months to make peace wi' it, Eden. The more I think on it, the more possibilities I see. I'll still have to work hard to make us a life here." He watched her intensely. "Will that do?"

Eden melted against him and lifted her lips to his, wanting him to feel her love all around him.

"It will do nicely, Ramsay. Very nicely, indeed."


It was another few hours, nearly sunset, before Eden and Ram finally emerged from their bedroom and descended to the parlor. Their faces were polished; one like blushing apples, one like glowing bronze. One look at them together and it was no work at all to deduce how they'd spent the afternoon. They swept into the parlor and Eden's eyes danced as her assembled family rose to greet her with collective relief. Arlo hugged Ram with wet eyes and then drew Eden into an embrace. Adam extended a hand of welcome to his son-in-law and Constance managed to smile approvingly at him, now that her daughter was smiling again.

"James!" Eden spotted his back, wedged between his younger brothers, and glanced up at Ram. "You didn't say he'd come with you!"

"There was probably a lot I didn't get to say," Ram grinned wickedly. Adam glanced stiffly at Constance and she averted her widened eyes.

"James!" Eden rushed across the room to greet him and he turned to catch her up in a full hug. "It's so good to —" She stopped dead. Around James's shoulder she spotted Carina's face and sparkling MacLean eyes. "Carina!" she pushed away from James enough to stare at Ram's little sister. She sat on the sofa like a demure jewel set in velvet. Eden abandoned James to fight through her other brothers to get to Carina's side. Carina jumped up and hugged Eden with tears in her eyes.

"Oh, Eden," she sniffed through her gentled burr, "It was so awful without you . . . Poor Ram — have ye made it up wi' him?"

"Yes," Eden thrust her back to look at her, "I've made it up wi' him. Let me look at you! You're positively ravishing!"

"Amen to that!" Chase hung over Eden's shoulder, appreciating Carina's voluptuous little figure a bit too openly. James yanked him back by the arm and took his place.

"And you're beautiful as ever, after the bairn," Carina

beamed at her. "And what a lovely home an' family you have!"

"Carina!" Eden suddenly frowned, "What are you doing here?"

Carina twinkled naughtily and raised her left hand, wiggling her fingers. Nestled against her palm was a shining gold band. Eden's jaw loosened and she turned to James, who looked rather perplexed himself. He ran his hands back through his hair and started to speak. But he caught Carina's warm, openly adoring gaze on him and softened visibly.

"I had to marry her. She wouldn't come unwedded — and I couldn't live without her."

"Nor I him." Carina shivered noticably and her eyes darkened at the way her husband looked at her. "But I made him wait until I was seventeen."

"The two longest damned weeks of my life," James growled, looking at Carina like he was still making up for them.

"Two MacLeans in the family," Eden laughed. "Poor Mama!"

They dined in celebration that evening, with fine foods, rare and wonderful wines, and a peaceful air of subdued joy. But when they adjourned to the parlor for coffee, there was a flurry about Carina that raised Constance' already strained brows even higher. James had to muscle between his fascinated brothers to be able to sit near his sensual little kitten of a bride. Their openly amorous remarks and questing glances drove James to install her on his lap, his lean hands curled possessively about her waist. And the results of his protective closeness soon became obvious.

Constance and Adam sat together on the sofa and

watched the turmoil amongst their lusty, unconventional offspring a bit numbly. Constance clutched Adam's hand in a death grip when Carina started on James's lap and looked down at her throbbing seat before she thought and raised her eyes quickly. Flushing, she turned to him breathlessly.

"Damme, James, why didn't you say somethin'?" She set his hands away and slid from his lap. She pulled him to the door with great finesse, camouflaging his embarrassment behind her skirts.

They left the room with a certain dignity before Ram burst out laughing and Ethan and Chase joined in. Eden did her best to keep a straight face, but even chewing her lips, it was hard. She ended by rising and pausing by Ram's chair to say something to him in a low tone. From where they sat, Adam and Constance couldn't hear, but Ethan and Chase began to laugh wickedly. Eden sailed out the door and it was no more than a heartbeat until Ram was on his feet, striding after her, grinning.

Adam cleared his throat and addressed his remaining sons tersely. "What was that all about?"

They rose, trying to sober themselves, pulling their vests down into place and having a hard time meeting his demanding look.

"She said—" Chase began, but erupted in laughter, so that Ethan had to finish for him. . . .

"Baaa."

The younger Marlow sons supported each other through the door and into the hallway where they retrieved their hats and staggered weakly out the main door, gasping Madame Rochelle's name.

Adam stared at his white-faced Constance. She'd just figured out Eden's cryptic invitation and her eyes were glazing over a bit. "Adam, if I didn't know better, I'd swear they weren't ours."

539

And they mounted the stairs to their shared rooms worrying about their shocking offspring and wondering how two such refined and cultured individuals as themselves could ever have produced them.

# DISCOVER DEANA JAMES!

**CAPTIVE ANGEL**                    (2524, $4.50/$5.50)

Abandoned, penniless, and suddenly responsible for the biggest tobacco plantation in Colleton County, distraught Caroline Gillard had no time to dissolve into tears. By day the willowy redhead labored to exhaustion beside her slaves . . . but each night left her restless with longing for her wayward husband. She'd make the sea captain regret his betrayal until he begged her to take him back!

**MASQUE OF SAPPHIRE**                (2885, $4.50/$5.50)

Judith Talbot-Harrow left England with a heavy heart. She was going to America to join a father she despised and a sister she distrusted. She was certainly in no mood to put up with the insulting actions of the arrogant Yankee privateer who boarded her ship, ransacked her things, then "apologized" with an indecent, brazen kiss! She vowed that someday he'd pay dearly for the liberties he had taken and the desires he had awakened.

**SPEAK ONLY LOVE**                   (3439, $4.95/$5.95)

Long ago, the shock of her mother's death had robbed Vivian Marleigh of the power of speech. Now she was being forced to marry a bitter man with brandy on his breath. But she could not say what was in her heart. It was up to the viscount to spark the fires that would melt her icy reserve.

**WILD TEXAS HEART**                  (3205, $4.95/$5.95)

Fan Breckenridge was terrified when the stranger found her near-naked and shivering beneath the Texas stars. Unable to remember who she was or what had happened, all she had in the world was the deed to a patch of land that might yield oil . . . and the fierce loving of this wildcatter who called himself Irons.

*Available wherever paperbacks are sold, or order direct from the Publisher. Send cover price plus 50¢ per copy for mailing and handling to Penguin USA, P.O. Box 999, c/o Dept. 17109, Bergenfield, NJ 07621. Residents of New York and Tennessee must include sales tax. DO NOT SEND CASH.*

### WHAT'S LOVE GOT TO DO WITH IT?

*Everything . . . Just ask Kathleen Drymon . . . and Zebra Books*

| | |
|---|---|
| *CASTAWAY ANGEL* | *(3569-1, $4.50/$5.50)* |
| *GENTLE SAVAGE* | *(3888-7, $4.50/$5.50)* |
| *MIDNIGHT BRIDE* | *(3265-X, $4.50/$5.50)* |
| *VELVET SAVAGE* | *(3886-0, $4.50/$5.50)* |
| *TEXAS BLOSSOM* | *(3887-9, $4.50/$5.50)* |
| *WARRIOR OF THE SUN* | *(3924-7, $4.99/$5.99)* |